Stephen O'Raw

Author's Note;

Upon a family outing to Hook Peninsula one fine summer's day my head was turned by a magnificently dilapidated old mansion all alone on the long barren outcrop.

I had heard the rumours of Loftus Hall and its claim to being the most haunted house in Ireland. Well, it certainly looks the part, like an unwanted leftover after a Hollywood horror movie shoot.

Feeling sorry for the old girl, I ventured in and I listened to her tale. Oh, how I wished I hadn't. She then made me swear to retell it, or become part of its savage history itself.

This is what she whispered to me…

CONTENTS

CONTENTS

Old dreams fade, New ones are born.

For Harley ~ My Lucky Charm.

TWISTED PATHS

Are you sitting comfortably? I hope so, I hope you're nestled on a recliner or sofa, between plump cushions with a hot cup of tea. Because, I'm afraid to say, you will find little by way of comfort within these pages.

As this grim story unfurls itself to you, you may find some respite in the dalliances of a delightful, yet deluded, maiden fair. You may also glean some smug satisfaction from the devious plottings of a desperate young man...you may.

But otherwise this is a tale of torment, misery and murder, which dates back over a century. Even today, its pernicious effects ripple ever outwards through the ether and time, leaving all it touches, traumatised, tarnished or scarred in some way.

Know also, before you commence, that the involved parties who were sucked, inexorably, into committing the fiendish acts detailed within, were once as innocent as you or I.

How innocent that is, is for us, and only us, to ever truly know.

"And may you be in heaven half an hour
before the devil knows you're dead."
~Old Irish Proverb

"For the devil has no power ...except in the dark."
~Madame Dorothea

"The devil doesn't come dressed
in a red cape and pointy horns.
He comes as everything you've ever wished for"
~Tucker Max

Loftus Country Hotel, Wexford 1983

Dawn's light was just beginning its daily conquest over darkness when the night porter was jolted by a ruckus from somewhere upstairs. He was just preparing to end his shift when the disturbance startled him, he craned his head, following the racket which continued to tumble down the old wooden staircase.

On the landing the young couple from room 307 then appeared, carelessly dressed, clumsily packed and looking petrified, their sole intention was to exit the hotel immediately and without hindrance.

The rookie receptionist recalled the pair from the previous night, begging to be relocated. At that time they were near their wits end, by now, it looked as though they had reached them.

I should say something, thought the jaded bellhop, *Mr Devereux will be furious.*

'Oh Good Morning,' he chirped, 'Did you sleep well Mr…'

But they were oblivious to his feeble geniality and already encased halfway through the revolving door, leaving a scant trail of their frantically stowed belongings in their wake.

Clearly not, thought the perturbed porter.

From the dining room window overlooking the newly gravelled driveway, a handful of the hotel's cock-crow guests turned their heads from their steaming eggs and black pudding towards the noise of the clamour out front.

Michael Devereux, hotel manager and maître'd, cocked himself quickly to the direction of the manicured yard. There, he saw the frenzied couple were stuffing their luggage into the back seats of their mint green Ford Capri with its distinct UK yellow registration plates. *Mr & Mrs Moss*, he believed.

Not Good. Not good. The red alert beeped in the manager's head and spurred him to action.

Without losing stride from his task of delivering a silver teapot to table six, he cordially excused himself and made for the lobby. Brow furrowed as he whizzed past the reception desk, he shot the bemused night porter a quizzical glare. Darting then, as graceful as a panicked springbok, towards the Capri which was already spewing exhaust fumes.

Reaching the car, and in as calm and pleasant a manner he could muster, he rapped on the passenger side window. The sudden rattle causing the already frayed Mrs Moss to shriek from behind the wet veil of morning condensation.

Mr Devereux, still aware of his duty as a hospitality provider, deftly wiped the morning dew away with his handkerchief. Mrs Moss's pretty face, last night aglow and trouble-free, was now stricken and wan beneath her raven, unkempt curls. She stared at the manager, pop-eyed until recognition dawned to her, then her facial muscles relaxed. At last she exhaled.

Amid the gathering noxious emissions Mr Devereux bowed and courteously mimed to her, with a spin of his wrist, to roll down her window. Checking first with her husband, she opened it halfway.

'Mrs Moss, Mr Moss, please forgive my intrusion, I can see you're in a hurry, is something the matter? Can I assist you at all?' He fawned.

Mr Devereux remembered Mr Moss signing in just yesterday, wheezy yet jocular. He had appeared to be coming down with a cold, but he was still high in spirits. He even recalled sharing a gag with him about the *Sex Pistols* of all things. *Ahh yes! Sid and Nancy Moss.*

There was no sign of that zeal now. Now he found the young husband strained around his temples and blankly staring at his knuckles, as though they were fit to tear the steering wheel from its column. Mrs Moss placed her cold, delicate palm over his taut fingers.

'Mr Moss...?' Mr Devereux began again.

Snapping from his trance, Mr Moss shuddered and fixed the manager with his nervous eyes. 'We're leaving, we're getting ourselves as far away from this wretched place as possible. This place...that room, there's something...something very wrong here. It's cursed, how...how could you open a place so evil to the public...' a coughing fit took hold and his wife soothed him, patting his thick, auburn hair.

She continued speaking for her husband who was now grinding gears trying to find reverse. 'We spent the night with *something*....something Dark Mr Devereux. It watched us, it, it touched us. Something cold and dark, and dead. This is no hotel Mr Devereux...it's a tomb.'

The morning shadows cast from the surrounding tree line clawed down the Victorian façade, the third floor windows began winking at the new day, and the relatively new owner. His mind scrambled to find an appeasing solution.

Recompense! Mr Devereux babbled some vague and gratis offers to in attempt to apologise, pacify and mollify the distraught couple. Alas, Mr Moss had at last, via an unhappy clutch, found a home for the gearstick, and began crunching gravel stones in reverse. Keeping astride with the closing nearside window, Mr Devereux uttered a few more 'pleases' before the chintzy car's tires changed spin direction and lunged forwards, exhaling smoke and spitting tiny stones as it sped. Some even managed to clack against the dining room windows, where the early birds and golf jocks were gaping at the forecourt drama.

Two flights above the dining room windows, the morning sun now fully reflects its coral majesty onto the upstairs panes of this very fine establishment. Had you been watching from the courtyard below you may well have noticed that one of the windows seemed less generous in reflecting the dawning light.

Room 307's ornate bay may have struck you as curious, and in contrast with the long row of gleaming windows, as a dull or smoky black, an anomalous chamber of shadow.

Witnessing this, you may well have chosen to pack your bags and bolt away too, or at least insist on a complementary upgrade to anywhere very far away from this particularly perturbing suite.

Behind the glass, within the 'double-bed with en-suite' guest room, *something* watched. Something vile and loathsome and ethereal floated and surveyed the grounds below. The fawning creature scuttling after the carriage held no interest for it. Its gaze was fixed on the green vehicle belting through the gates. An opportunity, a lame soul, cold and trembling within this carriage existed for the dark, vaporous being.

Its prey. Its quarry. Its vestibule.

The entity rose, spiriting through the ceiling and above the old roof, the car always in its sights. At the height where the low sun reflected on the calm Irish Sea, a small, dark, whirling plume gathered and began its aerial pursuit.

Below, in the fast moving but slowly heating up Capri, the couple's cold sweats began to dissipate, and their nerves, still jangling from their fretful night, became a little more manageable. Distancing themselves at pace from the damned hotel, Mr and Mrs Moss began to breathe again.

Their panting would not have relaxed nearly as quickly, had they noticed the strange, black cloud following them from high above their car, moving in the opposite direction as the oncoming northerly wind.

***

Not Good. Not good at all Mr Devereux. The manager fretted as he watched the dishevelled deserters run for the hills.

The alarm tolled doggedly on in his mind, which now faced the more immediate issue of diffusing any potential fallout from his spectators sipping Earl Grey from the breakfast buffet.

Though the hotels branding offered esteemed visitors *An Experience to Remember*, this was not what he had in mind.

Mr Devereux's business model was, 'Big Spends, Bigger Rewards.' His intention to quickly recoup the restoration and refurbishment fees via the *Luxury Hotel* price tag, meant that your deluxe weekend away in Wexford would cost you the same as a week's holiday in Spain. And although the county is renowned nationally for boasting more sunshine than any other county in Ireland – Mallorca it is not.

Mr Devereux was a dignified man, earnest, and mostly very honest in all his endeavours. Despite the present mini ignominy, he stood proud before his castle, the magnificent Loftus Hall. Now the Loftus Hall Country Hotel, the latest incarnation of the estate that had been built, toppled and rebuilt again over its 800 year history.

Like previous proprietors of the estate during its restoration phase, he was sure to take ultimate care and bestow exquisite taste with its furnishings and décor. Taste and exquisiteness however, requires fiscal expense. No way around that conundrum. One does not throw sugar at these houses by the teaspoon, one uses spades. Nice stuff costs money.

As wealthy and shrewd as Mr Devereux was, projects such as these involve digging oneself into a depth of debt. With less prudence than usual, he chose to dig himself about belt high, already he could feel the earth sinking deeper beneath him.

He thought this tight, claustrophobic feeling, like a constricting serpent around his waist, must be the very same feeling his long dead predecessor must have felt after his exorbitant investment into the lavish restoration of the same building over a hundred years previous. Did the coil of debt squeeze the life from him? Did the moneypit swallow him whole?

For now at least, Mr Devereux only had mud on his face, maybe he could still wade from the pit and slither from the mire, clean and respectable, front of house, preened and ready to receive and welcome his high paying guests very gratefully again.

He breathed and took perspective. All was not lost because of two spooked guests. The first few months since the reopening were wonderful. At least his esteemed guests actually arrived after his extravagant overhaul, unlike the royal VIPs once highly anticipated by the long expired Marquess. But that, is another story.

The hotel's red carpet launch night saw the Beaujolais nouveau and Chardonnay crates stacked high. The Lord Mayor got to work with his scissors, and in whooshed a swell of glamorous and gleeful guests. The elite clientèle, all keen to be seen in their velvet tuxes, hot-pink jumpsuits, and chunky gold adornments. Thick moustaches and big hair bounced in the heady air, a mixture of cigarette smoke and *Poison by Dior*. Their notion of the perfect hotel break was to dine and drink like hogs all night, and at dawn, either catch up with the F.T. or tee-off on the nearby links.

During the fine summer season, the neatly coiffed hedges that lined the parking areas housed some very choice motors. Amongst the Datsuns and Hillmans, a range of shiny Mercs, Beemers, Porsche, and the occasional Roller. *As yet, no Aston Martins*, Devereux had mused smugly. *As yet*.

During the restoration, the feeling of optimism and the upwind scent of success that dangled the carrot of him becoming the owner of a five-star rated hotel, buoyed and spurred him on. Yes, he was aware of the buildings structural shortcomings, and of its rich and fascinating ancestral heritage, and its sinister secrets. But his focus could not dwell on absurd tales from the crypt, his goal was grandeur and prosperity, and to get this old jewel to sparkle again.

Mr Devereux was not one to paper over the creepy cracks with bargain basement décor, nor sweep the tall tales beneath any old rug, and in accordance with his strident sense of duty, he ensured only the deepest piled carpets, and plushest of wallpapers and paints should be used to cover up the ghostly gossip. The decadent ornamentation enough to distract, and keep The Hall's many dark little secrets just that - secret.

Never the superstitious sort, he scoffed and poked jibes at the local lore when brokering the details of the sale. After seven years of advertising the sale of the grounds in the auctioneer's window, with few nibbling at the generous price tag, the estate agent was all too happy to laugh along agreeably at the new landlord's quips, all the time holding out his pen, his hand quivering to secure Mr Devereux's signature.

Mrs Devereux, two steps less zealous than her husband, bit on her reservations, and dutifully underwrote the deeds.

And now, standing in the skid-marks of the Ford racing towards the exit, he imagines room 307. Inside it feels cold. A tiny tear appears in the new wallpaper, perhaps behind the large seascape painting of Hook lighthouse. Creeping from this rip he sees charred, twig-like fingers. They curl and grip and pull open a small vent, an inoffensive wormhole in the fabric of time, a portal from where a shadow from the past can peer into the present. And wait for the next guests to unpack their cases.

Snapping from his eerie reverie, he became aware again of his current predicament.

Although a fan of comedy, he was now wary of ironic serendipity. After becoming a hotel owner, Mr Devereux had developed a fear that he may ever bear a hint of resemblance to Basil Fawlty in any situation, comedic or otherwise. Being in stature a little gangly, he made a point some months ago to remove his moustache to avoid any further parallels with the hapless TV lank. Yet here he was, on stage before his rapt diners, all waiting hungrily for their next act, and smoked kippers.

Of course he would play this down melodrama with jovial discard. He would butter their toast with low-fat humour and tell them an off-the-cuff spiel, which he'd create between the car-park and foyer. A light filler for now will work fine. Then let them eat cake and chase golf balls.

Devereux pondered his options. *Their room would have experienced some plumbing issues, creating eerie bumps during the Moss's night. Mrs Moss suffered with her nerves and frequently experienced night terrors under her medication. Mr Moss's poor mother of 106 took a bad turn and it's not looking great so they had to dash off.* This, that, the cat in the hat, any old yarn to stitch this unsightly seam in his precious oil painting would hold for now.

Maybe soon he would resurrect the house's legendary ghost story. He knew of course, of enthusiasts and ghoul chasers who follow the tourist trails of *Haunted Houses.* This had always been his fail-safe should anything hinting on paranormal disturb his beloved and lavishly paying guests. The repugnant tale he heard would be watered down and honeyed to make it more palatable to the public at large. He would present a coquettish sprite, akin to Casper, compelled to create occasional childlike devilment or some-such dialogue would suffice. It may well knock a star off of his aspirational five, and the re-branding would be tiresome...and costly...again with the costliness of it all.

Retreating to the lobby, he traced his gaze from the spot on the windows recently chipped by wheel-spin debris, up to the gawking diners He wryly cast his eyes heavenward to illustrate *a Hotel Manager's lot*, like a true ham.

And still, as he crunched his way back to his captive audience, the alarm droned on...*Not Good...Not Good...*

Dun Laoghaire. Co. Dublin

Should you ever parade along the mile long pier at the ferry terminal in Dun Laoghaire, County Dublin, pivot south west and crane your neck a little skywards, above the first thick copse of trees and into the Dublin Mountains. Scan across this tree-line and an unusual blue light may catch your eye.

The Dun Laoghaire pier is a busy port for passenger and cargo ferries to and from the UK. After their shift, many thirsty and land-lorn sailors seek sustenance for the skin and the soul in the vicinity. Sailors by trade, are both wary of, and drawn to sea sirens, and are used to keeping weather eyes alert for luminous signals that both warn and guide them at sea. Sailors, when not sailing, are also drawn to stout, song and sultry company, and so the story goes for the Blue Light Inn of Barnacullia, who mounted their azure beacon high to lure land-lubbing sea men to their hedonistic hideout in the hills.

It is a pleasant autumn evening in the south Dublin borough, mostly clear with no forecast of inclement conditions, and certainly no mention of thunder, and yet, from nowhere, a mighty boom and a flash of light rocks the little mountain. The cause of this freak electrical discharge was perplexing to all who witnessed the frightening event. Did something crash into an overhead power line? Is there a storm brewing? The sea is calm and the trees are still, and the shipping news broadcasts are to continue mild and holding.

The moment has passed, and all remains as it was just a moment ago. Life continues, a little unnerved, but uninterrupted by the sonic boom. Inside the Blue Light tavern, an elderly man shudders, he recollects hearing the very same terrifying rumble when he was just a boy.

Let us venture closer to the inn. Outside this comely pub is a hanging sign, nautical in theme, welcoming us to the hostelry. Beneath the unusual incandescent hue the walls glow ultramarine, turquoise and navy, flecked by the occasional whispery shadow from moths lured close to the humming bulb. Wiping your feet you approach the newly painted half-door, odd symbols carved in the wood are still visible behind the tacky gloss. We enter, and a congenial atmosphere greets us. The warmth of the open-fire places sunny kisses on your chilly cheeks. Rustic paraphernalia adorn the thick stone walls. Among the décor hang two pike, one, an eighteen pounder, hooked from the Dodder and stuffed, the other, a long barbed lance once used by Wexford rebels to impale British soldiers. The room, painted orange by firelight, made the inn look more like a cavern then a tavern. The shadows cast from the thick oak beams ghostly dance about as you close the door and leave the cold outside. You are greeted by the heavy odour of turf smoke and a lazy glance from a wet wolfhound drying at the hearth. And eyes - not suspicious, but curious eyes, follow your steps. They passively scan and gauge you, before returning to their cards and porter. Make yourself comfortable, rest by the hearth, order an ale, it could be a long night.

The innkeeper in September 1983 was a Mr Dennis Moody. Unlike his surname might suggest, he was seldom glum, He maintained a jovial disposition and a cheery smile on his pleasant ruddy face, despite smelling of beer rags and chimney soot most of the time. Today he smelled of turps, after attempting to conceal his recently scarred door with a fresh coat of black paint. He grumbled to himself about the teenage vandals and their graffiti as he washed his hands, then set about his daily devotions to his beloved bar.

Finally done and satisfied that his bar was suitably stainless and his barrels were brimming, he took a breath to savour this morning's industrious efforts. Dennis flapped his tea towel over his shoulder and inspected tonight's punters.

Playing whist in the glow of the red embers sat Charlie, Jack and Christie, the bald brothers, who were all at one point, privates in the Irish army. The elder two wore flat caps, and weighed the merits of their hands. Jack proudly flattened his comb-over, then smugly flattened his cards. He downed his ale then upped the ante on his brothers, sipping their single malt at a more measured pace. Jack may yet lose his shirt this night, and although brothers, either would be happy to wear it home.

Dug into the snug were Ambrose and Marie, dumb as dung, locally presumed inbred, and married since the day Kennedy was killed. Ambrose with a head like a prize beetroot and Marie as pretty as a parsnip, they would make a very presentable display at a fête. Amid their hushed chatter they are having a rare giggle to themselves. Maybe they've inherited a windfall from Madge, Ambrose's spinster sister from further up the hill. Madge, rarely seen, but always elegantly dressed when she was, and who, in forty years stepped inside this establishment just once to ask, very politely, for change for the bus.

And lastly, Rubin, the strange old Jew, perched like an owl at *his* end of the bar, his chimney pipe smouldering and brandy glass empty. The all wise and nebulous Rubin, who spoke with a brogue as Dublin as Ronnie Drew's coalman, tried hard not to adhere to Jewish norms, and although predominantly a lone soul, he was generous with a round of ale more often than most. However his habit of paying his tab with lose change, from hands donned with ragged fingerless gloves, did little to shed the stereotype. Dennis often imagined him wearing, within the lining of his tweed overcoat, a silk purse filled with diamonds.

He mostly read his obscure books at the end of the bar where the light was best. Books you would not find in any shelf in Easons. He kept today's heavy looking volume stowed in his satchel, guarding it closely.

And so, Dennis' mental role call checked everyone *anseo* for Monday evening. The familiarity gave him a positive sense of order. A calm which he drew a deep lungful of after a busy weekend of revelry in the popular watering hole.

He felt tempted to suggest to Rubin a top up for his depleted Hennessey, but he knew better to wait until he raised his bushy eyebrows and tapped the glass with his pipe stem. Instead, feeling suddenly a little colder, Dennis chose to throw more briquettes on the fire. As he neared the whist table he prepared to deliver a zingy one liner to rib the card sharks with, when the noise of a hastily halting car outside diverted his attention.

Peering through the original warped glass panes, and over the still abundant dahlias in the window box, he saw a poorly parked Ford Capri on the opposite side of the road. The couple within appeared to be fumbling for something, then, two glowing amber tips burned bright before yielding to thick puffs of smoke. The driver reclined his seat well back and returned the cigarette lighter to its socket. Eventually, the window rolled open a crack on either side to allow the fumes waft out of the mint green car, like steam from the ears of an angry iron beast, now bathed turquoise by the light of the blue lamp.

Dennis was going to announce the impending visit of strangers to his clientèle, but again, he thought better of it. A window full of gawking hill-billies would quickly send this already nervy looking pair spiralling back down the hill.

That's thrice, he noted, he denied himself from speaking. He grunted, a little miffed at his monastic decisions. He chose instead to hum his usual party piece, *The Whistlin' Gypsy Rover*. He had barely finished an *ahh-dee-doo*, when Ambrose, finding himself hilarious this evening, cut off his tune with a mimic of a dog howling in sonic agony. Setanta, the wolfhound in front of the fire, cocked his shaggy ears. Dennis sneered, chewed his cheeks, and resigned himself to silence and fuelling the waning flames. He pet Setanta, his coarse hair now all but dry.

Their ciggies smoked to the butt, the shaken duo edged warily into the pub. Dennis was used to seeing new comers self-consciously tip-toe past the scrutiny of his regulars, but this attractive pair's eyes darted about with a different sort of wariness, as though awaiting an ambush from the shadows.

As always, a puff of cold air snook in through the door with them, but even after it had been latched shut, the chill clung to them like a fog to a hill. A startled Setanta rumbled a deep woof towards them, and their audience of ne'er-do-wells and gamblers soaked in their countenance. Ambrose's greasy grin squared and the bald brothers' gazes finally diverted from their deck. Rubin, inhaled deeply as though in preparation. His dewy eyes shrunk and his parched lips pursed, he tapped his empty glass with his pipe.

Mr and Mrs Moss reached the bar. He, tall, lean and bred of good stock. She, doe eyed, diminutive and timeless of beauty. Mindful of their timid state Dennis warmed up his most cordial of greetings and once again he was cut off at the tip of his tongue.

'Two large brandies, please,' Mr Moss ordered in a soft welsh accent. His brow beading sweat, despite the chill.

'Coming right up, sir,' Dennis replied with a broad smile, comforted by the fact he could still verbalise his thoughts, 'And I'm not forgetting you, Rubin,' he nodded down the bar.

Eager to continue his long dormant ability to speak, and crack the icy silence that now froze the room, he chanced some banter, 'I'm detecting you might be from the valleys? Is it visiting us or leaving us you are?'

Mr Moss, remote and glazed, just plainly uttered, 'Can we get food?'

So much for a small-talk, Dennis thought and set down three large Cognacs. Accustomed as he was to informing new punters that Guinness and Tayto was the only nourishment on offer, he considered the couple's fragile state and steered against droll and towards Christianity, 'I'll be happy to make you cheese sandwiches.'

'Thank you. And can you bring another two brandies to our table with the food, oh, and a pack of cigarettes.'

'Yes, of course, Major?'

'What?'

'Major Cigarettes?' Dennis tapped the green and gold cigarette carton.

'Yes. Anything! Thank you,' his eyes twitching to the ceiling. He then clasped his wife's hand and they found a corner table to cower behind.

Dennis, pursued the man's gaze up to the rafters, and then towards Rubin, as if seeking an explanation for the couple's furtive behaviour. Rubin's intent eyes, hovering above his raised brandy glass, suggested he might actually have one.

Shrugging his shoulders Dennis shouted, 'Christie! Make yourself useful and get that fire blazing, 'tis as cold as clay in here,' and went muttering off, looking for a bread knife.

Outside in the dusk, we observe quite the quaint tableau of the traditional Irish pub. The old walls chilled by the fading light, whilst from the fire within, the windows warm with hues of pumpkin and pink-lady. Their welcoming glow invites you in to thaw your toes, and wet your thirsty whistle.

But pause now, wait. Maybe instead you may consider a wide berth around this comely tavern on this darkening day. See how the dahlias wither. Note the errant cloud gathering above the smoke-stack. Look now at the moths circling the blue lamp. Is it a mirage or do their numbers swarm? Notice their shadow, does their mottled umbra wax fuller on the gable and around the doorway. The growing shadow becoming more discernible and beastly in shape. Unsettling portents to behold I would think. Forestall your desire to rest here awhile. Defer that drink you desire. Quicken your step. Jog on. Run.

***

Within the thick stone walls, the good folk gathered here remain unaware of portentous occurrences above the roof tiles. They play cards and empty their glasses. The famished couple wash down their crusts with brandy, and light up again.

He coughs aggressively. She comforts his heaving back, while still managing to drag heartily on her own fag. Though remaining somewhat distracted, the gamblers return their stare to their cards again. The two tubers in the snug resume parley, more conspiratorial now, and without their earlier gaiety. And Rubin, now sitting upright and pensive, as though mentally solving a puzzle. Dennis, the dutiful barkeep and compère, monitors all with stealth and a whistle. *Ahh-dee-doo* had never sounded as eerie before...

Rubin necked his nectar with decisive surety. Rubin the resolute, ready to alight. Taking leave of his stool, but not his pipe, he followed the flagstone floor to the Moss's table. Odder still, he slipped off his boots and hid them behind a pew. Surprising as this act was, their ashen faces showed little change of expression when the hollow-cheeked sage landed quietly beside them.

The *Whistlin' Gypsy Rover* stopped whistling, the gamers in the stalls and the gossips in their allotment sat up, gawping like meerkats over the plain. Setanta slunk down and Dennis blurted out with poorly hidden alert, 'Ahh Rubin, let them alone to themselves wouldja.' But Rubin did not.

'Please forgive the intrusion,' he politely began. 'You don't know me from Adam, nor I you from Eve, but I am...concerned for you. I couldn't help but notice your state of apprehensiveness, your agitation, and I truly hope that I am wrong, but has *something* followed you here?'

The Moss's inhaled in unison, and regarded one another for permission to speak. Mr Moss nodded to his wife to allow her proceed. Then he broke into a cough, covering his mouth with his handkerchief.

When his hacking subsided Nancy Moss spoke, her slight hand fumbling at her trembling lips, and her oval, royal blue eyes always on the door. 'Look, we just want to get home, Sidney is poorly, and we've had an awful nights sleep last night. Really, we're fine, we'll be fine.'

'May I ask what is wrong with you Sidney?' Rubin kindly asked.

Wearily, Sidney replied, 'I've this thundering cough is all, I should never have taken the ferry, and with the lack of sleep...'

'And what, may I ask, disturbed your rest Sidney?'

Again, the handsome couple assessed each other before answering. It was Nancy who replied, she began fidgeting with her necklace and attempted to play down the question with a nervous wave of her hand. 'It was nothing,' she said in her pleasant welsh lilt, 'That Loftus Hall is a noisy old place. Full of clanging pipes and draughty windows. I'm sure no one could get a wink of sleep there.'

Rubin leaned forward, the mention of Loftus Hall turned his expression to stone, as though an old enemy had just winked at him. He exhaled fully and lowered his brow. 'Please, if you will, continue, what occurred during your stay that shook you so?'

Sidney nodded consent for Nancy to continue, her taught face still beautiful in the dim, shadowy light. She drew on her smoke and gripped her silver pendant, as though for protection, before elaborating. 'Well, the trip was to be our deferred Honeymoon.

We had…complications with a pregnancy, which messed us up for a long while. So, we thought that this holiday might pick us up, get us in the mood to…well, to try again.'

Rubin bowed sympathetically.

'Anyway. Sidney, whose father had been adopted, always maintained that his real grandfather had some connection to Loftus Hall. We think he may have been Lord William Loftus. We had heard rumours that it was a spooky old place before its renovation. We were intrigued, and very eager to check out any possible link to Sidney's ancestry, so when we heard it was re-opening we booked our trip.'

'We had planned to stay there for two nights, and even though Sid was poorly we were still excited when we arrived. So the first thing I did was prepare a bubble bath. The bedroom was a very chilly as the windows had been left wide open, so I pulled them closed and latched them, and then unpacked while the water was running. We, emm, shared the bath and spent a good while in the en-suite. When we were done, I found the window was open wide and the room frigid again. We were spooked, but not freaked out, we giggled about the haunted house rumours, but then we just blamed the wind.'

'As you do, we started to drift into a nap. As I was dozing, I heard the sound of a baby crying upstairs, it didn't bother me at first, but then I shot up on the bed and stared at the ceiling when I remembered that we were on the top floor. It stopped immediately then. I woke Sidney, he listened, but there was only silence by then. So we convinced ourselves it came from the adjacent room or outside.'

'I'm a keen knitter, I'm not afraid to admit, so to distract myself, I took out my knitting needles. I was making a little hat for my friend's baby, which is due in a couple of weeks. I finished it and left it on the bed. We then went for supper, but when we came back, the little hat had been unravelled and tossed into a tangle of wool on our bed. Now, we were properly freaked out.'

'We considered leaving right then but we had been drinking. We rang reception, they sent a porter to look around. He took a cursory glance and just shrugged his shoulders. So, no comfort there. They were fully booked up and could not relocate us. So, we could either sleep in the lobby or tough it out. We should have chose the lobby'

'Eventually we fell asleep, I'm nearly sorry we did. It was a restless sleep from which we both woke shaking and sweating during the dark, early hours. I told Sidney of my nightmare. I can still recall it vividly. It was in a muddy field, there was a pregnant woman in a crimson dress, she was trapped and tangled in the briar, a shadow approached her, it was that of a giant bull, as it bore down on the helpless woman it began to burn, turning into a fearsome fireball. The woman tried to fend off the beast with a knitting needle, but it just engulfed her. Then it turned towards me...that's when I woke. When I had finished recapping my dream to Sidney he just stared at me with a blank recognition - he had had the exact same dream.'

'We decided to stay awake and leave at first light. Petrified, we clung to each other. Sidney was burning up and he took his painkillers. Unintentionally we drifted off again. At some point we felt weight on our chests, and then growling, like an angry dog, it startled us again from our sleep. We woke up freezing at dawn, the room was frigid, we sat up to find the spare bedding had been layered over us and our bed had moved from the back wall and was positioned tightly under the open window.' Nancy signalled the end of her story by lighting up another smoke. 'Freaked us the fuck out.'

Wide eyed Rubin, his suspicions now fully confirmed, snatched the matches from her hand and set to stoking his pipe. He closed his eyes and puffed with intent, filing the air with smoke. His grim face appeared through the grey cloud, and then he spoke, the kindness in his tone, now replaced with solemnity. To Sidney, with his illness sailing him close to delirium, he seemed more prophet than man.

'Sid and Nancy,' Rubin addressed them sincerely. Dennis raised an ironic brow hearing their names coined so, but pop culture was lost on Rubin. 'Please trust me. I believe you may be in serious peril. I have listened to your story and connected the dots. Your fever, your nationality, and the chill that shrouds you. *And. your possible ancestral connection to Loftus Hall.* It all tallies. I would not say this lightly, nor am I trying to frighten you more than you both already are. But I *felt* something when you came in. A coldness. And not just a chilly cold, but an *otherworldly* cold. The type of cold that seeks to suck heat from a flame, and life from the living. Like your fever, it churns, first icy, then burning. Given hold will pollute your blood then devour your spirit. I would not mention these things had I not once previously experienced this same frigid fear crawl around my own spine, and know the legends and truths that I know.'

Mr and Mrs Moss were riveted to his unflinching stare.

'And these legends trace back to that damned mausoleum by the sea. I cursed the day it re-opened. Of course, the fact that *it is* haunted was never mentioned in their advertisements. But, I can tell you now for certain that it is a plagued palace. This is not a chance occurrence. Faith's hand is at play here today. As you were drawn there to face the dark, so too were you drawn here to escape it. I can help you. I have been waiting for you, and waiting fifty years for *his* return.'

Nancy was now awash with concern. Placing her faith in this stranger, like some palm reading gypsy, she probed him for answers. 'How do you know such things? What is it...what's after us? Why us? What did we do?'

His hands flat on the weathered table, Rubin ruminates, then speaks. 'I know such things because I have *seen* such things, first comes frost, then comes flame. It preys on the infected and the lame, the weak-willed and fantasy prone, the heirs of its tormentors. It seeks to snare the soul in flux and then assume itself in human form. The charming beast of seven cloaks. Usurper of gamblers and fools. The vengeful son of the bull, and King of Hell. He who pursues you is...Baal.'

'Jeeeesus Christ, Rubin,' the gob-smacked bartender wheezed. The gamblers and fools were equally stricken by the blood freezing proclamation.

'The demon seeks to absorb your husband's soul and to take earthly form. The sons of Eireann were granted protection from these demons by the Tuatha De Danann millennia ago. I have ways to delay this unholy communion. Though they are frail and only temporary. My hidden boots - an ancient superstition, serve as but a puny mousetrap for a creature of such power.' He reached to an inside pocket, 'Nancy, take this amulet and place it around your husbands neck.' The ugly adornment appeared to be bone. 'It is an ancient artefact. The Norse used it to as a shield against evil.. It is Odin's skull, it will help ease his fever and repel demons.

He turned to Dennis, who looked staggered by the unfolding drama. Opening his long overcoat Rubin plucked out from another pocket a small satchel. 'Take these crystals and spread them along threshold and sills'

'Well Holy Fuck! I was right.' Dennis blurted, staring at the small pink rocks.

'Its salt Dennis! It acts as a boundary and will buy us time, draw the curtains, when your done turn off the lights, and the outside lamp, then light candles, we don't need any more guests tonight'

And lastly from his coat, now more like a magicians robe, he unveiled a small ornate blade. He secured Nancy's delicate hand around it. 'This is a very sacred blade. I won't tell you of its origins. Pray you don't need to use it, but should the moment arise – do not hesitate.' Her face drew even further fearful.

Sidney, awaking somewhat from his stupor, began feeling warmth emanate around his chest where his grotesque new charm hung. He stared at Rubin incredulously. 'Who are you? What are you? Are you a priest?'

'Yes Rubin, Who the fuck are you.' gasped Dennis in disbelief.

***

For those stuffed into the strangled atmosphere of the cavernous inn, time seemed to decelerate. A candle lit scene of astonished faces playing in slow-motion. All of whom fearful to twitch, as though a giant king cobra had slithered from the fire, and reared up to hiss at them from the centre of the room.

Rubin did not address the room when he spoke, directing his replies squarely at the couple, his sole concern was to earn the trust of the frightened blow-ins, and find them safe passage from the terror that hunted them. Although, this didn't deter the audiences rapt attention from his every word. The cards, the inheritance, the dimming flames were now redundant. The convivial arena had morphed into an ethereal cabal. The stage now a set for a seance, or ouija board reading.

'I am not a priest. I have studied the ways of demons and witchcraft since I was a boy. These measures I've employed will frustrate the demon's access. The salt crystals, the amulet, the runes I carved into the door...'

'That was you?' huffed the aggrieved landlord.

'I am not a common vandal Dennis, I've read enough texts to suspect that the demon's path, and my own, were bound to cross again. Our first encounter was a half century ago to this exact day. I did not want to this morning's sun to rise for fear of the anniversary it heralded. But faith has entwined us, faith tethered the beast to Sidney's back, and faith has delivered them both to us tonight.'

The room warmed again, the chill sucked into the grate, out the chimney and into the night.

'We must get you both far from here, the next ferry leaves at dawn, and is only a short drive. The beast is bound by the sea, once on board you will be safe. But you must seek immediate medical help, Baal does not pursue a healthy host, I'm afraid your illness may prove to be more than just a thundering cough.'

Sidney, though his wits had returned, still look haggard. 'OK. This is all very far fetched, and if it hadn't been for our torment in that hotel last night I'd have considered you a raving maniac. But tell me, before we go scampering for the boat, tell me your story, you say you've seen this...Baal before, tell me what happened, what are we facing here?'

Dennis reached to the top shelf for the Black Bush, and passed it around. The party gathered closer together to hear his tale. He began…

***

"…At the age of twelve I was taken, rescued, from a Dublin orphanage - I'll spare you the sob story. The man who signed my release, and duty of care papers was a priest named Father Thomas Broaders. The terms of this agreement was to provide me with an education and a trade. Officially I was a book-binders understudy. But the truth was, Father Broaders needed an assistant for a quest which had consumed him for over forty years. I was a sturdy lad, quick to learn and resilient in spirit, traits he needed in a comrade to follow him down the chasms of darkness which he followed. Essentially I was the exorcist's apprentice.'

Oh yes, I was sceptic of his tales at first. At the very sight of this wizened priest you would scream 'Madman!' With his hair wild and white as ash and a scar that chased his face from his glass eye to his jugular. But his manner assured me was not that of the insane. Broaders was well spoken, educated and articulate - and focused, a driven man with a singular, thinly veiled obsession.

He told me he was once a very handsome man. A broad-minded gent from Kent. An inquisitive scholar. His vocation compelled him to banish evil in all its forms. He believed where there is life and light, death and darkness will always seek to corrupt and quash them. As a young man in

England and Rome, he studied obscure ancient texts, the metaphysical, the Sumerian scripts, the Grand Grimoire. He lived his life with a serious yet unburdened heart, until his own fateful encounter with Baal. The encounter that maimed him to the core. That fateful night was almost exactly one hundred years ago...in Loftus Hall.

That night he was summoned to oust the demon, he came too close to his hellish fire. He clashed with an evil none of his textbooks had prepared him for. He believed that he only half succeeded to thwart the beast that night. He fled from the house and sought isolation, he became reclusive and eccentric in his ways. He became consumed by Baal, and lived a dogged pursuit of him ever since. Like Ahab and the whale.

His pursuit became *our* pursuit. He tutored me in witchcraft, alchemy, astrology, demonology, purification rites and rituals. In between this he still made time to instruct me in the art of book binding, from saddle stitching to gilding, staying true to his oath to the orphanage.

Whether I believed he was delusional or not at this stage was now irrelevant, he took me from the cruddy kids home, tended to my welfare, and amid my bizarre schooling he showed me kindness and love. And I grew to love this arcane and enigmatic father-figure in turn.

He was certain in his belief that Baal would return. He restlessly sought a time and place, a date and coordinates, a stage and a curtain call. He upturned stones, raided crypts, burgled museums and drank in doss-houses, all to garner clues and tales about the miscreant. But aside from the nefarious dredging, there was always pure research and due diligence.

After three years his pupil, our divining and observations of increasing supernatural phenomena ushered us to a cairn on Montpelier Hill, not at all far from where we now sit. Cairns are large, heavy stones placed by man on certain hilltops, they are said to mark, commemorate and at times to restrain the dead. Some say they are laid to appease evil spirits.

Our pilgrimage to this site was hastened one night in September 1933, when an anomalous electrical surge reverberated across the city. The pulse seemed to trigger Broaders' sense of urgency. Early the following morning, we set off on foot from our Dublin dwellings to pursue, and hopefully conclude, our investigations. My duty was as a mute mule – to silently observe and cart our provisions and his wooden box of curious effects.

Up and up the hills took us, leaving the city below us in its smog. Father Broaders carried little more than his pipe, a map and a compass, while I toiled to the top like Sisyphus. When we reached our coordinates, we found no cairn, but in its stead was an ominous stone building. A lonesome hunting lodge had been built square over the burial site.

We had read of follies like this, sometimes used by the gentry as dens of inequity, for gambling, indulgence, and debauchery. Behind these walls the gentrified and civilised behaved like everything but, and here they committed sordid performances that I don't care too much to expand on.

Within the steamy mist on the hilltop, the damp air smelled eggy, the soft heather underfoot receded to bare rock, hot as though seared by the sun. The silhouetted structure protruded at the peak, jagged, like a giant stone tooth. Weeds writhed around its walls, and upon its apex gathered a murder of crows, eyeing our approach from the rooftop, then in turns they dived for carrion, which seemed plentiful on the ground.

A disquiet grew within us, but having come so far, we were not going let trepidation turn us around without seeking answers first. Broaders was teetering on exhaustion after the climb, and looked very poorly. Driven by our tiredness and hunger we approached the house and rapped on the door.

When at last it creaked open, and to our surprise, we were greeted warmly by a very tall and striking looking man, heavily dressed in luxurious garb.

We told him a mish-mash yarn, declaring ourselves as scholar and journeyman, taking a field trip, whilst conducting studies of historical landmarks of Ireland. Despite his fearful appearance, Broaders' intelligent tongue and respectable aura made him warm and affable when he needed to be.

Introducing himself as Lord Blake our immense host smiled, his long yellow teeth disconcerting, yet he seemed pleased to greet us into his home. 'Welcome to my house! Enter freely and of your own will.'

We followed his heavy footsteps clopping across the oak boards into the heart of the house.

In the drawing room there sat a small gathering, strikingly similar, in fact, to our present assemblage. The poker table, with three privates from the nearby barracks, paid us little heed. In a candlelit corner, two tawdry looking maidens, likely as working girls, eyed us, then turned away and whispered intimately to each other.

'Forgive the cold. We have only just started the fire,' came Blake's deep voice as he threw on logs and removed a layer of his plush clothing, the air immediately felt hotter. 'Great wood,' he grinned.

We were visibly tired and hungry. Blake turned and offered us food, 'Don't worry, the days of Holy Ghost Pie and Scaltheen have long since vanished from our menu. Make yourselves comfortable, I'll just be a moment.'

Broaders, now gaunt and aching, paid grace to our retreating host and hobbled toward the yawning stone fireplace to warm his frail fingers. He was scrutinising the huge mantle when a look of realisation came over him. He shot me a come-hither look, and unfolded an etching from his pocket. The print he held was of the cairn stone, a large obelisk, with distinct linear carvings. I followed Broaders eyes to the lintel above the hearth and observed the parallel markings. Without doubt, this granite bolster was the twin of the image in his hand.

Unearthing this ancient marker was akin to unplugging a portal to hell. Broaders urgently pulled out his notebook and anxiously flipped through the pages while mumbling names and dates. The priest shuddered as terror rose like a red dawn on his face.

At the card table, one of the privates erupted into a coughing seizure. The other players just mocked his phlegmy hacking.

'Boy!' he whispered.' We are in danger. Open the box, fetch me the vial of doves blood, and the dagger, and hide the ancient spearhead in your pocket, make haste!'

Unquestioning of my master I ran to it.

Blake returned with a silver tray laden with fresh fruit. 'Whatever is the matter Father? You look troubled...frightened even.'

'I've no time to explain, but we are all in imminent peril.' He gasped. 'You there, coughing at the card table, there is a beast coming for you,' he said, pointing at the young soldier.

His comrades just laughed at the crazed, jabbering old man. Ignoring them, Broaders opened the small bottle and poured an inky red circle around the bemused card player. Then he turned to Blake, 'Barricade the doors, nothing must gain entry this night. Boy, get the salt crystals for Mr...'

'Its already bolted' Blake calmly purred, placing down the silver tray of now corpulent fruit.

It was then, as I was bent over the wooden box, that I noticed beneath Blake's long robes. His strange elongated feet, bare and black and as cloven as a bull's hooves.

I cried out 'MASTER!' and gripped the iron spearhead concealed in my pocket. Blake sneered and grew taller still. He tore off another of his coats to reveal a shimmering layer of blood red clothing. The room becoming stifling. The walls started to smoulder, the heat was overwhelming. His guests, now appearing more evident as members of his loyal legion, sat in as though in worship, awestruck by his arcane majesty.

Broaders, once again eye to eye with his nemeses of five decades, mustered all the courage he had left in his frail body. 'Hand me the dagger son,' his hand extended to me as he gripped the ill soldier by the neck and bared his jugular. 'Baal, Prince of putrescence, I will spill this innocent man's blood and see his heart stop before I let you corrupt his soul with your foulness'

Blake, now the towering host of Hades, duke of the damned, smirked at his weakness and naivety. 'Spill his blood Priest, I will pour it into a grail and toast your death with it – after I swallow *your* wretched soul.'

The holy-man from Kent, ill of health, and now weakened and vulnerable, was a prime vestibule for the demon's depraved intent.

Broaders then realised his enormous mistake, the omens, the clues, the quest he had led, had all been in vain. It wasn't the poorly private playing cards that was the demon's quarry. No, it was Broaders had been unwittingly baited and lured to this desolate scalp. The vengeance he sought and the breadcrumbs he had followed to attain it, had all been insidiously placed in his path to cage him right there, right then.

A time and a place. Baal had been moving him like a piece on a chessboard and now he stood cornered. It was *check* to the demon.

Broaders' desperate mind frantically searched for some countermeasure, then an image of an ancient item crystallised in his thoughts...*The Holy Lance of Longinuse...There may yet be one last move.*

Exalting itself, the demon bayed and reared with menace. Broaders' eyes set calmly on me and then on the ancient spearhead, a precious artefact, stolen from the belly of Christ and then again, 1800 years later, stolen from the Weltliches Schatzkammer Museum during Broaders last pilgrimage to Vienna.

His resolute glare fixed on me, our telepathy strong. I had read the texts. I've had my training. I knew what I must do. And I must do it before doubt or any moral adjudicators within me raised a hand. The brass clasp around the iron blade glinted as I pointed it towards our demonic host.

It was puny against his hellish might, Blake looked mockingly at me as I raised my stubby weapon.

But it was not for him.

'Goodbye Father.' I whispered, before I plunged the blade deep into Broaders' heart, holding him dearly as his hot blood spilled in gouts over my hand. The mania that lined his face for so long, softened to a peaceful gaze as his spirit shed its mortal shell, foiling the demon's devious intentions.

Now enraged, the beast wailed in tortuous fury. With a whip of his giant arm he slapped me across the room. Desperately he clawed at Broaders' limp body before his aperture fused shut for another fifty years.

It was too late. Baal was thwarted. Checkmate Broaders.

In his rage and fury Blake ripped off the last of his garments and became a blaze of ferocious fire. I had landed next to the coal chute, and was nimble enough to scraper through it before the inferno took hold.

Safely outside I turned to witness the hill become a volcano. The flames and fumes created a brocken spectre of strangled light and shadows. I took flight down the hill and would not turn again, even as the agonised howls called out my name."

Rubin shot back his whiskey and scanned his captivated congregation.

'I've never returned to the place we all know now as the Hellfire Club, now a derelict shell for winos and pissants.'

***

The small gathering sat in frozen silence upon hearing this tale. The oppressive air fraught with menace. Jittery eyes flitted from window to door and to window again. Fingernails embedded into tabletops, jaws set hard and hairs rose on clammy prickly skin.

Coming to somewhat, they supped hard and fast on their spirits and lit up their smokes, fearing it may be their last time to do so.

Outside the evil grew dense, like thick smoke shrouding the old Inn. It preferred the threshold, to knock on the door, to be invited unwittingly, under guise or pretence. The Jew had foiled his element of surprise, but the delayed demon could wait, encircle and watch, and probe for a crack. Baal's host had been delivered and sat helpless inside. He would breathe his malice onto the walls and through the stone. Inside, they would succumb to fear and despair to escape their layer.

He would wait, yes, he would wait.

Inside the cauldron, the agitated patrons sweated and stewed. The pressure fluctuations squeezed and strained their thinly strung nerves, the inn felt like it was submerging fathoms below the ocean's surface.

Nancy nervously palmed her silver pendant, then grabbed her husband's arm, 'Right that's it, we have to leave Sidney, we have to get you to safety, and to a doctor, lets get to the port immediately and off of this cursed island.'

Rubin cocked his head upwards as though to smell the air. 'No', he warned, 'it is not safe now, you must take refuge here now till first light, I'm sorry, he waits outside like the wolf, prowling, sniffing for an opportunity to strike.'

'So what will we do till then, eh? Sing songs? Play cards? Drink ourselves to oblivion? Pray? Nancy snapped.

'We wait, keep alert, keep together. Prayer may help, so by all means pray, I too will chant the rites...but he will try to force his way in before dawn, he will not wait another fifty years to strike. We must prepare our minds, he seeks vulnerability, physical, mental and spiritual. We must dig deep, find our strength to survive the dark of this night.'

Marie rummaged in her handbag for her rosary beads. She blessed herself and began to recite the 'Our Father.' Her husband and the brothers gathered close, clasped hands and followed her chant in unison. *Prayer*, thought Rubin, *the last bastion for saints and sinners alike.*

Calmer now, Sidney tried to rationalise their precarious scenario. 'Rubin, you are certain it is this Baal demon! Why me? I am not special, nor righteous or religious, nor am I corrupt, nor malevolent. How do you know he appears every fifty years?'

'He cares not for the beliefs of man, and if I were to guess, he would prefer to corrupt the innocent. I know not the precise reason why he pursues you Sidney, other than than you fit the bill, and the chance that you may bear Loftus blood would appeal greatly to him - he is a vengeful deity, but you are merely a portal to him and his malicious will.' The wise old man said with empathy then added, 'Did you hear that thunderous roar earlier?'

Both Sid and Nancy both nodded their heads. They had nearly skid off the road upon hearing the ferocious bellow, such were there nerves. Dennis too, tipped his head in accord, 'Aye, it rattled the glassware, I nearly shat meself. That wasn't thunder I'm now presuming?'

'I heard the same crack as a boy. It woke me from my sleep the night before we set out to confront the demon fifty years ago. It is the clarion of his arrival, the violate trumpet of his return.' Rubin spat.

'Broaders' attention was first drawn to Baal today, September 23rd, one hundred years ago. He did not encounter his spirit until several months later. He wrote of the same hellish clap preceding the demon's footprints into our realm, even back then. He was a methodical chronicler. He kept a journal, a comprehensive report pieced together from his experiences, research, interviews, folklore. I have studied his findings exhaustively and delved as much into the past as I could to fill in many missing pieces of the jigsaw.' Rubin withdrew from his satchel a beautifully bound book, filled with notes, letters, photos and sundry articles Broaders and he had scraped together over one hundred years.

'Much of the story is lost to due to ramblings and embellishment, and the insanity and deaths that beset the trail of the beast. Strands of the story originate from your native country Sidney. But, it all started when a curious little girl once ventured too deeply down the rabbit-hole.'

Rubin struck a match and set fire to his bowl of tobacco, beneath his bushy eyebrows he squared his pale eyes with Sid and Nancy. 'It is quite the tale. It begins almost one hundred years ago, back at the damned hotel from where you have just come from. So, do you think you're prepared to hear this unsettling story?'

The stricken lovers regarded one another, agreed without speaking and nodded for him to continue.

<u>Loftus Hall, Wexford 1879</u>

Steeped in the turbulent Irish sea, guarded by an army of treacherous limestone teeth and a medieval sentinel, Hook peninsula protrudes. Home to Europe's oldest lighthouse, and graveyard to a thousand ships.

The beauty you may find on this jutting headland is not upon the jagged black rock, nor flat bleak marsh, rather it is a romantic beauty, a beauty you must *feel* more-so then see. So close your eyes, feel the chill sea-spray on your cheeks and behold with your mind this beauty. Allow it to refract the spectrum of your soul onto that screen where your memories, dreams and fantasies are projected.

On this almost deserted plateau one can't help but echo its cries of isolation. The remote outcrop, a thin boggy thread feebly connected to the disinterested mainland, as desperate and lost as the hopes of a spurned lover.

From the seas foaming wrath, travel north along the desolate plain, before long an imposing structure will draw your eyes west. Like a tombstone alone in a waste cemetery, Loftus Hall juts from the earth as though it was forced, unwanted, from the fiery underbelly of this world.

Grey as thunderheads the monolith stands, defiant of the gales, defiant of the barren landscape, and defiant of time. Spurned by royalty, she sits brooding on the bog. If Mrs Havisham was built of timber, block and mortar, then this is surely the monument where she pains, and pines for her lover to return.

The year of Our Lord is 1879, but to understand how this once fine abode came to this this grim juncture we must travel back in time a little further, less than ten years to see her in her grandeur, soaring proud and magnificent in her splendour after her extensive renovations. A stately country home fit for a king, or in the case of the Loftus and Tottenham families, their Queen.

During the summer of 1869 the Lord Charles Loftus received word, stamped with Her Majesty's royal seal, that his family may expect to receive the pleasure of a regal convocation with Queen Victoria at their home, while She attended to her royal duties during a state visit to Ireland.

Upon receipt of this news the Loftus and extended families rejoiced and were filled with a renewed sense of purpose, zeal and enthusiasm. The neglected building, as fine and grand as it was, was in dire need of a comprehensive overhaul and a considerate makeover to drag her dated countenance and dreary constitution out of the seventeenth century and propel her, splendiferously into the nineteenth.

The extents and expense Lord Charles undertook in preparation for Her visit were vast and lavish. Though he was an engineering and crafts enthusiast, Charles abhorred physical labour and intended never to as much as handle a hammer. But he was not opposed to spending big when it came to hiring the right tradesmen. Specialist masons and craftsmen were drafted from across Europe to ensure the highest standard of finishes.

Opulent materials such as Italian marble and Spanish tile were shipped in, regardless of cost. Tonnes of oak varieties were imported to craft the intricately designed, nail and bolt free, interlocking staircase, the show-piece of the undertaking, matched only in its identity by a replica in the Vatican, and a soon to be built, unsinkable sailing marvel called the Titanic. An ornate and uniquely designed tiled floor greets your first steps into the Hall. The hypnotic ocular pattern seems to examine you, as much as you scrutinise it, as you wander in.

Countless marble fireplaces, numerous bespoke Waterford crystal chandeliers, rich wallpapers and deep luxuriant carpets all adorned the halls. Tapestries denoting the proud Loftus ancestry and their ties to royalty were commissioned for a specially designated room within the three tiered mansion. The roof was completely restored and neatly framed by a broad balustrade parapet and guarded by magnificently sculpted eagles.

The land to the rear contained large furrowed vegetable gardens, the gardeners, like bees at the hive, tended to their prize parsnips and potatoes with as much devotion as they showed the rose beds. The family enjoyed home grown fruit and vegetables almost year round, and much of the produce, and salted meats could be preserved in the deep ice-pit to the rear of the allotment.

One exits the rear gardens via an archway, over which, engraved into the lintel, is the enigmatic family emblem, a Boar, its jaw and savage teeth raised in a snarl to the heavens. Continuing on, you wind along a twisting path into an immaculately tended world of well coiffed hedges and borders. Exotic plants and other wonderful varieties of native and non-native flora were plentiful, their perfumes divine. An ornate fountain trickles gently into the koi pond while beautiful Roman busts gaze idly beneath the shade of the willows and laburnum.

When it was complete, the Hall shone like a crown and looked as gilded, as elegant and as indulgent as royal wedding cake.

***

It was a time of great joy and excitement and camaraderie. With an honour of such magnitude bestowed upon the family, they all rallied joyfully towards a common purpose. United in their task, the family bond had never been stronger.

The goodwill even spread, to a degree, outwards into the local villages and town-lands. It was not that any of the native Irish had any great desire to welcome *Her* to their tiny corner of the world, but the labour involved in undertaking and completing the massive restoration project meant plenty of work, and plenty of money, for tradesmen and labourers, skilled or otherwise. While they may have spat on her face stamped onto their coins, it did not stop them filling their pockets with them.

But the dark legend of the Hall still lingered. Even through the heady years of the rebuild, when goodwill and well-being brought relative prosperity to the community, and pleasant discourse between the classes and nationalities, it could not hush the whispers. The ancient ivy that gripped and matted the walls of Loftus Hall was far easier to abolish than the well established tales, the spectral stories and phantasmic folklore that clung to the hearth of the manor, the roots of which they believed bore deep into the earth's bowels and down further yet, into Hell itself.

Fables of fire breathing demons, banshees on the balustrade, cloaked figures clouded in smoke, unearthly night-walkers and unholy graves, spoken in hushes throughout the townlands. Murmurs of madness and whispers of wickedness abound.

It was treated by the nobility in their grandiose houses that ghost stories and grand estates go hand in glove, par for the course. They come with the territory, mildew on the grapevine. No manor worth its salt would be found wanting for a haunting, a curse, or a rogue spirit gracing its corridors.

The family Loftus scoffed and tittered at the silly stories that stirred over the turf fires that lit up the local villages and hills. They noticed as *Oiche Shauna* approached so too the villagers distanced themselves from the vicinity of the Hall, unless on urgent errand. The patronising gentry thought it pleasantly parochial and quite a quaint custom amongst the naive natives. The subject of the Ghost of Loftus Hall was, without exception, a source of great amusement and levity at every reception and dinner party. Each of the guests denouncing, with scholarly derision, the latest spooky anecdote they had caught wind of.

After all, the great ancestral home of the Loftus, during the current generations residency, and in very recent history, there had occurred very little phenomena that didn't incur a rational explanation, nor any *supernatural* event that did not merit a logical deduction. On occasion, the very rare, yet peculiar incidents that did cause consternation or bafflement, were denounced as mere quirks of the manor's microcosm. The mystery of which, the haughty overlords assure us, will oneday be prudently unlocked by science. But until then, none may speak, nor whisper of them ever transpiring. Loose Lips deter Queens.

The good monarch however, was deterred. Or, maybe she just postponed her trip indefinitely. Maybe it was a matter of urgent national address that flipped her decision to visit the Emerald Isle. Or, maybe the whispers of haunted halls wafted all the way to her throne. One would assume Victoria would not be dissuaded by banshees, leprechauns or the Fir Bolg – the ancient ghostly garrison of Eire. But, maybe her intended visit was just a hollow promise, trumpeted by her royal emissary to keep Her subjects, Her Lords and Her Ladies in check, and all dutifully dancing to her tune.

If we were to glean any plus side to their misfortune, the anticipated imminence of Her Eminence did, at least, serve to drag the manor from an idle state of disrepair to a dwelling of palatial magnificence. Without Victoria's note expressing her keen interest to meet with Lord and Lady Loftus, the building would have inched far quicker to dereliction.

Alas as a consequence in the spring of 1879, this had become its fate. The rate of erosion and corpulence, for some unholy reason, seemed to accelerate here more so than on any other structure on the peninsula.

As well the dilapidated building, the fallout and disillusionment of the Queens truancy also quashed Lord Loftus once abundant zeal and vigour, and he slid into a pit of languor, and an even deeper pit of debt.

***

Dwelt within the walls of Loftus Halls were the Loftus and Tottenham families. Amongst these were, the current custodians the 4th Marquess of Ely - Lord Charles Loftus and Lady Anne Tottenham and their family of six children, four boys, William, George, Charles (Charlie) and Alfred, and two girls Elizabeth and little Anne, or Annie as she was affectionately called to avoid confusion with her mother.

Most of our focus will concern Annie, the most bonnie and vibrant of souls living within the dimming mansion.

Jane and Thomas Cliffe, cousins to the Tottenhams, were also in residence. Thomas was married to Beatrice Lyons with two sons, Cecil and Frederick.

Charles and Anne enjoyed an enviable marriage. Both were handsome and loving, and as devoted to one another as swans in springtime, their opulent nest teeming with healthy and happy offspring. The family kept good stead with Her Majesty's peripheral circles and were wholly respected amongst the peerage. A reception in Loftus Hall was a reception not to be missed. Stations and careers were well served by ingratiating oneself jovially with the social and political might that gathered for their lavish lunches and decadent dinner dates. The summer of the Loftus family's life was a vignette from a fairytale. Their winter though, would be anything but.

The boys, disciplined, elocuted and groomed to fulfil their expectant role of burgeoning statesmen still managed plenty of time for horseplay. None of whom enjoyed a particularly keen intellect and these limitations seemed to descend in direct correlation with their ages, William the oldest possessing the lions share of the grey cells while Alfred still wrestled to shed the primordial ooze of intellectual evolution. They were however affable and kindly, and under the strict doctrines of a blue-bloods education they managed to pass themselves off as semi-literate members of the gentry.

Jane and Thomas Cliffe and his family, resided at the Hall while protracted renovations to their own manor, on nearby Tottenham Green, continued. As the works grew nearer to their completion, Thomas eagerly itched to move out from under the feet of his very accommodating cousins, and enjoy the comforts of his own home while his children were still young. Jane however felt less exuberant to leave the house she had grown so accustomed to over the last six years. She was particularly fond of Charles and maybe a little green of eye when it came to his perfect romance with his demure and devoted wife. She hoped Anne had never noticed when she allowed her gaze to linger on Charles' magnetic smile for longer than the cousin of a married man ought to.

Elizabeth was the winsome one. The sober one. Indeed most folk would appear serious in comparison to her flighty little sister. Elizabeth strode upright gracefully, kept her conversation polite and her opinions in reserve. She met with all company respectfully, and it was ever a boon have her attend your receptions. With her tact and temperance she always knew the correct remark and delicate quip to deliver in civilized circles.

Elizabeth conscientiously took time to amuse her manic little sister. In fact, Annie's vibrancy was somewhat of an alleviation to the straight laced sibling. They would sit on the garden swing together, Elizabeth would feel herself unwind, feel her corset ties loosen and her hair blow freely. With love, she recalled the lazy, sun drenched days of swinging and singing into the heavens while their darling mother brought them lemonade and sponge-cake.

Lady Anne was a very hands on woman and would sometimes insist, outside of protocol, that she be allowed to carry out kitchen activities if she so desired. To bake a rhubarb tart or fairy cakes was a simple delight she might engage in once a month, and Annie would always assist in breaking the eggs and licking the spoon. It was highly irregular for the family to enter the kitchen or scullery, but even Jane, with her staunch views on propriety and place was sometimes surprisingly spotted, furtively brewing up a pot of tea when she thought no one was watching. Their presence in these quarters made the staff feel particularly uneasy, but they were always on ready standby to source the sugar bowl for them, or mop up their spilt milk.

In the mansion's hay-day, a small army of servants and grounds-keepers manned the kitchens, halls and gardens. The staff were all locally sourced, appreciative of the work and silently begrudging of their submissive station to their protestant superiors. Truth told, they were all treated respectfully and fairly, and quite content in their ranks. All within the Loftus employ diligently set to their duties to ensure that both the upkeep of the estate, and the whims of the family, were obediently met at every turn. The head roles were lead by Mr Delaney, Charles' devoted Butler. Missus Meades the faithful and biddable housemaid. Treasa the tireless young cook and Mr Casey the ageing head gardener.

Every room at one point homed occupants, a brother or a sister, an aunt or an uncle, there were cousins galore and friends and guests in abundance. Along with the commotion and racket during the renovations, the place flurried with life, with wonder and bustle and light and colour, and dear little Annie delighted in the pandemonium and hubbub of it all.

Any visit to the Hall during its zenith would have greeted you with a throng of activity, energy and gusto. Life in the Hall reached its pinnacle of happiness during the renovations, the children played in the blooming gardens while the grown ups rode a gilded wave of excitement and giddiness. Allowing themselves to patiently starve in their finery at the lavishly laden banquet table, sliver spoons at the ready, swallowing their pooling saliva as their bellies rumbled, waiting for their monarch to arrive.

After the royal axe felled the tree of their fruitful ambitions, the mood became sullen and at times morose, and how quickly their food spoiled and flowers wilted as a consequence. The children still played as children do, but their laughter now echoed dull and distantly on the richly wallpapered halls.

Eventually, even the vibrancy of youth skidded to an unexpected halt when their mother, Anne, took ill shortly after the disappointment of the visit that never was. After a spell of fatigue and listlessness, initially attributed to depression, Anne became addled, feverish and bedridden. Doctor Chisholm was summoned, and after some bafflement he eventually concluded that advanced dysentery had taken hold. The illness began to squeeze and diminish her, food would not remain inside her, and eventually it could barely be taken at all.

The children watched as their graceful, doting and always kind mother, began to fade and shrivel, the paling of her ruby cheeks like an early frost on the rose. She wasted hopelessly, beyond the cure of medicine, the care of the doctors and the love of her devoted family.

The blow the family incurred by their exclusion from their Queen dwarfed in comparison to the passing of Anne less than two years later. A broken promise to a broken heart.

The compounding effect of the death proved overwhelming, and the once pristine family veneer grew tarnished and cracked, chipped and dull. The boys seemed to grow into men overnight, they yearned to vacate the Hall, and one by one found colleges, careers or stations overseas, far from the confines of the grey manor walls.

Elizabeth and Annie remained, wandering the corridors and gardens, bereft and adrift, although Elizabeth too, had her eyes on faraway horizons.

Annie was just a sapling when her dear mother died. From this sad juncture, her already spry and curious mind began to skew more-so towards the fantastic and delusionary.

Furthermore, fresh misery lade onto the girls when Charles, with the very best intentions for his family and the estate's concerns, took a new wife. Their brief courtship and betrothal was complete in less than ten months after their mother died, a suitable enough time for Anne to cool in her grave. But only Just.

Jane Cliffe was Charles' cousin on the Tottenham side of the family. Although there were no blood ties, in Annie's fertile mind even the suggestion of an incestuous connotation in their relationship repulsed her. It made her think of some of the peculiar looking offspring that would fascinate her when her carriage trundled through rural Irish townlands and villages.

Jane made herself an immediate source of comfort to Charles, ever present with a supportive smile and always ready to offer a heartening embrace, bordering on wanton with her overtness. Charles, though fond of Jane, found ulterior intentions to marry, viewing the union as a means to help bolster the families weighty debts, and also to provide a caring governess for his remaining children. Jane however, blatantly held a tacit disinterest towards Charles' sweet girls, and met with them coolly and perfunctory, her indifference towards the pair barely concealed.

Elizabeth, mature beyond her years, managed to maintain with her a courteous contact and a modest distance. While Annie, ever flighty and whimsical, conjured fanciful illusions, drawn from Aesop and Grimm, of her wicked stepmother, dark, thorny and deceptive on her throne. Outwardly however, she enjoyed deploying her own duplicitous tactics, and always met Jane with overbearing joy and sickly-sweet manners.

Annie often wished the fragments of the ghost stories she overheard about her home were true and that her mother's apparition might some-night glide in through her curtains to comfort her. At times she would tip-toe along the dark corridors at night in the hope of finding a glowing spectre or even a floating sheet. Her faith in the netherworld waning as each night passed.

Disillusioned, she sometimes even donned a long white veil and ghosted through the halls herself, stopping at the giant mirror to regard her ethereal appearance in the moonlight.

It was on one of these nights, while Annie was performing as the spectre of her deceased mother - her face powdered and donned in her mother's ill-fitting wedding gown, that Jane too, came wandering down the hall. When she turned to see the miniature, resurrected spirit of Lady Anne dancing before the great mirror, Jane spun into convulsions of fear and fell backwards to the floor shrieking, and alerting the entire household to her distress.

Annie the wraith, the very semblance of her mother's visage, then approached Jane to try to console her, which only made her more hysterical, so Annie ran to hide in her bedroom.

When Father found her feigning sleep under her sheets, the wedding gown concealed poorly beneath her bed, and her face still pale with powder, he was livid, and called an immediate cease and desist to her midnight wanderings.

Still, Annie considered Jane's histrionics excessive and suspected that the replacement wife hid a weight of guilt for making herself so wantonly available to Charles so soon after Anne's passing. And, for generally being a ghastly substitute for her dear mother ever since.

Before their mother's death, the girls would amuse themselves together for hours on end. Swinging from ropes, chasing through the surrounding woodland, concocting prison escapes, gunpowder plots and romantic interludes. They collected ladybirds and cherry blossom petals, made perfumes and poisons, they tied daisy chains and sang, '*jinny joe-jinny joe, bring me back my Romeo,*' as they blew dandelion fluff into the wind.

Annie had derived many games of her own, her favourite being one she called *Chorigami*, whereby one player must chose a person, a place or a thing, and the other must attempt to represent it in the form of dance. On one occasion Annie's choreographic rendition of Elizabeth's suggestion to portray *water,* made Elizabeth giggle so much she got belly cramps and her cheeks hurt for a full hour afterwards.

But now, at seventeen, Elizabeth spent her days tending to the blossoms of her new romance with Arthur, from Sussex. Daily you would find her at her bureau, her quill earnestly tracing lamenting lines of love and devotion to her darling. Their intensive correspondence built the emotional footing upon which she would soon embark towards her new life.

Arthur Penbury was her beloved fiancé. An engineer and artist acquainted with the family through the restoration period. An affable fellow and aptly suited for the fair and kind Elizabeth, and visibly she heartened in his presence, audibly too - her voice gaining an octave on his arrival.

Annie felt no envy, nor begrudgery towards her darling sister's engagement and happiness. In the absence of her boisterous brothers, she too loved the conservative yet self-effacing Arthur and his goofy antics with her. Though the Arthurs of the world, she decided, were neither her type nor her ideal of a beloved counterpart. She believed in her mind that a far more feral and misunderstood creature would oneday rescue her from her dark, ivy clad tower.

This industrious exchange of letters and notes to and from Wexford and Sussex left little time for Elizabeth and Annie's close childhood friendship to endure and Annie found herself increasingly alone with her books, bobbins, and bows.

Their mother taught them to embroider and sew, to crochet and weave, and the three ladies enjoyed many nights tittering by the fires whilst creating doilies and doll hats. Now Annie sat alone in the voluminous tapestry room, regarded only by the intricately woven eyes of the men, boar and dragon draping heavily along its walls.

Here Annie would cart in her sewing box and set to some couture emergency for her many dolls and soft toys. Or she may gather a pile of books from the library and lose herself for hours in a tale about shrinking girls and white rabbits, or learn how to make potions or cast spells from The Little Book of Witchcraft. Any random tome would engage her, all kinds of everything piqued Annie's fertile young imagination.

Humming a tune she overheard one time at a wake about a raggle taggle gypsy, Annie leafed through a maritime yarn by Edgar Allen Poe, the premise of this tale, the author had decided, he had found encased inside a floating bottle.

She was today feeling particularity perturbed about Elizabeth's waning interest in her. Chess, chasing and charades were simply far less fun on one's own, Annie deduced, after several attempts at self-ammusment.

On a sheepskin rug before a blazing fire she lay with her dog. Baggy, her faithful border collie, sat at her side as she kicked her heels behind her. 'You'll never dessert me, will you Baggy?' The happy dog tilted his head curiously, then licked Annie's lips. She giggled and licked him back, oblivious to any sanitary concerns. They then rolled playfully together on the rug until Baggy barked a cheery yap, which Annie, believing she clearly understood animal linguistics, construed as conversation.

'Really Baggy? What a wonderful idea. Oh you are a clever collie...but, how Baggy?' she quizzed back to her pet. 'Hmm?'

Distracted now, she tried to return her attentions her book, the doomed vessel was just about to get swallowed by a vast whirlpool when Annie slammed it shut before the cataclysmic finale. She now knew what she must do. If Elizabeth can find love with pen and ink, then *By Golly* so could Annie.

***

At dawn, Loftus Hall casts its long shadow over a small family cemetery to its rear. In the gloom we see the faint names on the headstones, dating back over six hundred years. Many of the engraved titles have been eaten smooth by times tiny teeth, and now appear barely legible. But under scrutiny, we will find the distinguished name of the Loftus ancestry, Earls and Viscount, Duchess and Marquess, Lords and Ladies, all resting in peace.

The most recent addition to this stately subterranean gathering was the good Lady Anne Tottenham, who just a few years ago was tragically taken from her dearest sons and daughters before most of them became teens.

Due to regular tending and continual blooms, this allotment appears as the brightest, cleanest and most colourful amongst all the graves belonging to Anne's neglected peers. However, as you walk past, it may *seem* that the morning shadow appears to loom darker and hold its umbra denser around the pretty plot.

Surely this is more to do with sentiment. Our perception playing *trompe l'oiel* with our imagination. But certainly, the sadness caused by the loss of this wonderful lady upon the Loftus household runs far deeper than six feet beneath the lawn.

Within the home, the giant rooms in the hall grew even larger and emptier in her absence. The echoes of the children rang louder in the vastness, until one by one, her chicks grew tall and spread their wings. After they flew the coup, nothing remained but their broken shells in the silent halls of the great Loftus nest.

But now the sun ascends, gradually it gains dominion in the sky and the morning shadows shrink and scuttle to hide. Soon the little graveyard bathes in light. The morose mood diminishes, and the atmosphere there becomes fresh and green and airy. The blooms crane there slender necks along the solar path and the sundials arrow begins its arc.

Through the gaining chorus of birds we hear another merry song. The lilt approaches and with it an abundance of life floods into the garden of the dead. Annie Loftus-Tottenham, now almost in her teens yet still as vibrant and vivacious as a sea of sunflowers, skips and zig-zags and leapfrogs over the stone markers, barefoot in the short wet grass.

She winds her way wistfully to her mother's floral mound to wish her a very good morning, sliding to her knees as she comes to rest at the foot of the grave. 'Good morning Mummy, look what I've found for you,' she said, and took from her basket a clump of amber nasturtium, violet gentian, some chestnuts, a large red toadstool and a plump garden frog. 'Isn't he a wonderful fellow, I don't yet speak *frog* yet, but I do understand it. His name is Byron and he asked to meet you. However I've a feeling he's going to hop off soon.' But Byron just sat, quiet and patient on the foraged flora.

'Ick Mummy! Look at your lovely headrest, the snails are slithering their silvery mess everywhere,' the young girl jumped and flicked the little pests into the grass 'Now shoo! Scat before you're hedgehog food.'

Annie settled by the headstone, 'Mummy, My darling sister is soon to forsake me for her lover, you know of course all about this Arthur chap. Oh, I'm sure he's wonderfully proper and as suitable as a silk glove for our dear Elizabeth, and I do wish her so much happiness. Of course, his type is really not for me when I debut. I think for me it will be a hunter or soldier, brave and heroic, oh how he would fill my heart to its brim. Maybe, he might get awfully wounded at war, and possibly die, and my grief will know no end, and I'll live alone in the Hall with a thousand cats.' She fingered her button nose and wiped it clean in her brown petticoats. 'Anyway, she sails to England next Sunday to spend some time in Sussex, I'll miss her awfully Mummy, no one else seems to have any tolerance for my creative little diversions, nor the faintest inkling of how to enjoy life anymore. I won't even bore you again with my feelings on Jezebel Jane, the wanton, sham Queen of Loftus. Oh how I wish a fish-bone would prick her throat.' She breathed and reset herself.

'The point is, I'll need to replace Elizabeth with a sturdy and caring soul who will devote himself to me, but who else is there on this lonely shore. Baggy suggested I should find a pen pal to correspond with. He's such a clever doggy. So I shall prepare a special message, an SOS, detailing my plight and my loneliness. I shall send it with Elizabeth on her voyage, and should she meet a young cadet or circus acrobat, she may pass it on for him to begin our correspondence.' Annie sighed heavily, 'Until then maybe I'll just send smoke signals, or tie a note to a carrier pigeon.'

'I'm going to knit Elizabeth a shrug for her birthday, I find the ones she wears awfully prim. I shall fashion for her one with thick homely wool, rich in pattern and trimmed with a playful fringe. She tends to me so so readily and kindly. I love her dearly, and I, to this end wish to repay her kindness while also highlighting the many errors in her wardrobe,' she sighed. 'But I do wish you were around to assist me with the roses I intend to crochet, I am still quite the fidget with darning needles.'

The thrum of enthusiastic bees on the lavender was the only reply. This pleased the young girl but she maintained a lookout for a further communiqué. Byron the frog remained mute. Annie sat back against the supporting headstone and surveyed the skies. The sun-bleached billows blew slowly over the roof of the house. In the trees the warming dew steamed slowly through the brush, and from where the hedging skirted the lawn a small twitching creature caught Annie's eye.

She slunk behind the pillar, so not to scare off the little rabbit. From her hide she watched its fawn form scuttle yonder and fro between the stones, and rudely over the sleepers beneath. Sometimes still and alert, then curious and nibbling the shrubs again. 'Well, good morning Mrs Furrball,' Annie whispered to herself, 'What's your name? Lucy? Fuzzy Lucy?...I know, Lucy-Fur! Are you looking for a carrot?'

Annie mused and mentally scrolled through the many pages she had read. From a tender age she was fantastically keen on books of all classes and categories, and held within her a substantial database to access for a girl so young.

All country manors of substance and pride should house a comprehensive library, from which family members can advance the intellect and imagination. Loftus Hall was no exception and their library stacked on its shelves over three thousand tomes from Austen to Zangwill. Among these Annie had many well-leafed favourites, Little Women, The Anatomy of the Bones, The Fowler, The Complete Embroidery and Needlework Handbook, Alice in Wonderland, and The History of Magic.

Extracts from the latter two titles now swirled and knit in her vivid mind. Was Mrs Fur her own private messenger from the netherworld, hopping towards her to whisper her mother's wishes? Did her burrow wind deep underground, and did she make her home in the coffin below, nestling at night in her mother's burial gown, now sunk between her caved chest cavity?

A rabbit in a graveyard reminded her of another superstition she once read about. While she pondered this option, the rabbit was suddenly startled and scarpered quickly out of sight. Byron too, took the disturbance as an opportunity to spring away into the long grass. Disgruntled, Annie bit her top lip and turned to detect the cause of their concerns.

'Good morning young lady,' the lanky gardener announced, as his rusty barrow whined.

'Michael!' Annie scowled, 'you really must learn to be more stealthy in your approach. You would rouse the bones of the very dead beneath us with those clumpy boots and that old rickity rick.'

Slightly confused, Michael humbly apologised to the young madam. Then he gave her a friendly smile and ambled on. Yes, he was an affable fellow, quite a gormless young giant with his gentle face and curiously *crossed eyes*....

That's it! Annie's epiphany sparked and she realised with immediate clarity the fateful meaning behind the arrival of this morning's furry visitor.

'Young Master Casey! Halt and listen to me, my very fine fellow. I have been bestowed a task, a sacred task I might add, that you, and only you can assist me with, for you have the gift. I'll need your wits, cunning and utmost discretion. What do you say? Have you the stomach for it? Will you help me?'

The lumbering gardener was very fond of the little garden sprite and would have done anything he could to bring her cheer. 'Of course, Lady Annie. Happy to help you on your quest. What can I do for you?'

'Hazzah' she beamed. 'Quickly, to the tool-shed we must haste, we'll need a cage, twine, a loppers,' then extending the point of her finger to the tip of his nose she added, 'And a tasty carrot!'

She dashed off to raid the scullery in search of treasure. There she found buried in some bins, a trove of discarded wine and whiskey bottles to choose from.

***

Sir E.A. Wallis Budge, Annie recalled, was a noted figure in Egyptology, This philologist also possessed a wealth of knowledge on superstitions, amulets and talismans. It seemed to her to be a preordained fate, that she should read his detailed section on the *Rabbit's Foot* as a charm, just days before Lucy-Fur popped out of her hole to wriggle her nose and say hello to her.

In order to attain a *true* charmed rabbit's foot, one cannot simply lop one off, run to the whist table and gather your fortune. If that were true the countryside would be littered with millionaires and three legged bunnies. Nay, an alignment of factors must be in place to divine the magick.

Firstly, the rabbit must be captured in a cemetery. Next, the rabbit must be captured by one with a rare ocular defect - crossed eyes. It should also preferably be caught on a Friday or during a full moon, and as providence would have it, this day bore both.

Serendipity was moving great pieces on the chessboard of Annie's destiny today.

Michael had no moral issue capturing and killing rabbits, he and his father frequently sought them out for a decent stew. He was also eager to make little Annie smile, he was only a few years her senior, but he felt a brotherly protectiveness and great empathy towards the lonely child, her peculiarities fascinated him, so he was happy to indulge her.

All set, they sat and waited for their quarry that clear evening behind a couple of headstones. The sun was still far from set and the early moon was already full, and climbing from the sea into the dusky blue sky.

Annie kept lookout and Michael held the string that tethered the twig that held open the gate to the little cage with the big carrot inside. The cage was placed neatly inside an auspicious dark ring on the lawn, most likely the result of dancing fairies, if Annie's folklore knowledge was correct.

Annie scoured the deep shadowy borders for movement, but for now only the occasional bird foraging through the leaf litter.

Michael's kindly face remained keen for Annie's sake, though he was tiring and losing faith. His odd eyes moved back and forth between her and the cage, one slowly catching up with the other, before the speedy eye would dart again, leaving the tardy one to begin its pursuit anew.

Annie nibbled her nails and whispered down to her dead mother. 'Please Mummy, this is a matter of utmost urgency, can you send Lucy-Fur out to us again, we have the fattest carrot in the world for her.'

Annie's pursed lips pinched to a small smile as something started through the undergrowth, then from beneath the hydrangea little Lucy-Fur popped out her nose.

'Thanks Mummy.'

The hunters grew silent and as still as gargoyles amidst the flanking granite stones. The curious rabbit gingerly sniffed the air, and hopped ever closer towards the trap. She tried to chew the rusty bars of the cage then shook her head in distaste. Ears back and down she paused at the gate, the tasty orange root willing her in. Michael prepared to yank the string, Annie biting her finger to keep the squeaks of excitement escaping her.

Lucy had one foot over the threshold when Baggy spotted Annie covertly crouched behind the pillar. The joyous dog then bound into the cemetery towards her, barking with enthusiasm.

The startled bunny darted aimlessly in between the headstones where the assassins were hiding. Before the confused cony had the chance to say, 'Oh, Hello again Annie,' Michael's heavy muddy boot stomped down on her back. There wasn't even a squeal. Lucy-fur was dead.

Baggy growled at the flattened creature, Michael looked sheepishly at Annie, her face taut in an awkward grimace, her eyes fixed on the crime scene. She raised her look to Michael then uttered a great squeal of joy.

'*Go hunting for rabbits - be eaten by wolves!* Michael, thou art the most cunning of all predators!' She leapt and gave him a huge hug.

Michael felt immense pride and shared her joy, but kept himself subdued. He shoved Baggy's curious nose away from the carrion with the offensive boot and lifted limp little Lucy-fur into the cage. 'I'll take her away and get that paw removed and off to the stuffer Miss Annie.' He was referring to a taxidermist he father knew. 'A young lady wouldn't want to be witnessing such brutality.'

'Nonsense Michael, there be no lilly-livers in my belly. Plus I need to be certain you lop off the long eared lop's right foot, and by right I mean her left one. Right?' she giggled confusingly. 'Now, give me that carrot.'

Seizing the vegetable from him she snapped it in two, offered Michael one half and chomped a bite from hers, 'Huzzah for Lucy-Fur!'

***

The Saturday before Elizabeth's departure fizzed with a frenzied fervour and no short measure of apprehension. The open door to the beginning of a bright new life awaited her. Stepping through meant leaving behind the world in which she grew into a young woman, a world that now bore no familiarity to the effulgent place in her memory. Its sunshine forever lost behind the clouds and the cobwebs of life's catastrophes.

The difficult part wasn't stepping through the door, or 'walking the plank,' as her father put it in jest. The strain on her heart came when she envisioned letting go of Annie's hand, leaving her in the cavernous castle with her distracted Daddy and malcontent stepmother. She could not help but feel selfish and guilty, she longed to pack her inside her luggage case and stow her along with her on her voyage.

But there was excitement too, when she allowed herself to feel it. Arthur adored and cherished her, he was smart and gentle and his home in Sussex suffered from none of the stigmas, burdens or bleak histories that shadowed her family home. At times her heart flared brightly with the prospects of her future, and she felt that if she could simply fly to England from the rooftop then she'd forgo the boat trip entirely.

Elizabeth's first visit was planned to last a month. With the aid from her maid and a servant girl they managed to pack a cartful of cases for her journey. Elizabeth was very keen to have Annie involved in the process, and whatever bauble, trinket or garment Annie took a fancy to, Elizabeth made her abundantly welcome to have and keep them.

There was very little in her wardrobe that Annie felt was her style, but she did like the materials used, and thought, that with some help from a scissors and thread she could transform some of the extravagant dresses into fashionable works of art.

'I'll take this one darling sister if you please,' Annie said folding the copious taffeta of a maroon ball-gown. It was one of Elizabeth's favourites, but she feigned genuine delight in donating it to her. 'And I have something for you Bizzy-Lizzy, so leave some room in that case.' She shot off to her bedroom to fetch a package.

Annie returned and unwrapped from brown paper a beautiful aquamarine cardigan. The rich woollen shrug was a very neat cashmere knit of chunky turquoise yarn. It felt as soft as a kitten and as warm as hot cocoa. Fat and shiny chocolate buttons kept it fastened and a delicately scalloped lace neatly defined its trim. It was everything that amiable Annie represented in Loftus Hall, a colourful and comforting curiosity in an otherwise chill and dull dimension.

'I did not manage to get it completely finished dear, you see here at the shoulders,' Annie pointed, 'Here will perch apricot coloured blossoms, I find crochet quite fiddly still, and I think you can assist me with that when you return. Shall I jot you in for an appointment in the tapestry room?'

Elizabeth pulled its fluffy pile to her cheeks and warm tears filled her eyes. 'Oh yes Annie of course you can, book me in for four weeks to the day. I simply adore it, it's so beautiful, I shall wear it tomorrow on the cold boat to remind me of you. It will warm me as your sweet smile warms my heart. I cannot bear to leave you here alone. Already I dread departing. It is my entire intention to return to you as often as I can. Soon, you may be able to join me on my journeys.' She rubbed Annie's porcelain cheek, 'Though maybe you will have your own suitor to occupy your time by then. Just look at your beautiful face Annie, soon they will be queuing out the gate for you, all laden down with roses and jewels.'

Annie raised a brow sceptically. 'The inbreeds and bog boys? No thank you Sister. But on this very subject I have a particularly urgent errand for you to carry out for me on your voyage. And you simply must not decline me!'

Elizabeth was piqued, 'Of course darling, whatever you want Annie, what is this clandestine chore, pray tell?'

Annie produced a tightly corked glass bottle from behind her back, then fixed Elizabeth's eyes with stern sincerity. 'I am placing my utmost trust in you Sister dear. You must pledge to me to complete your quest. This, you must deliver unto the sea, for within lies the path for my true love to follow and find me. A treasure map that leads him to his Princess, alone and forlorn in her castle. I know the waves and Gods divinity will deliver it to his shore, and then he to mine. A number of fine writers have whispered this to me, and Baggy concurs,' She passed the bottle over. 'As you travel across the water I need you to cast it far. I don't wish to find washed up on the beach behind the house or bobbing along at Slade harbour, do I?'

Intrigued, Elizabeth held the bottle up and peered in at the paper scroll tied neat with red ribbon and some ghastly object, distorted by the warped glass. It looked like a dead mouse tied to a small chain. The links clinked lightly as she rolled the bottle. 'Eew, what is that?'

'It's a lucky charm, donated by Lucy the rabbit, to protect my beloved from ill-will and peril while on his quest to find me. Now what say you to the quest Lady Elizabeth? Do I hear an Aye?'

Scrunching her nose nauseously at the bottles contents Elizabeth absently murmured, 'Aye.'

Annie stood high on her tippy-toes and emitting a tiny *eep* of delight she kissed Elizabeth's cheek. Spinning then, she sped off with her new, luxuriant burgundy dress under her arm in search of a big scissors.

<u>Anglesey, Wales 1879</u>

Above a blacksmiths forge in Beaumaris, near the Menai strait in North Wales, a troubled young boy lies on a grubby mattress, and sleep, though he is exhausted, is far from his addled mind.

What to do, what to do, the question whirled round his head like a carousel and dizzied him. He should be feeling rage at this moment, there should not be a doubt in his mind about the swift, savage and vengeful action he should take. But, he had always been such a good boy, eager to help, eager to learn, eager to obey. Even after his mother passed away two years ago, he remained diligent and dutiful to the uncle that kindly took patronage over the poor orphaned mite.

Alas, the uncle had not been kind, maybe a little initially, just to soften the boy up, to make him dependant on the new grown-up in his life. But, between being enslaved by his relentless duties in the forge, the mountain of domestic chores that the house demanded, and the midnight visits, when his uncle stank of ale and pipe-smoke, no, now there was no kindness at all in this unfortunate child's life.

His drunken uncle had stumbled from the boy's room over two hours ago. The boy used to cry himself to sleep and pray to visions of his dear mother, but now he was just numb. Broken, tired and numb.

He was a clever lad, once very bookish and curious in another, happier life. The smarts never left him, and the answer to the riddle that he had deliberated so intently for over a year was obvious, *one plus one equals kill your uncle and run away. Q.E.D. Well done my little cockle.*

And yet, he wrestled with the answer. The principled boy of yesteryear, crouched in the dark recess of his tormented mind feebly spoke - *that is wrong, Mum thought us right from wrong, and murder is very wrong.*

He didn't feel scared to carry out the task, not anymore, he just needed to rationalise it, square it with the trembling young boy and the ghost of his dear Mum. But they both just continued to play tug-o-war with his thoughts.

He resolved to seek council from God. Bible studies were important to his mother, and catechism was practised both during school and home hours, so the boy knew damn-well the commandments. Hands clasped, he prayed for divine reasoning, an enlightened solution to his mortal dilemma, a sacred sanction to execute his task, and his uncle. But God's echo just reverberated that thorny sixth commandment, *Thou Shalt Not Kill,* round and round in his head. So, no help from the Good Lord either.

Exhaustion overcame his aching body and sleep at last began to seduce his worn spirit. Before he conceded his murderous notions to the pious, righteous and moral opinions that heckled from the clouded corners of his deliberations, he thought he might reach out to another metaphysical advisor, and far darker entity. Ready to barter his soul, he considered council with the horned Lord of the fiery underworld may yield a more definitive answer to his most pressing question.

Sleep came.

As soon as his heavy eyelids dropped, *He* appeared, smiling pleasantly, dressed in gentleman's attire, like an illustration he once saw of Professor Moriarty. They sat on a park bench, the svelte stranger held out a gloved hand and the boy handed him a golden key. *He* graciously tucked it inside his coat and removed his top hat. *He* placed the hat upon his lap and from it *He* pulled by the ears a three pawed rabbit. *He* smiled, *Ask the Bunny*. The boy then addressed the twitchy nosed pet with queries concerning his current conundrum. Before it answered, the boy's mother and his younger self appeared and gathered around the seated agent, posing as though for a family portrait. The rabbit then opened its tiny mouth, but it did not speak. A red light appeared in its yawning throat, then its mouth grew impossibly wide as a ball of flame grew and belched forth from the creature like a blazing meteorite. The family tableau now swam in flame, yet they all smiled happily in unison, unaffected by the scourge.

The dream there ended, and the boy drifted into a blissful sleep.

He woke brightly and full of vim for the day ahead. He had no conscious recollection of his dream but was revitalised by its subconscious message. Before the cock had crowed, the eggs were boiled and the tea brewed, he hummed happily as he poured the teas, his mind buoyant by the prospect of an exciting new future. Freedom and adventure beckoned and his lucky uncle was getting breakfast in bed.

'Good morning Llewellyn, I'll leave your breakfast here and get the fire going in the forge,' he chirped and skipped off, leaving the sore-headed, sodomite slob, listless and bemused.

Looking forward to his last day of work, the boy stoked the furnace and whistled a merry tune about a vagabond gypsy.

Elizabeth Leaves

With her array of suitcases loaded and secured, the coach and horses waited patiently on Elizabeth. Their destination was Rosslare harbour, and from there the passenger liner would sail her to Southampton before her final leg took her to Gravetye Manor in Sussex.

Elizabeth's nerves had steadied overnight, and now the excitement built as the remaining family and staff gathered in the courtyard to see her off.

Charles appeared proud and commanding, fully collected after the tears that escaped him in his private bathroom earlier. He would not let Elizabeth know that her leaving brought forth forlorn feelings for his wife, and her departure, floating back to the surface. No, he sinks these sentiments deep down into the sediment, ballast into the brine, the good ship Lord Loftus must float peerless, and unsinkable on the surface.

The staunch Marquess of Ely and his second wife Jane waited in the hall on the cold Spanish tiles to say farewell to his eldest daughter. Mr Delaney, Missus Meades, Treasa, Pat and his wayward eyed son, gathered to from a small aisle to see off their beloved Elizabeth. All of whom doing their utmost to subdue their heavy hearts whilst wishing her well in her future, and all sharing the fear of the great impending emptiness that would remain in her absence. Elizabeth brought grace, sensibility and continuity to the depleted Loftus legacy, they feared her departure would unglue and topple the fragile remains of their little empire.

Their little empire had already fallen, they just hadn't gotten the memorandum yet.

Annie came gambolling along beside Elizabeth, chattering away, oblivious to the meagre ceremony. She was holding her big sister's hand as though she was leaving with her. Elizabeth's spirits were high, but when Mr Delaney swung open the coach door for her, her excitement faltered and gave way to leaden butterflies as the moment of her departure drew to hand.

She shook the hands of the staff kindly as they wished her Godspeed. Her family then all exchanged gentle, yet sincere, embraces and offered messages of good fortune, health and prosperity, until they all, very soon, met up again. Even Jane managed to come across with a degree of warmth and earnestness with her farewells.

Goodbyes for some, are far more pleasant affairs than hellos.

Annie clasped Elizabeth's fingers tightly as she boarded the hansom. 'I'm not going to get upset Elizabeth, because I know that you will keep your word and be back to visit me soon, unlike our brothers who seem to have forgotten entirely all about us. You're quite aware already that I truly love you and will miss you infinitely, but I shall step up, and tend to the enormous vacuum your selfish departure will create.'

'Oh Annie,' Elizabeth smiled through the welling tears, 'life will be endlessly dull without you, my little wildflower. I shall begin a letter to you as soon as we set sail, I'd start on the coach if it were not so bumpy.'

The two girls giggled and embraced. While Annie had her close she whispered, 'don't forget your quest, promise me again.'

'I promise Annie, I've packed your message very carefully and shall cast it as far as my arm can throw', she whispered in return.

Taking her seat, Mr Delaney closed her door gently, boarded his box and gripped the harness. With a final cheer and flurry of waving handkerchiefs, Elizabeth was off. She peered and waved through the back window at the merry gathering, happiness and sadness mingled on all their faces, except Annie's, who looked quite pleased with herself.

***

By the time Elizabeth had boarded the ferry and found herself a seat with a pleasant view in the dining room of her ferry her mood had stabilised, she now felt revitalised, brimming with feelings of freedom and adventure.

Mr Delaney left her at the gangway, and now she was experiencing a wonderful sense of singularity. She had always been surrounded by family, cousins and in-laws, friends and associates, servants, caterers and attendants, and now, now she was adrift on a boat full of strangers, not a familiar face for miles and days. It was exhilarating, for the first time ever, she felt alone. Not a bad or a sad alone. Not the feeling of aloneness and abandonment she felt after her mother died, no, this was a good alone, a challenging alone, a liberating alone. Of course she could not wait to see Arthur and be alone with him, but this uncaged sensation thrilled her.

The clearness of the air and the emptiness of the horizon mirrored her mood, free of the usual mundane distractions, free of everything, with a huge blank canvas to paint her world with any colours she wanted.

Instead of tea with her crumpet, she ordered port, this was a measure of how grown up she was currently feeling. The young waiter poured her a glass and she courteously thanked and smiled at him, treading the borders of flirtation. 'Do be a wonderful boy and leave the bottle,' she purred.

'Of course, m'lady,' he blushed, set the port on her table and retreated. She watched the ruby contents of the squat, topple-proof bottle lurch with the swaying of the ship.

Elizabeth drank one measure down, and feeling everso pleased with herself, poured herself another. Not accustomed to the effects of alcohol she felt a pleasant light-headedness wash over her. She languidly stroked the carafe of port, and as her mind drifted and meandered she was reminded of her urgent task. She recalled Annie at the coach, her keen eyes resolute, and firmly intent on Elizabeth completing her mission.

My playful little pirate. It was time to keep her promise.

Reaching into her carry bag Elizabeth withdrew her new turquoise cardie and snuggled into it, feeling Annie's warm embrace again. She next reached inside for the bottled communiqué and once more regarded its curious contents. Bizarre yet fascinating and wholly whimsical, a bottled metaphor of her darling sibling. She finished her third glass and ventured forth bravely on her quest.

Battling against the strong wind, she navigated her way to the rear passenger deck of the great steamer. The chill sea haze sprayed onto her face and quickly doused the port-infused rosiness from her cheeks. Glad she was again of her snug knitware.

Elizabeth was fascinated by the churning foam wake that the vessel ripped into the sea, its trail dissipating far behind her, now no sign of headland on the horizon. Wexford, Loftus and burdensome memories at last out of her sight and beyond her worries, behind the crest of the vast watery hill.

Looking around, there was no land in sight in any direction, this seemed like as good a time as any to cast her capsule overboard. She felt furtive and giddy, aware that a fellow passenger may see this well dressed young lady casting debris into the sea. She tittered to herself and had to quickly catch the handrail as the ship lunged over a large wave.

'Oops-a-daisy,' Elizabeth laughed out loud, checking to see there was no one around. 'Am I drunk? Is this how drunk feels?' she giggled.

Taking a firm hold the rail and gripping the neck of Annie's bottle, ready to hurl it on its passage of destiny she thought of Annie and dandelions and yelled to sea, '*Jinny-joe, jinny-joe, bring Annie back her Romeo*,' and with a mighty lunge the bottle took flight. At that moment another rogue wave belted the prow of the ship and lifted the already off balance Elizabeth off of her feet and tumbling overboard after the bottle.

She barely had time to scream before the torrid froth beneath engulfed her and swallowed her deep into its dark icy belly. Her thick woollen shrug and the rich folds of her layered skirts pulling her inexorably to the seabed.

As beautiful as a regal mermaid, as heavy as a naval anchor.

There, the last balloon of air escaped from her lungs and out through her terror stricken mouth, the bubble floated to the surface where it came to rest, and then pop alongside the peacefully floating bottle.

Bangor 1879

Across the grey and undulating Irish Sea, in the country of Wales, near the coastal town of Bangor, a raggedy young boy of around thirteen or fourteen sits, his legs dangling over the harbour wall. His fine features, still striking despite his filth. He casts his fishing line with desperate hope into the unpredictable tides of the Menai Straits. It has been two days since he has eaten and hunger gnaws angrily at his concave belly.

The runaway has never fished before, but he was well read in theory of several fishing techniques. He once had a home lined with a great variety of books and a very devoted teacher to school him academically. Here in the real world nothing was biting except his hunger pains.

He had scavenged some line and wooden floats, and fashioned makeshift hooks from wire. Worms and sinkers were a doddle. Still his lures were not luring. He decided then, or rather, his grumbling belly decided, that he would resort to theft to feed himself should his maiden fishing trip prove fruitless.

The strange eddies and whirlpools that the reversing tides conjure in this unique saline channel beguiled the fresh faced urchin, the hypnotic rhythm of the river deepening his reverie, his thoughts rewinding to the flames and screams.

Sitting on the worn stone steps of the harbour, amongst the sweaty stink of turning seaweed, he caught the faint smell of smoke still clinging to his smudged clothes. He was unsure whether it was from the rudimentary camp-fire he had lit the night before, or the house-fire he caused a few nights previous. He chose to believe the latter, he imagined Uncle Llewellyn screaming in pain as he was eaten by flame, and this made him smile. With his waning patience now somewhat revitalised by this thought, he whispered, 'Come on fishy, have a nibble, I won't bite.'

As he rolled his line back in he felt a tug. His heart raced. His first fish – and it felt like a biggie. He didn't even have a knife to gut it. But that was a worry for later, right now he had to land this monstrous meal, it was pulling him strongly with the tow of the tide.

To the last I grapple with thee...

He heaved his weighty snare slowly in, his limber young arms wrestling with the line as the tide fought back. The strain and struggle to land the catch was immense. He prayed his frayed line would hold strong. At last a dark mass appeared just under the surface, a long tail waved gently behind it. Fear mingled with intense excitement for the novice angler.

Knife? I'll need a machete to gut this.

With both hands he hauled the snagged shadowy shape from the water and onto the dock. His heart sinking as he recognised his quarry as not the son of Moby Dick, nor even the father of a tasty sprat. Before him lay dripping on the stone step was some cast off rigging or trawler net, so entangled and strewn with gunk and seaweed that it gave the effect of a fishtail under the water. It was hard to tell exactly what the coagulated glob was comprised of.

Seemingly destined to begin a life of larceny, the maligned boy cursed his luck and kicked the defenceless tangle. 'Ow,' he yelped, as his foot connected with something solid, which cracked within the soaking ropes.

Seething further, he rubbed his bruised toe then set to locate and unearth his smashed, inanimate assailant. Cautious not to add more injuries to his woes the boy picked out the broken pieces of glass, a large section remained intact and was clearly visible as a bottle end. Within this lay a rather morose looking treasure. A dead rodent of some description wrapped in a small chain.

Lifting it by the chain, the sodden, hairy object rolled free to reveal itself...it appeared to be a rabbit's foot. It was fastened to the chain by a ringed metal clasp with a peculiar stamp on it.

There was also some pulped paper at the end of the bottle, the boy tried unfolding it but the mush just fell to pieces.

'Hmm, well I suppose I caught *something,* not enough to make rabbit stew with, but *something,'* admiring his ghoulish find, he opened the chain, hung it around his neck and got back to the task at hand – putting food in his empty belly.

He considered the market his easiest bet of snatching some bread or fruit, where he'd sleep was another matter, probably a home for juvenile delinquents. He cursed his luck again. Still holding the bottle end, the former apprentice farrier flung it in temper onto the cobbled street where it split into nasty shards.

Mounting the steps to where the dangerous debris lay, he paused to let a horse and cart pass by, when suddenly, the horse whinnied and bucked like it had caught fire. A large splinter of pointed glass pierced through its hoof and remained wedged between the arc of its horseshoe. It threw its rider tumbling to the road and sent its cargo of fruit and vegetables flying as the beast bolted off, still baying in agony.

The rider, gaining his senses, rushed after the frenzied animal as it sped through the parting pedestrians, not noticing his spilled bill-fold lying on the stones behind him. The hungry boy noticed, and, as other opportune urchins helped themselves to the toppled turnips and plundered the pink potatoes, the young fisherman calmly walked amid the chaos and then slipped away again, tucking the well wadded wallet under his shirt, alongside his new pendant.

He'd eat and sleep well tonight.

Grinning contently, he considered his change in fortune and gratefully stroked his lucky new friend.

This larceny lark may be easier than I first thought.

Post Mortem

An unusually late snow fell on the battlements of Loftus Hall shortly after Elizabeth's disappearance. It came just as the yellow sprouts of spring pierced through the thawed winter soil. Any prospects of the warm hues of summer arriving to cheer up the grey plateau were quashed by a relentless blizzard and heavy layers of compact ice. The conditions entombing the residents in a frozen prison for weeks.

It felt like no quarter, no respite, no peace, would ever be granted on the forlorn and embattled family, any sprig of hope crushed by compounding attacks of cursed luck or ill fate.

All they could do was wait, trapped by the ice and their misery, and wish and pray for a warm wind to blow onto their shore, and thaw the cage of their plight.

They may tarry and pray in their ruin for many years, but at all times when bartering with the Gods for a brighter future, we should make our wishes cautiously and much deliberation.

A prayer for warm wind – may summon a dragon.

"If you travel far enough, you'll eventually meet yourself."
~Joseph Campbell

*"If you've never met the devil in the road of life, it's because
you're both heading in the same direction."*
~anon

Pembrokeshire, Wales 1883

With a litheness in his step and only the slightest itch niggling at his conscience, Dafydd reached the brow of the lush grass hilltop.

At this gentle summit his vista changed dramatically from rich, rolling pastures to the majesty of the still and silvery sea. The morning sun fractured into millions of brilliant sparkles on its mirrory surface. The light reaching towards the infinite and illuminating Dafydd's flushed cheeks. He inhaled deeply and felt the fresh, saline breeze fill his lungs as it would fill hoisted sails, blowing renewed gusto into his earthly vessel and pushing him eagerly windward to his next berth.

What a sight to welcome the weary walker. Tenby bay, broad and briny, and bustling with maritime life. Already audible from this lofty distance the sounds of the hour bells, the clanging of rigging and the seagulls hungry heckle, a chorus that created music for Dafydd after his long and silent trek.

Call me Ishmael. Dafydd dreamed, his spirit buoyed by the sight of the shoreline hamlet and civilisation tending to its circadian chores.

Could he already catch the aminic scent of the trawlers haul sweating on the dock? Or did his exhilarated imagination just conjure the aroma in anticipation of the wealth of smells awaiting his arrival at the harbour.

Roping his burlap satchel tighter to his wiry frame, he merrily began his descent, skipping to a canter, carving a swathe in the swirling meadow like a schooner through grass green waves. Atop his voice he sang *The Raggle Taggle Gypsy,* scattering the morning dew and the nesting sandpipers as he sped.

***

Dafydd's paper thin leather soles slapped the old stone cobbles between the narrow streets of Tenby. The smells he had imagined materialised and flurried around him in a rich saline smog. Sweaty old rope and wood and foreign odours, cargoed from distant places. The heavy blend of seaweed rooting on the shore, putrefying fish heads, and smoke from the puffers was far from the perfumed recipe he fancied. But stowed within this broth of emanations he filtered out flavoured smells that woke his shrivelled innards that now wailed for sustenance.

Food. Hot yeast from a bakery. Frying lard and seared bacon. Even the char of wood-smoke and stale malt of yesterday's empty beer kegs caused his stomach to lunge and cramp. He swallowed the spit pooling in his jowls and walked nose-ward down Frog Street to the nearest inn.

The Coach and Horses Inn was the first and most aromatic building he arrived at. Unkemptness was an excusable state for patrons in most of the taverns in Tenby, accustomed as they were to the ripe smelling deckhands and ripped clothed riggers.

Voyage weary sea-dogs and washed up curs littered the harbour village like strays, some came looking for work, penniless and eager, some worked regularly and drank their pay, some didn't work and went hungry on the streets. At this moment, Dafydd fit somewhere between this mix, shabby and starving, and staring longingly into the aromatic tavern.

And though it rumbled loudly, his belly was still full with fire. Undaunted by his own scruffy appearance he opened the door and marched into the inn. With the tavern still void of any punters he chose a table in a dingy nook and rested his bony backside for the first time in five hours.

He hummed his tune and his murmur summoned Maude, the roomy serving maid. Indifferent to the sight of the dishevelled scamp, and long since scrutinous or suspicious of the rag tag clientèle that the tide washed in, this salty, yet sweet dumpling engaged him. 'You hungry love?' she piped.

His voice hoarse from lack of use cracked. 'Ravenous dear, can you please bring whatever you have stewing in the pot, and a tanked of ale.'

'Of course my lovely.' Then squaring his eye, 'tell me, young sir, you can pay for it can you?'

Rummaging through his purse he produced a shiny silver crown. 'My last one.'

'That'll do very nice love,' and she padded off to the kitchen.

From the service hatch the maid now paused to consider him. Not yet twenty she guessed. A runaway for sure. His frayed and stained clothes may once have been reasonably tailored. His calloused hands and ruddy cheeks pocked by sparks or flint. He looked like a royal climbing boy, forced once too often by the sweep up the soot clogged flue.

Trailing steam from the savoury plates, she returned with the food. She watched him feast on broiled ham and crusty buttered bread. He reminded her now of a famished dog, some halfbreed, mostly mongrel, but smart, maybe some traces of border collie.

She smiled at his avarice. Though wary to disturb a feeding dog, if he were clean she might fancy to pet him.

His pale blue eyes sparkled, viably gladdened by the fresh sugars coursing through his veins he winked to her a happy *thank you,* and gulped down a half pint of ale.

'Anything else love?' she cheeped.

Reclining on the wooden bench, he turned his head to gaze into the street, 'Dwellings. A place to rest, with what change you might fetch me from my guinea,' he said absently.

'Change? You'll be lucky sir. But...' she considered, 'the Buccaneer, over by the slipway is affordable to most. The swabbies usually muster there for shore leave. It can get rowdy at night mind you, all that pent up spunk leads to all manner of trouble.' Cockling her full lips and eyeing him closer, 'You lookin' for passage or work? Or is it sport you're lookin' for?'

Alert now, he pivoted his gaze towards her, holding her eyes and the crown in the palm of his hands. 'Work, fair woman, work! On a boat, a schooner or trawler, if she's wet and floats Ill board her, scrub her deck, haul in her nets, and load her hold till she groans,' he paused to allow the *double-entendre* to sink in and allowed her to witness his gaze drift down to her cleavage. 'I'm certain a fine damsel like you has connections in stations of power and influence. Maybe there is a friendly name you can equip me with as I make my enquiries?'

Forgetting his scruff and whiff she flushed and subconsciously licked her bottom lip. 'Oh I know 'em all,' she boasted. 'Manys the Lord who fancied a bit of dessert off of me after they've filled their boots here.' She rolled her ample hips she curled her amber hair as she trawled her mental diary, 'Well, I'll tell you so I will, Captain Stanley Roberts is the name to shout when your looking for graft, and I'm sure his crew are due back today. He's a hardy blighter, with no time for slackers, so be sure to impress him with your gumption. As for your lodgings, the hotel is above the Buccaneer, and, well Mr Matthews is a while dead now, and Judith, his widow runs the business now. You tell her Maude sent you and you might get a wee discount, mind, you'll have naught left for supper, you won't.'

He softened his dreamy gaze upon her further. 'My dear Maude, my content belly purrs, not only do you serve the sweetest meat, you are a mind of knowledge. I shall try my luck with the cards and dice with what's left jingling in my purse. Should I secure a bed and use of a bath I will be complete. And, if the sporting whim takes me when I'm rested and washed anew, I will soar like a dove back here to return the kindness you've shown to me.' Placing the crown into her clammy hand he bowed and gently kissed its back.

Maude, fluttered and flattered, had forgotten the scamp in rags and felt as though he had just placed a glass slipper onto her plump foot. Grinning girlishly she cooed before regaining her composure, 'Oh my, aren't you the Romeo? Not that I'm not used to the advances of men, I am,'

He finally withdrew his hand from hers and offered her his inescapable hangdog eyes. Righting himself then as a peacock might, Dafydd swept his greasy raven hair back into a knot. *Lord, aren't you handsome.* The spider veins blushed redder on her cheeks.

'Madam, it is you who has made me feel like a Prince, albeit a very poor one.'

Smiling then, he made to leave. He turned to fetch his knapsack while Maude, pondered his behind in his grubby pants.

Petting her soft décolletage she sighed and called him to pause, 'I must be going soft in the head, young sir.' She returned to him his coin. 'You come back now, and see me when you've scrubbed and we'll play some dice ourselves,' she coyly purred.

'I knew you were an angel.' Dafydd cheered and gave her a sincere *cwtch*, heedless to his state and stink.

Maude flushed once again and Dafydd downed the last of his beverage. With a hearty burp he swung open the door and announced, 'Maude, today is a beautiful day. I pray it shines sweetly on you. Farewell'

As he skipped towards the water, Maude shouted, 'I didn't get your name?' But he had already scampered away. Maude sighed, already slightly rueing her generous gesture. *Maybe there's a lot more collie in that lad than I first thought.* She then wistfully returned to her chores, humming a tune about a raggle taggle gypsy.

***

Dafydd sieved himself through the stew of street stenches to reach the slipway. Now free of imposing smells, he felt nothing but the freshest of air imbibe his spirit. The sea's restful meniscus as calm as a monk's inkwell. He gleamed, wide-eyed and chasing the far off horizon, his heart brimming with wonder and excitement. He fantasised about his forthcoming freedom, and yearned for the escape that the seductive seascape whispered to him.

Remembering then the clammy coin still clasped in his palm, he unstrung his purse and returned the money. There it clinked and came to rest alongside the other purloined two dozen crowns and sovereigns.

***

We have all at one point, or at many points in our lives, felt the urge to unclasp ourselves from the shackles of our diurnal toil. Who amongst us, in our moments during our mundane and monotonous chores, hasn't slipped off in to a reverie of pure escapism. Willing the windows to fly open and allowing ourselves to soar as the clouds soar into golden skies. Farewell to the hungry husband ever grumbling over guineas, farewell to the worrisome wife ever eyeing the dust, farewell to the scruffy sprogs ever demanding and noisome. Farewell to char, to grind, to the skillet and stove, to the hammer and forge, to the mooches and meddlers, to the judicious and cynical. Oh to unburden ourselves from life's ballast and banality, to shed the encumbrance, untie the millstone and become as a gannet or tern, and just fly, with nothing in the vast empty heavens nor the seven bottomless seas to deny our ascent. How like Icarus on feathered wings, kissing the sun, we could become.

On a Tenby beach under a tepid sun lay he in bliss, Dafydd Alwyn Jones. Having playfully swept the sand about him, the gull's eye finds him flat and framed, spreadeagled in a sunken symmetrical mattress. Skyward he gazes, dreamily pointing his finger to a cloud, he wished to scrawl his name in it, as you would upon steamed pane. The feathery outline his writhing shaped in the beach could well be that of a winged angel. Some may imagine it a shallow grave. Eitherway, we shall mark this sandy carving as the ephemeral conception of his new life.

Content as a swill-full swine, he lazily contemplated his cross country flee and basked in a delirious sense of freedom. He began to drift. The shadow of the gull flitting across his closing eyelids.

Sleep came.

The marshy valleys of Snowdonia are painted purple and gold as he gaily waltzes with Charlotte. The onlooking fellows in their court, dour faced, envious and nude. Dafydd, fully aware that their absent finery was now adorned on him, and Charlotte - the very vision of beauty and grace - their stolen prize. Although seething, his audience are compelled to clap as the joyous couple whirl ecstatically upon the gilded grass. Charlotte's bosom, brimming from her luxurious dress, her smiling mouth moist, like dew on the tulip and as inviting as a rabbit hole to a fox. And the crowd cheered him on, as his dance quickened and their silks and linens shed as he spun, the couple began sinking into sodden grassy carpet...a piercing heat stinging his feet...

The encroaching tide had lapped up a purple jellyfish, it lay at Dafydd's filthy feet, its sting peeling him from his slumber. The whispery ghosts of his dream fizzing from conscious thought as he pinched the smallest of tentacles from his toe. A sharp numbness grew. A tale he once heard suggested peeing on it was worth a shot. One myth debunking wee later he washed his feet, and now his burning fingers, in seawater. The pain slowly began to subside. He considered the vast length of the translucent beast, then his prospects for gaining work, and went to scavenging along the shore.

***

After tying up his knapsack he reckoned he'd done enough dawdling. Priority one, he thought, digs, priority two – get off the mainland. Righting himself, he set foot for the Buccaneer Hotel.

Judith Matthews, widow of Will Matthews was a Coldey Island native, a woman as hard and distant as the isolated rock where she was reared. Sitting behind her desk, she tongued the hole where a bottom tooth once was, she was eyeing Dafydd in his filthy rags as he entered the tumbledown hotel. Foul as he was, she'd seen worse.

Her sceptical frown and close beady eyes impressed upon the observer that she was not a lady to be be crossed. And didn't Dafydd sense it. 'Help you son?' she rasped.

'I do hope so good woman, I have travelled upon hoof for days without the softness of a bed, I pray you have one available.' There would by no fooling this serpent lady but manners are free, and grace begets goodness.

She regarded the urchin, and was unimpressed by his charm, but nevertheless she appreciated his effort, far as it was from the usual grunts and grumbles of her regular visitors. 'We've a bunk in the attic dorm, two shilling,' she eyed his filth, 'you'll want water heated to clean up, that's half shilling, supper's another half. You'd want to pay now. Captain Roberts and his lot are soon due to dock, place'll fill right up then.'

Having already gleaned the price of bed and board from a passer-by on the way over, Dafydd already knew the cost, and had three exact shillings to hand. 'Of course kind woman. I've no doubt that the clean sheets and soapy water will be worth my last three shillings.'

'Clean sheets?' Hah!' Judith clawed his coins and slid him the guest book, 'Hot water at five, supper at six. Sign.'

Dafydd Jones promptly scrawled the name Dafydd Starbuck into the register, thanked the crone and quick-stepped up the loft.

Clean sheets they were not. But after three nights under bush and crag, the respite of a woollen throw on sheeted straw, stained or otherwise, was most very welcome.

***

In his blackberry blotched knapsack, amongst the detritus and a makeshift kelp purse full of mischief, he hid a handful of possessions he managed to steal and stow before his urgent departure from Bangor. His coin-purse of course, its contents he kept individually wrapped in rags to avoid their jingle drawing attention. A thin velvet cloak which had served as his coverlet while roughing through the dales, a chisel he swiped from his uncle's forgery, handy for digging, prying, and, if necessary, a weapon, albeit a feeble one. His special dice. A pouch for water, and a battered edition of Moby Dick. Apart from his loot, of value he had but only one other item, a shiny silver locket he borrowed from a maiden in Bangor, specifically, from the daughter of General Charles Warren. After a quick polish he flicked it open, inside are set photos of a very handsome pair, their names - Charlotte and Dafydd.

The locket he considered his safety net, a pawnable item if his loot ran out. Anyway, he needed no accessories to remind him of the past or adorn his neck, for there resided a more reliable pendant. Dafydd held his lucky rabbit's foot and stroked it like an old pet.

Dafydd pondered the silver trinket and the sentiment within, then snapped it shut and returned it into his bag, retrieving his book on the way out.

Flopping onto his bunk he flipped through the sepia tinted pages and let his mind set sail to fantasise, as was his way his whole life. Presently his tiredness overcame him and he drifted again.

It was the heft and clump of boots on boards that jolted him from his dream of Charlotte, swathe in red at the brow of a lush grass hilltop.

Roberts' crew, reeking and ravenous, each saw to their bunks. They bared no interest in the slight young man. Dafydd thought this a good time to address his state of hygiene. He grabbed his borrowed belongings and with a few courteous greetings to his new room-mates, all duly ignored, he hurried to the washroom for his half shillings worth of hot water before his greasy counterparts could cram in alongside him.

In the washroom there was a central fire with a sturdy spit for boiling water. He was fortunate to find soap and an abandoned cut-throat razor. The maid filled one of the four tubs with four gallon pots of steaming water and left him to bathe. Dafydd immersed himself, fully dressed - bar his shoes, into the soothing hot water. After lathering his clothes he stripped, wrung them out and arranged them beside the fire, then returned to soak, the water now milky brown and tepid. He considered his locket and the crimson lady upon the hill.

The moments he spent in his mind stretched time. Soon the unwashed herd from the attic came thundering downstairs. A good time to exit, he grabbed his warm garb, wrapped himself up in his cloak-cum-robe and left to get dressed.

As the sun fell to the horizon and gilded the glassy surface gold, the hotel attendants tended to the gas-lamps. Between the various fires and candles and steam the Tudor building became a reasonably cosy abode.

He tied his black hair back in a thin bow, his clothes now all but dry and the fair skin beneath his high cheekbones clean-shaven free of fluff. He added the razor-blade to his inventory and slipped his lucky dice into his pocket. Carefully then, he removed his seaweed wrap. Completing his furtive mission in a jiffy, he then skipped down to the dining area while the sailors still sang in their baths.

***

He found Judith, now acting barmaid, and asked her to bring him his supper, pleases and thank yous all in order. He secreted himself into a corner by a window. When she arrived with his stew and bread, slightly less po-faced than before, he asked her if Capitan Roberts might be dining here tonight.

'He'll be here son, sits in yonder snug, face like a tempest mostly, best not to approach till after he's ate, or not at all.'

He kindly thanked the witchy old woman and ate heartily.

Spirits high, he decided to break another silver crown for ale. He reckoned he deserved it after his wayward hike, and he was quids in after this morning's breakfast on Maude. Judith returned him a tankard and change. She made a point to fix him a canny eye as she passed the coins, fully recollecting his earlier lie of being bereft of cash. He smiled at her boyishly, not amusing her in the slightest.

Can't win em all.

He paid a quick visit to the gaming table then returned to his window seat and the dusky sky.

The bar slowly filled with bodies and noise. Good natured wupping and banter, the clang and clatter of plates and forks. The arrival of food subdued the clamour greatly. First grub, then smoke, then ale, then noise again, shanties, song and stamping boots. The maid scraped the greasy leftovers into a large slop pot leaving the tables clear to become stages for the working girls. Once done, the troupe of whores arrived in a whoosh of cheap colours, frills and lace. They danced and whirled and teased and the tavern heaved and hoed. Every seat taken, except that of Capitan Roberts.

Hidden behind an oak column, Dafydd managed to avoid the advances of the wenches. As fine and merry as they were, had his sculpted features caught their eye they surely would have saddled his lap in the hope of winning his custom, and he figured on prudence with his remaining swag.

A notable hush muted the din in the tavern. The crowd parted, forming an avenue for a stalwart brute to pass through, suddenly all on their best behaviour.

'Evenin' Cap'n. How are thee tonight?' was the general murmur.

Captain Roberts, wide and silent as a barge, docked at his cubbyhole and sat. Dressed in his best for dinner, a dark broad belt over a scarlet tunic strained to contain his girth. His impeccable white shirt, frilled collars and cuffs and all his gold adornments belied his true menace, like a warlord in drag. The daunting prospect of approaching him writhed in Dafydd's stomach.

Wait till he's eaten. Dafydd remembered, nervously eager to make an impression.

And so he did. Patiently he sipped his sup like a duchess, avoiding interference with the sex starved seamen and the trollops as they began drifting to the private chambers. The room emptied slowly, like a leaking beer-keg, leaving nothing but puddles and a stink.

Some stragglers remain. The old, the sloshed and the unwanted. Two gruesome looking men sat down to play dice. The box accordion wheezes a lullaby under clouds of second hand smoke. And Roberts, his hostile face weathered as slate, boots up, fed and watered, brooding alone, his mind churning and his pipe embers burning.

Make haste. Make hay. Dafydd deepened his husk and hoisted his mainsail on approach the foreboding Captain.

Tapping lightly on the partition glass he ventured, 'Captain Roberts? May I buy you an ale?'

Raising a stern eye to this boy acting like a man, Roberts considered the whelp. Few ever dared to trouble the Captain. He put his impetuousness down to fool innocence and no small degree of courage. Knowing already what the whippet was after the Captain decided to play along. With a breath of smoke, Roberts rumbled, 'I drink rye after meals, large measures.'

'An excellent tipple sir.' Turning to a maid Dafydd shouted, 'Two very large whiskeys, Madam.'

Admiring his moxy, she fetched his order. 'My name is Dafydd. May I join you sir? I promise not to unduly bother your hard-earned peace.'

The gristled sea-dog motioned him to sit and drink.

'sir, you've probably already guessed why I disturb you. I have travelled a long way in search of honest work and new adventure. I hear you suffer no fools in your ranks and all under your command toil hard and equally so. There is more to my meagre appearance than you might first assume. I have strength in my back and sharpness to my wit. I am sprightly, fleet and though somewhat emaciated, I abound in good health.'

The captain stroked his greying black whiskers and rumbled, 'A good pitch son. Tell me so, I smell no salt from you, what history have you at sea?

Dafydd drank then spoke, 'You have a keen nose sir. Well, I have shuttled nets in Bangor, and gutted the catch for a monger there too. My trade was as a farrier's apprentice, I found the forge and furnace suffocating. Every day, as the fires charred my cheeks and the sparks splintered my skin I dreamed of water and the wide open seas.'

Roberts noted the boy's blemished cheeks, then grabbed his hands for inspection. His thick leathery fingers kneading Dafydd's, fragile by comparison.

'Aye son, you've done some work, and you've hidden brawn I can tell. And you're no numbskull, like half of me crew. But me manifest is full. All them blighters upstairs, tending to their wretched desires, are dependin' on me for labour. Unless one or two of 'em drop dead overnight then I'm afraid you're outta luck.'

Down, but not out, Dafydd remained calm and charming. 'Sir, I thank you for you candour and company. I may be out of luck here but I'll keep my dander up. Who knows, maybe I'll steal a penny at the dice table.'

Uncharacteristically, Roberts chuffed at the young lad's optimism. He downed his fire-water and held up the boy. 'Laddie, you'll do well keeping your keel line high as you do. Tarry there, and I'll roll the die too. I too can afford to win or lose a penny or two tonight.'

Dafydd's fair face lit up, 'Very good sir, Lead the way Captain.'

***

They joined the undesirable looking dice-men at their table. One bigger and uglier than the other. They looked like they lived in caves.

'Captain Roberts!' the uglier one stood up to greet him, visibly subordinate in the wake of captain's shadow.

'Evening gents. Horace, you handsome devil, mind if we join ye?'

'Of course sir. Welcome to sir. Sit sit, please. Get you a drink sir?' Horace grovelled. 'Me n' Max didn't feel much fetch for the girls tonight. My guts ain't the best these few days. But fear not sir, I'll be right by mornin'.'

'Indeed Horace. Their loss no doubt. Ryes all round then. Good man.'

As the offer didn't apply to the scrawny stranger, Horace eye-balled him good and seethed off to the bar. 'Thank You Horace,' Dafydd yelled after him, he noted the giants jaundiced jowls and fevered bloodshot eyes, hardly helping his already unfortunate features.

'That hulk is my deckhand, dumb as sponge, strong as rope. He really shouldn't gamble,' said Roberts.

'I'm not much of a dice-man either, all a matter of luck I'd wager.'

'And wager you will, Master Starbuck.' Roberts winked, 'Aye, I can read, I copped your *nom-de-plume* on the register young Dafydd, on the run are we?'

Roberts is a sharp one. 'Not at all sir. Just a bit of a dreamer. I'm reading this book you see...'

'I know what book you're reading Starbuck, as I said, I can read, and often I do. Chasing whales are you? Hah!' he bellowed. 'You wouldn't be the first fugitive to flee the law by ways a boat, my lads are far from spotless, but on my boat, it's my law, and by God they're squeaky clean on my watch.'

Dafydd rolled with his good humour and diverted. 'Well, lets get started, who's got the dice?'

The game got under-way. Between the tankards and the bowl of piling pipe ashes the dice fell and clicked and determined their game of chance. Horace threw well despite his sweat and nausea and made early gains, and sneered at the runt. Max threw mostly onto the floor and struck out until the ale finally anaesthetised his feeble mind and he fell asleep. Roberts held steady, while Dafydd slid nearer to bankruptcy.

It would have pleased Horace to purge the pup entirely and allow the game fall down to just two players. And if he was given the chance he'd happily, and unwisely, bag the captain's cache too. 'Well, pretty boy, better keep your last shilling for breakfast,' he wheezed.

With the ante in, the captain surveyed the boy as he might a distant squall, wondering would it break or bite. Dafydd figured it was time. He feigned to leave, then eased back down. 'I'll fish for my breakfast. Count me in. I call high.'

'You'll cat from the slop pot for breakfast,' Horace sneered and coughed.

Adjusting his throw, Dafydd palmed the dice high, claiming his first win of the night. Horace grumbled, his reddened eyes rolling under his thick brow. Dafydd kissed his rabbit's foot.

Thus began the winning streak, Dafydd seemed to palm high or low at will. Though happy to reduce Horace's stack he was mindful not to completely deplete the captain's moderate pile of coins.

Horace fumed as he fingered his last coin, his early flourish now gleaming under Dafydd's chin. 'Call it a night Gents?' the captain suggested, no, provoked.

'All in on sevens boy?'

'What about your breakfast Horace?'

The feverish goliath stewed. 'I'll have you for breakfast. All in or what?'

'All in, my good man.'

Dafydd called and threw a straight set of sevens. A feat only a conjurer could manage. He slowly slid Horace's last coin across the table. 'You're a sport Horace, breakfast is on me.'

'Cheat. Thief.' He spat and towered over him. Dafydd deftly bagged the stakes, and shimmied over to the bar. Horace lurched after him, his giant head swimming with rage. Roberts, ever the anthropologist, chose to observe rather than interfere in the outcome. With his toe, Dafydd tipped over the slop pot and took two paces back from the spillage.

'Now Horace, I never cheated, those are the house dice, you used them yourself, please be reasonable.'

Horace, no friend to reason, fumed and lunged at the smug young pup. But before he could swing his massive fist, his boots slid on the oily slick and sent him arse first onto the floor, the small of his back striking it with an excruciating crack. Before he had a chance to recover Dafydd was pinning him down with his knees.

'You'll never best me, fool,' he whispered as he grabbed the ashtray from the table and emptied the still smouldering embers onto the brutes face.

Horace howled in agony. Completely blinded, he flailed about like a harpooned whale. His strength still mighty, he caught hold of Dafydd's ankle and savagely bit into his calf muscle. Dafydd winced and screamed as he attempted to pry himself from his rabid snare.

Then, from nowhere came an almighty clunk, and Horace bit no more. Unconscious and spent, like Gulliver on the shore, the beast lay still. Dafydd looked to see Captain Roberts standing over him, a stout iron skillet in hand.

'Looks like you cost me a deckhand boy.' The captain squared with him. 'I may need you in the morning after all. See to that wound before it rots. You don't want to know where this cur has been. Come to my room of the morrow,' before he turned his broad frame to the stairs he whispered, 'and don't forget *your* dice.'

Roberts is a very sharp one. Despite the ache from his chewed limb Dafydd felt the cold fear of being exposed, very similar to the sensation he felt recently, when he was caught by General Warrens right hand man, naked in an outhouse with the Generals daughter. *He could own me now. Not Good. Not Good.*

***

Judith, accustomed to brawlers, felt a measure of compassion for the victorious underdog, and was decent enough to tend to Dafydd's gash with her potions. Alcohol, iodine and a poltis of oats and herbs to draw any infection.

109

Thanking her kindly he returned to the drunken snores of satisfied sailors in the loft. Suddenly he remembered his earlier ruse, his first and now redundant ploy to create a vacancy on Roberts' ship, and wished he could unlight that taper. He grimaced and reluctantly crept onto his straw bedding.

Although his leg seemed to throb more in the dark, he lay awaiting another sharp pain. When at last it came it was almost as a relief, a familiar sting burned his left hand. That done, he let himself sleep. Maybe the lady in crimson might visit and distract him from tomorrows impending dramas. Maybe.

...Dafydd washed to shore atop a giant jellyfish, safe from its long nettle limbs dangling below, from his pink cushion he peered inland over the smoking chimneys of Tenby, upwards over the meadow to the brow of the hills. Charlotte came in her crimson, an army of naked soldiers at her flanks, marching in unison. The trains of her dress catching wind and billowing like dragon wings against the sky, the words Charlotte Loves Dafydd etched in the clouds. She reaches to him on the shoreline, guilt and anguish and regret rises from his gut and pools in his eyes. He takes the locket from his neck and offers it to her. Charlotte then clasps her hems, lifting the front to reveal her legs, her thighs, she widens them...the head of a small, fire breathing beast bursts forth from between and takes flight towards him, as the army charges downhill to the sea...

***

Morning broke with howls and wails in the attic. Dafydd woke to find the sailors all upright and dancing frantically beside their bunks. Squirming and crying in yelps of pain and discomfort.

While they slept, the ale and spirits helped to numb and delay the effects of the venom laced bedding. But once they awoke, the toxins released by the tiny thistles secreted into their straw coursed quickly through their blood and stinging cilia began to sear and agonise the nervous systems of the unwitting crewmen.

Dafydd too, whined alongside the suffering sailors, baring his blistered arm for all to see. 'What devils lurk in this hay? Chiggers? Weevils? Or have they been matted with nettle instead of straw? Damn! Damn the hellish hostel.'

The half naked sailor's blisters were far more rampant and angrier than his own, carpeting their backs and bellies. Dafydd noted too, they all bore long and short welts on their backs, some old, some new. They furiously scratched and rubbed, serving only to spread the tiny infectious hairs and make matters worse. Dafydd exaggerated his pain and mimicked their motions.

When they ran for the bathroom, Dafydd followed, and all began washing and soaping feverishly with freezing water. With the pain searing him even further, and nearly out of his mind in agony, the first naked sailor bolted downstairs, out through the front door, down to the dock and plunged into the sea. Like lemmings, the others quickly followed suit.

Dafydd, almost giggled, but remained in character, and raced behind them. Judith, awoken by from the clamour, caught sight of Dafydd's skinny rear just before he ran outside. 'What on earth is going on young man?' she demanded in astonishment.

Faking pain, Dafydd turned, 'Mrs Williams, we are on fire, see to it that our contaminated bedding is destroyed at once, and pray woman wear sturdy gloves, the devils nettles dwell within.'

Judith was struck mute and gazed incredulously at the early morning bathers wailing by the dock wall. Snapping to, she spun to fetch her oven gloves.

The men eventually returned, draped in the fresh blankets Judith had left by the entrance for them. Their external symptoms retreating and cooling. They gathered in the washroom where Judith was burning the bedding in the fire. '*ych-a-fi, ych-a-fi,*' she muttered.

'Gentlemen, I can't apologise enough, I cannot explain what ungodly pests invaded your bedding. Nobody else has been accursed so, and I've not changed the straw for a over a week. Ahem, I mean only a few days. The hay looks innocent even as it burns. Please forgive me.'

The shivering men didn't bear the look of leniency. Dafydd volunteered as spokesman, 'Mrs Williams, I have never witnessed such an awful awakening, and neither have my comrades. You may offer apologies and excuses, and indeed we may never know what beasts took nest in our cots. As we heal, I feel some recompense is warranted. Should you feed us free of charge this morning and return our overnight fees, that may go some way towards soothing our anger and sealing our lips.'

Judith, beside the fire, the boiling pot like a cauldron, a poker in her hand, turned sour. She could no look more like a witch were she on a stage. Unblinking she stared at the upstart.

'Young sir...' she began.

'Loose lips sink ships Judith, and we all need to keep our business alloat.'

Judith regaining composure began again but was shot down by one of the sailors, 'Aye, we wants compensation, what man wants to visit an infested hovel on his leave. None, that's what.'

A chorus of 'Ayes' followed wearily along in support of their mate.

Judith caught Dafydd in her hideous stare and puckered. 'Very well, gentlemen, I'll return your money and send you off with bellies full...and I hope this isolated event will not sully my reputation with you or any of your acquaintances in the future. You're always welcome here at the Buccaneer.'

Finally breaking her gaze from Dafydd she paced intently towards the kitchen.

Feeling a little better as their chill retreated from the fire, the crew's spirit began to lift like the smoke rising from the burning bedding. Small smirks crept across their faces as they eyed one another and tittered at the ludicrous adventure they'd just had. Opening there blankets they hugged each other by the flames of the burning bedding. 'Get in here young master,' they chuckled to Dafydd, 'that's one way to cure a hangover, eh?'

As Judith angrily lumped a heft of bacon from the scullery the band of nude brothers erupted into convulsions of laughter.

Chortling with his new pals, Dafydd recollected to himself his ruse to sideline a shipmate in order to create a vacancy for himself on Roberts' ship, and how just yesterday, he carefully spread the jellyfish tentacles into their beds from the satchel he had fashioned from broad leaved seaweed. Adding just a sprinkle to his own for his alibi.

That worked out very well indeed.

***

The crew gathered for breakfast which Judith delivered to their table, smiling bitterly through her remaining gritted teeth. All of whom hale and hungry and unaffected by the rude awakening, except for the small one, Pock they called him, who still looked a little pink and bloated.

Chewing on the salty meat Dafydd recounted life as a young cockle in Beaumaris village. No doubt he grew up hard, but no harder than most folk in the town. He never knew his father, a merry merchant sailor he was told, kindly to his mother until her belly got fat. His interest drained quickly when the anchor of a child was presented to him and he disappeared on the evening tide. His Mother told him he had *gone to hunt his white whale.* Dafydd grew up wanting to hate the rogue that abandoned them both, but often found himself daydreaming about his father, imagining him as a pirate, brandishing a cutlass with his long black beard, swinging from the mizzen mast and hoisting the jolly roger. *Oy'll be back with a holdfull of booty for you son!*

His mother was a school teacher, and taught him well both in school and at home, and through her he engendered a great love of fictional literature. Melville's epic remaining his favourite amongst many. She also taught him to clean and cook and bred him with no small degree of good manners and etiquette. She imagined a life as a naval officer for him, an admiral out to hunt down rogues and pirates.

Tuberculosis came and took her from him at eleven years of age. He was spared the orphanage by her brother Llewellyn, a blacksmith and farrier in Llan-faes. There they lived over the workshop where Llewellyn made thorough use of the young boy by the forge, his apprenticeship far more about labour than learning.

Though he fed and kept him well and warm, his uncle was more often cruel than kind. Sometimes, on cold nights after ale, Uncle Lew' would become too kind, and seek warmth where no man should seek warmth.

Here is where Dafydd chooses to suppress, rather than revisit his past. This is the point where Dafydd cut these wretched memories from his thoughts. This is turning point when he decided to become somebody else. This is when he knew he must escape. A decision firmly endorsed and encouraged by none other than Professor Moriarty himself.

At fourteen, Dafydd got out of bed and left for Bangor. Taking with him his few belongings, his uncle's savings and some items from the workshop, before setting it alight. He imagined the phoenix rising behind him as he hurdled his way over hedge and fencepost towards his new life of mischief and adventure.

Mischief and adventure, as it turned out, hung low and in great abundance on the branch for the hungry young snapper. After a patchy start to his new life, his fortunes tended always tended to shine favourably on him, most notably after his fishing find one fine afternoon in Bangor.

Since that day, he did not go hungry, he found mostly legitimate work and slept comfortably more often than not. And, when he felt in any way cornered by circumstance or his antagonists, either by twist of faith or slight of hand, he would emerge victorious from his dilemmas, his adversary usually left cursing having ever crossed his path.

A short stint assisting a farrier in Bangor even landed the love of a beautiful young woman in his lap. While shoeing the horses in the stables of the police headquarters in Bangor he met

Charlotte, the police commissioner's daughter. Captivating in her crimson cape, truly if there was ever a reward for his tormented past, this was it. She shone, as warm, demure and exotic as a midsummer evening. Smitten, his gypsy lust for swag and booty became a minstrel's infatuation with her grace and beauty.

She too, tired of the restraints of her strict and expectant upbringing, was taken by the grubby young farrier, with his face as fair as a winters morning and his eyes divine. Those eyes entranced her, the way those of Christ might entrance her.

And so it proceeded, as love stories often do, with the least likely of suitors. The cautious courtship began with secretive seductions and trepidatious trysts. The young fugitive's romance was fuelled by their furtive forays and midnight meetings beneath the gas-lamps and willow trees.

***

Judith interrupted his reverie with a snap. 'Roberts wants you boy!'

His early appointment had slipped his mind amidst the morning's excitement. 'Thank you Judith, breakfast was excellent.'

Back at his bunk he was feeling a growing throb around his shin. Dafydd examined the angry bite-marks and applied a clean dressing. He then took himself to the captain's private room, knocked, and was evenly welcomed.

'Master Starbuck no less. How's the peg?'

'Not a bother sir. a mere kitten bite. Forgotten all about it.' He lied.

'Sure you have son. Though I hear Horace's memory is quite clear on the matter. Seems he's much worse for wear after your little tussle. Can't open his eyes nor sit straight for the pain. Bayin' for your blood big ol' Horace is. Off to the infirmary today.'

Dafydd imagined Samson, bitter, blindfold and enfeebled. 'I'm sorry to hear that Captain, I had no intention...'

'Of course you didn't, frail lad like you, a Goliath like Horace. Nay. Of course you didn't. But luck was with you all the same, during the brawl, during the game...you're quite the charmed one eh?' Roberts eyed him up and down and licked his salty lips. 'Tell me son, tell me what think you of the white whale lad? Did the beast fear ol' peg-leg Ahab? Or was he mocking him, baiting him, luring him, pursuing his own pursuer?'

'He certainly seemed to the pilot of Ahab's destiny sir.' He said humbly and added, 'I deeply regret costing you a crew member. I pray I can still be of service on your vessel.'

'I hear you also had a spot of bother this morning too, all manner of hijinks going on as I slept. Got your bed and board refunded by all accounts. In my lifetime I've never 'ad a free breakfast here. Making friends with me hearties too. You are a lucky charmer eh! Maybe that paw around your neck has you blessed.'

'Yes sir, I don't know about all that. All water under the bridge now I hope, and may I say you have a very fine crew, a hardier bunch of boys I've yet to meet.'

'Enough son, enough', Roberts interjected, smirking through his chapped lips, 'I've eyes in me head and me wits about me, and I reckon full well that you're as slippery as a sack of eels. However, there's few to none of me boys with any smarts and I know a grafter when I sees one. C'mere boy.' Roberts motioned him closer.

A familiar fear lunged in Dafydd's gut.

'You cost me a hard worker so you'll replace me hard worker. The only benefit you'll bring me over Horace is that you're easier on the eye.' Roberts snatched Dafydd's hands tightly into his own and pulled him close, Dafydd smelt his foul breath, yesterday's stale whiskey and meat. His stomach churned. 'You'll come aboard the Rapscallion this afternoon and I'll take good care of you...*if you take good care of me, savvy?* Lessin' of course you want your new best maties to find out you blinded their ugly 'ol shipmate and swindled away his winnings. Hmm?

What do say my lovely? Do we have an accord Master Starbuck?'

Well shiver me timbers, Captain Roberts is a damn pirate. Dafydd suddenly felt cold and adrift, and this sly 'ol skipper had just thrown him a noose to climb into. He had to think fast between the beats of his thumping heart.

'Of course sir.' He stroked the captain's thick hair, bistered and as coarse as a boars, 'I'd be honoured to serve under your command.'

'Don't play me boy! Don't play me and there'll be no need to rock the boat. Rock the boat and you may go swimming, savvy?'

'Aye sir.'

'Aye, we cast off at high tide, be aboard and be merry about it. You wanted work didn't you? Hah! And if you decide to go AWOL, I'll send message to a good sergeant friend of mine about a scrawny fugitive who's duping and plundering the good folk of Tenby. I've a feeling you don't want to get into a conversation with the local constabulary eh?'

'No sir, I'm grateful for the favour you have shown me.'

'Hah! Favour Indeed!' he scoffed. 'Welcome aboard the Rapscallion Starbuck!'

***

Dafydd had much to do, the tide was already rising. The latest inconvenience of Captain Buggery needed urgent and immediate consideration. Remaining a land lubber was not an option. He had marched four days and two hundred miles over brush and burrow. He had managed to get himself across the gangway, albeit with a few bothersome clauses in his verbal agreement. Now, he just had to figure out his passage off of the boat, preferably alive and unadulterated.

During breakfast Dafydd learned from the crew that their next voyage would take them south and east through the Irish Sea, around the south coast of Ireland where they were to unload their cargo at Cork harbour. There they would rendezvous with another supplier. After a night or two in Cork, depending on tide and weather, they would reload the Rapscallion with their return cargo and haul anchor for the turnaround trip. Docking to unload and for a week's shore leave, this time in Aberystwyth, where Roberts' family lived.

If Dafydd could survive long enough to disembark in Cork harbour he could abscond there. General Warren's naked army would surely not pursue him overseas, no matter how vexed the chief of police was with him, surely?

Well I can fry that fish another day. Right now I've some provisions and clothes to purchase, a letter to post and a sodomite to defer, oh the days chores are endless.

It was time for Dafydd to spend honestly some of the money he had stolen from the police headquarters in Bangor. Firstly he needed new attire, necessary to heighten his appeal to Randy Roberts, and a decent satchel to store his stash. New court shoes were a must, finding these, he quickly discarded his ragged old pumps. Next he desperately needed to find an Apothecary, his leg was sore as hell and he would need, amongst other items, pain relief, sterile lotions, healing balms and lots of clean dressings. A Stationers was next, then a quick tea while he penned his letter. Then to the post office for stamps.

His next chore he felt mixed emotions about completing, he needed to secure a discreet courier for the first leg of his letter's journey. He returned to the Coach and Horses in his finery to greet Maude, in her dirty aprons. She would need payment in advance to ensure completion of his requests, so in the stinking lane behind the pub he gave her her full dues which she very gratefully received. With Robert's vile advances still echoing in his mind it was actually quite a pleasurable conjugation with a member of the sex of his preference. So, everybody was happy. He only hoped he hadn't infected the saucy concubine with Horace's rabies. The very last errand on his to do list before he scuttled off of dry land and onto the love boat, was a quick visit to a nearby pasture to forage. It was a little early in the season but he might be lucky...

A letter to Charlotte Warren 21st September 1883

The below correspondence arrived to the Warren Household in Bangor, 5th October 1883. Although addressed to Charlotte Warren it was opened without her consent by her father, Charles Warren. Charlotte found the open envelope and its contents on her bureau the following day.

My Dearest Charlotte,

What must you think of me! What ever rapacious and malign terms you have conjured for me in your thoughts and words I can only heartily agree, that you are correct in all your assumptions.

I am a cad, and a coward, and a cheat and a fraud. I never deserved the grace of your company, let alone your love. Your proud and honest father saw me for what I truly was, a wolf in the guise of a sheep. Alas, I am not even worthy of the title of a wolf. I am more akin to vermin. A wolf would standby his mate, a wolf would protect her, and their litter, a wolf would kill to feed its pups. But I flee. Shame and shame again, a lifetime of shame will rain down on me.

My reckless behaviour and actions have cursed me, I feel damnation awaiting my every turn, and though I cannot turn back, I pray you believe, that this is more for your good than mine. Though I may be cursed, you are blessed, blessed with grace, kindness and beauty, and you can continue to live a blessed life as a beautiful mother. The truth is, our child will excel in life through your goodness and care and love. All it would learn from from me is deceit and immorality.

Your father, though furious with me now, when he becomes aware you are with child, will breath freely knowing that I have vanished and will play no part in its upbringing, and he is right to believe so. Although, this will not stop him from sending the hounds to every corner of the kingdom to hunt me down, my intention is to be off the mainland soon.

I have encountered a depraved sea captain, whom I'll not name for my safety and seclusion from the long arms of the law. I believe him more pirate than sailor and suspect he smuggles contraband for a living, now I aide and abet him. Via this tyrant I have gained passage to sea, but I fearfully take it under duress and the threat of violence and molestation, nevertheless, I see this as part of my penance for my ill deeds, and I fear further damnation awaits me at every turn and tide.

Would it be of any comfort to know that I loved you? For what it's worth I truly did, and still I do. My time with you was the gladdest I've known, and this is the memory I keep locked in my heart, as I return this locket to you. Although I am impoverished I could not bring myself to pawn it, and knowing that you may take care of it offers me more comfort than coins.

Hold no flame for me Charlotte, I am gone and will not return, the Rapscallion waits for me now, (a suitably named vessel for a bounder like me!) If I survive the sodomy and torture that awaits me there, then maybe, just maybe, I can find freedom in a distant land.

Your beautiful image is indelibly seared into my mind and haunts my dreams. In these dreams you will remain eternally beautiful and young and pure.

I pray you will live long, with a healthy and very happy child.

May God's Light Bless You,

My Deepest Regrets,

Dafydd.

Life and Death at Sea

The Rapscallion rolled gently on the swelling sea awaiting her cargo and crew. Roberts already aboard, his back to the helm, puffing on his pipe.

Wary of the captain's wrath, the deckhands always arrived much sooner then punctual. They boarded the ketch, a modified wind driven schooner with distinct red sails. They unloaded their scant baggage and set to work filling the hold. One of the crew held up to converse with the captain, the subject matter throwing him into mood of malcontent.

Scowling down the dock, his black eyes angered and peeled with intensity for the troublesome boy.

The deckhands busily loaded up the freight. Contained within the crates and sacks were oils and spirits, grain and cheeses, cured meats, olives, rice, semolina, spices and cases of wine. Roberts' trade associates in Cork catered for the upper-crust in Irish society, mostly of English descent. The landlords and ladies never went without, even when they watched their tenants wither and die in their blight ridden fields.

Roberts ran a risky operation, his overloaded hold sank his keel line deep through the unpredictable conditions off the southern Irish coast. Very few traders attempted to run this route in vessels of this meagre size, to most mariners it was a raft at the mercy of Llyr.

Though steam powered sea vessels were still in their infancy, the advent of puffers with iron clad hulls saw vast cargoes shipped slowly and safely in bulk to more distant ports. The ketch was light and fast and needed deft management when the sea grew angry, so Roberts recruited more than the minimum number of hands, all worthy and brave, to steer their crossings in speedy time. Though regularly perilous, the trade off paid handsomely, with only the wages for another two or three hands, his overflowing vessel could cross the channel back and forth while more cumbersome ships were still on their outward journey.

At last Dafydd stepped gaily into sight. With the exception of his old cloak, the boy in rags had gone. Now looking almost regal in his new attire he strode merrily towards the captain.

'Ready to set sail Captain!' he confidently announced.

The vexed captain's nostrils flared as the boy smelled incredibly sweet. The fragrant scent, paradoxical amongst the harbour stenches dazed the captain, and he was momentarily dumbstruck. The savage briefly smitten, held captive by something distant and familiar in the princely boy's eyes. Just as quickly, the captain regained his former furious disposition.

'Come hither fool and listen to me. I see you've enjoyed spending Horace's money, but that clobber will be as torn and filthy as a tramps bloomers by dawn. I had you pegged as a smart 'un. Hah! Wash off that vile stench, or I'll boot you into the drink meself, there's no place for vanity on my boat boy, I'm looking forward to you finding that out.'

'Sir, I'm sorry if my outfit offends, it has been such a long time since fresh cloth draped my skin. I have kept my old clothes for work-wear.' Dafydd proffered the captain a peek in his new tote bag.

Seemingly disinterested, the captain ranted on. '*Twmffat!* Heed me boy, for I am vexed. Me boys have given me news that me cook won't be joining us. Seems that Pock's taken a fierce reaction to this morning's sting, swelled up like a pig in the sun, can barely breath, gone with Horace to the infirmary. Last time I've seen him react like that was from a jellyfish sting. Curious that, isn't it boy, eh?

'Very sir, I'm sorry. I truly hope he'll recover.'

'*Cachu hwch*!' Roberts spat, 'You may very well be! Now I'm two men down and no time to scout for another. You'll be taking up Pock's galley duties as well as scrubbing me decks, you hear me?'

Call me Pip. Dafydd sighed, then it dawned that this is in fact a very fortunate turn of events, and rubbed his rabbit's foot. 'Of course Captain, I'm quite capable in a kitchen. Right now I'm eager to change garb and help the lads load up, may I throw my bag in my bunk and get started?'

'You may and you will, but hold up boy, show me that satchel, I don't want any *contraband* smuggled onto me ship' he said with suspicion.

Rummaging though Dafydd's rags the captain found nothing of concern, some ointment and bandages, some money and his book. The captain seemed somewhat relieved. 'Do you think we'd leave without medical supplies? More injuries on a sea voyage than in the trenches. And what's this? He held up a small vial of cologne.

'I got it for you sir, in appreciation for you kindness.'

The captain's eyes fired with rage. 'What do you take me for fool, this isn't a pleasure cruise, by Christ boy you're here to work, it's not a favour I'm doing you, nor you I,' he flung the bottle into the water. 'See to your quarters and be quick about it, there's work to be done.'

'Aye Captain.' He scampered aboard and scuttled below deck.

Puffing furious plumes from his pipe, the captain watched the little bottle of perfume bob and sail away to sea and recalled its potent sweetness, its scent having once beguiled him many moons ago. Some genies are better kept inside their bottles.

Alone at his bunk, Dafydd removed his robe and began to strip, under his shirt, tied tightly to his back was his old knapsack. He peeked in at his goods, some old, some new.

Smiling to himself he hid his stash, donned his old rags and set off to work.

Day 1. Tenby Harbour. Conditions calm

Setting their rudder to shore when tide was full and the sun in the third quarter, captain and crew made a frustratingly slow passage across the unusually sedate sea. The sails at times slack as the conditions held mild, and a sluggish, but trouble-free, voyage was anticipated.

Dafydd recalled his euphoric emotions of yesterday morn, as he rolled downhill through the dew damp daisies, he remembered the sheen of the sea that mirrored his golden hopes and dreams. He weighed these emotions now against his current circumstance. Yes, he attained work and was safely off dry land, drifting further and further from General Warrens hound dogs. While scrubbing the deck of the Rapscallion he mused, was this fire he now found himself floating in, hotter than the proverbial frying pan he had just escaped?

The congenial attitude of the crew towards him had shifted somewhat. The good humoured banter they exchanged over the breakfast table had turned silent. Maybe they too, once under the iron hand of their captain, behaved as congregation before pastor, diligent and dutiful and dour. Maybe word spread about Horace and Dafydd's involvement in his blindness. Maybe they're just hungry, and wary of the new chap's cooking ability.

Maybe their stings still prickle. Maybe it's for the best that they just never find out the truth behind the matter.

The captain had so far kept to himself, sometimes manning the wheel, sometimes in his small private quarters. For Dafydd the monotony of the deck scrub allowed his mind a little peace to form a strategy. As best he could, and as long as he could, he must keep all aboard sweet to his company. Did he detect a crack on the captain's stony face on the dock? Could he salvage any camaraderie with the crew? He was too far at sea to sour the atmosphere, *cook overboard* was still maritime tradition, although he was hoping the pirate rule that all grievances should be settled on land would play a stronger hand. Heck, he would gladly take marooning as an option if he could. Four to six nights at sea was the estimated return schedule, he planned to survive three of them then jump ship. Eitherway, he thought, as he watched the coastline fade fainter behind him, *this is the last time you'll ever see Wales.*

As he believed a whistle while you work makes the hours fly by, he thought he'd try alleviating the mood on deck. He puckered and began to whistle. No sooner than a few bars of the *raggle taggle gypsy* breezed past his lips than he was shot down by the first mate. 'Cook! Button that blow-hole and we'll hear not another sound from you. Idiot boy! Don't you know it's bad luck to whistle into the wind. Is it a storm you want to bring raging down upon us? Shut up and scrub, you whelp!'

So much for music.

'Aye sir. Excuse my ignorance sir.'

***

Eventually, after five hours of labour Dafydd was summoned to the galley. Meals were at dawn and noon and sundown. But tea was brewed ceaselessly. To Dafydd preparing meals was not a difficult chore, regularly he helped his mother wash and peel, and stir and season, and daily he readied breakfast and supper for dear Uncle Llewellyn, R.I.P. He had never cooked for more than two before, but he reckoned it was as simple as finding a bigger pot.

The common rule at sea regarding provision was *sufficient without any waste,* the Rapscallion treated this rule with generous pinches of salt. As their cargo hold was bursting with fine food and drink, they often kept a little of the good stuff aside for themselves. So there was no scrimping for decent fare in the pantry. With a wealth of flavours at his disposal Dafydd set to preparing a rich herby stew for the crew. *The easiest way to a man's heart,* Dafydd reckoned, and so it was in the beginning.

After seven hours swabbing and hauling ropes the crew gathered in the galley to dine. The ravenous bunch consisted of Max the deckhand, fourth and third hand Williams and O'Brien, the Mate was Effan, and Walters was the Master, the duties of the boy fell upon Dafydd. Captain Roberts ate in his private quarters. Dafydd had prepared an especially large helping for the captain's table, which Walters took to him.

Scoffing down their tucker and wiping their plates clean with bread and tongues and fingers, their audible eruptions and hearty grunts indicated a noticeable gain in spirits. After food, some pipes were lit and a little ale shared. Captain allowed a little imbibement on calm waters. 'Not bad boy, said Effan, 'I tell thee Pock might have to find another ship to boil his broth on, if the poor sod ever recovers.'

'Aye,' hailed the crew and clashed tankards, was it to the loss of Pock or the offerings of the new cook, Dafydd wasn't sure. Night was just upon them and the vessel was peaceful. O'Brien played shanties and Williams took watch. Dafydd, feeling weary from work and Horace's virus multiplying under his skin, saw to the dishes.

As he scrubbed the pots Walters approached and whispered, 'Captain will see you in his chambers when you're done lad.' A mixed look of pity and repugnance creased his swarthy face.

Behind the galley was a small, simple room where the captain dwelt most of the day. Dimly illuminated by oil lamp, it housed a small bed, a table and a seat, all fastened to the deck. A cupboard, some boxes, and on the wall hung some scant regalia, including a whaling harpoon and a cat o' nine tails. Roberts exhaled smoke and drank rye. *Rye for captain, ale for crew*. The gaslight pricked tiny lights in his shadowed eyes.

'You can cook boy,' the captain grumbled, nonplussed, 'and fair dues, you swabbed your worth today, I reckon you may be of worth to me yet. But you know your duties to your master and commander don't finish there, don't you boy?'

Dafydd felt wretched, his leg stung and his fever grew. He thought of Uncle Llewellyn screaming from above the blazes in his foundry and composed himself for his performance.

'Of course, my captain, how can I be of service to you?'

Dafydd's continued willingness toward the tyrant threw Roberts off balance. For him, part of the pleasure, or maybe all of it, was in his show of authority, his crude misuse of power and vulgar use of strength. The capitulating youth before him, with his beauty and charms had the effect of blowing a still wind into his mainsail and capsizing the captain's base intentions.

Another catalyst to these churning emotions the captain was experiencing, was also likely to be the small amounts of opium and heroin Dafydd stirred into his extra large supper.

The crew were also subject to a few special ingredients in their soup-bowls, foraged fungus from the Pembrokeshire hills, added less for their flavour and more for effect.

For now, we'll stay focused on the captain and cabin boy. Dafydd the obliging servant and apparent willing lover, and the odious ogre who would serve to defile and enslave him.

***

Upon presentation of his leg-wound in the apothecary in Tenby, Dafydd was allowed collect the drugs on his shopping list without prejudice or inquisition. Amongst the gauzes and ointments the dispenser sold to him was *Bayers Heroin Hydrochloride* for the combat of infection, and Laudanum, containing over 10% opium, for effective relief from pain. As Dafydd responsibly informed the druggist he would be at sea for an indefinite period, he was permitted to purchase several vials for his journey. They also sold colognes and perfumes.

The effects of the medicines in tandem with mouthfuls of rye were beginning to take hold. (Dafydd added a half cup of brine to the captain's stew to ensure him a mighty thirst). Deep in the filthy swamp of Roberts' mind now slithered two serpents of the cooks design. The goal of these manipulative worms was to reduce his carnal cravings, while simultaneously increasing his emotional needs. *One side will make you grow taller, and the other side will make you grow shorter.*

The captain's thick head rocked loosely and his eyes rolled star-ward. He slurred a *come hither* to Dafydd, trying to maintain a semblance of his command, then accidentally tipped over his tumbler.

Showtime. Dafydd quickly recharged his glass and took a seat on the captain's lap. Ignoring his oily stink, he doted on his massive shoulders and stroked his wiry hair. 'Captain, forgive my forwardness. I know how you see me, as other men have seen me, who would debase me as would deviant dogs in the street. Tell me, tell me that I saw in your eyes a kindness towards me, when we met before departure, I know I felt for a moment, than more than just your latest concubine. Please say there's more. Please.' Dafydd passed him his tumbler and fed him glugs of rye.

The captain's eyes now at half mast, and his bowsprit limp as kelp. He slurred and touched Dafydd's cheek tenderly, the boy's reapplied scent enrapturing him. 'You're a prince boy, a prince aboard my ship. But who could love this hog? Ain't no one has no warmth in their heart for the captain. Captain Blackheart. Who would love him. Will you care for me son? Would you truly?'

Earlier that day Dafydd splashed not cologne about his cheeks but a fragrance called *Lance Parfum* - a perfume he remembered his mother swearing *could reduce a ravenous wolf to a puppy licking at your toes*. Dafydd certainly noticed it had had some effect on the captain back on the dock. The cologne that was flung away was merely a distraction to aid him smuggle his private goods, including a spare bottle of the fragrance, stealthily on board.

'Of course sir, I will be your servant at sea, and lover on land. But I beg you to treat me kindly till we dock. Then we can dress ourselves like royalty and parade proudly above the dullards and the dross. Do not degrade what we have. Your crew are loyal and expect you to treat me as a cur. Show them that you are merciful, that you protect that which is precious to you. And, as you are precious to me, I will serve at your side like no other and deliver you pleasures untold.' He kissed the Captain's rubbery cheek.

The captain was held in a trance of quixotic bliss. The suggestions whispered in his ear manifested and took dreamlike form in his mind. Dressed like a King, with his beautiful pet, swanning in purple, red and gold swathes through the streets of adoring well-wishers. No more the salty dog of the sea. A life of an artisan, filled with riches and respect. The notion sweetened his bitter mind, warmed his cold heart and soothed his voracious lust. The seed was sown.

'Aye son, Aye', he said sleepily and held him tenderly, 'I'm tired of wretches and strays. Swear your love and loyalty to me and I'll guard you like gold. Sleep with me boy. Sleeeeep....'

'I swear my Captain, I am yours, and yours alone.' Dafydd watched as the captain's drug-burdened brow could no longer hold awake, his lids draped heavily down, like the soaked sails of a war weary ship.

Dafydd's face returned to its usual countenance. He shuddered in hideous disgust and unclung himself from the contemptible captain. So far, his strategy was proving quite successful, *very successful,* his goal to spare himself rape on his first night in private quarters, gratefully achieved. The pain and fever was mounting though, and how long he could hide his symptoms from captain and crew remained to be seen. Tradition held that cooks were the first to be jettisoned overboard by malcontent mariners, and second thoughts would not be spared nor much weight of mercy shown towards a skinny, infectious rookie. No matter how enamoured the captain may be with him, nor how well he cooks a stew.

***

Returning to the subject of Dafydd's stew, and the portions served to the rest of the seamen of the Rapscallion. It was his intention, for the duration of the voyage, to keep the captain in as much of an isolated stupor as possible, while also playing on the crew's sense of superstition. He wished to create within their psyche, an acute wariness of the weather and water on this particular crossing. He also hoped to maintain some degree of camaraderie with the shipmates. Another reason he could quickly become flotsam was if they were to ascertain that Pock and Horace's ill faith, was off his very own making.

Before he left dry land, Dafydd was very fortunate to find, in the short grasslands just above above Tenby, a field with a bumper crop of *Psylosibin Fanaticus*. An autumnal fungus, identifiable by its fawn crown and donned with a distinct nipple. The effects of this mushroom upon a person varies with dosage. A small dose might imbue a light sense of giddiness and mild sensory alteration, ranging to a high dosage which can lead to vivid hallucinations or even wild, insane mania. Right now the crew were enjoying a few unexpected giggles after their dinner. Maybe soon, the waves may take some ethereal form or the wind whisper of fell portents that imminently loom.

The permutations of the plan were far from predictable, but he would ride each storm as it came, as long as he had some favour and goodwill amongst the crew he may yet mange to go AWOL in Cork. In any case the introduction of chaos, doubt and nervousness kept some of the control out of the captain's hands. Also, with the captain doped, and while Dafydd remained sober, and maintained as much control over his illness as he could muster, (by now he suspected typhoid) the young maestro may have some sway in conducting the *largo* and *agitato* of his stupefied orchestra.

During calm conditions, as they were currently enjoying, the thin walls under the deck allowed sound to pass quite freely. Dafydd expected the crew may have been accustomed to Roberts' *trysts* and maybe even experienced his gross manoeuvres first hand. He considered they may have been expecting cries of help or distress to come screaming from the cabin once *The boy* received his invite. Maybe they sat relieved of the silence, maybe they cared not a jot, maybe they were just laughing in very spite of their miserable circumstances. Eitherway, they were laughing.

Snores befitting swine gurgled from the captain. Dafydd looked in disgust upon him, and would run him through now if it served his ambitions. But foremost he needed fresh dressings and pain relief. He also needed to avoid the captain gaining his full wits again. *Heroin for his hangover, a greater dose perhaps.*

Dafydd needed to return to his bunk to fetch his accoutrements. He had been lucky to find a cubby-hole above a rafter to secrete his bag of illicit goods, and he thanked his rabbit's foot. After tending to his pustules wound he decided he needed more immediate access to his special ingredients. He took them to the kitchen where he camouflaged them amongst other, more savoury flavours. He was on third watch so had time to *season* the fish for breakfast before he got some shut eye. Once done, he returned to the captain's cabin.

Still unconscious, Dafydd set about polluting all his rye stash with doses of heroin-hydrozide. *I'll keep the opium for your dessert, Piggy.* Exhausted and feverish he lay beside the snoring captain, wishing his illness was highly contagious.

Dafydd's lucid dreams became more surreal, abstract and fragmented. Any semblance of metaphor, allegory, or metaphysical representation seemed now to blur and crack into the ludicrous. The fire-child borne from Charlotte's womb, was now akin to a tadpole regressing to spawn. The naked army played cards on a banquet table and laughed hysterically. Charlotte was their serpent queen whore, waiting legs akimbo for each of her nude servants to take and ravish her.

If we are to discern any logical reference from Dafydd's visceral delusions, we must know a little more about his recent past. We are well informed that he is on the lamb, or gur, as some folk say. He had left Bangor unplanned and without warning. The reasons of his leaving abundantly clear in his letter to Charlotte. The details of the night of his hasty departure rest with the police sergeant who reported to Commissioner Warren. Late on the evening in question, Dafydd and Charlotte were caught in an intimate exchange in the stables adjoining the police barracks. Duty-bound to arrest the youth and detain him until Charlotte's father was notified of the matter, Dafydd was confined in a holding cell, wearing nothing but his briefs. After considerable begging, the sergeant granted Charlotte a brief visit to her imprisoned lover. They whispered their vows of undying love, and then Dafydd persuaded her to leave with him her silver locket. He then instructed her to fetch his pouch from his holdall and drop it through the small grilled window at the rear of the cell, then to leave his knapsack beneath the sill, pledging to meet her at dawn by the bridge. Besotted with her urchin blacksmith and sire to her tiny foetus, she obliged. In his pouch were some of the tools from the old workshop - small pins and picks that quite easily turned the latch. Once free of his cell, Dafydd reluctantly needed to knock the attending guard unconscious. Luckily he had left his baton within easy reach and had his back turned. Dafydd petted his rabbit foot still dangling from his neck. With the little time he had to find clothing he stripped the guard and donned his uniform. He then had the notion to find civvies in the policemen's lockers. When he heard the loose coins jingling in the pockets of several garments he couldn't resist bundling them up and fleeing with as many as he could carry. He then collected his bag and scampered away into the night - leaving his accomplice, lover and unborn child to wait alone in the rising sun.

Day 2. Southern Irish Sea. Conditions Foggy

Dafydd arose at four bells and placed a flask of lightly medicated water beside the captain. Roberts roused groggily and was aghast to find the boy still in his quarters, floundering to recall the previous night events. 'Blast ye boy, what do you think you're doing in here.'

'You asked me to stay, Captain. Can I bring you anything before I take watch?'

'Water dammit! Lest I parch, *drewgi siffilitig.*'

'At your side, sir.'

Roberts gulped from the flagon and Dafydd took to the prow of the ship.

Dawn was yet to begin its glow on the horizon but change was upon them. The air was biting and wet with fog and whipped fast about his face. The stars erased to black and the darkness was all encompassing. Keeping watch was as futile as fishing in fondue. The ketch now rose and fell with greater purpose. Dafydd thought back to a recent night on a bare tor in Snowdonia, and how the rain pelted down on his puny coverlet. This was even colder and the damp sank deeper into his skin. He wrapped in an old coat that the night-watch shared. These were not the ideal conditions under which a sufferer of typhoid might choose to recuperate. He coughed and shivered and took a drop of Laudanum and prayed his strength would hold.

At first light Williams appeared and spoke to Dafydd, gentle and timid. '*Bore da*, young Dafydd, how goes the watch?'

'*Bore da,* Master Williams, 'I've never seen a fog as thick.'

'Aye, nor we. I tell thee last night we met with some strange omens. Still as the water was, the waves seemed to talk, the windless air whispered, the very timber of the boat seemed alive, we think there's trouble ahead aye. Dare we suggest an about turn to the Captain?' Upon speaking of Roberts he remembered the boy's visit to his cabin and looked embarrassed. 'I'm sorry son, I too have had to keep him private company,' he spat on the deck, 'let us not speak of it, why don't you prepare morning tea and I'll take watch, I'm piggin' parchin'.'

Dafydd tried to focus on Williams, but his features appeared distant, contorted and watery. He was starting to loose control, exhaustion and delirium were beginning to kick in. He shook himself alert and thanked young Master Williams, whose eyes and thoughts were already lost on the dusky horizon, and set about preparing breakfast.

***

The Rapscallion gained in the quickening winds, moving now at a steady nine knots they rounded about ninety miles south of the Wexford coast and began marking a direct passage to Cork Harbour. The black fog had become a thick grey veil, making visibility poor, and zero over a hundred yards.

The crew, in sullen form, grumbled as they scoffed their delicious kippers and eggs. Though they enjoyed his meals, Dafydd was certain that their mood towards him was souring fast. They would not deduce any logical reason for their suspicions and irrational apprehensiveness. Rather they would draw conclusions in their minds from their gossip, time-honoured sailor's superstitions and mariner's tales, of which there were plenty.

The dried and milled hallucinogens blended neatly with the parsley and thyme and were indistinguishable from the flavoursome fish. A slightly larger measure to up the ante, and keep his shipmates with one eye over their shoulders. First mate Walters took the captain his morning fare. His, marinated with a more sedative seasoning.

Walters returned, 'Captains' out of sorts today, so I'll be assuming command till he's right again, savvy?'

'Aye sir,' the galley replied in unison, then scowled from under hard set brows towards the cook.

'More tea gentlemen?' he brightly offered. But the master ordered them to there stations and Dafydd to hurry the galley clean and back to swabbing duties.

The fog cleared but the morning grew only darker beneath heavy, foreboding skies. The ship's bow dug deeper channels into the surges and spray spat high over the taffrail, making Dafydd's scrubbing efforts pointless. The watch called the master, alerting him of a distant squall that could impede their current vector.

The master called to reduce speed and maintain course. Roberts would be furious should Master Walters decide to take decisive action and divert from the approaching weather system. Fearing his wrath, he sought council with his absent commander.

After a moment, the pugnacious captain stormed onto deck yelling blasphemies. Dafydd remained hunkered over his scour-brush and kept about his futile business. Then from nowhere, a blinding pain tore across his spine, causing him to wail in agony. He thought a sail tether had flown loose and flayed him, or that even lightning had struck his back.

When he turned around he saw he was in Roberts' despotic shadow, his face red with rage, the cat o' nine tails gripped furiously in his colossal hands. Dafydd recalled the welts he witnessed on the backs of the crew in Judith's washroom. Initiation rites, or plain savagery? Eitherway Dafydd was now one of the crew, branded and owned, his sliced skin bleeding onto his newly scrubbed deck.

'Whelp!' He barked. 'I'm told you've been summoning ill winds and fell tides upon me boat. Me crew are nervy, look at 'em. Cowering at the sight of rain, hearing sirens wail in the night. They'll be expecting the kraken next!'

Dafydd winced and tried to stifle back the pain, 'Captain I...'

'Quiet boy!' Roberts cut him off and turned to his loyal and edgy crew, 'Men, I'll hear no more of your wives' tales or ghost stories. It wasn't for fear of superstitions that I crossed the seas a thousand times. Keep your wits about and your tongues still. The runt may be proving a bane to you blockheads, but by Neptune he is no Jonah. Harm him and you will feel my sting. savvy? Now, have back to work, you decrepit dogs!'

Dutifully they scarpered back to their posts, remembering well their own encounters with the whip. Dafydd, a wet and bloody mess of anguish and agony down on his knees, grimaced up at his oppressor, willing back his tears.

'Up pup! Don't you get delicate over my disciplines. No place on my ship for soft bellied ponces. Get to the tea now or swim home.'

'Aye Captain.' Roberts slung a boot to his backside as he passed him and howled a hideous laugh.

'Master Walters, I don't like the look of that westerly, plot a change of course, take us north and reduce speed to seven knots, we'll skirt near the southern coast of Wexford and Waterford. It should only take a few hours off of our time.' The captain commanded loud and lucidly.

He then whispered to Walters out of earshot from Dafydd, 'Keep the boy bound below deck when we make land in Cork, I'll be turning him in to the law when we return home, he makes a decent stew but he's more trouble than he's worth. Might even be a reward in it for us,' he winked.

*****

It was time to up the medication. Dafydd simmered water while his blood boiled and his soul screamed for vengeance. He could barely disguise his worsening conditions. He ached everywhere, his throat closed tighter and his breathing was laboured. At times he felt like retching, then he'd feel faint and just wanted to collapse. He could not maintain the act of courteous cook and devoted concubine for another two nights. And the delirium was affecting his grip on reality, his dreams of Charlotte plagued his waking hours now, he saw her in the waves, pinwheeling in the centre of her copious crimson dress, she sang seductively to him, urging him to join her.

North, Dafydd overheard, *how close to land will they venture, swimming distance?* The southern Irish coast is fierce and merciless to schooners and galleons, let alone flesh and bone. Alarm rose within his breast and he fought to breathe it away. An urgency to action was now upon him, however he must stow panic and maintain his polite persona for as long as possible. Hysteria now would surely sink him.

He stirred the heroin tonic into the captain's mug and brought unadulterated tea to the others. As they approached challenging weather he needed the crew to have their navigational wits and naval skills about them. By now, the effects of the mushrooms were visibly affecting their functionality.

***

Roberts, already on a come down after his brief display of authority, retired once more to his cabin with his brew. There he would sleep for the rest of the day, leaving Walters to helm and guide the ship safely around the storm. Walters, nor the rest of the crew, would now not even acknowledge Dafydd, save only to order him to secure this, haul that, and fetch the other for them. With Roberts out of commission, he sensed they could well make a mutinous decision, and turn Dafydd into a human anchor.

The boat battled hard and brave in the strenuous conditions, but it was just the fringe of the foray, and the men, even in their semi-lucid state, had the seamanship to steer the craft safely onto her new bearing and away from any impending dangers. Dafydd must also steer himself to safety, as storm-clouds loom threateningly on his horizons too.

When he had the chance to steal a glance at the charts he tried to mentally note their approximate location. Unaware of how close to land the new course would take them, Dafydd would need to rely on line of sight. And, as he was having visages of mermaids and firebabies, even his eyes now proved to be unreliable assets.

It was all or nothing time. No slight of hand nor loaded dice. The ante was high and he must wager all to have any chance of winning. Game On.

Between duties, he asked Walters could he prepare a trolling line. He claimed he wished to offer the hard-working lads a proper feast of fresh fish to help raise spirits. The notion of a fresh catch appealed to the hungry master. He grunted, 'some luck you'll need, you'll not catch sprat in this weather boy, but by all means sling it out.' On approval Dafydd dashed below deck to fetch line, tackle and lures. While out of sight he also grabbed a cork-jacket and found a convenient spot to stash it for quick access when the time was right.

Once the simple troll line was cast he returned to his tasks. The endless chores sapped what little energy he had. He felt that the deckhands could see him fading, his gaunt pallor and his stifled coughs. Eyeing him as hyenas might eye an injured lion cub. He wanted to cave to his urge to take some morphine and just drift away. Instead he drank water and bore down against his maladies, scraping his deepest recesses to find the strength and the will to see his plan through. The stinging wound on his back fired the rage he felt towards Roberts, and this rage fed the last of his adrenalin into his contaminated bloodstream, like the last bucket of coal fed to a steam train. He pressed on.

After the ninth or tenth brew of the day he checked the line. Again, his charmed rabbit's foot did not disappoint. He had hooked eight good sized mackerel, a double helping all round. The resentful crew fought to hide there pleasure at the sight of the writhing delights. 'Well, what are you waiting for, Applause? Get 'em in the pan before we starve boy.'

'Yes Master, right away,' he smiled. You'll be dining in heaven tonight.'

On returning to the galley he paused and held himself in silence and just within earshot of the crew's conversation. The whispers of the crew above floated through the thin partitions.

Deep in cahoots they plotted, louder than they must have realised, most likely due to their unsolicited intoxication.

'Capn's gone Barmy, Aye he's kept himself to himself before plenty, but never seen him gone a whole day wasted like this. Tis witchcraft. Tis sorcery. I'd never go against 'is will, but that boy's a Jonah and no doubt, summoning the wind as he did. Angrying up the water. Blackest fog I've e'er seen. Horace. Pock. Our burning beds in Tenby. And all these ghostly warnings we've been witnessing. Nay, he's a jinx. A real bad egg. Have you even seen 'im. Like a ghost he walks. Has Roberts under a spell if you're askin' me. Nay, I say the Capn's diminished. If Roberts don't show his face after supper the Jonah's going down to Davy Jones. What say ye lads. Aye. Aye. Aye. Aye.

And so the die was cast. Operation castaway began.

Day 2. Southern Irish Sea, Conditions Treacherous

In the galley Dafydd had privacy to prepare their supper and to tend to his wounds, and to drop his façade. Grimacing, he tried to nurse his lesions. There was little he could do for the ripped skin on his back except try keep it clean. He then removed his leg dressing, the ointment and sterilisers may have served their purpose, the pink rage had seemed to dissipate somewhat. The scab that came off with the dressing was a dark crust, the size of a large toad, globs of fetid yellow pus and fresh infected blood clung to it. It would make a fine ingredient in tonight's chowder.

Before ringing the dinner bell Dafydd scanned to the north horizon for any signs of dry land in the waning daylight. There was still none. Regardless, he had ran out of time to wait, this show must go on. The white whale neared now. *I know not all that may be coming, but be it what it will, I'll go to it laughing.*

Ding Ding. Supper is served.

The ravenous seamen rushed to feed, salivating towards the alluring aroma of the intoxicating meal. They piled around the table and their steaming bowls.

Plenty of onions, leeks, herbs and aniseed, along with the naturally strong flavour of mackerel and heaps of seasoning masked, without effort, the less savoury elements of his unctuous soup.

After gutting the fish he added their raw innards to a dish he had already placed his scab into. Into this he then stirred all of the remaining hallucinogens, possibly three hundred. Two ampoules of Laudunum and a vial of Bayers rest remedy also followed into the mix. This was the garnish he then gently stirred into the simmering pot of fish stew. Upon its ravenous consumption the effects of the broth should yield uncharted results, though the hopes for infection, food poisoning, visceral hallucinations, hysteria, panic and lunacy were high and very promising.

Dafydd kindly offered to take Williams' watch in return for this morning's favour, the offer gratefully taken. The entire crew sat and ate like swine at the trough. As they sopped their plates and quaffed back reckless amounts of ale they heard the captain bellow from his cabin. Walters rushed in with his helping. Next they heard a furious ruction explode, shouts and clattering arose and then a door slammed. Walters came trotting up to the watch.

'Boy, better get down there and pacify the captain, his baying for you, whether it's your flesh or your blood he lusts I'm not even sure, just be sure to please him whatever way he wants. Or it'll be the whip for us all.'

The final act. Dafydd on the brink of exhaustion braced himself. Dashing to his bunk he donned himself once again in his recently purchased finery, splashed on the exquisite Lance–Parfum, grabbed his effects and then strolled towards to the captain's dirty den of iniquity.

'What took you runt?' Roberts was livid, his face swollen with fury, spittle foamed on his fat lips. 'Never tarry on your captain's command!'

His supper was upturned on the floor and his whiskey bottle tipped over and near to empty. 'None of your tomfoolery this night boy, you will serve me, you will serve your master damn you.'

Dafydd could see that Roberts was swaying and disorientated. The lethargy still clung to his brow and his speech rattled drunk and hollow. He sounded more like a boy speaking with a man's ill fitting tongue. Dafydd bowed his head in deference and bent to clean up the mess, uprighting the bottle swiftly. Roberts took his prone position as an invitation and rounded on him. His meaty paws clenching hard on Dafydd's aching hips. Grinding his flaccid organ against his cleft.

Revulsion overcame Dafydd, the beleaguered boy could never overpower the burly captain even in his addled state. He had to endeavour once again to swallow his bile and repugnance for this monster and feign adoration one last time. Coaxing and coercion were his only hope. The captain fumbled angrily with his britches while venting vitriol at his subordinate trophy.

On all fours Dafydd could act unseen by the captain, and with stealth and dexterity he drained his last full vial of Bayers into the dregs of the whiskey bottle. The captain, now unleashed, raged at his inefficient member, placid as a windsock in a summer breeze.

'Captain, don't anguish so. I can help you, let me help you,' Dafydd said soothingly and slipped from his grip and rose to meet the captain's rank mouth. The bewitching waft of the boy's perfume entranced and dazed Roberts, sending his mind back to a floral-scented maiden fair he impregnated and abandoned long ago. He remembered love, and his heart changed tempo. His violent *Furioso* tempered now to a lamenting *Lacrimoso*. Dafydd took his limp baton in his hand and began playing his opus.

'There my dear Captain, I know your love for me forbids such a bestial congress, we have all night, the crew are inebriate and we are undisturbed, let me love you, already I can feel your passion for me grow. Allow me kiss you sire.'

With his free hand Dafydd gulped the last tainted sup from the whiskey bottle, then held the captain's face and kissed him fervently, opening his mouth to allow the liquor to fully drain into Roberts' mouth. Then coyly sealing the captain's lips to ensure he swallowed the toxic cocktail.

Roberts, euphoric with pleasure, smiled rancidly at the boy. Dafydd seized the moment to take a step back from him and play for time. 'Watch me sire, let me dance for you, watch me sire.'

The salacious captain leered as the lithe young man sashayed and pranced in the tiny cabin for his captain's pleasure. The scent and sight of the youth in his fine regalia overwhelming his muddled senses. He gripped himself as Dafydd began to undress.

'There Captain, there,' he whispered coquettishly, 'it won't be long now.'

Roberts now at half mast staggered towards him. Dafydd held him off at shoulders length and teased. 'Are you ready sire?'

Lecherous laughter spat from the blow-hole of the beast, and in that same moment, the cocktail of Heroin-Hydroxide fused with the nerves in his cerebral cortex and exploded like a mute grenade. *Thar she blows.* The lobotomising dose crippled his mast, his mizzen and every other function on his damned vessel. The captain toppled backwards onto his bunk where he lay still as a millpond, paralytic in a waking coma.

Dafydd regarded the reprobate as he re-buttoned his shirt and pulled from his satchel a torn rag that was once his shirt. He stood over the captain's limp torso and from Roberts' perspective he was akin to a golden god, but the captain could only gurgle his adorations. His garbling became muted grunts as Dafydd stuffed his bloody shirt into his ugly, foaming mouth.

I am the white whale.

'My dear Captain, you are the greatest swine I have ever encountered, and I feel a great honour of ridding the world of your stain.'

'I believe it's bad luck to say *Goodbye* on a ship?' Dafydd unhooked the whaling harpoon from the wall and waved his new baton like a flag to begin the *Crescendo*. The captain twitched and mumbled frantically, and then he squirmed no more, as Dafydd took careful aim and speared the harpoon deep into Roberts' black heart.

'Goodbye Ahab, Goodbye.'

Disembarkment

Dafydd stepped away from the growing carmine puddle while the pig captain bled out. Dead now, he felt as though a life's burden had evaporated into the ether, taking comfort in the knowledge that Roberts' miserable soul will long scream and burn in Hell.

Dafydd surveyed the porthole. Desperately scrutinising the black night, a blink of light caught his eye. Was he hallucinating, were his senses beginning to give way to fantasy again? No, it was a light, faraway but clearly visible, too bright for house-light it had to be a lighthouse. He thumbed his lucky paw. In Dafydd's dire state, and at this distance it was a suicide mission, the rabbit's foot could not shape-shift him into a dolphin. Still, he must try. *Time to jump ship.*

After some maniacal laughter in the galley the worms of madness began to burrow and proliferate into his bewildered shipmates psyche. Their grasp on reality loosening, as was their grasp on their bowels. Dafydd could hear the rising hysteria as everything the salty crew held tangible and actual in their world, deteriorated into their every insidious nightmare. Every superstition, every fear or phobia took ghastly form. Faces and hands melted and shrunk and grew. Cadaverous eyes watched them from every knot and hole in the wood. They were grappling with a whole new dimension in pain and suffering.

The nausea and cramps merged with their evaporating sanity, creating a hellish scene worthy of any ghost ship.

Dafydd recalled one of the sailors whispering, *"if he didn't see the captain's face after supper,"* he'd lump Dafydd into the drink. He reckoned he may have one more parlour trick for his pals before he walked the plank. Delving once again into his satchel he withdrew the cut-throat razor that was kindly left for him in Tenby. It glinted and caught Dafydd's grim reflection, he hardly recognised himself. *Oh well, time for a shave Captain Roberts.*

Like a sack of rats sinking into the mud, the sailors clawed at their flesh and dug on every solid surface, seeking passage back to the world they once knew, tearing fingernails and splitting skin in the process. Then, their lunacy suddenly quelled as an authoritative voice roared for heed.

They imagined the sound as an echo, reverberating from the very bones of the ship, until the captain's door swung open, and out clomped a very strange looking figure.

They huddled close and blessed themselves as the monstrous aberration clodded towards them. The clothing was instantly recognisable as the captain's garb, but his shrivelled form appeared as though his bones had been shrunk beneath his skin. His boots slid and fell awkwardly on the floor, his pants hung and gathered in folds at the ankles, his red tunic - a farcical, baggy shroud from which no fingers or hands emerged, and most macabre of all the head, Captain Roberts' face hung loosely and expressionless, its contours and folds all fell at absurd angles, but behind the fleshy veil were two sunken eyes that pierced the petrified spectators with menace.

The arms of the ill fitting garments rose up, then drew back and whipped forth the cat o' nine tails. The lash catching Walters just below the eye, causing red tears to run down his cheek. From the abomination's unmoving lips the captain's face belted out his orders, 'On deck, you decrepit dogs, what am I paying ye for. Walters, *cont gwirion*, get these pigs to their stations and bear south, set the stuns, lest ye all yearn to feel the sting of my tail till doomsday...NOW,' he screamed.

The crew, dislodged utterly from reality, were now crying with fear and scrambling about, sliding and falling on vomit and excrement, while frantically trying to make sense of their morbid new world. Walters attempted to second the ghost captain's orders, but all that came forth was insane babble. The lunatics clambered in disarray up the steps to the deck, manned random stations, and wrestled mindlessly with ropes and sails in the pitch black of night.

The spectre of their dread leader shuffled to deck and slowly wandered amongst them, and then turned and lumbered towards stern. Reaching the wheel, he turned to address the gormless grunts. The grim helmsman declared unto them, 'Fare thee well me hearties,' and with that he stepped out of his billowing outfit, a cork-jacket and satchel secured tightly around his midriff. Then lastly, in the manner of tipping one's hat to bid another farewell, he grabbed his scalp and removed the flayed cowl of flesh he had peeled from the dead captain's skull.

Dafydd's elegant and blood-smeared face smiled piteously at his witless witnesses, then peered over the taffrail into the undulating black mirror below. The only reflection he saw was that of a huge crimson circle, surfing gently on the waves, pinned in its centre was Charlotte. Her sweet, kindly face and her delicate hands beckoning his invitation, to take his place with her in her briny bed. She began to sink and her drapes swirled into a vortex. Dafydd leaped, and sank deep into her dark and icy embrace. Her love engulfing him like a thousand dead fingers.

***

We should take this moment at this juncture, as Dafydd floats unconscious and indiscriminately on the whim of the wind and tide, to mention a few noteworthy post scripts.

We have followed the auspicious misfortunes of those who wandered into Dafydd's wake. Guile and good luck have spared him thus far, and although his present plight is perilous, he has survived, whether by his hand or the hand of his rabbit limb pendant.

However, there were those yet to suffer further fallout from Dafydd's manoeuvres. Judge them innocent or no, the bit-players in this tale were not to leave the ghastly stage unscathed.

Firstly let us address the fate of the Rapscallion and its leaderless crew. The effects of their poisoning was to last for another five hours. In this time, their demented attempts to sail their boat steered them on a random southward course. During this time Williams, while spewing over the starboard bow, toppled overboard after his vomit. Max cleaved off his hand with a Bowie knife, fearing it to be possessed by an unholy force. Walters, hoping to restore leadership to the helm, tried reapplying the captain's flayed face to Roberts' bare skull. All this time the boat was getting sucked into the eye of a devastating storm. The Rapscallion was obliterated, with n'er a sail nor soul ever recovered from the depths.

Judith, back at the Buccaneer, suffered a damning loss of trade due to rumours of her squalid and virulent lodgings. Unable to make a living she turned first to ruin, then to drink, then to suicide. She was found hanging from beams in the derelict attic where she first lodged Dafydd.

Up the hill, we would have found Maude, merrily serving her customers, had she not have contracted typhus from her carnal exchange in the back lane with Dafydd. The fever consumed her within two months. She died half the size she was when he first met her.

Horace too perished, but his fever was not the culprit. One night, in a blind and drunken rage he went stumbling after his long vanished antagonist. The following day he washed up on the slipway, crabs feeding on his flesh. Pock too, fell off the perch, his throat ballooning, and suffocating him due to a severe anaphylactic reaction to jellyfish stings.

Misfortune too tolled for the night-guard on duty when Dafydd flew his holding cell. He suffered a haemorrhage from the clout Dafydd delivered to the back of his head and he never woke again. But truly, Dafydd really only meant to stun him.

Further ardour reached as far as Roberts often estranged family in Aberystwyth. Dafydd had rightfully perceived that Charlotte's father, Police Commissioner Warren, would intercept his hastily crafted letter. Aware that the dogged detective, who at one time worked the notorious Jack the Ripper case, would not easily abandon his duties to the law, nor to his expectant, deserted, and broken hearted daughter. He left just enough breadcrumbs in the letter for the hound-dog to catch a scent. Dafydd purposely omitted Roberts' name, but included the name of his ship. He had also gotten Maude to travel to Aberystwyth to post the letter from there so it would bear the stamp from that office. His intention was to have Roberts seized on his return with the Rapscallion. However, as he never did return to dock, Warren's men paid a visit to his family home and his haggard wife and his two scruffy children. As contraband was mentioned in Dafydd's note, (a complete fabrication), a search was conducted of the household, and uncannily enough, a large horde of stolen tobacco and alcohol was unearthed from his basement. Roberts' wife was named as accessory and taken to prison, screaming her innocence. Their children were forced to spend their youth in an orphanage, and Roberts' name as a smuggler and paedophile spread like syphilis. His neighbours torched his vacant house on Guy Fawkes night.

And finally to Charlotte. After being abandoned on the bridge in Bangor, the distraught young maiden directed her rage and anguish towards her father, blaming him on driving her love away. She took flight one night in the sixth month of her pregnancy. General Warren never seen, nor heard from his daughter or grandchild again.

The list of mayhem and casualties, as far as I know, end more or less there. Though the consequential ripples from all such terrible events reverberate endlessly. But, here is one more point of remarkable interest.

Dafydd butchered Roberts with ease, easier then shooting a plague ridden rat. But pause now to consider this. Do you think he may have hesitated if he'd known that it was his own father's heart that he was impaling with such calm and precision?

None now will ever know. But most might agree – probably not.

'...And I will stay till my dying day
with my whistlin' gypsy rover...'
~Leo Maguire

"I imagine a line, a white line, painted on the sand
and on the ocean, from me to you."
~Jonathan Safran Foer

Loftus Hall 1883, Wexford

In less than fifteen years after Queen Victoria announced she would visit the Loftus family in their stately home, it had transformed from a modestly kept manor, to an opulent palatial home, to a forsaken and neglected home. The bright paint stained and ran from the sills leaving blood coloured tears. The proud eagles overlooking the courtyard bowed, humbled and meek. The rust gathered and stiffened the seldom used gates. The prematurely deceased and the youngsters' departures stole any remaining joy from the family nest, leaving behind only eggshells. Broken and empty memories of a thing that was once perfect, promising and brimming with life.

When the news of Elizabeth's misadventure arrived back to the Hall in 1879, it hit the family like a battering ram. Charles, the stalwart and bolstering head of the family, having so long tried to keep estate and family together after their previous disruptions and tragedies, crumbled like a salt pillar when news returned from Southampton that his beloved daughter never met with her dearest fiancé. The assumption that she slipped overboard, a correct one.

Arthur too, capitulated and caved after the death of his darling. His devotions for her turned into devotion for isolation, and for alcohol. He never functioned again as an engineer, and although his wealthy family did all they could to support him and help guide back from the darkness, he remained distant and listless when sober, dissolute and lecherous when drunk. He slowly vanished into the underworld of taverns and brothels, never to be recognised again.

Annie, who already lived in the safety of her own little dream-world, was just twelve when she heard that her last true companion on this earth had drowned. To support herself through her challenging childhood Annie crafted a sturdy inner framework, forged of pirate ship masts, unicorn horns and knitting needles. The dreadful news of Elizabeth tested this delicate scaffold like the wolf blowing on the little pigs houses. It shuddered and rattled and teetered, but, it did not succumb as you may expect a house of cards to. It weathered and endured, the supple sapling more pliant than the rigour of the old oak.

Undoubtedly she was grief-stricken, but the trauma had the effect of redoubling her retreat into her fertile fantasy world. Here, she could resurrect Elizabeth, alongside her mother, they could be Queens and Princesses, rabbits or wolves, fairies or goblins. Annie's inner wonderland grew rich and expansive, throughout her rainbow coloured realm dwelt all manner of personae, mostly carefree and happy, with the occasional nefarious villain. As the narrative of this world was Annie's to dictate, she could invent and oust the rotters at will, so happy ever afters were always a guarantee.

But he real world often came a-knocking. School and teachers, homework and violin practice, Father and Jane, - her most wicked stepmother and most cunning nemesis - whom she vanquished over and over. Annie had a filter for all these interruptions. All of her prosaic chores and temporal responsibilities were carried out by a facsimile she created of herself, - Anne the obliging servant girl.

Anne would be summoned to deal with humdrum affairs, while Annie, as we know her, becomes Wendy, the White Witch of Elizaland. Here, Queen Elizabeth reigned supreme and serene, but only via the wisdom and protection of her enchanted fairy sister Wendy, who thwarted all who might bid her ill-will or attempt to usurp her throne.

So outwardly, one might encounter Anne the servant girl tending to Annie's chores and errands, merrily and dutifully going about her day, few detecting that she was but an automaton, devised to allow Annie to play unfettered in the wilds of her imagination.

Her tasks complete, Annie spent more and more time alone in the tapestry room with her needles and threads, and her towers of books, which she now digested rapaciously. We all have our coping mechanisms, the alternative for Annie would have been a straight-jacket in a secure institution.

The brothers arrived home for Elizabeth's funeral ceremony. They appeared like grown-up ghosts of their former selves. Outwardly they smiled for the large congregation that gathered, and took some comfort in each others company, all together in their family home after their prolonged absences. There only seemed to be a flicker of genuine joy when Annie appeared to squeeze them with her earnest hugs, and witter into their ears some secretive nonsense, or conspiracies about the planned assassination of Lady Jane Grey.

However, even after one night's stay back at the Hall, they itched to get back to the distractions of their labours, and the lives that they had forged for themselves on faraway shores. Within two days of the gathering the house was as hollow as a pumpkin again. The eerie silence filled its rows of vacant bedrooms, and echoed along the long corridors and the hollow staircase.

Since this time, The Hall has sat and wasted, the housekeepers and groundsmen whittled away, as the burden of debt and wages became irreconcilable. The endless demands of the mansion and its grounds now rested with a staff of just five. The duties of the remaining staff doubling and tripling at times. Mr Delaney, now acting footman and coachman, Missus Meades cleaned and laundered, and Treasa scullery duties extended to housekeeping and running grocery errands too. They kept living quarters in the coach-houses on the estate. While Pat Casey - the groundsman, and his son Michael worked there six days weekly, but resided off-site, nearby in Fethard-on-Sea.

The remaining residents within the cavernous castle were Lord Charles, Lady Jane and Annie, now sixteen years old.

Miraculously their marriage remained intact despite the burdens the house and the harrowing luck brought on them. Elizabeth's death tested further her father's resilience, and his original political reasoning for wedlock to Jane softened, and the pairs' alliance warmed. Witnessing his vulnerability brought out a caring instinct in Jane she did not even know existed within her. Even towards Annie she felt now some small weight of pity and sympathy. She tried to treat her kinder and warmer as best she could, though the child's capricious peculiarities continued to baffle and bemuse her bourgeois sensibilities.

They faced however, the insurmountable issue of the family debt. The Tottenham-Cliffe wealth could no longer to buttress the extensive Loftus liabilities. Time and favours had run out, and their last remaining option was declare bankruptcy, and sell the estate. Charles and Jane held long and pragmatic deliberations far out of earshot of Annie, who probably would have not tuned in even if she was sitting on the desk between them. These discussions, though weighty and sombre, never grew tense nor near to argument. Their common level-headedness served to build a friendship they had never envisioned, and both strived to find an amicable arrangement for their future. But in the end, all their meetings and best intentions boiled down to a matter of choice – and they had but only one.

They would wait until Annie was seventeen before selling the ancestral home. 700 years of family legacy would be handed over to the highest bidder. They would move to modest accommodation in England, where Annie would take board in a private college of her preference. They hoped to tell her of their intentions when she matured a little, not that that looked likely anytime soon.

This was the plan. And so they sat and they waited. Keeping up appearances and doing the bare minimum to keep the estate ticking over.

They say we die twice, the first when we shed our mortal coil and are buried in the ground, the second is when the last person who knew us on this earth also dies, and with them dies our eternal memory. Loftus Hall stands amongst her overgrowing gardens, like the headstone of a long deceased family member, spurned and unattended, it lies still, silent and forgotten, waiting for its second death.

***

Over the winters and summers, Annie, remaining very much suspended in her delusionary childhood mentality, outwardly became an exquisitely beautiful young lady. Almost seventeen now, she bore her mother's fair countenance with a desirable and delicate bloom all of her own.

Her father considered her akin to a very unkempt Cleopatra. The amateur geologist in him theorised she was like anthracite, or a rough semi-precious stone, whom, with the application of enough pressure and expertly honed cuts, could eventually sparkle like a diamond. But he knew he was too soft on her to ever harden her so, regardless, she always shone in his eyes.

Trips to town, seldom as they were, brought admiring glances and craning necks from men young and old, even women of an envious, or sapphic disposition found themselves staring at her longer than propriety expects.

Annie, was mostly oblivious to her admirers. She would study the decaying leaves on the trees, or the tempestuous patterns in clouds or skip between the treacherous cracks on the pavements. It was not her intention to appear rude or aloof, but so often did the everyday folk of the everyday world, appear to her humdrum, grey and dreary. Annie simply just took no interest in the conveyor belt of people who passed her by, who opened her doors, who tipped their hats in her direction, hoping in return for a glance or a smile.

Sometimes the thick eared, bug eyed and badly shaven farming boys who loitered around the cattle mart would amuse her inquisitive mind. She would gawk openly at their unfortunate features, fancying them as swamp trolls or dwarfs that she could place into the adventures of her fantasy world.

Though she was not entirely distracted, nor blind to the opposite sex, and her eyes did seek out the prerequisite characteristics that she determined as necessary ideals in a male partner. There were just so few of them to witness in the world.

In the tapestry room, between her reading and her needlecraft, she often sketched. Floral and fanciful visualisations brought forth from her vivid and industrious carnival of dreams. She kept these private mostly, as a young lady would expect to keep her diary private.

Within this portfolio lay sketches of the man she would oneday wed. Composites of characters she read of over the years, his features developing and refining as she matured. The first sketches of a clean and handsome, sword bearing prince swathe in colourful clothes, evolving into a more swashbuckling, decadent character, clad in black and red capes, with dark and wild hair.

Once, having half-read Wuthering Heights and the plight of Cathy and Heathcliffe, Annie decided she would fall in love with a savage brute, of whom only she could see the gentle soul within. She was adamant now to crave only this clichéd paramour, only he could pave her path to true love. So, even against her instinct, she forced herself to take fancies on dark, rugged and burly types.

There was Michael, the groundsman's son, lanky and dishevelled wheeling his barrow. The boy was kindly faced, and bore a rustic sort of attraction about his ever filthy face, but the crux with the late adolescent gardener was with his unfortunate strabismus condition, with one always slowly chasing the other, she found it just too distracting.

The hulking fisherman in Kilmore, gutting his catch in his dirty woollens and waders caught her interest when they went to visit the fish markets. She thought him very coarse and manly, puffing smoke like a steam engine while he chewed his pipe stem, his thick fingers smeared with fish slime and blood. She surmised his first love was to the sea, a marriage she decided not to intrude upon and let him be.

The family doctor, not yet thirty, loomed tall and broad with a shock of wild unkempt hair, not at all the preconceived bearing of a neat and diminutive medical professional. No, he was not an exact facsimile of Heathcliffe, but still, she chose to narrow her desperate pursuit down to the imposing, yet domesticated Doctor Hargreaves, deciding to overlook his tamed breeding and cultivated manners.

In order to attain his closer attentions she would feign illness of melodramatic proportions and have him summoned. Bouts of the lurgy, consumption and cholera all befell the young lady. From encyclopaedia she would glean the symptoms of various ailments, then she used, to limited effect, her powders and paints to administer and emphasise her theatrical symptoms. Pock marks, flaking skin and ghostly pallor could all be easily simulated. She particularly enjoyed the time she applied a burning rash effect on her inner thighs, then demurely rising her skirts to display this fevered fabrication to the reticent examiner. She fascinated to witness his blushes. Once, she even poured actual dog vomit, alive with worms, beside the bed. The good doctor, reluctant to inform her parents of her chicanery, grew vexed and impatient with her exaggerated performances and props. On his final visit, upon examining her breast, a lazily applied blackberry juice bruise smeared onto his fingers. He fumed at her, then vented his opinion of her to her father and stomped away. His bereft patient, quickly alive and well, chased barefoot after his carriage all a-thither and distressed. Then began to giggle when he was gone. Realising that laughter was an entirely unsuitable reaction from a jilted lady, she began to wail aloud and ran back through the puddles to her boudoir, examining the sincerity of her tears in her mirror before throwing herself, and her muddy feet, onto the bed for a wonderfully long cry.

Vinegar Hill 1883

Darkness shrouds the Hook peninsula, and between a snarl of razor-sharp rocks there nestles a tiny strip of moonlit sand, like a missing tooth in the shark's overcrowded mouth. Over the years it has been littered with driftwood, wreckage and the shredded debris that the fanged fringe has chewed up and spat out.

The odds on anything reaching the spit intact are minuscule, the sole purpose of the sea and the rocks here is to pummel and destroy. A foreboding front-line of defence against all unwitting flotsam or jetsam.

So what is this small, ragged mass, lying still on the sand, with the blue foam of the night sea lapping around it? Is it man or mineral? Is it alive or dead? It does not move, 'cept for the water urging it towards land.

What faith conspires to navigate this body safely betwixt the menacing maze of shards and place it unscathed, apart from its many scars from other adventures, onto this safe slip of strand beneath the ever vigilant eye of Hook lighthouse.

Was it ordained for Dafydd to be delivered unbroken? Was it grace or grim destiny that laid him, still breathing on the beach? Was it blind luck, good luck, or a lucky rabbit's foot that guided his path? Or was it the hoof of a horned devil that shielded his passage to shore? Maybe it was no fluke that he slipped past the savage teeth of the beast. Maybe now he lies asleep, on the dragons tongue, waiting to be swallowed whole.

Barely concious, barely alive, Dafydd coughed, spluttered out seawater from his lungs, and breathed in the Irish air.

***

There are certain locations, elevated and alone, steeped in foulness, misery and despair that are favoured by nefarious, otherworldly beings as portals to this world. Decayed and desolate tors where humanity lost its way, committed unspeakable crimes, embraced insanity and evil and danced blood-soaked around the devils bonfires.

Fifty miles from the beach where Dafydd lies is Vinegar Hill, the battleground where the British redcoat invaders bulldozed through the Irish rebel stronghold. The pikemen of Wexford fought bravely but were savagely overwhelmed by enemy numbers, who claimed another ill-gotten gain for the Crown.

The hill itself now sits silent. It is long since the screams of battle and the cries of anguish have hushed. It is long since the blood, spilled from the vicious atrocities that were executed on this small highland a century ago, soaked into its ochre soil.

Perched atop the modest knoll, looking like a giant stone fez, are the gnarled remains of an old windmill. High above this ruin, a small sooty eddy mysteriously materialises and swirls ominously.

The dark vortex gathers in size and momentum against the clear night sky. The centrifugal plume growing and twisting and churning in mesmerising revolutions. The swirling cloud could not be mistaken for any meteorological anomaly or geographical idiosyncrasy. This was not of science. This, was not of this earth.

The furious flurry becomes a turbulent maelstrom, and from within its electrified belly, sparks and flares begin to rupture and ignite. The whirling black cyclone amassing in intensity and fizzing with dark energy. A rumble then, like distant thunder groaned and seemed to speed nearer to this source, gaining resonance and rage as it sped.

The swelling roar reached the black vortex and detonated with a bellow and fury that would worry Thor himself. From the epicentre of the spinning cloud a blazing bolt of fire spat forth like lightning, casting over the landscape for an instant, a blood-red stain. The force of the impact rippled across the countryside like dragon's wrath. Far over the fields in cottage windows, candles were lit, and concerned faces dared to peep. Livestock, wiser than folk, bawled and took cover. Then all was still once more. Not a dog howled.

In an instant the plume evaporated into the moonlit night, leaving nothing behind but an orange glow inside the topless ruin of the windmill, like a giant smouldering candle-holder.

A moment of silence, before suddenly, the old oak door burst outwards and flew from its hinges. The vision now was of a crimson pyre burning fiercely within. From the dead space at the wick of the flame a shadow began to grow, a shimmering blue black cone, gathering in form, terrific in its horror. The doom-laden spectre began to hiss pestilently, like fat blistering on the fire, while mutating into some abhorrent humanoid pretence.

The phantasmic silhouette stepped forward from the blaze within the ruin and the fires immediately subsided. Now, the black menace stood, ember and flame still clinging to its cloaks, turning then, it panned the night horizon slowly from north to south with its red slit eyes.

Baal's avatar halted its gaze to the south, and to the sea that binds him to the shores of Eireann. Acknowledging its destination, it arched back, and with a grotesque fusion of triumph and unholy rage the demon erupted with an omnipotent bestial roar. Any curious faces still peering through distant windows now quickly dipped, candles quenched, and crucifixes gripped.

Bathed by the benevolent moon, Baal slowly strode down the hill, following in his wake, a trail of burning footprints.

Hook Lighthouse

Salutem Omnium

For over 700 years the passage of all god-fearing maritime vessels making the often perilous journey across the south Irish Sea has been safeguarded by the colossal monolith that is Hook lighthouse.

It has grown from the ashes of the bonfires that Brother Dubhan lit in 453A.D. The beacon born from the flare that the monk kept lit to ward boats clear of the merciless, rocky ridge that guards the peninsula like a natural fortress. From this far-seeing friar it inherited its name - Rinn Dubhan.

Over the years the shipwrecks and vanishings became fewer and fewer, owing to the success of this solitary flame on the horizon. A tower was raised to hold the torch higher. The tower was fortified and made habitable, and became as much a symbolic extension of the nearby monastery. as it was a lantern for those lost or wary at sea. Now in 1883 she stood bold and brave, immovable and insubordinate to everything the wind, rain and raging sea has thrown at her, century after century.

The monks have long since passed the torch into the hands of civilians, but the duties of maintaining the light has never lost its crucial sense of import during the transfer. Each generation of family tasked with its responsibility treated their duty with as much a sense of vocation as the first monks that dwelt there.

Beneath the full moon and scuttling clouds the magnificent dominance of the girthy tower appears, then disappears, as the moonbeams alternate upon her breast. The powerful glow of her all seeing eye, like a great, squat candle, shines defiant and unquenchable, high above the turbulent tides.

In September 1883 it was the Gardiner and McCarthy families who tended to her every need, and of those there were many. The painting; a task that was never really finished, one coat just led to the next, and by day the tower shone white, and distinctively bound thrice by red bands. The magnifying glasses that encompassed the powerful bulb were treated and cleaned like crystal chandeliers, and gleamed always. The internal quarters were kept pristine; while smoke from the round the clock fires did its share to thwart the daily scouring. And all the while, they kept their steadfast vigil, ever fixed on the horizon.

Will Gardiner was a happy lighthouse keeper. He had all he ever wanted within arms reach, a secure job, fuel to rid the cold and a well stocked larder to rid hunger. He had his responsibilities and his relaxation time when the relief keeper took his shift. Most importantly, he had his family by his side in the purpose built dwellings that flanked the giant beacon. Glad was he, not to stationed on Fastnet or Ballycotton, as isolated and alone as a marooned pirate.

Though content, Will did not sleep well last night after the strange rumble had woke him from his slumber. He was used to torrid seas pounding their fists on the lighthouse walls. He was used to wily winds howling their ghostly chorus as they tried to sneak through the door-frames. But last nights commotion, albeit brief, seemed to rumble from *beneath* and unsettled this hardened keepers gut, and kept his slumber fretful till dawn.

First light was welcomed with relief, and Will began his daily routine. A cursory glance seaward told him the sky had not fallen nor the seas dried up. He began preparing breakfast, the bubble of the boiling kettle and the cat purring for attention comforted him. He grabbed the log book and binoculars. The sea calmly undulating, south west wind at four knots, visibility - moderate, overcast and cool, rocks still lethal, lighthouse still intact, and all was right in the world.

He continued his magnified patrol over the frothy surf, panning north then adjusting his focus on a tiny sand spit, not long enough to deem worthy the title of a beach. The tide had delivered something new, and had retreated. Could the amorphous shape be a small boat? No, too small. A stranded seal? No, strips of red and white clung to it. A body? His instinct told him yes. His stomach would prefer another no.

Shooing the cat from his trouser-leg and delaying the kettle, he hurried to alert the assistant keeper John McCarthy.

Once the details of the unusual sighting were conveyed to his trustworthy partner, McCarthy grabbed the wheelbarrow and off the two beachcombers sped through the misty fields, towards the mysterious shoreline deposit.

The shape took the recognisable form of a person upon approach, adrenalin burned in the rescuers bellies as they lumped the cart awkwardly over the rocks. They reached the body, lying face down. Will gripped the wrist to determine a pulse. The clammy skin was bluey white and as cold as the sea. He could not feel anything and turned over the body, it was a man, a young man, eighteen or nineteen, well dressed beneath the cork life jacket that bobbed him to shore. He was limp as seaweed and bore no signs of life. Will put pressure on his jugular, while McCarthy blessed himself and muttered a Hail Mary. For a moment there was nothing but a seagulls caw. Will closed his eyes and desperately tried to feel more than just the cold.

Was it the faintest of pulses he felt, or was it imagined? Will held the lad up in his arms and listened to his chest and waited and hoped, like pressing an ear to the ground in the hope of hearing a rabbit's footfall. Nothing.

Then, just one beat, -lub-dub!

'He's alive!'

'Oh thank Jaysis,' McCarthy said to the skies.

Before hoisting him back to the lighthouse they wrapped him in the blankets they had brought and tried rubbing warmth into his frozen chest. Upon this action, Will found a furry pendant clinging to the lad's neck. *How curious*, Will thought as he pinched it closer.

It was a rabbit's foot.

Will held it, regarded the corpse-like boy, and then his hazardous hinterland. 'Well Saints preserve us, McCarthy! This sure is one lucky fecking fellah.'

Matt Malloys Funeral.

The first glow of a new day dimly appeared in the chilled autumn darkness and the stars faded fast after an unsettled and restless night at The Hall. Unusual climatic or electrical activity rocked the old walls, and roused the meagre contingent of remaining inhabitants in the vast mansion.

Thereafter the fearful clap, sleep did not come easily to the nervy Loftus family and staff. The thunder that shook the panes and rattled the crystalware was, at first, perceived as an otherworldly harbinger, laying siege on the infamously fabled homestead. After hours waiting for the other supernatural shoe to fall, the perturbing event was classed as meteorological, and eyelids slowly drifted downwards to dream again. Although to Annie, the booming, apocalyptical experience was thrilling, more so than terrifying.

All occupants of the manor were delivered safely unto morning. No maids found hung in the hallway, no butler serving his own head on a silver platter, no wicked stepmother impaled on the suit of armour's sword. All remained as it was within the once very fine estate.

Outside the blackbird sings, crimson begonia flutter, and the second flush of roses yawn at the promising morn. For not all joy has forsaken her gables and gardens. The fruit does not rot on the branches, nor does the fuchsias skirt pale less red. Nor have the extravagant dreams of young Lady Annie been doused by the drum of despair. Her dreams endure, dreams of sunrises, warm breezes and love.

A sash window rises swiftly on the third floor and the exquisite young woman peeks out to greet the dawn and delight in the blackbird's aria. A radiant aura seemed to follow Annie like a spotlight from the heavens. As long as she chirped and skipped along the halls and stairs of the mansion, the wolf stayed clear of its gates. Though, should one ever steal inside, the inquisitive maiden would quite fancy to stroke it.

Let us follow the blackbirds trill to the sill, where the eager teenager, fully assured that she can converse with the cheery bird, returns her mimicked song, and smiles to the sun rising over the Irish Sea.

Annie drank in the morning's brilliance from the end of her bed, which she preferred to have pushed tight against the wall beneath her open window. She enjoyed the contrast of the chill night air with the pocket of warmth that kept her snug beneath countless layers of bedding, and Baggy, her faithful collie companion. Her room often frigid as a consequence, but her father had given up having the windows closed and her bed moved back to its original position a long time ago.

There was nothing particularly special about this day, it was neither a Friday, Saturday nor Sunday, not a birthday nor Holy day, no distinguished guests were due at the door nor were any outings with friends or acquaintances penned in her diary. No, nothing of note. But to Annie, the fresh morning air abounds with song, scent, sunshine and promise. An endless day full of possibilities invited her to gallop and dance and laugh. She turned and ran in her night-skirts, merrily along the landing, rapping on its many doors, and greeting each empty room with a rapturous, 'Good morning!'

Her greeting finally echoed back from the master bedroom, though with far less exuberance. 'Good morning my dear,' grumbled her father, Charles. Beside him, his wife Jane – Annie's stepmother, and second cousin, offered her no such utterances.

Annie's opinion, apart from the aspect that Daddy should have never ever taken another for his wife, to take a family relation - this just seemed bizarre. The word *yuck,* sprang out in Annie's mind like a cuckoo clock every time her Daddy pecked Jane on the cheek.

Irked by Annie's lively alarm call, Jane wearily roused herself. Charles, already dressed, kissed her gently and followed the chirps of his beloved daughter downstairs to the dining room where Missus Meades was bringing the morning tea.

Annie shouted from the kitchen where she was helping Treasa with breakfast, 'I'll be with you in a jiffy Daddy. Runny or hard boiled? Yes, hard boiled, I know I know!'

Charles had ceased asking Annie to maintain her position of peerage and desist from menial household chores, or assisting the help. It seemed all hierarchy, roles and norms were slowly abandoned after Elizabeth's passing.

The disciplined maids too, always tried to maintain within the limits of their station, and behaved nervously when Annie offered to lend a hand, especially if their master approached. But over time, even they calmed down in her presence, their fondness for her growing with every encounter.

The Lord, in his more contemplative moments, supposed that the age of aristocracy was in its last stages, soon to become as extinct and fossilised as the dinosaurs. Classism, he had lately philosophised, is fast becoming an outdated principal, a second cousin to slavery, and no model from which to launch civilisation into the twentieth century. The Loftus's may be bowing out of the royalty race a little early, but they were bowing out with a degree of foresight, and, with a head start they may well lead the way into the brave new world.

Also, with no one but old Baggy to amuse Annie, it is of no wonder that she sought to amuse herself in whatever way she could in their rattling old house. If beating rugs with bats, planting vegetables or boiling eggs helped her while away the boredom, then he'd let her coalesce with staff all she liked, just to see her preoccupied and amused.

To everyone's great anticipation the sons were reconvening at the Hall this evening. It would be the first time they would all be under the same roof since Elizabeth's funeral mass. This would provide a welcome distraction for Annie, and she was visibly thrilled by the news of their forthcoming arrival. Charles had planned for an evening of merriment and games, and already Treasa was preparing the courses for dinner. It would also give Charles a chance to discuss with them, in confidence, his fateful plans for the estate. He was quite sure the news would not displease them in the slightest. After all, by now they had all carved their very own industrious niches in the world, niches that demanded their fullest attentions. Annie alone remained the most attached to the family home, and required the deftest of approaches with this news.

He was hoping that a suitor may yet be found for her, before they divulged their news to her. Charles knew she had romantic notions, usually fantastical and difficult for Jane and he to get their heads around. But should she fall in love with a decent fellow, it might serve to soften the blow that the news of the sale and the move, could affect upon her.

Charles believed that this fellow would need to have the most patient, understanding and tolerant disposition, as well as being handsome, of reputable stock and wholly solvent. Some may call such a rare creature a unicorn, but Annie liked unicorns.

The prospects of nabbing one were not good. The couple of potential courtiers that Jane and he had managed to lure over to the old Hall to sit with Annie, politely declined the invitation of a return visit. It was not a question of her feminine attraction, as Annie was as fair as calla lillies, blushed cheeks on moonlit skin, beneath a swathe of unkempt raven curls. The young men were instantly enamoured by her beauty. The crux at these engagements was distilled from her unusual personality. The rules of courtship and civil conversation were alien to Annie. Politics to a Pixie.

If for example, while she sipped tea and ate tart with Rupert, after he realised that commerce or real estate were not subjects she shared a remote interest in, he may ask her what might her favourite filling in pie might be. Finally engaged, Annie would lunge into a vivid description of giant rhubarb forests, wherein the magical ingredients for rhubarb flavours were a heavily guarded secret. Then, she may attempt to describe the flavour of the sour taste of the stalky plant via the art-from of dance. Rupert, being unfamiliar with the game of *Chorigami* might then, very quickly finish his tea and bid the Lord and Ladies a very good day. *Rhubarb indeed*, Rupert might tsk.

Annie and Treasa brought hot eggs and toast to the dining room where Charles was reading the morning papers. Annie placed his at his setting and kissed his cheek. 'Happy breakfast-time Daddy.' His daffy darling never failed to warm his heart and mellow his mood.

'Good morning dear, My, this smells good. I'm ravenous. I could eat a unicorn,' he teased.

Annie squinted and pursed her lips playfully at him. 'Well, it's no wonder they're extinct with galumphing great beasts like you going around scoffing them up.'

The good mood was tempered somewhat by Jane's arrival to the table.

'Good morning Lady Jane,' Annie pipped, confident that her stepmother would not relate to her historical reference.

'Good morning, Annie,'

'You're eggs are runny, just how you like them,'

'I like them hard boiled Annie dearest, I thought you knew this,' Jane said through a pseudo smile.

'Oh dear, I'm stupendously sorry. Here, allow me to knock your head off for you,' Annie said holding a butter knife and alluding to her hot uncracked egg, enjoying her private joke to herself.

'That'll be fine dear, let's just eat shall we.'

Charles gave Annie a droll glance, sharp enough to say naughty naughty, wry enough to suggest he enjoyed the sinister insinuation.

***

Annie, the epitome of optimism, believed that this particular morning would herald the provenance of her destiny, as she frequently did. First she would get the gloomy funeral business out of the way. Matt Malloy, the local thatcher, publican, popular chap and all round nice fellow, who had become acquainted with the family while working on the roof of Loftus Hall during its renovations, had recently passed.

She had considered sending Anne, her obedient servant girl alter ego, in her stead, allowing Annie to adventure without distraction in fantasy-land, but Annie fancied some fresh air and had an ulterior motive to cosy up to Daddy. Once the poor old beggar was resting comfortably beneath his new blanket of turf,

Annie planned to thoroughly harass her father to organise for her private tuitions in the dulcet language of French.

Of recent, she believed her destiny lay as a couturier in Paris, specifically millinery. She also hoped that her tutor would have an adorable accent, reek of garlic and ask her if she would sit for him to paint her portrait, naked of course. This was the plan, alas, *qui vivra verra*. Of course all pleadings would be made in the absence of the nay-saying *Lady Jane Grey*. She wished their marriage as little longevity as the Eighth King Henry's to his once dear, and now decapitated wife. Annie imagined one of her own hats, perhaps a cloche, crafted from dirty grey signet feathers floating over Jane's vacant shoulders.

Annie's fondest memories were of knitting in the tapestry room, tending to her needlecraft with her mother and sister. Despite her flighty nature, in millinery, and indeed most artful tasks, Annie had a good measure of adroitness. Like most of her creations they often leant towards the obscure.

One example of her avant-garde ambitions being the time she hung the sheepskin rug up for her canvas on the wall in the tapestry room. She then endeavoured to create on it an illustration of a burning boar, using a red hot poker in lieu of a paintbrush. It was looking quite well - figuratively, until it caught fire – literally, whence she tore it down and threw the entire rug into the Inglenook to burn the artistic evidence - permanently.

Having sheared through all her floral clothes of youth for use in her early headpiece designs Annie determined that she needed more innovative raw materials at her disposal were she to create truly great hats. After helping herself to snippets of curtains, carpets, and Jane's cashmeres, she began scavenging the grounds for nature's moltings. She quickly amassed an assortment of plumage and pelts. Peacock quills, raven, grouse and pheasant feathers, fox and rabbit furs all served to decorate her exciting new line...*Any relic of the dead is precious if they were once valued living*...was an Emily Brontë quote she favoured dearly.

Her autumn collection begot a darker, more gothic allure. Her Davy Crockett effort, fashioned of fox, was bleakly comical, with poor Mr Fox's head still sleeping atop the crown of ginger fur, his tail tangling like an oversized earring. One of her successes was her crow top hat, wrapped with dark and deftly filed feathers, shimmering with inky iridescence, a band of black beads mirroring the rook's eyes, and a veil fashioned from dyed curtain netting.

As she chose her wardrobe for the day, she believed this topper would be perfectly suitable for today's sombre event.

Donning dark garments was nothing unusual for Annie. As a child her mother kept her pretty in lemons and lavenders, but before long she realised that Annie's penchant for mud was to be an enduring one, a relationship where dainty dresses and lace socks would always come second. So, she began to clothe her in more forgiving hues, blacks, browns and burgundies, and they've maintained their earthy symbiosis ever since.

Mr Delaney announced the readiness of the coach and horses, and the funeral party, suitably glum bar one, were promptly on their way to see off ol' Matt.

Although they were keen on the former publican, attending funerals was a delicate matter of form and manners for the gentry in Ireland. Mr Delaney would inform the family whether it best or not to attend impending burials. For example, when the deceased was formerly an active member of the Irish Republican Brotherhood, or lamented the attack on Vinegar Hill, or felt strongly that it was the aristocracy (and not the blight) that allowed his recent ancestors to starve and perish - all viable and legitimate grievances - then the attendance of her majesties favoured subjects would be most unadvised.

In the case of this morning's send off, it was a perfectly safe, and a politically sound gesture to gather alongside with Matt's mourners. Although, whenever they convened with common folk, pleasant as they were *face á face*, there always rose a suspicious trial of whispers in their wake. The natives held dear to their myths and superstitious tales, and the vaults of Loftus Hall was never in short supply of these.

Irish funerals are often populous affairs. You would need to arrive quite early to find yourself a good vantage spot inside the church. To whit, most folk remained funnelled outside the cramped chapel. There they would gape, hail or shine, at the church doors and stained windows as though part of the internal congregation. The Loftus contingent arrived very early and found a seat inside near the rear.

Annie enjoyed how her splendid feathered topper drew keen attention from passers by. She chose to keep down the netted veil to shield her face, as she could not muster any discernible sadness today.

Catholic mass etiquette bemused the protestant family who waited on the cue of the regulars to sit, stand or kneel. Annie of course enjoyed the pantomime of it all, but she would have preferred a seat nearer the immediate family in their grief. The nuances of the bereaved fascinated her, and she was desperate to see which person was most afflicted by the eulogies, softly delivered by those dearest to Matt.

Ad nauseam the sermon droned on. Finally the priest signalled its completion and voices sang. Annie whispered in chorus with the other attendants '*In aminin aher vic august speerod nive Amen.*' An organ bled sad notes and the crowd filed silently aside into dark walls, between which the coffin was borne.

The small chapel was situated in a picturesque setting overlooking the sea, fortunately for the pallbearers the graveyard was dug into the sanctified grounds that encompassed the church, so no undue lugging was needed.

Matt was gently lowered earthwards as his widow wailed. Without much thirst raised, a whiskey bottle was opened, the diggers filled the coffin shaped hole, and a melancholic song in gaelige lilted on the breeze. Annie delighted in the melodrama and sang along quietly her own unique gibberish version of the ballad. Some scathing eyes squinted in her direction, then silence fell as the rosary began.

Anon, a blackbird's pleasant trill cut through the monotonous drone of prayer. Perched on a low branch Annie believed she recognised her yellow beaked friend from her garden. Delighted to see her chirpy pal again she began to twitter his *hellos* back to him. For the most part the attendants just stared disbelieving, in stony silence at her. Though some knit their lips in effort to stifle their inappropriate giggles.

An angry storm swelled within Jane's bosom, while Annie's encumbered father closed his eyes in mortification.

The ceremony complete, it was finally time to disperse. Any thoughts Charles had of loitering awhile in the pub to make pleasantries with the common folk had fleeted quickly from thought. He would bury himself in an open grave now if he could. However, when they walked away, certain encounters, greetings and condolences were unavoidable.

Charles and Jane, exemplars of civility and manners, shook hands and offered their heartfelt respects and good wishes to all concerned. All parties avoiding any mention of their daughters irregular behaviour. Thankfully, Annie was now keeping to herself, sitting alone on a headstone, legs swinging, lost in a daydream as she gazed outwards to sea.

Lord Charles was also grateful that a lot of the locals seemed to be somewhat distracted. Grouping in small clusters and muttering about a matter neither concerning his kooky daughter nor the late Matt Malloy, RIP. Relieved by their preoccupation with whatever gossip they were sharing, and no doubt exaggerating, Charles tried to eavesdrop. But between the strong local accent and occasional use of their native tongue, he could not catch enough of the conversation to piece together the full story.

Jane took a lull in congress as an opportunity to bid her polite and swift goodbyes, and made her way over to the carriage where Mr Delaney was waiting. Charles, dawdling somewhat, signalled Mr Delaney over to his side and asked his loyal footman to ascertain what scandal has them chattering so intensely. It was far easier for Mr Delaney to mingle on ground level, and in little time he returned with the news.

At the same time Annie returned, eager now to ask about her french scholarship and mentor. Mr Delaney was about to speak when Annie exclaimed, '*Papa, je suis desole, je ne pas parle Fraçais tres bien.* Please, you simply must find me a language teacher to equip my tongue fluently in French, or I shall never survive in the savage world of Parisienne couture.'

Completely bemused by this barrage, the perplexed Lord grunted, 'Quiet Annie, you've embarrassed us all quite enough for one day. Mr Delaney, please ignore my *darling* daughter. Carry on. Do you know what's going on?'

'Yes sir. It seems a young man was found washed ashore down at Hook head. Over there is John McCarthy, one of the lighthouse keepers, apparently he found him only this morning on a slip of beach between two vicious rocky outcrops. It's a miracle he wasn't impaled and broken on the rocks. There was no sign of any wreckage, nor ships nor boats on the horizon. Just him, alone, and barely alive by the sounds of it. He hasn't spoken a word, he just mumbles delusionary nonsense. A fever seizes him hot and cold, so they are sustaining him there as best they can, but he is apparently at the door of death. McCarthy is trying to get hold of Doctor Chisholm, and hopes to take him with him on his homeward journey to the lighthouse.'

Charles looked suitably grim upon hearing the tale. 'Gracious, this is an awfully unfortunate business. Isn't Doctor Chisholm abroad still. Can we assist in any way?' he proposed absently.

Annie stood gaping, mesmerised by this fantastic tale. Images sparking of a heroic mariner, fending off beasts from the deep, scaling mountainous waves, his drained body thrown to the shore, waiting in rags to be rescued, and she, rushing across the sand to save him. It was all too exciting.

She blurted. 'Yes Daddy, we must help this poor soul, Daddy we must. We simply have no time to spare, his very salvation depends on our charity.'

'Please Annie. Hush, slow down, I'm sure we can offer some help.'

'Yes Daddy, we must have him sent for, and brought immediately to the Hall. We shall mend him, our warm fires will chase away his fever, our food nourish him back to health, Doctor Hargreaves can...'

Charles snapped a frown down towards her.

'Well OK, maybe not Doctor Hargreaves, but we'll summon Chisholm or courier a locum from New Ross or Rosslare. We'll see to it that this brave sailor survives this tragedy, and the good Lord in the heavens will be ever-pleased with us and reward us for our kindness.'

Once again, Lord Charles found himself chagrin by his daughters impulsiveness. Standing in the midst of the villagers, who had paused there gabbing to overhear Annie's very vocal and avid pleas. Mr Delaney scanned his polished shoes while Charles, squirming in the spotlight searched desperately for the correct reply.

Naturally there was only one option, he had already brought ridicule to the ceremony, how could he now possibly be seen to shun his daughter's benevolent proposal in front of the expectant audience. A degree of philanthropy was expected from the peerage towards the rabble, who were liable to arrive at their home with pitchforks ablaze, should he reply to Annie with anything less than a heartfelt affirmation of her plan.

'Of course my darling, we must do all we can to help the poor fellow. It's what any of us would do for another in such dire circumstances.' he announced. Several *here-heres* rose from the proletariat.

Visibly relieved, Mr Delaney nodded in his direction and silently conveyed his thoughts, *Well done old boy. That, was a terribly awkward situation.*

Acknowledging his thoughts, Lord Charles addressed Mr Delaney. 'Mr Delaney, be a good man and offer Mr McCarthy transit with us to the Hall, from there we can take the coach to Hook to collect the patient. Also, find someone to send an urgent message from the exchange. Get hold of Chisholm, or find any immediate doctor and summon him to the Hall. We'll foot any expense.'

Annie lifted her veil to offer her wonderfully kind Daddy her sparkling hazel eyes, now wide with delight. Choosing then to wrap both arms around his waist and squeeze him tight she whispered, 'I love you Daddy. You're my hero.'

A rising warmth engulfed Charles' throat, he coughed it clear, smiled and returned his daughters embrace. 'I love you too ragdoll.' A pet name he hadn't used in many years.

A collective approval rose earnestly from the gathering and hands were outstretched to shake Charles' as he made his way back to his ride.

He took his seat beside his wife and Annie sat opposite, veiled again to hide her giddiness. They waited for Mr Delaney. 'There seems to be quite the hullabaloo for a funeral. Are we ready to off dear?' Jane asked.

Grimly aware of Jane's forthcoming displeasure, Charles said grimly, 'Just a moment sweetheart, Mr McCarthy will be accompanying us home.'

'Oh!' she startled.

'Yes, darling, I'll explain on the way,' he mumbled reluctantly as Mr Delaney and McCarthy ambled towards them.

Annie could not contain herself a moment longer and burst out, 'Jane, isn't it thrilling? We are going to take in a half-dead pirate and nurse him back to life. What say ye to that me hearty? All in favour say Aye!'

Jane, dumbfounded, very slowly turned to Charles, hoping for some expression of clarity.

Charles, resigned and impotent, just shrugged and sighed. 'Aye!'

The Twisted Path

Within in the thick lighthouse walls a log fire blazed on the second storey. This level, sandwiched between the fuel storage chamber and the one time living quarters, was kept uncomfortably hot while the shipwrecked stranger wrestled with his fever.

The patient had not regained conciousness since his arrival on his wheelbarrow gurney at dawn. It was decided to keep him quarantined from the lighthouse family houses until some form of diagnosis had been established. Though truly, they expected a diagnosis of death to be proclaimed by the time any doctor could reach the remote promontory.

Will Gardiner's caring wife, Fiona, despite her husband's protestation, kept a bedside vigil on the weakening soul of the desperate young man. Though she herself was stifling in the sauna-like conditions of the chamber, when the lad's fever burned with a fury she tended to his brow with a cloth she kept in an ice-cold bucket of seawater. His frequent fits would cause him to grind his teeth like millstones, and to spasm and jerk his limbs to the point of needing restraint. When his frenzy had passed, he sank back into his deathlike sleep.

Under Hook's burning eye, their hope was that McCarthy may arrive back from the funeral in Fethard-on-Sea with Doctor Hargreaves, should he have been attending the ceremony. Failing that, he would carry on to Wellington Bridge, and return with the good Doctor Chisholm or his locum as soon as he could.

Considering the condition of the patient, all assumed the errand would be a trip in vain, wiser to send for a hearse, thought Will.

***

John McCarthy sits, bobbing along in the luxuriant coach on the slipshod road, beside him Lord Charles looks pensive. Above them on the box seat, Mr Delaney hastens the horses through the misty rain towards Hook head.

They sped in silence, a gloomy pall upon them. Charles looked especially grim, he supposed he was on a fool's errand from the information he gleaned from McCarthy while in transit. He had come very close to snapping with Annie and her fervour to ride along with them. Apart from the fact that there just wouldn't be room for her with the patient within the carriage, she had Charles' nerves frayed to wisps, and he needed breathing room away from the maniacal little madam.

As well as sending word and a carriage for Doctor Chisholm, Charles also, as a wise precaution, summoned for a priest too. The last rites quite likely a requirement for this mercy mission. It was his faint hope that they would be waiting at Loftus Hall upon their return with the patient, and maybe even transport him to a hospital, sparing him his charitable undertaking.

In the Hall, Jane had Missus Meades prepared a bed and fire in one of the smaller rooms on the seldom used third floor, far from this evenings visiting family members. Michael stocked this room with logs and Treasa prepared a broth, but by all accounts it would be a long time, if ever, this stranded stranger regained his appetite.

'Will you be returning to the house with us Mr McCarthy?' Charles piped up, suddenly wary of being alone in the back with the potentially infectious passenger.

'Wishin' I could, but I can't sir, I'm late for my shift already and Mr Gardiner will be in dire need of his sleep. I'm afraid you'll be on your own on the way back sir.'

'No, no, of course, that's absolutely fine Mr McCarthy. Myself and Mr Delaney will manage quite ably I'm sure. I'm just hopeful the poor fellow will survive this awful road.' The mental image of a pustules leper or lifeless corpse bouncing around beside him unnerved the Lord.

'Aye, sir, you'll be grand I'm sure, we're nearly here now.' He pointed to the spinning halo atop the tower that had saved so many souls, and prayed it might save just one more this night.

From the lighthouse parapet Will's eagle eye spotted the carriage coming and raised a brow, recognising the coach as that of one of the gentry's. He dashed down the endlessly coiling stone steps to greet them, alerting his wife to their arrival as he passed. He waited nervously in the large yard which fronted the family homes adjacent to the lighthouse. He impatiently watched the coach, and its faint gas-lamp, grow nearer through the blue mist of the dimming evening.

He was not alone surveying the vehicle, but even Will Gardiner's keen eyes could not detect the penumbral being, striding deliberately towards the lighthouse far across the boggy headland.

The clopping and breath of the labouring horses caught the shrouded figure's attention, its hooded head turning slowly in the direction of the galloping beasts and the vessel they towed. It slowed to a pause as the carriage drew up to the tower. Its footsteps burning less voraciously now than before, leaving only a trail of quickly extinguishing blue flames in the prints it hollowed into the bog-land. It stopped, shrouded in the thick fog, its unnaturally sharp sight piercing through the mounting dark. There it contemplated the ensuing furore at the lighthouse door. There it watched. There it waited.

***

Will Gardiner was perplexed when Lord Charles alighted the carriage, he tipped his head involuntarily while shaking the Lord's hand. Will was not displeased to see the Lord, rather he had somehow expected, by way of some good fortune, that the doctor may have stepped out of the fine coach. An irrational fear knotted within him at first, a fear similar to that that might be brought on by the unexpected knocking of a peeler on his moonlit door.

McCarthy hastily brought him up to speed with developments, and upon explanation Will relaxed. He then felt very relieved that his stricken occupant would very soon be taken away to become someone else's problem. Suddenly he was very eager to cart the body down the stairs and out the door.

On a makeshift stretcher, Will and John awkwardly lifted the patient down the winding turret and out to the yard where the

Lord anxiously awaited them. Mr Delaney assisted them from the doorway.

The young man was very tightly bound to a quickly fashioned plinth. At the coach steps Charles caught his first glimpse of the deathly young lad strapped to the narrow board. In the gaslight he looked more corpse than a living being, his thin blue mouth rent upon his sickly pale skin, now dyed coral by the gaslight. His eyelids were black and sunk deep into the ocular cavities of his almost visible skull. Dark hair clung to his gaunt features by cold sweat droplets, like seaweed to a shoreline rock. Charles visibly shook when the rotating light from above flashed these horrid features alive, white, and ghost-like for a moment, before passing again and returning him to his dormant coma.

Noticing this near swoon, Mr Delaney began barking orders to the lighthouse men hurry up. 'Get a move on Lads, every moment is precious to this poor man. Not to worry sir. We'll have him home and under the care of the Doc. in no time at all. He won't give you any trouble at all in the back, of that I'm certain,' he added wryly.

With him strapped to the stretcher they could only manage to stow him on the floorspace between the seats. Charles would have to sit with his legs resting on the facing seat, which was nothing new to him, as he often did this when alone in the coach. But this time he nearly offered to ride beside Mr Delaney on the box up top. He feared however that this would convey an image of cowardice to his subordinates, so he bit his lip. He thanked and commended the good men with honourable sincerity, and then, with commanding authority he shouted, 'Let's be off Mr Delaney, time and darkness is most pressing upon us now.'

As he slammed the door closed and propped his feet up over the cadaverous form, Fiona came dashing to the carriage with the patients satchel of belongings and held them at arms length through the window. 'Begging your pardon sir, he was found with this knapsack strapped to his body, might be some clues as to who he is in there somewhere.' Then she held out a small sack, 'and here are his clothes, dried and folded, we decided it best to clean him and dress him in some fresh nightshirts'

Gingerly taking the bags from her with forefinger and thumb as though it contained drowned kittens, he thanked her and tipped her his hat. 'Let us not tarry Mr Delaney, haste now, don't spare the horses.' He unpinched the knapsack onto the patient's midsection, and heard a slight clink of coins. Charles wiped his fingers in his handkerchief as Mr Delaney whipped the steeds, spurring them homewards to the cheers of *Godspeed*.

***

Beneath the slow strobe of the spinning watch-light the lighthouse families watched the carriage disappear. When it was out of sight they hurried out of the chill night and into the warmth of their homesteads and hopefully to a quick return to the normality of the sea-watchers lives.

Tonight they would celebrate the success of their *meitheal*. Much tea, ale and whiskey would be drunk that night by the hearth while they endeavour to calculate the boy's chances, ponder his providence, and rhetorically relive the adventures of their memorable day. The sooner it became an embellished tale of yesterday, rather than the arduous event of today, the better.

Last inside was Will Gardiner, before he turned the key to shut out the cold, dark night, he scanned, out of habit, across the rocky outcrop and boggy plain that led to the buildings. In the darkness he thought he noticed something candle-like, faintly flickering in the distance. He squinted into the night and believed his eyes were seeing tiny blue flames glowing in a line leading towards him. He smiled a little to himself, he had heard tales of the *will-o-the-wisp*, but never thought he'd witness this rare peat-land phenomena first hand. He stared for a moment until the rotating light whirled around again. Will's stomach seized when the beam caught in its sight the unmistakable shape of the tall shrouded menace looming towards him, an otherworldly shadow with glowing embers for eyes. In that instant Will swore he was staring Satan's mask in the eye, he froze, as cold and immovable as a menhir, his heart dared not to beat such was the fear struck upon him.

The light continued its circular path, and the world was plunged into blackness again, Will wondered if he was dead, and remained petrified, as cold as coffin nails and in dread of the light returning and revealing him face to face with the soul-harvesting reaper. But on its return, there was nothing, nothing but the wet wisps of marram swaying into the distance. No reaper, no demon, no flaming footprints.

Snapping from his stupor he dashed inside, bolted the door behind him, and tried to remember how to breathe again. He joined the safety of the others gathered round the fire. Their stories were told long into the night over the drinks and card-games, but Will chose to keep his cards very close to his chest. None of his companions, now basking in relief, were ready to hear about the unexpected joker in the pack.

***

Out on the bog, barely visible, the faint cerulean blue flames change their direction. Now north they steadily plot a new course. Roughly in the same direction of the would-be ambulance bound for Loftus Hall.

Via his 'Geddaps' and 'Yas', the driver commands his horses to bolt homewards along the twisted path to Loftus Hall. Inside the coach the Lord steals his queasy gaze away from the wan figure on the deck and out into the hazy, featureless night. Gnawing at his thumbnail for the first time since Elizabeth's funeral, he loses himself to her memory, and begins a lamenting and apologetic conversation with her in his mind.

Unseen to him, the frail figure beneath his outstretched legs can feel the weight of the satchel on his emaciated middle. His skeletal fingers twitch, then his white hands slowly climb towards the canvas sack like two blind spiders. Finding comfort in the folds of the familiar bag they clutch it and come to rest, as though it were a childhood toy.

The Patient Arrives

On the third tier of windows in Loftus Hall a solitary pane glows through the damp night air. Within, a remote room had been prepared for the sick arrival, the intention to sequester him here, far from the family bedrooms on the second floor. In the window, silhouetted against the glow, was the still outline of Annie, occasionally twitching at the sight of any movement on the road. She kept a constant lookout, not dissimilar to the vigilant nearby lighthouse, for her Daddy's return on the road south to Hook. It was nearing her third hour waiting.

During this time, her brothers had arrived for the family reunion and were settling in their rooms. William, Charlie and Alfred arrived without their spouses, only George managed to persuade his rubenesque wife, Agatha, to accompany him to his ancestral home. They were all hungry, and quite disgruntled not to be welcomed by their father, who was off on his altruistic errand. Treasa, the diminutive red-headed maid, tirelessly outdid herself in the kitchen all day, but the heady, herby aroma of roasting lamb mingled with the cabbagy steam emitted by her medicinal broth, offered little temptation to their ravenous tummies.

Even Annie, who ran downstairs shrieking in delight to find her handsome siblings gathered by the fire in the hallway, was less attentive and clingy than they had remembered and expected her to be. After hugging them all dearly, while spewing out in rapid-fire the days ongoing dramas, she kissed their cheeks and flew back to her lookout perch, singing some pirate shanty about a bottle of rum. Baggy, her ageing allegiant collie, barely keeping up with her strides. Jane, who had met and welcomed them home, filled in the multitude of blanks that Annie had omitted.

From what they could gather about the days events, they quietly held their meddlesome little sister in account for their father's absence from the welcome mat and dining table. Their aristocraticical leanings were also highly opposed to the notion of dragging a diseased or dying castaway into their family home. *Oh how the times have changed the order of things, are we now just as common and kind as the caring peasants of Wexford.*

Jane was pleased by their snobbery and heartened towards their mild animosity towards their little sister.

Having settled in, the guests could no longer stave off their hunger and gathered around the candlelit dining table. Here they greeted Missus Meades like a dear old aunt, then told her to fill their glasses high, and load their plates with all the fare the crockery could accommodate.

There was little by way of conversation as the sliced salty meats and steaming buttery vegetables were wolfed down and the wine guzzled heartily. Shortly, the mood became lighter and a few jibes and jokes of childhood pranks and mishaps were shared.

'So,' William declared. 'What do you lot think of this vagrant soon to be within our midst, Hmm?'

'I'll be keeping my distance, he could be malignant,' grumbled Alfred through a mouthful of mashed veg.

'You mean *contagious* don't you Alfred old boy?' said George sipping his wine beside his giggling wife.

'Yes, Yes, that too. Fact is, it's not our duty to take in every poor sod that washes up on the shore, it's a matter for the authorities, hospitals and the like.' was Alfred's conjecture.

'Does the tide often drag half-dead bodies to the shore Alfred? Is it endemic around these parts?' Agatha mused playfully, toying with the youngest brother.

Alfred, not sure what endemic meant, shot her a snooty glance but remained mute.

Charlie chimed in humorously, 'Yes Agatha, it truly is. Of course, with you not hailing from this strange part of the world you wouldn't be familiar with the tidal offerings. As youths, the hordes of half-dead or lifeless bodies would wash up like great big wobbling jellyfish, strewn all over our beach, we used to poke them with sticks and rifle through their pockets for loose change.'

The table burst into laughter, and with that the tone of the evening was lifted. Promptly, Missus Meades served dessert - jelly and honeyed fruits. The diners laughed again at their wobbling dishes.

***

At last, the faint burn from the coach's gas-lamp came into view from the third floor. Annie jerked her head like an owl, hands to the cold glass pane as she watched it nearing, she could feel her pulse drum in her ears. Baggy barked, sensing her excitement and stood upright, paws on the sill to peek out too. When the coach rounded the bend and onto the long drive, Annie hoisted up her skirts and bounded downstairs shouting, 'Incoming, incoming. They're here, they're here. All hands on deck.'

All were alerted by her frantic cries and gathered in the large hallway. The family and meagre staff spied the coach nearing through the panelled glass either side of the door. It had suddenly turned unseasonably cold. The mist had thickened to heavy rain that pelted the roof of the carriage. Annie bounced to the front, her head popping from window to window, then to the latch, swinging the door open she ran out barefoot into the rain. William reluctantly suggested someone should go out and give them a hand unloading the cadaverous cargo, the anticipation of receiving the diseased stranger squat heavily on his full tummy.

Being the eldest, he knew it meant him. He could hardly send Missus Meades or Treasa out. Surprisingly, Alfred offered to help. Missus Meades was quick to source them rain gear and then, guiltily, Charlie and George followed them into the rain under their umbrellas. Jane, and the servants waited out of the deluge.

'Good to see you again boys', Mr Delaney exclaimed through his exhaustion as he alighted from the reins.

'You too Mr Delaney,' said William, 'Well, best get on with the business at hand, time for pleasantries later I hope.'

Annie tried to peer into the carriage, like a child prematurely opening a wrapped present. She couldn't see a thing.

'Please Annie, keep well back. Back behind your brothers, don't get in the way now.' Lord Charles spoke gruffly from the carriage window.

Mr Delaney swung open the door, the brothers grimaced and took a step back from the limp and colourless body on the floor. Annie struggled to catch a peek through the soaked, huddled men. Her eyes huge and expectant, the rain dripping from the end of her nose and loose hair.

The sons regarded their father's stern, business-like countenance, this grim matter was one he just wanted to get on and over with. 'Boys, glad you could all make it, sorry about the circumstances, but let's just get on with it shall we? William, be a good lad and pull the foot of the plinth out, Mr Delaney can grab it from the head once it's out.'

William did so, but Alfred insisted that he take the other end of the stretcher and allow the visibly worn Mr Delaney to stand back.

At last Annie, caught a brief glance at her pirate, not at all what she was expecting, no beard, no patch, not even a fully grown man, only a boy, a weak and scrawny boy, unconscious on a thin gurney. She ran beside her brothers as they hurried him across the courtyard, oblivious to the sharp gravel stones scraping her feet. Her gaze fixated on his face, scavenging for more clues as to his person in the gloom and glutting rain. Suddenly an unexpected flash of lightning bathed all for a split second in daylight, in this instance the young man's face appeared upright, his eyes wide and transfixed on Annie, like a wakened cadaver, his black oily mouth spilling eels from the seabed.

As quickly as world returned to night the mirage had vanished. The body on the stretcher bumping over the threshold remained limp and inanimate. Annie, momentarily stunned, quickly consulted Queen Elizabeth in the palace of her mind's labyrinth. Her imaginary monarch cautioned her to be wary of the snakes within, but assured her that her destiny awaited, and would deliver unto her incredible tidings.

***

'Has Doctor Chisholm arrived yet?' the flustered Lord Charles demanded optimistically.

Jane braved the negative reply, 'No dear, as yet we are still unsure if he has returned from leave, but carriage has been sent to retrieve the nearest locum, we have even sent for Doctor Hargreaves, we can just hope they arrive sooner rather than later.'

Visibly irate, and out of his comfort zone, Lord Charles had the boys bring the patient to the prepared chamber. Annie had been hovering but since disappeared out of sight. He asked Missus Meades and Treasa to tend to him until medical help arrived, or until he could conjure alternative arrangements. This task clearly beyond their remit, they reluctantly accepted the request.

The flames blazed in the temporary ward, and the patient, as light as pillows, was placed on his mattress. The brothers vacated the eerie scene hastily and returned to the lounge where they could reconvene with their father and some stiffer drinks. There was much to discuss.

The boy's condition had stabilised somewhat. He muttered occasionally with the odd muscular spasm, but after tending his bed, mopping his brow and tipping a few spoonfuls of sugared water into his listless mouth there was little more Treasa or Missus Meades could do except keep vigil, and both were already exhausted after the very long, adrenalin fuelled day. By now they were asleep on their feet.

They decided to inform the master of the boy's restful state, and to both get some sleep before taking two-hourly bedside shifts until dawn, or a doctor arrived. Returning the fire-guard, they too vacated the room, leaving nothing but the fevered boy and firelight dancing on the walls and drapes.

After the door latched shut, something else caused the curtains to dance, then from behind the drapes stepped Annie. Knowing full well her father would forbid her there, she secreted herself into the room before the patient's placement in his temporary ward.

She felt like a child tip-toeing downstairs at Christmas, desperate not to summon a creak from the timbers or hinges, for fear of waking her parents, a fear mingled with the seductive allure of unopened, beautifully wrapped gifts. She could feel her heart pound uncontrollably against her slight chest. She clasped a hand there to wrestle still its rapid rhythm, but to no avail. Her legs felt heavy as she slowly drew her muddied feet across the thick carpet rug, her eyes immovable from the sleeping sailor.

The ghastly image her mind had earlier conjured held no lasting fear for her now, a new excitement grew in her breast, this was not the wizened old dog she imagined. In the fractured shadows of the firelight lay a young man, a boy, probably closer to her age than not. This presented a whole new world of possibilities to the fair faced fantasist now looming at his side.

At last she could see his face in profile, resting on its side. Her nerves whizzed so much electricity through her that she trembled. She could hear blood coursing to her temples like great cascades, a dreamlike dizziness close to overwhelming her.

She dared to touch his face, now cold and clammy. Her graceful fingers reached his cheek, the contact of her skin on his acted like a lightning rod, sending bolts of emotional energy between the pair. She gasped and bit, then licked her lips, but she did not draw her hand back and dared herself even further, to turn his head. Her fine hand lifted his feeble face with ease, and bringing his ashen features towards her she absorbed this miraculous young man's full countenance for the very first time.

She audibly sighed as she soaked up the beauty of his face behind his deathly mask. Nothing in the vast wonderland of her imagination of knights and knaves, heroines and hellions, vanquishes and victories, came even close to the erupting, molten emotions she was currently experiencing.

Annie, allowed herself to caress his chill cheeks, steadying his limp crown with her palm. The burgeoning well of emotions within her spilling forth tears from her eyes. The touch of her warm hand on his cold skin, the palpable frisson - like static power they created upon their touch, a genesis, stirred the boy into a brief and blurry consciousness. His dark eyelids lifting slowly and slightly, he beheld the obscure vision of a beautiful young woman dancing in flames and touching his face. Feebly raising his arm towards her he uttered a name. 'Charlotte...'

Swallowing hard, Annie took hold of his hand and smiled sadly as she shook her head, 'I'm Annie...who are you?'

'Annie?' he whispered, 'Dafydd...I'm Dafydd, Annie.' He smiled weakly then passed out again.

Annie was quivering now. Overcome by the epiphenomenal resonance of the encounter, she silently cried. Then, as she wiped her eyes, a single tear fell to his chest.

Annie, touching where it landed, caught sight of a thin chain resting beneath his open white cotton shirt. Her curious fingers toyed with the small silver links, wondering should she pry further upon the helpless fellow's privacy. She felt the chain tug upon a small weight, a pendant of some sort. Despite the inappropriateness, she could not deny her inquisitive urges, and reeled out from under his shirt an odd looking trinket. Something familiar, something from her childhood, something that she had almost forgotten all about.

When the curious object spun into recognition, a series of quick-fire memories jolted through Annie's mind - from the family cemetery, Michael stomping on a bunny, Elizabeth eyeing the necklace in the old bottle. Annie, dumbstruck, was overwhelmed by a whirling dizziness as the rabbit's foot spun in her hand like a hypnotists watch. 'You…You found me.' She spoke as though in a trance.

Just before Annie blacked out and thumped to the floor she recalled Elizabeth's last words to her. A promise she made to complete Annie's quest. *"I promise Annie, I've packed your message very carefully and shall cast it as far as my arm can throw."*

She had, and now it had returned, just like Annie said it would.

***

Treasa and Missus Meades had prepared for themselves temporary sleeping quarters in the adjacent bedroom. While Missus Meades snored, Treasa, though exhausted, found herself uneasy due to the stranger's presence in the Hall and sleep did not come easy for her that night. The thump of something falling in the next room jolted her from her restless recline. She immediately assumed the patient had fallen out of bed, and was most likely dead. Though fearful, she wrapped herself in her gown and tread softly, without wishing to wake Missus Meades in the room next door.

Fraught to see what she may find, she creaked the door slowly open and the uncomfortable heat wafted over her.

Peering in, she pulled her hand to her mouth when she spotted the still form lying on the floor beside the bed. She was about to dash to summon the others to lift him back, when she noticed an arm hanging from the bed. The patient still rested there, unconscious and unmoving. *So who was this lying on the floor.*

Just then, the crumpled body began to stir, and at last, recognizing it as Annie who was sprawled there, Treasa slid into the room, quietly closing the door behind her.

'Miss Annie, are you OK? Have you been hurt? What are you doing in here? Here, let me help you.'

Disorientated, Annie tried to make sense of her situation. 'Yes, yes, oh hello Treasa. Yes, please help me up, it's the heat in here, it's simply unbearable.'

Treasa held her up, the young girl quickly regaining her strength and wits. 'You shouldn't be in here Ma'am, if you don't mind me saying. Master would go through the roof if he found out.'

Catching sight of Dafydd again, her features drew stiff as it all came back to her, his face, the rabbit's foot, her fainting. Forcing herself to smile to Treasa she said, 'Yes Treasa, I believe you're quite right, my curiosity just got the better of me it seems, and then with the heat, I must have fainted. Oh please, can we keep this lapse in judgement between ourselves, Father would roast me alive if he knew.'

'Of course we can Ma'am. No harm done. But best to be off to your room, and no more sneaking about eh?'

'Of course, you're a wonder Treasa,' Annie hugged her quickly and sped light-footed away.

Treasa smiled after the impetuous young Lady and went to close over the door, casting an unfavourable glance at the inert figure asleep by the dimming firelight. She noticed too as she left, the curtains, which now curiously hung half open.

***

Two flights below, oblivious to the thumps and pitter-patter of stealthy footsteps upstairs, a merry gathering began to rollick and roister in the games room.

The day had been long and stressful all around, and with their mysterious tenant now tucked neatly away, beyond sight and mind, and in the capable hands of the help, they all began to relax and unwind. After all, they had much catching up to do, anecdotes and jokes to share, and possibilities to ponder.

Mr Delaney wheeled in a drinks trolley loaded with whiskey, port, brandy, gin and wine. Lord Charles insisted his heroic coachman stay to join them. He then regaled the embarrassing events at the funeral with good humour, and then their epic trek, their mission of mercy to Hook through the battling elements. Mr Delaney stayed for one whiskey then politely bade all good night, leaving family members to discuss family matters.

On the elegant chaise-lounge, Jane and Agatha gossiped furiously over glasses of gin, while the men steered clear of any weighty matters and ramped up raucous merriment around the grand marble fireside. Charles rested his port on the mantle and poked at the fire before adding more logs. He stood back to regard the tableau and smiled. The scene reminiscent of old, the gentlemen in their dining dress, merrily quaffing away the night, sharing tales of their success, the ladies in their evening gowns furtively engaging in their tittle-tattle, all under the dusty chandeliers and cracked cornicing of the families ancestral home.

Lord Charles indulged himself to romance in it all. Yes, sleeping upstairs there was a fly in their gourmet soup, but for the moment this must be cast aside. He took his mental photograph of the gay ensemble. *This was how it was meant to be*. He so longed to preserve the night and relive it over and over. Nevertheless his decision was set, the Hall would be forfeit, and a new and very different life would begin for Lord and Lady Loftus. This however, was not a subject for discussion on this carefree evening. Over omelette and the Sunday papers he would broach the brothers with this momentous matter.

'Cards, my fine young men. Let us play a while, the night is yet young, and I want to see if any of you scallywags learned any crafty new plays while off on your worldly travels. Though I should imagine, you will still need more than a few tricks up your sleeves to best your Old Man at the whist table.' Charles laughed.

'Very well Old boy, You may well be very surprised at my shark-like shrewdness with the deck. But I'll remain quiet before you can gauge if I'm bluffing or not,' George blagged.

'Yes Father,' chimed in Charlie, 'You've no idea how skilled and merciless your boys have become, so don't go wagering the keys to the castle, you may end up homeless by morning.'

All the brothers guffawed in unison, Lord Charles and Jane looked at each other wryly, and weakly joined in their laughter.

***

Annie lay on her bed staring at the ceiling in the darkness. The weather conditions outside had intensified and rain pelted the window-frame above her bed. The heavy droplets on the glass joining together to form meandering rivulets which coursed down to the ledge and cascaded away into the garden below. Her room sporadically flooding with brilliant light as the storm turned electric. Each time it flashed the ghoulish image of Dafydd's head, alert on the gurney, sprang to the fore of her swarming thoughts.

She could not control nor organise the multiple narratives streaming in her mind. Like the streams of rain falling down the windowpane, so her thoughts gathered, streamed and fell away from her, only to land, gather and stream again. Desperately she tried to separate the twisting strands and gain control over her restless, chaotic conscience.

Fear, Love and Destiny, she considered. This was the order of the night's sensations.

Fear. The horrid mirage on the stretcher she dismissed from being a warning sign, to *une illusion d'optique,* a trick of the light, a flight of fancy from spending too much time in Elizaland. She would not remind herself of that sight again.

Love. Her approach from behind the curtains. Never before had she remotely felt burning excitement akin to these few moments, the pulse she felt upon touching his skin, the beautiful sadness that made tears well in her eyes upon seeing his terrific, troubled face. If this was not how true love felt then she may cut out her own heart, for what other use could it ever be to her.

Destiny. Most unmistakeable of all. The pendant he wore. The pendant she had her long deceased sister cast to sea all those years ago. The pendant that cost her her life. It had returned. This was the most irrefutable, the most undeniable and the most serendipitous factor of all. She had summoned him and he was delivered to her doorstep. Annie and Dafydd were meant to be. Giddiness overcame her and a smile stretched across her perfect face. She squirmed excitedly beneath her sheets, then nestled down, falling into a blissful sleep.

It was only to be a short one.

***

Into the small hours the gamers carried on. Jane bid them all goodnight as soon as the cards were unboxed. Agatha, somewhat the lush, stayed on to spectate with a freshly poured gin. The men gathered round the card table to commence the grown up affairs of playing games and gambling money. The initial boisterousness and gusto was presently replaced by more serious scrutiny and candid calculations of the cards. Under a thickening cloud of pipe and cigar smoke they won and lost their coins.

Alfred, was first to drop out, then stumbled across the gnatty Persian rug to join his drunk wife, where they engaged in some slurred and incomprehensible dialogue. At the card table the others were not fairing much better, slouched half eyed over their cards. Any winnings now would be down to sheer luck. Deft skill and adroit choices had been washed away two whiskey bottles ago. Yet on they played.

Charles was about to deal fresh hands, when a sudden, loud knock beat out through the still house. The players froze.

A second knock sobered the party up somewhat, the eerie clang sounding out through the empty halls, they propped themselves up alert and regarded each other nervously. 'What the devil time is it,' Lord Charles blurted, 'it must be Chisholm. Bloody nuisance. Well, better late than never eh? Maybe he'll cart the blighter away with him. Charlie, be a good man and open the door.'

Charlie, gawked at his father apprehensively, visibly fearful to tend to the booming doorway.

As the knock pounded a third time, Mr Delaney was heard shouting towards the games room. 'Its all right sirs, I'll see to it, it's probably Chisholm, and about time too.' Relieved, Charlie settled back into his chair.

Mr Delaney reached the heavy door and swung it open, allowing a torrent of wind and rain to sweep in. Mr Delaney was taken aback by the large figure standing in the stoop, the sheet lightning illustrating, in silhouette, the breadth of his mighty frame. 'Doctor Hargreaves? Oh! I was expecting Doctor Chis….nevermind, please, do come in, welcome, welcome, let me shut the door behind you, dreadful evening,' the manservant muttered.

Once inside and out of the dark, the lanterns revealed to Mr Delaney that this was clearly not Doctor Hargreaves. Momentarily mute by fright, he caught his breath and managed to stifle the shock caused by the sight of the striking stranger he had just welcomed into his hallway. 'Oh excuse me, we were expecting…' regaining some composure he continued, 'I'm sorry, who are you, what do you want here?'

'Forgive my unannounced intrusion sir. My name is Doctor Blake. I am Doctor Chisholm's locum. I believe you have a poorly young man in your care.' He spoke deliberately, in a very deep, very calm voice.

Mr Delaney took in his sharp, chiselled features. Under his copious hood, dripping with rain, he half hid his unusually long face. His tight skin was swarthy as though recently burned by the sun, he smiled broadly, with long, straight, perfect teeth. He appeared to have many more than a regular mouth might. Mr Delaney noticed too that he was very heavily clothed, draped in long dark cloaks that trailed the ground. Around his sturdy shoulders, where the rain had landed, the wet appeared to steam and rise, like a stallions hide after a steeplechase. Mr Delaney did not notice a carriage either. *Did this strange man run here?*

Blake offered a hand to Mr Delaney, and asked him where the patient was, reminding him that time was pressing. Shaking his hand he found it bore an impossible heat and he pulled it quickly away. 'He's on the third floor, fourth door on the left. I'll have the master of the house follow you up immediately.'

'Thank you, that really won't be necessary, I would like a preliminary appraisal of him alone if you don't mind,' Blake hissed sonorously at the butler.

'Very well, sir, but I shall need to alert him, and his four sons, as to your arrival,' Mr Delaney replied, using the masculine presence in the household to try usher a warning to this fearsome stranger.

'Do as you must good sir. I shall see to my work now,' Blake spoke quietly as he strode upstairs noisily, as though wearing heavy wooden clogs. Mr Delaney noticed that steam rose from where his wet feet had trod.

***

Annie, sat upright. The wisps of her fantastical dreams whizzing from memory like ghosts into the night. A heavy thump, like a giant's footstep had woken her from her brief slumber. Wiping her eyes awake she quickly remembered that the love of her life was sleeping in the room directly above hers. Wrapping herself in a thin gown, she dashed barefoot upstairs again, insisting Baggy stay put on her bed.

Pausing on the third floor landing to scan for any night vigils – Missus Meades or Treasa, she found it all clear, and stole ahead towards the fourth door on the left. Dafydd's Room. Her Dafydd. *Dafydd - What a wonderful name!*

With the stealth of a cat she crept inside again. He was as she remembered, still her sleeping beauty. She just knew he would revive. Faith would not have dragged him thus far to see him perish on her porch. She would give her blood and her last breath to see him well, she would carry him to hospital to have him healed if she must.

Taking his hand in hers she thought it fit as well as one hand could possibly fit into another. The room was a still red from the dying embers, but her eyes were now her night eyes, adjusted to the dark, she absorbed his fine features now more attentively than during her earlier frantic and panicked gaze. She vowed to restore him. She would feel his skin warm with life, she would see the colour bloom on his sunken cheeks, she would return life, and vigour and strength to his feeble frame. She would love him forever, and he in turn would love and adore her too.

She reached again for the furry pendant lying idle around his neck, she took it in her hand and held it to her face, brushed it against her cheek, smelled it, smiled effusively then kissed it. 'At last life has stop taking from me. Dearest Mother, darling Elizabeth, gone forever, but through them I have been delivered you. And I shall see to it that you become mended and that you are never taken from me. Thank you Mummy, thank you Elizabeth...and thank you Lucy-Fur.'

Some conversation drifted upstairs to her from the hallway. She moved quickly to the doorway to try to eavesdrop. The sounds muffled until she heard heavy footfall pound purposefully up the oak stairways.

Startled, and convinced it was her father, fuming with her and her reckless disobedience, she darted back behind the heavy curtains where she had earlier hidden. There she waited, forcing herself silent save for her heart thumping against her chest.

The bedroom door creaked slowly inwards. The heavy, clodding feet entered the gloomy room. From the gait, Annie knew this was not her father. Then she remembered the doctor had been summoned. *It must be Chisholm.* She sniffed the air quietly, the gaining sulphuric smell Annie mistook for some medicinal potions. She dared herself to peek out between a small parting in curtains. She swallowed at the size of the brute looming over Dafydd's vulnerable body. *Could this be Hargreaves? He certainly had his height.*

No, not Hargreaves either. This giant overshadowed the mild mannered doctor. The way he was lumbering and rocking over Dafydd was particularly odd. Lolling, swaying, it reminded her of a vulture on a branch about to swoop on a dying deer. This was not a doctor. This was danger.

***

Mr Delaney, looking very uncertain and timid, entered the games room, where Lord Charles and co. waited somewhat sheepishly to hear what news of Chisholm.

Lord Charles spoke up. 'A fine hour for Chisholm to call Mr Delaney. We heard him hammer up those stairs, like a bloody antelope he was. People are asleep, curse him, no sense of time that fellow. Let me finish my glass and then I'll follow him on, I'm in no hurry to see that wretched boy again,'

Meekly, Mr Delaney replied, 'that wasn't Doctor Chisholm sir, it was his locum. A Doctor Blake. And a very curious fellow too I'd like to add.'

'What! Who?' George barked, 'What stranger have you let roam through our home man?'

'I thought it was Doctor Hargreaves in the poor light at first. I didn't…'

Lord Charles interjected, 'No need to explain yourself Mr Delaney. There was very clear mention that Chisholm was away and a locum was taking over his jurisdiction. Very sporting of the chap to visit us so late on such a dreadful night.'

'Oh' said George, a degree calmer, 'Sorry for snapping Mr Delaney Old boy, we're all a bit tired, and somewhat frayed I may add.'

'Not at all sir,' Mr Delaney said addressing George, 'but I do share a degree of concern, I did mention he was an odd fellow.'

'Odd ?' Charlie said, 'How odd? Odd in what way?'

'He just didn't seem to fit the bill sir. A goliath of a man. Heat coming off of him like a sauna. His face long, drawn like a reptile. Didn't half put the frighteners on me I don't mind telling you.'

'But he announced himself as the locum ? How else could he know of our patient?' said Lord Charles.

'Quite sir. He seemed very keen to tend to him, alone I might add. Still, may not hurt to go check to see how he's getting on.'

'Yes, yes, Of course. Come on men, down the hatch and back to the front. And careful not to wake the ladies eh?' Lord Charles tried to rally his soused sons, all of whom looked a tad reticent, but quickly donned a soldierly aspect and made for the stairs. Torches and pitchforks would not have looked out of place with this emboldened bunch.

***

Baal surveyed his quarry with malice and pleasure. He haunched over the unconscious, decrepit vestibule. Here lay his conduit into his latest term of wanton corruption within the realm of man. Beneath him lay his mortal coil, the frail earthly vessel that would disguise and endure Baal's vile and immoral spirit for the duration of his next pernicious spree in Eden.

The transfer takes but a moment, gripping the mortal first to assess their living soul, Baal, a beast of pure flame, allows the fire of his self to pass into the receptacle. For a brief instant during the transfer, Baal's spirit, while in flux, is vulnerable. Until the host body receives the whole of his malevolence, like a bath filling to its brim, it suffers searing pain, like lightning through his veins. When the transfer is complete, all that remains is a pile of smoking clothes and the bewildered host, left baring reddish burn-marks from the demon's grip. It may be days before the beast awakens within the host, slowly the host begins to carry out his will. Losing his mind, morals and eventually his spirit to the arcane monster within.

Baal took a vice-like grip on Dafydd's limp arm with his sinuous hand, more like a talon fleshed with oven crisped skin. He sneers as Dafydd's data, his stuffing, his deeds and his intentions, all pass telepathically into the demon. Baal remembered the boy well, bartering a deal with him for advice on the murder of his incestuous uncle. He had come a long way since his first dirty deed. Once trod upon, sinners tend to find the immoral path one they care never to veer too far from. Deception, arson, thievery, fraud, murder, destruction, there seemed little left in this ailing boy to corrupt. Baal was about to begin the ritual of the possession when suddenly he felt a long shard piercing into his back.

Brave Annie had stealthily crept behind the preoccupied blackguard, and speared his spine with all her might with the use of a knitting needle she found behind the curtain. The knave did not even flinch, the effect of the needle being akin to a poker amongst a grate of hot coals, and from the small rent in his cloaks a jet of steam hissed out. Baal turned, peering down to witness his tiny terrorist. His rows of long crocodile teeth drew wide in a vile smile beneath his burning orange eyes.

Annie, like Lot's wife, as though instantly calcified, became as a pillar of salt, unable to tear her gaze from the volcanic demon. Baal twisted his form unnaturally and snatched the needle from her, it crisped to charcoal and crumbled immediately as ash. Seizing her hand to regard the daring pixie closer, he channelled into her capricious mind, her lost soul and her yearning heart. Losing conciousness again, she collapsed onto the floor.

He was considering the naivety of the fanciful and romantic sprite when he heard a clamour at the bedroom door. The cavalry had arrived and were trying the doorknob, calling for Doctor Blake as they rapped. Baal's arm stretched six foot across the room and squeezed the knob, heating the brass to a scalding temperature. Lord Charles yelped on the opposite side and yanked back his steaming, blistered palm. The iron fixture buckled from the heat and rendered the door unopenable.

Perplexed and furious now, the irate brothers yelled out for Blake to open up, they began kicking and shoulder barging the heavy oak door. Baal, unfazed by the interruptions and clamour, mused the revised situation. Soon the door would be broken through, he could sear them all and burst through the roof in a fireball if he chose. But there may still be time to complete the unholy transfusion.

Gripping the frail wrist he began the transfer, the heat leaving him and cascading into the unwitting host. Deprived of his obsidian energy Baal allowed a mischievous smile stretch across his snakelike face as watched the door start to lift from its hinges. The neanderthal brothers would be upon him soon, beating their chests and pounding their clubs on his weakened state. There was time, he was sure of it.

On the third floor landing Alfred, the youngest and burliest of the brethren took his turn to ram the loosened partition, as his brothers wheezed. The women in the household, alerted by the pandemonium, scampered to assistance, though witnessing the fury at which the men rattled the doorframe, they held back timidly and cupped their hands to their mouths. Jane, kneeling beside her husband grimacing in pain, tended to his scalded hand, commanding Treasa to fetch the medical kit for aloe vera oil, dressings, and a basin of cold water.

Alfred's first mighty blow brought the door off of its joints, yet it held in the jamb at a peculiar angle by its mangled handle. Invisible clouds of heat billowed out of the shadowy chamber. With a powerful kick Alfred had the entrance free, and the pumped up young lords in their open chested dinner shirts piled into the room, baying for Doctor Blake's blood.

The nefarious doctor was not easily visible in the smoky, claustrophobic atmosphere, 'Blake you blackguard, reveal yourself!' George commanded, brandishing a knobbled hawthorn cane.

'Georgie? Is that you?' a meek voice cried out from the corner of the room.

'Annie? Annie, is that you?' George sped to his sister's side, she was curled up behind the curtain, tears spilling down her petrified face. 'My God Annie, what on earth are you doing in here? Are you all right sweetheart?' He held on to her tight then lifted her up and out of the room. She stole a look at Dafydd as she passed his bed, wondering if he'd ever wake again.

'I'm fine. See to Dafydd, won't you, tell me he's fine.' She said as she passed her brothers who were still bemused as to the whereabouts of the so-called locum. Alfred was investigating if the windows had been opened, while Charlie examined the wardrobes.

'Who the blazes is Dafydd,' asked William staring at the stricken patient, 'Has the boy spoke?' the question went unheeded.

'Annie darling, the doctor, the tall gentleman, he came up here not ten minutes ago. Have you seen him? Did you see where he went darling?' Charlie asked in as calm a voice as his breathless lungs could muster.

'He's gone Charlie, He's gone,' she said from over Georges shoulder as he carried her out the door, she pointed weakly to the floor in front of Dafydd's bed.

The brothers gathered around a dark steaming mound on the floorboards. George poked at it gingerly with his cane. It was heavy cloth and leather of some fashion. Scooping a length up with the end of the stick he recognised it by its steep collars as a huge overcoat. It smouldered and stank like rotten eggs. The brothers grimaced in horror. They scanned the room once more, fearful that there may be a naked maniac secreted in a dark corner or under the bed, but in their heart of hearts they knew he was gone, and that he wasn't a he, he was an *IT*.

'That was *his* coat sir, or one of them anyway', Mr Delaney observed.

The brothers stood gormlessly around the smouldering heap of repugnant clothes. Agatha, aghast, who had been monitoring the bizarre events from the safety of the doorway, stared in revulsion at the demon's smoking remnants. 'Burn them,' she blurted through her drawn lips, 'Burn them all.'

And into the flames they returned.

***

Sleep came to few that night, and when it did, it was tormented by terror and very short-lived.

After much debate and commotion, those under the roof of the plagued mansion eventually crept warily to their bedrooms. Those who had been arranged to sleep in single rooms chose to double up. Even the staff, normally confined to quarters in the coach-houses, took lodgings together on the second floor with the family that night.

The dark had summoned a fiery shadow like a pagan seance, but the dawn arrived at Loftus Hall like a hallelujah.

All were gathered around the breakfast table before the sun was fully risen, wrapped in their pyjamas and towel nightgowns, pale with exhaustion and twitchy of nerve. Treasa, who could barely hold a pan, prepared bacon and eggs. But tea and coffee, and plenty of it, were the order of the day, then maybe a nip of brandy after their stomachs stopped churning. A silent, curdled pall hung over the frazzled family until the caffeine finally perked them up a little.

Lord Charles, drinking coffee with his left hand, as his right was wrapped in gauze and still very tender, was the first to speak. 'We may all have our own personal assumptions as to the events of last night. True, it was bizarre beyond our immediate comprehension, and, having said that, there may still be a logical explanation to these occurrences that we have yet to decipher.' Agatha opened her mouth to interject but Charles waved her quiet. 'Yes, I know Agatha, and as I said, we all have our opinions on the matter. But before we run off the cliff with any supernatural conclusions, we must rule out all rational phenomena. Therefore, I will send Mr Delaney to have a detective dispatched from Wexford Town to carry out a full forensic investigation of the nights events. Goodness knows this old house has a poor enough reputation with ghosts and goblins, so I am hoping for a level of discretion. Although, I know as soon as Treasa speaks to the grocery boy, the jungle drums will boom across the hills. I'm sorry, I don't wish to sound condescending or reactionary, I am as confounded and addled by all this as anyone else sitting here. But we must do this before drawing any far-fetched conclusions. Who knows what evidence the police might find, maybe he was some crazed illusionist that escaped from Ely. Damn shame we burned the evidence now. They'll think us cuckoo.'

His declaration set off a great debate, where every outlandish scenario was speculated. The men posthumously pondered, and the ladies added supernatural slick to the already slithery subject. But the resulting consensus brought overall general concurrence with the Lord's pragmatic strategy.

Only Annie remained mute, which was highly irregular of her. The gothic and bizarre counsel, gathered around morning coffee debating abstract and arcane theory, a complete novelty in the

Loftus household and usually an arena in which she would revel and delight.

'And what about Dafydd? Has anyone checked on him this morning? Or have you all forgotten about the dying man alone on the third floor?' she remarked effusively.

Jane, sipped her tea and narrowed her eyes to scornful slits. *This, this drama and upheaval, this was all HER fault.*

Lord Charles replied, 'Of course not dear, I was going to get to that, I think it's best we have him moved to professional care as soon as possible. And besides that, you'll have to tell us, and the police I suppose, exactly what you were doing in his room last night. Is that his name? David? Did he wake?'

'No Daddy, it's Da-fydd! Yes he woke, well, sort of woke, I just went in to check on him. He barely opened his eyes.' she defended herself.

'Let us talk about it privately dear. You must be tremendously shaken after that grim fellow entered the room. Good job you had the wits to hide behind the curtains. Lord knows what may have become of you had the swine found you. I thank God you escaped unscathed.'

Annie subconsciously reached for her right hand, still stinging from the demon's grip, the pale welts hidden well beneath her long sleeves. She calmed her ire before delivering her measured response. 'Yes Daddy. I'm fine. Honestly. But I really think we should see how he is fairing now. I'm amazed the trauma neither awoke nor killed him off altogether. If he remains as poorly as he was on his arrival then he should be taken to a hospital, but if he has improved or comes to, maybe we can re-evaluate the situation.'

Lord Charles mused. *For so long Annie has sought sanctuary in her juvenile dreamworld. Lord knows she has experienced enough trauma in her young life to fantasise for herself a better one. But this dreadful business has really seemed to jolt Annie from her escapist, childish ways. Maybe sometimes it takes a traumatic event to catapult a lost soul back into the real world.*

'Excellent thinking Annie, we shall assess the situation after we dress ourselves like civilised folk. Well, let us make haste, there is much to be done.'

Jane's lips thinned at Annie's new found rationale. The hiss of suspicion coiled in her thoughts.

Just then an urgent rapping came to the front door, nowhere near as thunderous as the previous night's singular slams, but nonetheless it was enough to rattle the present company's already jangled nerves.

Mr Delaney, probably the most collected of them all, strode purposefully to answer, while the others gawped comically in their pyjamas and gowns, from a safe distance at the dining room doorway.

Relief swept over them as the diminutive yet portly physique of Doctor Chisholm stood impatiently in the stoop. Behind him, in a black suit and homburg hat, advanced the lean and learned Father O'Dowd.

Lord Charles stepped forward, extending his hand to welcome his callers, and allowing the others to scurry to their rooms and don attire more appropriate for aristocrats.

'Good morning Doctor, Father. So very wonderful to see you gentlemen on this fine morning. How decent of you both to come all this way, and your timing could not be better. I was just about to check on our patient, please, if you will, please follow me.'

***

In the temporary respite room on the third floor, Lord Charles, Doctor Chisholm and Father O'Dowd gathered around the sleeping man's bed. Annie, normally like an uncontrollable puppy in these situations, waited and listened patiently outside.

The visitors regarded the odd scene, the doorless room, the buckled and cracked doorframe, the scorched carpet and small mountain of ash pouring from the grate. The faint but lingering scent of a camp-fire mingled with struck matches, and the frail and pallid young man, oblivious to it all.

Charles noticed that he looked more restful than he had previously. Now, with a more human-like hue about his skin. But, he supposed, he had only before seen him in the darkness, by gaslight and flame.

The doctor began his examination, fastidiously exploring his scars and wounds with his array of medical instruments. Moving then to explore cardial, pulmonary and oesophageal systems. Chisholm indeed was a very thorough practitioner.

Meanwhile, the tall priest continued to find interest in the inconstancies of his aggravated surroundings. Lord Charles tried to distract him. 'It seems you may not have to read from your Bible after all Father?'

'I pray not, Lord Charles. May I ask what transpired here last…'

The reverend was interrupted by Chisholm, who had concluded his exam, and was now cleaning his small round spectacles against the light.

'This fellow,' he began, 'would appear to have been suffering pneumonia, typhus, streptococcus, numerous lacerations, hypothermia and exposure. In most cases I would be asking the good Father here to open his little red book while I cover his face and order a mortician,' his great double chin wobbled as he spoke. 'But it seems I am studying the tail ends of all of these symptoms, his vitals are good, and his infections abating. This lad is either a miracle, or an aberration of nature. It truly is the damnedest thing. Someone in heaven or hell has granted this fellow nine lives. Though, he must have used up half of them alone to manage to evade the rocks at Hook. It's a miracle Lord Charles, a miracle.' He gobbled. 'Or maybe that filthy charm around his neck actually works. But whatever force is watching over him, I do believe this plucky lad will pull through.' The squat doctor declared.

Lord Charles tried to look pleased. 'Wonderful news Doctor, Wonderful. You are a saviour.'

'Nonsense, I've done nothing. I shall leave you some remedies and a prescription for the dispenser to speed his recovery and boost his energy, and I'll call in again in a week. You are a good man Lord Charles, to show such Christianity to a complete stranger.' He held out his hand to conclude business and hasten from the unseemly bedroom. 'Are you ready Father O'Dowd? Thankfully your divine services were surplus to requirements. Let us be off. Our carriage awaits.'

The priest dawdled behind the hotfooted medic. 'Lord Charles, this room, may I ask…'

'Oh yes, dreadful thing, an unguarded fire. A coal must have spilled out, we caught the smell and hurried up to find the door jammed by the heat. Had to kick it in. I'm not sure what sort of a Christian I am, barricading a dying man into a furnace. Imagine the poor fellow coming all this way just to have his host finish him off in a fire,' Charles tried to digress with humour. O'Dowd looked not entirely convinced.

'Anyway, best not to keep the busy doctor waiting. Mr Delaney, please fetch the Father's hat,' Charles said, ushering his guest downstairs. 'I'll call by to update you after mass on Sunday, and I'll say many prayers for our patient until then.'

'I think we'll both need to pray for him.' The cleric said auspiciously. 'If you can meet me sooner I would very much appreciate it' he added, his white whiskery eyebrows twitching down towards the anxious looking Lord.

'Yes, yes. Of course I have a busy schedule now, with the boys over, and all the hubbub at the minute. But if I find the time I will. Thank you both so much for calling.'

The ponderous priest eventually took the hint and mounted the hansom where Chisholm impatiently waited. 'Please do, it could be a point of quite importance.' And with that they trundled off down the driveway.

<u>David Awakens</u>

Annie waited patiently until the third floor was clear before she ventured into Dafydd's room again. While she readied herself in her bedroom on the floor below, she listened intently as the gentlemen discussed his improving status. Sitting before her seldom used vanity mirror, she considered exploring her rich interior fantasy world, she was curious about Wendy in Elizaland, and how the arrival of the bedraggled young prince and wicked dragon-man had affected the peaceful realm and its population of harmonious inhabitants.

But she felt no pleasure now in escaping to fantasy. It was as though a great grey door had sealed her off from her fantastical retreat. So much had transpired in the real world that her mind could not stave away, nor distract herself from. As she softly applied some rouge to her cheeks, Wendy echoed feebly from behind the sealed portal, lost and afraid that she may never be seen again.

She had chosen to wear one of the few remaining garments she procured from Elizabeth's idle wardrobe. A slim-fitting dress, with a heart shaped bodice above flowing chiffon skirts. Her elegant reflection was now that of an alluring, confident woman. One would now not assume that she was the very same scruffy tyke that coursed the muddy fields, and waded knee deep into murky puddles throwing sticks for her dog. The perfectly fitting, graceful, scarlet ensemble seemed to banish

Annie, the childlike girl from memory and cast her from existence, along with her imaginary alter ego, Wendy.

The mirror's visage was to herald the arrival of Anne, Anne the Lady, Anne the woman, Anne the temptress.

Now she would see if she could rouse her prince from his dormant stupor. Long has he spent in his illness induced coma. But longer has she spent hiding from reality. In her fairytales, a kiss would wake one's true love, she would now test this magical miracle with her storybooks closed and stacked neatly back in alphabetical order.

She entered his room.

Standing over him, as the beast had done the previous night, she held his hand again. She noted his already gaining pallor, his blood warming, his skin nearing in hue to that of her own. Her soft pale bosom swelled and heaved against the restrictive corset.

Through her fingers she felt it again, the energy swimming from her body to his, his eyes now darting beneath his closed lids. Blood rushing to fill his lips and banishing all other deathly hues. The effect she had on him like electrolysis, stirring him from stasis, raising his submerged soul like a leviathan from the icy depths into which he plunged from the doomed Rapscallion.

Leaning her face over to his, he inhaled her natural perfume, his breathing quickened, little gasps passing from his twitching lips. Anne had clasped the rabbit's foot tightly and gently placed her soft lips onto his. A mermaids embrace, breathing life and salvation into his lungs, he inhales her breadth, he tastes her lips, he opens his eyes and he breathes.

Stranger than fiction, stronger than fairy-tales.

The pair observed each other in mute silence. They had both been in a sate of delirium when he had first briefly woke. Now Dafydd lay alert, confused, disorientated and amnesic but alert nonetheless. His wide eyes soaked up, in terrific detail, every delicate hue, sparkle and contour of this beauty holding his hand. He vaguely remembered diving off a ship, awaiting his lovers embrace. This angel in red was not Charlotte. *Am I in heaven? Did she just kiss me?* His head hurt trying to recollect. He winced.

'Do not hurry your recovery Dafydd. You are safe now, you have travelled far and endured great pain to find me, let me care for you now. Your quest…our quest…has come to an end. But our lives together are just beginning. Do you remember me? Do you remember my name?'

Dumbfounded and in pain he shook his head slowly on his pillow. 'No, no I'm afraid not.'

'I'm Anne, formerly known as Annie, and I sent *this* to find you, many years ago.' She held up his charm.

My rabbit's foot. I remember that. That's mine. What does she want with it? I found it. Where did I find it? In the sea. Where? It's precious to me. Let it go! Where? Floating. Where? Try to remember. In a net. What else. IN A BOTTLE! It's mine. Let it go! But who put it in the bottle? Who? HER? No!

Impossible! Really? Me being alive is impossible. Didn't I have typhus or consumption? I should be dead. Focus Dafydd. This woman, this beautiful woman? Could she have hurled it to sea? Somebody had to. So...yes. But how, how did I arrive at her shore? Same way. Washed in from the sea. No. The odds are impossible. You know it in your heart to be true. Believe it. It was your destiny. Somebody wanted you here. And some THING saw to it that you arrived here alive.

'You?' his weak voice whispered, 'It was you who cast the bottle to sea?'

'Yes. Yes, of course Dafydd. Well, I had someone throw it for me. But it was I who personally tracked down its former owner, and snipped off the fluffy appendage with a pair of Fiskars finest, all by myself. Do you see this stamp in the clasp? It's the Loftus Family emblem. It's a boar. There is but one of these pendants in existence, and it was sent to find you. And now here you are, four years later, at my side. You found me at last.' She purred dreamily to him, petting his cheek. 'Did you keep the note and the map? We managed to retrieve your satchel, though I'd say much has perished within'

'Note? I don't remember. No. I never found a note. Pulp.' Dafydd's body still ached but his synapses were beginning to fire. *Best not to say too much at present. Find your bearings. Make a plan.*

Anne, sensing his reserve backed off a little. 'Who is Charlotte, may I ask?'

Crikey. She's a live one. Stay on her good side Cockle. Roll over. Lie down. Play Dumb. 'Charlotte? I'm sorry Anne, I have no idea. But right know I can barely remember my own name. I do think I'll need more rest.'

Anne let it go and considered the pulped note. She concluded with even further determination, that his arrival to her arms was preordained and truly divine. If he had no idea who sent the rabbit's foot, or from where it originated, then without a guide or map, his treacherous path across time and tide truly had to have been orchestrated by a power beyond both of their comprehension.

'Of course dear, you must still be drained. Please try to listen to me for a moment while I fill you in on how you came to arrive here, and where here is for that matter. I'll omit certain details for now. I don't have much time. Others will want to quiz you soon. When I'm finished I'd just like to ask you not to say anything definitive until you're sure of your story, I mean, until your memory has fully recovered.' She drank in his fair features and touched his hand again, then drew her fingers along his hairless chest to his cheek. 'Truly, The Gods have delivered me a Prince.'

OK, she may be barmy, but she is the most beautiful basketcase I have ever seen, and everytime she touches me I feel a surge of energy, of strength. And if I am lying in her bedroom then we MUST have been fated to meet. Go with the flow Dafydd. I sure hope she can't read my mind.

'And you are my salvation Anne, the angel that has rescued me, saved my life and nursed me well again, bless you my dear.'

***

Dafydd drifted in and out of sleep after Anne had left. While awake he contemplated Anne's version of events and her grasp on reality.

By the time she had finished enlightening him as to his plight and his rescue, and his tenure at Loftus Hall, she managed to dispel a lot of the whispers of crazy he first detected from her. She came across as quick witted, intelligent and perfectly rational. He already felt immensely drawn to her and was reluctant for her to leave. She assured him it was for the best for now. He sensed that she was telling him more than just the facts, as though she was suggesting he read between her lines, and prepare himself for a barrage of questioning. But about the disconcerting subject of Doctor Blake she chose not to broach with him yet.

Wrapping his mind around the astonishing journey that has taken him to this juncture and the possibility of it being divine intervention whirled round and round in his head. Divine was surely the wrong word, arcane sounded like a better fit after his years of mischief and wrongdoings. He could now add another murder to that already very long list. Alive though he was, he was still in a pickle. *Play Dumb*, he reminded himself.

Around noon, Missus Meades brought hot broth to his side, along with the medicines Chisholm had prescribed. When she noticed him stirring she ran to fetch the Lord, eager to quit the fell chamber in haste. Lord Charles, William and Mr Delaney promptly arrived in the room. They regarded his waking state with astonishment.

'Good to see you awake young man, and indeed in gaining health. We figured you for dead more than once.' Charles said gently as Mr Delaney sat him up and placed the tray with his soup onto his lap. 'Are you hungry, thirsty? Can you speak?'

Dafydd exaggerated his hoarse weakened voice. 'I think so. Thirsty. Very thirsty.' He then gulped down his glass of water. The witnesses regarding even this feat, as a miraculous act.

'Good God Man, I can scarcely believe it. A feat worthy of Lazarus. Bravo.' exclaimed William.

Dafydd smiled weakly and tried his soup. 'I can't thank you enough. Where am I? Who are you kind gentlemen? Feigning ignorance and a thin smile.

'You are in safe hands young man. We'll tell you all in good time. Drink your soup, take your remedies, regain your strength. I'm sure you have an amazing story to tell. My youngest said your name was Dafydd, is this correct?'

'Yes sir, But I'm afraid I cannot recall much more before waking to the smell of this soup.'

'That's perfectly fine young man, I'm sure it will all come back as you recuperate. You were knocking on heaven's door just a few short hours ago.'

William cut in with a smarmy grin, 'Or Hell's gates, depending on your perspective.'

'Enough silliness William.' disregarding his remark. He then surveyed the bleak room, 'We must move you from this vile room at once. We had a blasted fire last night, of all nights. But we got it under control in no time, I promise we weren't trying to prematurely cremate you.'

'Now who's being silly Father,' smirked William.

'Indeed. Sorry about that. We recovered the attire you were wearing when you were found, some very fine clothing I'd like to add. Alas it contained no indication of your identity. Also a satchel of your belongings, we haven't pried. But maybe you'll find something to jog your memory when you poke through it.' Lord Charles continued a little awkwardly then, 'Ahem, there will be a police representative calling later, maybe he can help you piece together your last steps, your voyage, the ship you sailed? We're just trying to help you find a relative or loved one who may assume you had perished. What great news they await eh? Anyway David,' he mispronounced, 'we'll let you alone to finish your lunch. Just pull that cord if you need anything.'

'I can't thank you gentlemen enough. Bless you all.' Dafydd said, his soup-bowl empty.

The gentlemen left the room, still troubled, but in higher spirits than they had felt all day. Lord Charles was niggled, something was amiss. Passing by Annie's room it finally dawned on him what was all wrong about this picture. Why wasn't his quixotic daughter springing up and down the stairs to their reviving guest like a jack rabbit? Her alacrity now glaringly obvious by its absence. Charles gently rapped on her bedroom door. 'Darling, may I come in?'

'Of course Father.'

Anne was standing before her long looking glass sizing herself up against one of her mother's most beautiful dresses, behind it she was completely naked. 'Would you think me fetching in this one Father?'

Lord Charles spun on his heels and shielded his eyes, 'Gracious Annie, you should have told me you were changing. Erm, yes I'm sure you'll look quite wonderful in it my dear.'

'Oh Father, you're such a fuddy-duddy. And please stop calling me Annie, I rather find it quite suitable for a child and not a young lady burgeoning on womanhood, don't you? Please call me Anne from now on Father, just like Mother – Anne.'

Lord Charles found himself perplexed, awkward and eager to leave 'Yes, yes, of course dear. Please join us downstairs at your convenience. There is much to discuss. It seems your David is bounding back into good health.'

'David, is he?' Anne said nonchalantly. 'That's wonderful news Father. With your permission I would like to call on him later. Maybe after brunch. Right now I could eat a hog.' She giggled and spun with the slightly dated teal dress as though in a waltz. Her father turned just at this moment to glimpse a flash of her bare bottom.

Horrified, he spun away again, 'Oh for goodness sake Annie… I mean, Anne! Put some clothes on you.' He then stormed off downstairs, grumbling to himself concerning his life's heavy lot.

***

Dafydd sat upright on fresh sheets in his new quarters overlooking Dollar Bay and the private beach owned by the Loftus Family. He recalled Anne's recollection of events, and imagined his body crumpled on the sand. The crisp autumn day, like his memory and confused state, was beginning to clear and become bright again. *He had survived.*

Calculating his fortune and present circumstances he marvelled once again at his luck. This time it had chanced him upon the good grace and kindness of esteemed members of the nobility. He gauged himself to be currently sat on the third floor of their abounding mansion, albeit in need of a coat of paint and some fresh putty around the window frames. But who was he to complain, after his grimy quarters aboard the Rapscallion and in the Buccaneer he was well aware a few cobwebs and fungus stains had never harmed anyone.

This cat had fallen from the tree, hit every thorn and stinging bough on the way down and landed half-dead, not on his feet, but on a velvet cushion. He could grow very accustomed to a lifestyle in the ranks of high society. But once again, as always, he would need a plan.

The girl...the woman, Anne, she seemed fixated on him. And, truth be told, he felt a very strong allure towards her too. His first instinct told him that she was rather kooky, and for now she was certainly also a sure ally, but she was not to be crossed, considering how casually she sheared off Mr Bunny's foot. He'd wager she may have also boiled him for soup afterwards, the thought sending a shrinking fear to his loins. He also had the uneasy feeling she could read his thoughts.

Lord Charles too seemed quite affable for now, but no doubt he had his reservations and concerns, and would be surly eager to see him up on his feet again, bounding towards fine health, and striding out of his front door as soon possible.

And yet he did feel unnaturally healthy, it had only been a matter of days and already his appetite was relentless, his faculties were almost fully replenished and his wits were buoyant about him again. Dare he say, he even felt healthier than ever, and his multitude of scars were rapidly healing and already starting to diminish. Upon his forearm Dafydd noted three raw linear blisters, like rope-burns. He had no recollection of how these came to be. He wished he could forget how all of them had been inflicted upon him. A flashback of Horace chewing on his shin, like a rabid dog on a bone, raced to his thoughts. He swept it away just as quick.

Returning to his present circumstances and the bobbies en route to *ask him a few questions*, a polite interrogation may be more accurate. He was after all, to their ignorance, a fugitive. Back in Wales, almost all of his dirty deeds were unknown and unreported, but it only takes one of them to warrant an arrest warrant, and Police Commissioner General Warren was a tenacious taskmaster who might need more than the small matter of the stormy Irish Sea to call off his dogs.

There was zero possibility of the authorities posting any WANTED posters up for him, but his back-story leading to his arrival here was such an outrageous and vile one that a complete new identity needed to be conjured. Beyond doubt, Dafydd, aka David, to his honourable new hosts, needed an alter ego.

After some mental meandering, he recalled an encounter he made with a handsome young socialite whilst on one of his secret trysts with Charlotte. David Chesterfield, law school drop-out, fair of hair and eager of face was about two years Dafydd's senior. It was at box social in a rowing club in Glyn Garth on the west banks of the Menai. David was one of life's enthusiasts, an adventurer, and somewhat of a jack-o-napes. During their brief encounter they shared a few glasses of champagne, some laughs and some tales.

David Chesterfield, it seemed, was the troublesome son of an ailing coal mining magnate in North Wales. He held absolutely no interest in inheriting the management of a filthy coal mine nor the malcontent miners within. He told them that he'd rather strap dynamite to the canary and collapse the murky, bituminous pits entirely, blue-collars and all. So instead, his father, with one foot in the grave, chose to put his faith, and the reins of his empire into the hands of his hungry young nephew, and bequeathed his only, and most disappointing son, with a large inheritance. Within a month of this his father passed away, and directly after potting him into the earth, David took flight with his pockets bulging, keen to begin his luxuriant new life of indulgence and revelry. He had spent the best part of the last year merrily squandering it all from party to party. His next stop, he said, was Ireland. Where he heard the drinking was simply legendary.

Young Chesterfield, ever generous with his father's wealth bought drink after drink and was not coy nor careful about keeping his coins or bills concealed from hungry eyes. Indeed it gave him great pleasure to display his riches in public. Later that evening down by the waters edge, he and Dafydd reconvened by chance. David was suffering the inebriating effects of way too many glasses of Bolly. He was slurring and barely able to hold himself upright. With one caring arm, Dafydd steadied him on his feet, and with the other devious one, he emptied the wayward young socialite's pockets.

Dafydd now, sunk against his pillows, watching the waves break on the shore outside of his new domicile, was strongly considering stealing his identity as well. After all, young Master Chesterfield has long since had any need of it.

The last thing Dafydd remembered of David was him sitting precariously by the banks of the tidal straits, then hearing a heavy plunking splash and some watery gurgles for help. With his pockets full of the drowning man's silver, Dafydd would have been a very poor source of buoyancy for the flailing young heir, so he watched him go under a few times before the infamous swirling tide of the Menai strait swallowed him whole.

And so, he decided, from this juncture forward, that Dafydd shall be introduced to his peers and colleagues as David

Chesterfield Esquire. *Hmm, feels good to be back to my good old duplicitous self,* he smiled. *Though I'll still need a lot of sweet talk, and a tram-full of luck to squeeze out of this jam.* Dafydd involuntarily reached for his rabbit's foot, only to find it missing from his breast for the first time in four years. A wave of anxiety swept over him, he then snorted to himself. 'Anne!'

***

The interview with the police was a far less grilling inquisition than the newly titled David had anticipated. He had undertaken Anne's advice and volunteered as little information as possible, claiming fatigue and a fugue mind to be the culprits for omitted details. Considering the finely cut clothes he was found in, and the tidy sum of coins in his satchel, the credibility of his new persona was, on the face of it, a very viable one.

The lack of identification papers was credibly put down to them becoming lost in whatever misadventure had brought him here. Detective Tynan, bunged up with flu and eager to leave, was satisfied with the replies, Lord Charles even more so, envisioning a scenario whereby this well-to-do young fellow could present himself as a very appropriate suitor to his fast maturing daughter. And, if he was not mistaken, she did seem quite keen of him, hence he decided, her apparent urgency to suddenly grow-up.

The nasally detective scribbled in his notepad. 'Now, Mr Chesterton, oh, I'm sorry Mr Chesterfield, you have no recollection at all of the transport you took? Where it sailed from? Where it was heading?'

'At the moment no sir, I remember drinking, a bit too heavily, in an inn near Southampton…or was it Portsmouth…I remember I had been meaning to visit your beautiful green country for quite some time…after this I swear it is all a black void. I do wish I could be off more help.'

'That's fine, that's fine,' Tynan said taking a tissue to his snuffly nose, 'I shouldn't even be here with this blasted cold and you being as ill as you are. Well, our working theory is that you sailed by one of the less reputable ferries, there were no identification markings of the cork jacket you wore. You didn't topple overboard as you had time to strap yourself up. You don't remember the boat taking on water do you?' David shrugged. 'Anyway, it's also possible you fell into bad company. Seems some dirty blighter put his teeth into your leg, nasty business, maybe you decided to jump ship at the first sight of land. I'm sure it will return to you eventually. All in all, you're a very lucky man, and you have quite a lot of good folk around here to thank for taking you into their care.'

'Oh, I know and I am abundantly grateful. I can't ever thank these saintly people enough, I shall be forever in their debt.'

'Do you need us to notify anyone for you, surely there must be somebody worried about you?'

'Not a soul I believe, as I mentioned I'm an only child and my parents have both passed on. I've been foot-loose and fancy free for quite some years now. Probably time I should put down some roots I should imagine.' he then exaggerated a cough, eager now to be left alone. 'My recovery is miraculous, but still I tire easily.'

'Not a bad idea son. A good lady will keep you out of all kinds of mischief. Well, we're all very pleased by your recovery, already the townsfolk are singing Lord Charles' praise for rescuing and nursing you back to health. I am keen to let you return to your rest, but I just need to know if you recall anything at all about this dreadful Doctor Blake business?' The large snouted detective probed.

The question completely perplexed David who answered while knotting his brow, 'I'm sorry, whom?'

'Ahh, as I was told. You slept through the whole rotten calamity. And no doubt to your benefit as well young man. Sounded like a right nasty lout to be sure. I'll let the family fill you in on the details when you're good and ready to hear them. We'll leave you to rest now.' The sniffling detective did not offer to shake David's hand but tipped his hat and bid him a kindly farewell. 'If you think of anything further, we're not too far away.'

As they departed Anne appeared in the doorway.

With his wits now fully about him, he found she looked even more radiant in the rose coloured beams of the setting September sun. Whatever ploy he next supposed upon embarking, Anne's grace and beauty had truly disarmed and undone him. He felt naked before her. *Pull it together Dafydd...David...*already fluffing his lines.

'David, you look well, may I sit with you?' she asked, taking the end of his bed.

'Yes, by all means Anne, that would be a delight. I am eager to talk with you again.'

She smiled and gazed adoringly at him, the flush already filling out his cheeks. Clasping his hand she said, 'this is Loftus Hall David, it has been in our family for over six hundred years, many say it's haunted, or cursed, right now I believe it is blessed. *Cead Mile Failte*. Make Yourself at home.'

'I feel like I've known you, like you've been with me for years, steering me to safely. Your gift, I fished from the sea in Wales, it spared me from danger and death, it delivered me here without map nor compass. Tell me. Our rabbit's foot, is it safe? Do you have it? I feel naked without it, as though your warm hand has been torn from around my heart,' he said trying to control many emotions at once.

'Yes dear, it's quite safe, and so are you, and will continue to be safe under this roof for as long as you please. It pleases you doesn't it? Being here? He nodded, smiling at the once opulent room. For me to ensure your stay you'll just need to tell me your story. The whole story,' she encouraged.

'Of course Anne, though much still alludes my recall. My full name is David Chesterfield…'

Anne clenched his hand tighter, but her gaze remained soft and kind, 'The truth please, *Dafydd*, we have all night uninterrupted, Father is happy for us to commune while he and my brothers take dinner. He wishes us to court, unaware we have been entwined already for many years.' She drew her eyes out towards the sea and the dusky horizon, 'When I was a girl I sought freedom and adventure, and the love of a rogue or a pirate, and though I have now put innocent things behind me, my desires remain the same, I did not cast that bottle to sea wishing for a prince, but nevertheless, a princely looking man arrived on my shore. I suspect your beauty betrays many scars within.'

She turned back to him, 'I suspect you are dark prince Dafydd. I suspect you have a demon in you.'

You have no idea.

She implored, 'Pray tell me your secrets Dafydd. I will not judge you nor surrender you nor divulge a word from my lips. A power beyond our comprehension has forged our union. I have loved you since I first knew of love. There have been no others nor shall there ever be any others. We are bound to one another as darkness is bound to night, as wet is bound to water. All of this, and so much more, can be ours. You have trusted none in your life, have you? Trust in me, for us to pave our twisted paths together I must know your secrets. I promise you, nothing you confess will make me love you less.'

David's façade dropped leaving Dafydd exposed and vulnerable. Closing his eyes, the feeling washed over him like a wave of relief. She saw him. Saw his wretchedness and loved him regardless. The lies and the pretence were exhausting, smiling and maintaining personae and strings of lies. *Let it go, let go of the anchor, let it go and just float...maybe even fly.*

So he told her. He told her everything. He let it all go and bared his true self to her, feckless to the consequences. So be it if she shopped him to face the gallows. The verbal release of his vile deeds and wickedness spewed forth guiltlessly from him, and at times with pride. With each crime confessed he felt lighter, freer, and more like a real human being.

The purge was magnificent. Upon complete deliverance of his vagabondage, the room had become dark, bar the haunting light of candles. Dafydd, emerged from his trance-like state and felt as though he was born again. With his heart on his sleeve and life in her hands he measured her fair countenance for signs of revulsion or fear. None was evident, only the same look of love that she had regarded him with when she first took his hand.

'Thank you Dafydd, thank you. You are a brave warrior who has survived an epic quest and slain loathsome foes. In my life I have never had to scratch for food nor suffer exploitation from such predators. You are an innocent, and now you are free of the deeds that have anchored you so, it's time to rise up anew. Let us rise together.'

She smiled and moved so close they could feel each others breath upon their lips. 'Now, now you must say goodbye to Dafydd. Your life as David Chesterfield can begin in earnest. She then cheerily mused, 'Hmm, Lord and Lady Chesterfield, I do like the sound of that, don't you?'

He smiled the broadest smile and whispered, 'I do.'

Before their lips even met, their fate was sealed.

An Enjoyable Lull

Over the next few days David Chesterfield returned to full health. Doctor Chisholm returned to inspect on his well-being and, upon witnessing his vigour, remarked that he should present himself to the Royal College of Surgeons as an atypical case of extraordinary recovery, and to donate his exceptional blood and tissue samples to science towards research into the fields of medicine.

Before the brothers and Agatha returned to their four corners of the world they spent many a merry mealtime getting acquainted with the charming young Esquire. Lord Charles had finally gotten his opportunity to divulge to his sons his and Jane's plans to sell up the property and lands, and then, to quite likely move to England to be nearer them and start anew. The news came less as a shock and more as a relief to the boys, who had concerns about their dear father growing old in this almost vacant old shell. 'Wonderful, I'd be happy to leave it to the ghosts,' exclaimed Charlie.

They were also made privy to their father's desire to see Annie, now Anne, paired suitably off, to help ease the transition for her. It seemed, that to their great fortune, the arrival of David was both exceptionally timely and positively influential for Anne's coming-of-age. Indeed her transition, much like David's recovery, had been remarkable. Though her metamorphosis left them all to mourn somewhat the departure of their favourite little troublesome tyke, which they had for so long loved, and despaired for.

Their grieving was brief as Anne quickly took her stead. Initially the name adjustment to Anne caused numerous missteps, but on the whole, this composed, attentive and well dressed young Lady was a welcome replacement for the ever-trying scamp. Lord Charles adored her all the more, reminding him so much now of his dearly departed wife. The knot he constantly felt in his chest as Annie used to scarper furiously about had now entirely vanished. He now found himself laughing more, walking more and eating more.

Lord Charles also openly encouraged the courtship between the affable Mr Chesterfield and his daughter to flourish. Allowing them privacy to acquaint themselves and establish a natural bond. The pair needed little encouragement, and appeared to quickly become sweethearts, while dutifully maintaining the bounds of propriety, most of the time at least. They were inseparable, taking walks in the gardens or along the beach come rain or shine, or alone in the tapestry room where they could often be heard giggling and plinking the piano keys hilariously off-key together. It was heartening to see that some of Annie's spirit endured.

Not all embraced Anne's metamorphoses, Jane of course, ever sneering and reserved, followed her development suspiciously. Her now uncanny resemblance to her mother caused her to shiver each time she looked at her. Anne had even started to wear some of her mother's old clothes, reminding Jane of the time Annie scared her half to death while parading as her mother's ghost along the dark corridors. Anne, remained indifferent to the half-eyed looks she sometimes caught seething from her step-mother. Anne's aloofness towards her making her feel very small and unnecessary indeed. Of course, Jane did nothing to impede her blossoming relationship with David, and even smiled encouragingly when she needed to. Pairing these two off would have Anne out of her life far quicker than should she remain an eligible teenager.

Baggy too, now greying around the snout spent almost no time with her, his reserve for her growing as she spent more and more time with David. He even at times growled when they neared and backed away barking at them. David bore the blame for this, and jovially told people that it was an ongoing feud he suffered with all dogs, as they sensed that in a former life he had been a cat.

Detective Tynan paid a cursory visit, more out of curiosity than any further pressing enquiries. With Anne behaving charming and delightful with the healthy again policeman, and fully endorsing David's back-story, and along with the families apparent stamp of approval, the detective was more than happy to sign off on the missing persons case. The hunt for Doctor Blake however, would remain open, should further information arise.

Over numerous meals and drinks and cigarettes while the brothers were staying, David became fully informed with the bizarre and fearsome events of the night of his arrival. The disturbing effects caused by the mysterious caller's visit unclenching slowly in their stomachs as the days passed. Anne claimed to have blacked out with fright, and could retell nothing bar the fear for her life while hiding behind the curtain. On consultation with the detective, they concluded an almost plausible working theory. Mr Delaney had accidentally allowed a lunatic, possibly with delusions of being an actual doctor, into the house. The lunatic had overheard, probably after Matt Malloy's funeral, the story of a sick man being brought to Loftus Hall. He entered the room where Anne was hiding before she subsequently passed out. The fire was blazing and he stripped off, for what? Goodness knows. When he heard the footsteps of the brothers barraging up the stairs he bolted out of the room and downstairs, using the rear staircases and disappeared out through the back door. The heat of the room had swollen the frame of the door tight and jammed, giving the impression of being locked from within. When eventually the door was burst through, it only appeared he had vanished. His clothes, wet and steaming from the heat beside the roaring fire. adding to the macabre illusion. Of course this left a few questions open to scrutiny, and the locals in the pub already began chatter of it being the work of the Devil, but for most, this rendition of events helped them sleep better at night, though none since ventured onto the third floor willingly.

***

Life returned to a degree of normality within the decaying mansion. Memories of recent events were swept aside, the poorly cobbled together rationale attached to the odd occurrences was accepted and all doubts were confined to the damp cellars of the mind. It was a time for looking forward, the past had weighed on progress for long enough. Loftus Hall was sinking but Lord Charles would not go down with his ship. He had his escape plan and lifeboat ready to cast off, he had just yet to tell Anne about it.

He would wait until after Christmas, certain that by then the blooming romance will have been bound by an engagement ring and plans to marry in the Spring. Charles would nurture any such ideals and gladly cover the expense of a wedding in England, near any of the son's estates, and never return to this damned house again.

***

Not far away in Fethard-on-Sea, in a small empty chapel, Father O'Dowd stared absently at a stained glass window. His mind had been unsettled since his visit to Loftus Hall after that stormy night. The fractured, colourful panes illustrated a depiction of St. Patrick, the Irish patron saint, in his green robes and mitre, brandishing his curling staff while authoritatively banishing the serpent at his feet, forever from his shamrock covered island. Father O'Dowd sensed a snake in the shrubbery now, coiling around the ankle of Lord Charles' daughter. The thought chilled him so.

Unlike the Loftus family he could not attest to any pragmatic solution to Doctor Blake's sinister visitation and sudden vanishing. He had heard, over the years, from all his loose lipped parishioners, the haunting legends and tales from the mansion. Codswallop and blarney he had always assumed, but politely kept his logical opinions to himself. Now he was formulating a more esoteric assessment of recent events.

The old priest had waited patiently for Lord Charles to visit, but he had never called by. O'Dowd now felt that he needed to push ahead with his inquiries and bring the matter to the attention of a sage young priest of some repute within ecumenical circles. A priest who was both learned and wise in the arcane extremities of religious history. Set aside from his parochial duties, his principal interests lay in the ancient and unorthodox aspects of the creed, the matters that lay off of the spectrum of biblical teachings. Here, there be dragons.

Decisively, O'Dowd grabbed his cane and set off on foot, an uneasy sense of urgency growing within him, the late October chill and the mushy leaves underfoot only serving to dampen further his sombre mood.

Quite by chance, Father O'Dowd was made aware that this priest had recently taken sabbatical to further his knowledge and enlightenment of the metaphysical and mythological. He came to Wexford, following upon a special invitation to visit the vast underground library of ancient tomes located in nearby Tintern Abbey. The Abbey, long abandoned by the Cistercians and laying close to ruin, was maintained by a handful of Benedictine monks, devout caretakers, who dwelt there simply and silently, guarding the priceless illuminated manuscripts in the vaulted cellars.

O'Dowd arrived at the old abbey gates, he entered the wooded grounds and eventually found an old monk, clad in the traditional black habit. He was pulling up roots and tubers from the cold soil in a small vegetable garden. Quite aware of the humble monk's vow of silence, O'Dowd respectfully conveyed to him, in almost a whisper and much hand gesturing, the reason for his uninvited visit to the grounds.

The old monk considered the priest's request, he smiled and proudly held up a large and peculiarly shaped carrot. He then spoke. 'The lord creates life in all variety of odd and irregular designs, but I'll tell you that this carrot will taste as sweet as any other. Please have it Father. I will take you to the priest. I think he will welcome the company, he has locked himself away for almost two weeks. Come.'

'Thank you so much Brother. You are very kind.' Obliged but feeling rather awkward, Father O'Dowd took the bulbous vegetable, then followed the monk's robes trailing in the mud.

A heavy door was set three steps down into a stone wall to the rear of the Abbey. The monk knocked once and waited in silence with the priest. After a while O'Dowd believed there would be no answer, but the monk smiled patiently towards him. Then suddenly came the sound of a rusted lock being twisted and a heavy latch lifted.

The young priest squinted into the daylight, shielding his eyes as he scrutinised his arrival. 'Brother MacThomais. How lovely to see you,' he said with a dry mouth. 'Please, what can I help you with?'

The Monk just gestured towards his visitor, smiled and silently returned to his garden, leaving O'Dowd to explain himself. Caught in a pause, O'Dowd found himself staring down at the fresh faced lad in the doorway, surprised by the youthfulness of this handsome, clear skinned priest.

'Oh, Hello...Father?' The young priest said, noting O'Dowd's collar and his huge carrot. He twisted his face in confusion at the odd sight. 'I'm sorry. I'm really very busy and wasn't expecting visitors. Is that carrot for me?' He smiled, his polite, schooled English accent becoming evident.

Snapping alert, O'Dowd flapped and hid the embarrassing object behind his back, 'Goodness no son. But by all means you're welcome to it. Forgive me please, I apologise profusely for disturbing your studies. But when I heard you were nearby I found it...serendipitous, to a local matter that I find myself in quite a quandary over. I felt I just had to try and meet with you. My Name is Father O'Dowd, from the Parish of Fethard-on-Sea. I'd be forever grateful to borrow a few moments of your time.'

The young priest considered the old man's sincerity and smiled again, 'well, as long as you're only borrowing it Father, please come in, and feel free to bring your carrot,' he joked.

O'Dowd blushed again as he descended the three steep steps, 'Thank you son, you are so very kind.'

He held out his soft, ink stained hand to O'Dowd, 'Not at all Father. Good to have company. My name is Father Thomas Broaders. Pleased to meet you.'

***

Autumn became winter and mud became solid and frosted white, and still the lovebirds strolled the gardens arm in arm. Michael was just finished some pruning, he had now, more or less, taken over his arthritic father's gardening duties. He suspiciously eyed Miss Anne's new companion with some degree of jealousy and no short measure of protectiveness, even though Anne now appeared far abler than the girl for whom he once collected only the most perfect sticks for throwing for Baggy.

The old dog no longer followed her around, but Lord Charles found him a loyal tag-along, as he discovered a new zest for his daily walk around the grounds.

There was little to tend to in the gardens during the bitter months before spring. Most of the allotments and hedging had become overgrown and unmanageable anyway, so Michael busied himself with sundry repairs to outbuildings, gates and fences. He tipped his cap to the pair as they passed his creaky gate and entered the arboretum. Here they found their favourite bench beneath the ornate arched gazebo and parked themselves close together on the cold slats.

'So, my darling here we are again, huddled together like winter squirrels,' he rubbed his nose against hers. 'What a wondrous thing, the divine guardian who plotted my course and led me to your side, how blessed I am to have been washed to your shore.'

'We are both blessed my Love, before you, I lived in a contrived dream,' she took his hand to her frigid cheek, 'you are my reality, my most beautiful dream made flesh. I truly worship you David.'

'And I you, my angel. But I don't think that gardener stores too much affection for me. It's very likely he's soft on you, and who could blame the poor bugger,' he said lightly. 'Old Baggy too, takes to baring his teeth at me when he sees us promenading together, fancies himself as Cerberus I should imagine.

Anne's eyes flashed angry briefly, then quickly softened, 'Oh my love, don't allow these trifles to discourage you in any way. Michael, has always been like a brother to me, I think he just feels protective. And it's rather likely that Baggy too just wants to keep me guarded. They've never before seen me keep a man's company you see.'

'You're right, it's something over nothing, I'm sure they'll warm to my sunny charisma soon enough,'

'Of course, sweetheart. Sure who wants to be left out in the cold anyway?' she laughed. 'On the subject of cold, I fear my bottom may freeze to this bench if we don't get inside quickly. I'll get Treasa to heat us some cocoa eh?'

'Sounds divine. And I'll see to it as my chivalrous honour to stoke your bottom warm again,' he winked mischievously.'

Anne covered her mouth to conceal her tickled smile, 'Oh, you are a rogue David. Come now. In to the fire we go.'

Returning the way they came they passed the wonky eyed gardener again, on his knees wrestling with a pliers and a gatepost. Michael grunted as he twisted the tough wire, when the couple approached he raised his head to fix the newcomer with another poker faced glance. The eyes however that were waiting to greet his were so full of fiery malice and ill intent that he ducked down immediately again, like a dog afraid of being struck by a cruel master. He remained in frozen genuflection till they passed. He dared not even follow their footsteps when they had passed. Trembling then, he vowed to himself to never again to raise an eye in their direction.

***

Mr Delaney walked unhurriedly towards the knocking on the front door of the Hall. Opening, he found the long familiar figure of Father O'Dowd, and a younger priest whom he the did not recognise, standing under the porch together in the milky morning sunlight.

After brief introductions the priests were led into the hallway. Mr Delaney went to fetch Lord Charles from his study. Duly he arrived to greet the priests, not looking remotely in the mood for unsolicited company.

'Good morning Fathers. What brings you both knocking on my door on this frightfully busy day?' he said.

'I do apologise, it seems I'm making a habit of visiting folk uninvited lately. I do hate to disturb you Lord Charles, it's about the last months misadventure. The incident with the stranger? I wouldn't bother you unless I believed it a matter of some urgency. This is Father Broaders, he's visiting our fair land for a short spell, he's studying subjects concerning the, well the more metaphysical, elements of our religion,' the ageing priest bumbled.

Charles regarded Broaders suspiciously as he shook his hand. 'Hmm, very good. And what can I do for you both. We've managed to clear up most of the damned mystery with the police. Have we overlooked anything do you think?' We're all quite satisfied with their investigation and would prefer not to revisit that tale for quite some time, it was a very disturbing matter for us all.'

Broaders spoke up, his small unassuming stature belying his very confident tone. 'Lord Charles, it is far from my intention to pick at any recently healed wounds. I am very sure you have suffered quite enough anguish lately, and I'm encouraged to hear you're all moving on. I am only here to ensure that the incident was an isolated one without any possible ramifications further down the line. Father O'Dowd briefed me on the unusual details of that night, and the inconsistencies that he witnessed in the room, and there were a couple of finer points to his recap that grabbed my attention. If I can clear up these matters I could assure you then that you may continue to sleep peacefully in your beds without any further fear of threat.'

The busy Lord slumped. He had heard and understood the young priest's concerns hiding behind his upbeat introduction. Truth be told Charles shared them. It wasn't common knowledge that they would soon abandon their gloomy Hall. He just wished they could just survive or stave off further intrusion or incident for another few months. 'Look, I'm frightfully busy as I said,' he saw the earnestness in Broaders' eyes, 'Oh, very well, you can poke around for five minutes, just to give me peace of mind. What is it you do again?'

On the way to the third floor Broaders described himself as a simple priest, with an intense interest and vast knowledge of paranormal and cabalistic history. He said that he has also visited numerous sites across Europe and North Africa where verified satanic appearances occurred. He admitted that he himself had never witnessed a demon, nor a person possessed by one. He had studied the rites of exorcisms, but had never performed one nor was he sanctioned to perform one by the Vatican. At the moment he was merely a well versed observer.

Lord Charles, inwardly attentive, outwardly dismissive, led them to the landing, pointed to the room and turned again for his study. 'Please, gentlemen, five minutes only. I must return to my papers. Unless you discover anything dramatic please let yourselves out. Good Day.'

'Thank you Lord Charles. You have been very kind. We hope we need not bother you further.' O'Dowd croaked as Broaders stole on ahead along the echoing corridor.

The smashed door, never mended, led them into the dilapidated room. The acrid taste of smoke still clung to the curtains and linens. Broaders closed his eyes and inhaled deeply, his keen exocrine glands ciphering through the lingering smells, upbraiding them in to separate strands in his mind, woodsmoke, scorched carpet, soiled bedsheets, purulence, soured soup and egg…no...not egg…sulphur.

Next he studied the room, not sure what he was looking for, apart from its general state of disarray for a stately dorm, nothing jumped out at him. He asked O'Dowd to hold the broken door upright. His attention was drawn to the inside handle, how the brass knob appeared misshapen, as though squeezed too hard.

Broaders then joined O'Dowd at the window overlooking the lawns. A young couple were walking together along the pathway. 'Are they the ones you told me about Father?' asked Broaders. O'Dowd nodded an affirmation.

He then took the poker and sifted through the ashes and cinders. Small fragments of charred leather remained, something about them made his stomach churn. He glanced at Father O'Dowd, who returned his revolted look and shrugged his shoulders. Broaders tucked a small sample into his case.

Aware that time was passing and the Lord was more likely to be in his study staring up at his ceiling, willing them to leave, rather than tending to his correspondence, the priests readied themselves to exit. Scanning the room one more time, Broaders stopped in the centre of the hole in the burnt carpet and brushed away some ash with his feet. The varnished floorboards beneath had been blackened, the blaze melted the thickly varnished layer and it since hardened again into a solid tar. Broaders cocked his head and got to his knees. The smell of sulphur grew stronger here. He puffed and blew the remaining ashes away, he traced his fingers across the black floor as you would a Braille manuscript.

'Father, pass me my case would you please?'

He handed the valise over to the kneeling priest, Broaders urgently opened it and withdrew a sheet of rice paper, he placed it onto the floor and reached into the grate for a small piece of burnt wood. Then, using it as charcoal he began rubbing it over the texture on the floor. As the pattern was revealed, his face turned grim and ashen. He held the rubbing up to the light for O'Dowd to inspect. 'What does that look like to you Father?'

Father O'Dowd pinched his spectacles high on his nose, awestruck his weak voice whispered, 'Hoof-prints!'

***

'Should we inform the Lord of our finding?' O'Dowd asked, panic in his voice.

'Not yet, you said you noticed odd markings on the young man's arm. I'm wondering if we could catch them up for a little chat,' said Broaders.

'You catch them up, those stairs have me exhausted, I'll follow behind.' The weary priest replied.

'Can you do one thing before you leave please? O'Dowd tilted his head. 'Bless this room. Here is holy water. I know you've cleansed a thousand houses. But by God Father, this one really needs it.' Broaders shook his head despairingly and left the old priest to his task.

Below in the gardens, Broaders encountered the giddy and very handsome young lovebirds. A couple could not appear more innocent and full of life than these two, exuberant in the first flushes of love. 'Good morning, Lady Anne and Master Chesterfield? Am I correct?'

'Bingo!' chirped David, 'you have us nabbed Father, I hope you're not on a recruitment spree. We've already found our vocation, haven't we darling?'

'Indeed we have. I don't believe we've met Father?'

Broaders continued his introduction in a jovial tone to the pair not far off of his own age. He alluded to them that he was here more out of an extension of his own private research rather than conducting an investigation into recent occurrences, the house after all, had an historic reputation of hauntings that preceded it. The enthusiastic pair seemed fascinated with his interests. Broaders joined them on their extended walk and from a distance they may have appeared like college pals engrossed in a post-lecture debate on theology or philosophy.

By the end of their long stroll, they were quite chummy and a little out of breath. The gents had removed their jackets and arrived back at the front courtyard where Father O'Dowd sat waiting with his pipe at an outdoor dining set.

'Father O'Dowd,' Anne called, 'how nice to see you again and in such cheerier circumstances too. Your spooky little pal here is a hoot. If he weren't leaving again soon I'd have him around for games night.'

'I think the Lord's reputation around the card table would send him running. Anyway, a priest's stipend is hardly much of an ante in the first place,' the old priest laughed.

'I'm more of a dice man myself,' smiled David, recalling Horace's enraged face.

Spotting his opportunity Broaders said, 'Oh I'm a terrible card player too, but I'm quite the good sport nonetheless, there wasn't a one who could best me in the seminary when it came to an arm wrestle. Mind you, us priests are not known for our brawn.'

'Oh really,' said David, his curiosity rising, 'do you reckon you could take me then, old sport?'

'Well, it's been a while, but I'd say there's still some life in the old hammer, but no wager, I'd hate to take your money and your pride,' Broaders jibed.

The testosterone fuelled fellows prepared to duel. Anne looked concerned, 'Oh really boys, is this necessary, I'm sure you're both equally strong and handsome.'

'Not to worry dear I could dispatch this scamp with one hand while sipping tea with the other,' bragged David.

Broaders sat facing him at the small dining bench, coyly eyed his opponent and rolled up his sleeve. Smirking then, David mimicked his actions. Anne's face turned serious and she puckered towards the priest, 'Tear his arm off, honey,' she cheered David on caustically.

'Steady on Miss, 'tis only a bit of sport' said Broaders, and the match commenced. Their sweaty palms grappled initially with a degree of tension, but David's longer forearm proved insurmountable and he quickly pinned Broaders and claimed an easy win.

'You're losing it old boy. Better luck next time eh,' David said as they shook hands sportingly.

Presently, Broaders and O'Dowd began their farewells, and mounted their trap. Taking the reins, O'Dowd said as they trotted down the driveway. 'That was rather clever of you young man. Did you see?'

'The burn-marks on his forearm? Indeed I did. A cause for grave concern.' Broaders said solemnly while massaging his sore wrist, 'I'll also have you know that that was my first ever arm wrestle.'

***

Some days after Charles watched the men in black gallop away from his home his sense of unease had abated once again. He sat by the fireside in his panelled study, scribing letters to his sons seeking temporary lodgings in the new year. He tapped his pen absently against his teeth and considered his sense of relief that the priest did not return to inform him of any doom-laden portents they had unearthed. Hearing Mr Delaney's footfall approach he said aloud, 'Has that blooming postman arrived yet, I'd swear he's getting later every day.'

'Indeed it would seem Lord Charles. But yes, he's been. I was just bringing the post to your attention now, along with your tea.'

'Ahh, wonderful, where would I be without you, my good man.'

'England?' Mr Delaney mused with a small degree of impudence. He had noticed the increasing correspondence between his sons and he. Mr Delaney had his suspicions, and not without reason, it was the logical course of action. He himself would have sold up shop long ago.

Lord Charles raised a brow and curled his tidy red moustache. 'I see what you're thinking my shrewd friend. Well, it's all speculation and conjecture at the moment. If there's anything concrete decided I'll promise to keep you informed. I trust that for now, you'll keep your idle musings to yourself?'

'Indeed sir. Apologies for my assumptions. I'll leave you to your work.' Mr Delaney humbly retreated.

Lord Charles regarded his neatly piled selection of letters while pouring his tea. Just one looked unusual amongst the familiar folds of manilla bonds and beige papers. He pulled out a modest parchment envelope, the inked address applied by quill. Flipping it over he found it sealed in wax, the stamp impression was of Tintern Abbey.

Lord Charles' stomach clenched, in dread of the possible connotations within. Returning his cup to the tray, he reached for his silver letter opener. He paused, feeling an urge to consign it directly to flames. He breathed and reconsidered. How immature that would be. Sliding the opener between the paper fold he sliced it open.

It read.

My good Lord Charles,

You may recall my visit to your beautiful home not less than a week from the date above. I write to you now as your friend and ally, Father Thomas Broaders.

Your welcome was most gracious upon our unannounced intrusion during your very busy schedule, I feel sending you this letter is a similar violation of your privacy, and for this I again apologise, but I do deem it necessary and a matter of great urgency. I pray it reaches you with an open mind.

You asked us not to disturb you unless we found anything substantive to report to you. Although Father O'Dowd and I noted many curious remnants of that nights events, we felt it best not to bother you further with our observations until we had thoroughly researched our findings.

Please bear in mind, that the conclusions I have drawn are my conclusions, based on ancient texts and archived reports of unusual phenomena. After reading, you may chose to continue to have faith in the opinion you, and the police detective, have already deduced.

Within that room, the specific details I found amiss and worthy of further probing were as follows.

The smell. Often mistaken as rotten eggs, a faint sulphuric scent lingered within those walls. This is also referred to as the smell of brimstone, which has been reported as a constant when investigating demonic visitations into the human realm.

The door handle. I believe the peculiar shaped handle could not warp so by the heat within the room alone. I believe a great degree of force would be required to render it so. Also, the heat required to soften brass would have killed any persons within the room, or more likely, engulfed it entirely in flames.

The clothing remnants. This is tenuous I shall admit. I tweezed from the hearth a small piece of some leather-like cloth. I had but a magnifying glass to study it and would prefer a microscope for a more thorough examination. All I shall say is, it is tougher than any material I have ever encountered and is comprised of dense fibres of which are quite alien to my learned eyes.

The embossed floor markings. I found strange prints moulded into the tar-like residue on the scorched floor. I took a rubbing of these strange shapes and have enclosed it for your consideration. I have made a copy for my own records. I will let you draw your own opinion of the traced contours. But I wish to add at this point, that many eyewitness accounts of certain demonic encounters relay the that beast walketh the earth on cloven hoof, like that of a goat, or a bull.

And lastly concerns the Hall's newest lodger, David. I found that he bore a peculiar scarring on his right forearm. I have been made aware that he has suffered a great deal of injury and these scars may very well be accounted for. However, it is written that a fire demon's clasp, should he choose to take possession of an earthly soul, will sear indelible welts, quite similar to his own, into the skin. If this is the case, as I fear, than David may already be carrying the spirit of the demon within, this fear I extend to the well-being of your daughter, who is clearly smitten by him.

I understand, you may find all this overwhelming and preposterous. I too hope my findings are erroneous and miscalculated. The procedure that follows, should my theory have merit, is to perform an exorcism, both on your house, and the afflicted party. I am versed in the practice, but forbidden by Vatican law to conduct this arcane ritual.

Should you chose to discard this note, it is your prerogative. But I pray you remain circumspect and vigilant. I have also enclosed a copy of an engraving of the demon I believe invaded your family home. I'm sure you will find reference to him in your vast library should you chose to pursue further the signs which I have highlighted in this letter.

I am at your service and disposal, I pray I can serve you in this disconcerting circumstance.

Yours in kind,

Thomas Broaders+

Distraught, Lord Charles placed down the note, and unfolded the parchment enclosed in the envelope, his fingers trembling. His eyes twitched nervously as he studied the smudged markings, the random contours, swirls and semi-circles could be interpreted as anything, but the immediate similarity that came to mind was that a bovine hoof. Charles inhaled sharply, feeling his skin turn prickly.

He then nervously slid the illustration from the paper sheath. His first reaction was to gasp in horror at the hideous etching. A monochromatic image, an ancient depiction of an immense and muscular creature. Horned as the bull, upright as man and poised on cloven feet, its vile abominate face held unwavering fiery eyes under heavy knotted brows, a leering smile curled on its thick lips. In its hirsute arms and grotesque, claw-like hands, it held a child, an innocent rocking in the cradle of evil. Overturned, it read simply *-Baal, Phoenician Deity.* Lord Charles flung it away as if it suddenly stung him. His stomach lunched and he wretched dryly.

He reached for a cigarette from his bureau drawer and inhaled deeply, dizzying himself in a cloud of calming vapours. When he caught his breath and gathered his wits. He stood up and paced around his desk, occasionally glancing towards the unsolicited mail.

'Nonsense,' at last he barked towards the offending missive.

The mental conflict he was experiencing between rationale and superstition had already decided its true victor. But Lord Charles would not admit this to himself, and declared logic as the undeserving winner. Life was chugging along quite nicely while all this supernatural nonsense was locked and buried away in the basement. He maintained his allegiance to the police's contrived explanation of events, crumpled the illustration into a ball and hurled it into the fire. Though enraged, he recomposed himself and remained prudent enough to keep the letter intact.

He drew deeply on his smoke once more, watching the paper burn with a hollow sense of power. As the flames licked the edges of the image, Baal uncurled and stared back at him. The sketch of the demon did not look at all out of its comfort zone while wreathed in flame. Into Hell he was cast, and from the flames he shall rise again.

The Season of Goodwill

Christmas was nearing now and the period of merriment endured. Goodwill frosted over any frictions and secrets like icing sugar over an undercooked fruitcake. The procrastinating Lord Charles resolved to tell Anne of the big move in January. In the meantime, spirits were high and efforts were made to adorn the lower rooms of Loftus Hall with some seasonal foliage, ribbons and candles, and early on Christmas Eve Anne suggested they fell a poplar from the perimeter of their grounds.

'Good Idea dear,' said Lord Charles, 'I'll get Michael to fetch an axe.'

'I'd like to offer to help him sir,' offered David willingly. 'Chopping timber together may afford us a masculine opportunity to bond, not entirely sure Michael has taken a shine to me.'

Lord Charles took on a pompous frown, 'Really? Well, it's far from his position to form opinions on any of his superiors. He is but a servant to this family. I shall have stern words if he has made you feel at all uncomfortable.'

'Daddy is vexed, David,' Anne was amused.

'Not at all Lord Charles, I'm quite assured that he has only your beautiful daughter's best interests in his heart. It rather pleases me actually that he minds her so. Really, I think if we both share some time, a bow-saw and some sweat together, we'll walk home like brothers after a hunt.' David smiled.

Lord Charles chuckled, 'And I about to have him flogged. You are wise beyond your years Master Chesterfield, I'll wager you are correct in your thinking.'

'Just be careful where you bury the hatchet Sweetheart,' Anne toyed again.

With the two young men wrapped up as lumberjacks they trod away through the hoary grass, crunching towards the small woods. It pleased Anne and Charles very much to watch them leave together, more surprising still, Baggy also started to trot slowly after them. 'The season of goodwill eh?' smiled Charles. 'Let's have coffee by the fire dear, I always find the hearth far cosier knowing some poor sod is perishing in the cold.'

Presently, Missus Meades brought the tray. Steam rose from a neat silver coffee pot, sat beside it were two delicate china cups and some shortcake biscuits. Father and daughter dipped and sipped contently together, staring into the flames.

'So, my dear Anne, I am heartened to see that young Mr Chesterfield has brought you such happiness. You are calmer and more settled than ever I have witnessed. I have always doted on you my darling, but it fills me with joy to see you in such a harmonious state. Not to mention your appearance, gone is my mucky little ragdoll. You have become a vision of elegance and grace of late. Looking at you I see your mother and sister combined, Lord rest them. I see you swan along the corridors and I see them, I feel they are alive within you, and this too brings happy tears to my eyes.

'Oh Father, you are a softy. But I am pleased you are happy, and you are correct, I am overjoyed to have David in my life, I was lonelier than I had even realised. David has awoken a whole new life within me' Anne smiled.

'Forgive me, I don't mean to be forward at all. But has David, well, has he declared his intentions to you in anyway? You know, your dear sister was about your age when she became engaged to Arthur,' said Charles hesitantly, afraid to cause her to blush.

Anne did not shy. 'Not directly Father. Well, not yet. I do suspect he's hatching something. Mr Delaney has taken him on furtive missions to town to buy some Christmas presents, maybe there's something twinkling in a small box for me. I'll just have to wait to see what Santa leaves under the tree for me,' she winked. 'Oh I do hope they find a big one. I should go and check on them if they're not back soon. Goodness knows what manner of tree they'll choose to hack upon. Likely they'll return with a measly stick of a thing.'

Lord Charles snorted and returned to his thoughts, comforted by the notion that the cogs of fair destiny were finally aligning for him.

After a while, when the sun painted the streaked sky cherry and orange, and the white fields peach, David returned into the house alone. He was sweating beneath his thick layers but looking very pleased behind his rosy cheeks.

'The woodsman returneth my dear. Where is my bloody steak and comely maiden?'

Anne ran to him smiling, 'Oh don't you look…and smell, very masculine. Ick! Go and bathe, I'll see to it that Treasa has a full boar roasted for you when you return sanitised. How did you two get on? Chums at last? Where is Michael now? And most important, where is my tree. You've done the easy bit. But now it must be decorated.'

He hugged her tightly. 'We got on terrifically my love. Michael is quite a sporting chap, though his poor eyes are the damnedest things to focus upon. Seems he only has your welfare at heart, simple fellow that he is. He is packing now for his Christmas leave, told me he wants to get home to spend time with his family, it could be his father's last one he thinks. And the tree, well, she's a beauty, We hauled her into the woodshed, I'll need a hand getting it in the rest of the way.'

'Oh dear, I was hoping to wish him a Merry Christmas, and there's a small bonus for him too, I'm surprised he dashed off without it. Go get your bath, I'll chase after him maybe I can still catch him.'

David looked dubiously at her, 'Darling it's freezing out there, I'm sure he's bolted by now,' but she looked quite determined, 'OK then, go after him. I'll go wash and I'll see you when I smell slightly less ursine.'

***

That evening, the night before Christmas, could not have looked more idyllic. True to her word Anne laboured long and lovingly over the fir. Tying red ribbons, bells, biscuits, oranges and tiny lanterns to its lush green boughs.

Jane was in good spirits, the constant supply of port to her lips put pay to her usual reserve, as she hummed carols and teased Lord Charles over what baubles he'd gotten her for Christmas. David placed a couple of neatly wrapped boxes beneath the tree.

'Ooo,' hooted Jane gaily, 'I hope the big one is for me Master Chesterfield.'

'Only if you've behaved yourself this year, though I'm sure you've always been on the nice list, Jane,' he quipped. Jane cackled back merrily, her bleary eyes lingering on the fetching young gentleman stacking his gifts.

Anne spotted her lechrous leers at David while he was bent under the tree and chimed in, 'I think I already suspect what gift Jane fancies from you David. And it's not wrapped in paper. '

Jane was mortified by the remark and spun her head towards her unruly stepdaughter, about to launch into a horrified tirade. But instead of rebuking, she corrected her teetering posture and laughed sarcastically in Anne's direction. 'My Charles has everything I need. Don't you, my darling?'

'Quite so, my dear,' he said, nodding mechanically at his half sloshed wife.

'Well anyway, David dear,' said Anne, 'I personally don't particularly care for cumbersome gifts, I would be over the moon if my present came wrapped in a very tiny box,' she hinted playfully.

'Now, now, girls, you're both verging very close to the naughty list. Go find some mistletoe and let's all be friends,' David joked. Oh that reminds me, Anne, did you manage to find Michael?

'No, sadly he was no where to be found, I do hope he got home safely.'

'I'm sure he did. He's a very capable fellow. I don't think he'll topple drunkenly into the sea, like some we have the good breeding not to mention. Now what's for supper, I'm ravenous.'

'No, sweetheart, you're ravishing. Isn't that right Jane?' Jane ignored her.

'We shall be enjoying hot fruit pudding and custard, doused in brandy and set ablaze,' said Lord Charles, 'Treasa has been hanging it for weeks now, the scullery smells wonderful. She's gone now to claim a pork belly from the ice-pit for Christmas dinner. When she returns I'll summon Missus Meades to bring dessert.'

Anne raised an approving brow, looking forward to the theatre to follow. The idea of flaming food appealed to her inner pagan. She rubbed her begging belly and asked it to be patient just a little longer.

The evening continued just so until Mr Delaney and Missus Meades walked in, their faces drawn and sullen. 'My dear friends, why the long faces, has our pudding been burnt to a cinder?' joked Charles.

'No sir,' said Mr Delaney lowering his head, 'I'm afraid we've a bit of sad news. It seems little Annie's, I'm sorry, Lady Anne's poor dog, has had an awful accident. I'm sorry Anne. Baggy has been found dead.'

Anne brought her hand to her mouth and turned to the window to cry. David dashed to console her. It transpired that Treasa happened upon the dog in the deep cold pit where they stored provisions. Treasa was in an awful state. Apparently she has always been fearful to climb down into the deep dark hole, even by day, let alone by candle light. While fumbling for the pork belly in the flickering light her hand traced over the dead dogs hairy remains. Turning the light, she found Baggy's twisted corpse staring back at her. She screamed and clambered frantically back up the ladder. It seems he'd somehow fallen and twisted his head at an impossible angle, his neck folded back over his back like a snapped branch. Treasa was still crying and shaking by the AGA in the kitchen, steadying her nerves with brandy.

'The poor old hound. What a terribly grim discovery. Let the poor girl be off to her bed now if she so wishes.'

Mr Delaney and Missus Meades then departed, leaving the party to console Anne, Jane held her ground at the fireside.

'There, there,' Charles said as he took her in his arms, 'That's ruined our night now hasn't it? You may want to head off to bed now too dear. We shall have more cheer of the morrow.'

Anne lifted her head to her father and sniffled, though her eyes were not red and her cheeks were not wet. 'No Father, it's Christmas eve, we are together and warm and safe and merry. I wish to continue in the vein of earlier. Please have Missus Meades bring pudding and lashings of custard, and brandy, lots of the stuff for our shock.'

Charles drew back in surprise, but was pleased by her indomitable spirit. 'Very well Anne, if you're sure.'

'Its an hour to midnight, what do you say we break with tradition and open our presents early, I'm sure that will uplift our spirits.' Anne pipped.

They all agreed, and after double helpings of dessert and many glasses of mead they began passing around parcels. The festive spirit had again been restored, and after all gifts had been torn open and delighted over, there was but one Lady with a pouting face left waiting for hers.

'Oh Anne, where's the gift I got you? I left it right here beside the logs, I hope it wasn't tossed into the fire,' David joked wide-eyed at her. She raised a brow, unamused.

He then reached into his pocket and took to his knee. 'This trinket will never replace your beloved pet Anne, but I promise, if you say yes, that I will forever be your loyal and loving companion. Anne Loftus-Tottenham, will you marry me?'

Anne cupped her hands to her face, agape and overjoyed by the twinkling diamond in the small box. Anne squealed and gleefully agreed. 'Of course I will, you handsome devil.'

Charles and Jane shared in their delight as they recharged their glasses and duly indulged in some merry carolling by the fire. After a while, Jane, by now slurring and heavy eyed, left the baritones to duet together and took a moment to quietly congratulate Anne. Her excessive drinking lowered her defences and she waffled on and on, while Anne politely tuned out. She proffered countless apologies, slurring condolences about Anne's poor departed mother and offered her self-recriminating excuses for being such a poor substitute, eventually moving on to *how much better things will be in the new year*. Anne glazed over but pretended to listen pleasantly and intently.

Anne never realised how infrequently they touched, but when Jane placed her hand on Anne's shoulder to embrace her, Anne felt a sudden surge, a connection, a portal had opened, allowing her to briefly intrude into Jane's mind, into her memories, and her feelings.

The image she visualised was like that of a dark cave, loaded with treasure, trinkets and jewels, spices and teas, like a pirates horde. It was grim and dripping, its crevices crept with rats and its waters swam with snakes. Amidst all the gold lay a single skeleton wearing a beautiful brocaded dress.

Her mother's dress.

Anne drew sharply from the embrace and quickly erased the initial shock from her face, then resumed her pleasant pretence.

She put her finger delicately beneath Jane's chin to steady her lolling head in her direction. Though the smile remained painted across Anne's pretty face, her eyes bore down on Jane with unholy menace. 'I should have made you a hat for Christmas Lady Jane. Something nice to stick your head into,' Anne said plainly as she swiped her forefinger across Jane's neck. Jane froze in terror.

'W-whatever do you mean child? I love the gift you got me....'

'Nevermind Jane. Tell me, people lately are saying more and more that I remind them of my mother. Do I remind you of her Jane?' she toyed with her petrified mouse.

'What? Well, yes, no, yes you do somewhat...' Jane swallowed hard.

'I think I'll have tea for breakfast Jane. Mother was the only one who drank Earl Grey wasn't she Jane. I think I shall take up where she left off. You were often good enough to bring your darling cousin a cuppa, weren't you Jane. How very odd of you to be sneaking around the scullery, performing such altruistic chores. You're such a sweet, considerate angel. Would you care to bring me a boiling pot for breakfast, hmm?'

Jane recoiled, aghast, as her blood drained from her face. Imprisoned by the damning eyes of her young tormentor, she felt like she was staring, face to face, with the vengeful spirit of the woman she had slowly poisoned with arsenic almost a decade ago.

Losing bodily control she slumped, dropped her glass and pissed her knickers.

Lord Charles, on the *ninth day of Christmas*, glimpsed her starting to stumble and leapt to her rescue. She crawled into his arms sobbing. 'Whatever is the matter dear Jane? What's going on?'

'I think poor Jane has over indulged on the brandy pudding Daddy,' smiled Anne, motioning his attention to the puddle on the floor.

'Oh dear, oh dear. Don't worry dear, lets get you up to bed now.' Charles said heroically, concealing his chagrin. 'I'll have Mr Delaney and Missus Meades see to tidying up. Lets be off now.'

***

After they had left, David and Anne embraced again before the glowing logs. 'Well, my darling fiancée, what was all that about, your wicked stepmother looked quite like she'd seen a ghost?'

'Oh, it's nothing darling, it just seems that Lady Jane may be on the naughty list after all.'

David smiled and kissed her, 'Well, I've already admitted all my sins to you, and in contrition I have since earnestly attempted to redeem myself. I must prove myself a worthy, noble and steadfast husband for my soon to be beautiful, elegant and heavenly wife,' he smiled. 'Have I flattered my name on to your nice list yet my dearest?'

Anne raised her crystal, hazel green eyes to his, flecks of firelight augmenting their lustre, 'Your name is, has, and always will be, indelibly written across my heart. But don't become too wholesome on me, all ladies crave a bit of pirate from time to time. Besides, we have already both been a little naughty together, haven't we?' she winked.

'Ahem,' David blushed, 'I am glad your father is out of earshot. Well, on that appropriate segue-way, I don't know if you noticed, it approaches the stroke of midnight, and our Lord and saviour is about to be born in his manger, the wise men await him with gifts, but poor old David here, seems to be missing a parcel,' he pried coquettishly.

'Oh!' Anne feigned surprise, 'Are there no presents beneath the tree for you? Poor, forgotten little urchin. Well, nevermind dear, I have something very special wrapped up for you, and how very timely you should mention the arrival of little baby Jesus.'

David stood befuddled, 'Oh you are a cryptic one, don't be such a tease, I'm piqued with excitement. Do spill. Where is it? Can I open it now?'

'Not yet dear, I'm afraid you'll have to wait,' she said rubbing her tummy, 'approximately six months by my counting. Just as well you asked me to marry you,' she beamed.

He stared at her in astonishment. The momentous surprise taking a moment to piece together in his mind. His initial expression of shock slowly lifting in one of heart-melting joy. David was going to be a father.

From an outside window we witness them, cast in a silhouetted embrace in front of the glow of the fire, snow flutters gently down, gathers on the sill and begins to carpet the frozen ground white.

What a wonderfully perfect Christmas Eve it had been. Delicious food, mulled wine, carols around a toasty fire and presents under the twinkling tree. An engagement, and a new arrival to crown it all. It was such a nuisance that Baggy had died, and Treasa had been emotionally traumatised by the discovery. But she was lucky in a way, just imagine how she would have reacted had she discovered Michael's corpse, his blue, convulsed expression peeping out through the top of the frozen pond, she would have been positively and irrevocably inconsolable.

The Long Winter

'Missus Meades, that pork belly was outstanding. Thank you again for covering for Treasa, I do hope her nerves are steadier today. Now please, you have done more than enough for us on this Holy day, off with you and enjoy some time with your family, you've left us with ample cold cuts and mince pies,' said Lord Charles kindly, even though the Christmas dinner was rather anticlimactic.

'You're very welcome sir, I'm glad you all enjoyed your dinner.' She replied and graciously took her leave.

Anne and David had agreed to keep their news secret for a while. Father was brimming with good humour, perfectly poised to launch into the new year, secure in the knowledge that the little loose thread, that had so long niggled and obstructed his intentions, was now neatly tied in a bow.

Jane however, was far less buoyant this Christmas day. Yes, she was paying the price for yesterdays overindulgence, but this was not the bane that plagued her most heavily today. She was last out of bed, though there was nothing unusual about that, and other than a few sips of coffee she didn't eat any breakfast, and only picked at her sumptuous dinner. She was drawn, skittish and silent and dared not raise an eye to Anne.

Charles laughed it off, refusing to submit to any maladies, and chalked her mood down to a healthy combination of good port and good cheer. To avoid any social interaction, Jane made her excuses and returned to her bed.

The house became quiet and fires were stoked to life again. It was, at one point, optimistically hoped that Charles' boys may return to spend time at the Hall over the festive season, but now with families of their own, visits to Ireland were but an annual treat.

Jane was not long retired for the evening when the front door rattled for attention. Mr Delaney, always on call, saw to it quickly, apprehensive as to who could come knocking on this snowy Christmas day, he waved the dread memory of Dr. Blake's image quickly from thought.

Eileen Casey, wife of Pat, the retiring gardener, stood looking fraught in the doorway, though her anguish did not rise from the chill of the steady blizzard. 'Is my son here? Is Michael here?'

'Michael? Why no Eileen. He finished his duties here yesterday.' he answered gently.

Growing quickly more agitated she began to cry. Mr Delaney hurried her in to the fire in the games room where the others were gathered. Eileen had walked from Fethard-on-Sea, her thin lips almost blue and cold air radiated from her slight frame. Lord Charles insisted Mr Delaney fetch her a hot brandy, the footman took her snow caked overcoat and left the room.

Tears held a well in her rheumy eyes and she held a handkerchief to her mouth as she relayed her reason for calling. Michael had never returned home yesterday. They had assumed he went to Malloys for a few pints to celebrate the season, but when his bed was found empty this morning their panic set in.

David told her of their tree chopping excursion together, and that when he last talked to Michael he was in high spirits and looking forward to Christmas with his family, and added that the last time he had seen him was in the woodshed. Anne corroborated this event and went to console the distraught woman, growing more frantic by the minute.

Comforting possibilities were offered to Eileen as she sipped her hot toddy, the aroma of cloves wafting through the air. Lord Charles promised to arrange a thorough scouring of the grounds when the blizzard subsided, awkwardly pointing out that nothing could be found under the thick blanket of snow that had fallen overnight. She wept again.

After a while, Mr Delaney was directed to take her home in the coach and she was escorted away, leaving the family to lament and ponder the possible circumstances around the faithful young man's disappearance. Silently, Anne raised her eyebrows to David as though to ask if he knew more on the matter. David pouted his bottom lip and shrugged back towards her innocently.

'Dropping like flies. We'll have no staff left by New Year,' Lord Charles grumbled. 'Damned house is already empty enough.'

Anne saw an opportunity to brace her father on another matter, 'Father dear, David has been made terrifically welcome since his unexpected arrival, and we are both eternally grateful for all the generosities you have shown. I know we have played this situation very much by ear up till now, as David has no friends nor family in Ireland, well, that is, until we are wed. I can tell you gentlemen are terrifically fond of each other, and isn't it wonderful to have some new life in this draughty old castle at last.'

'Yes, yes, wonderful to have him, cheeky fellow that he is,' agreed Charles.

'Well, as you know this cheeky little fellow, up until he met Anne Loftus, the dazzling love of his life, was quite the tearaway. Who knew that one could squander such a vast fortune in society in such a short time-frame. I'm sure he has many debauched tales of wild spending sprees, I'm grateful his memory is almost obliterated to be honest. There are certain things a Lady never needs to know.'

David and Charles stifled their titters.

'Anyway, apart from the small cash horde he managed to stow away with, he is now, all but bankrupt. The point I'm getting to Father, is that he is sharp as a tack and eager to build his wealth again, and if you would be so kind to further extend your generosity he would dearly love to work with you and extend his stay, and our lives here at Loftus Hall for a few years longer.'

Lord Charles had been placed in a tight spot, but he felt comfortable he could offer an equally inviting solution, which would benefit everyone's predicament. He began awkwardly, 'Of course Anne, you are quite correct with all you say, David has been a godsend to us all here, livened the place up, brought the woman out in you and your engagement has filled me joy. But there is a matter I have been putting off telling you for quite some time…'

Lord Charles at last divulged to them the irreconcilable debt the Hall has left them in, highlighting the cost of maintenance, its state of disrepair and various overheads. He added that if they were not to take action now they would face foreclosure and bankruptcy. While they maintained the deeds and if they acted prudently and swiftly there was a good chance of getting off the sinking ship with their heads still above water.

Anne's face seethed, then settled to a look of mild despair, 'but what of us Father, have you considered...'

'Of course I have darling, I have done nothing but. I have long delayed the sale. You seemed, in maturity, so ill-prepared to deal with this decision up until recently. I have waited and hoped that you and David would choose to make your relationship permanent, and now that you have I can tell you there is absolutely no need for despair.' Lord Charles approached her and held her gently. 'I have been relentlessly corresponding with your brothers in England with a view to making provisional living arrangements until we all find our feet again. And all are delighted that we are selling up and more than happy to accommodate us in their homes for as long as we desire, and you know they have no shortage of spare rooms themselves,' he smiled encouragingly.

David looked fearful but tried to hide it. He knew William lived in a manor house in north Wales. It would not suit him at all to return, especially under the pretence of David Chesterfield. He smiled reservedly but not wishing to sound at all ungrateful he said, 'Thank You Lord Charles, you are considerate beyond words.'

Anne chewed on the new developments, quickly calculating the permutations of her next response. 'David's right Father, you have been nothing but altruistic towards David and myself in all matters. It is selfish of me to think for a moment that you have in anyway acted underhand. I too remember little Annie, she would not have dealt with this news at all well. May I ask how quickly you would see us selling up and moving?'

Relieved by her mature, measured reaction, he poured himself a drink. 'Oh we don't have to wait until this place is sold. We could be on our way to greener pastures as soon as Spring. Our solicitor will look after all the legalities. I am so alleviated to hear you concur with the plan. It has burdened me terribly.'

'Oh,' Anne said hesitantly, 'that soon? Father, I was hoping we could postpone for maybe another year, at the most. You see, we have a bit of news of our own that we feel reluctant to divulge to you, and should we do you must promise to continue to show the kindness you have shown us and not get angry.'

'Angry? With you my darling why I never could, you can confide with me in good faith always.'

Anne told him the news of her pregnancy out straight. He fell silent and poured another drink. A larger measure this time. 'Father, please say something, there is no shame in this, we are in love and to be married. You swore you would not get angry.' Anne pleaded.

He supped his spirit from his tightly clenched tumbler and considered, his face stiffening like concrete in the sun. Finally he spoke. 'Of course dear, this is quite a...lot for me to take in. Leave me now to my deliberations. Please, I'm just quite exhausted, I swear I'm not angry.'

David took Anne's hand and they soberly left the room, turning the heavy door behind them. They paused just outside holding each other, unsure now of their predicament and future. A moment later they heard the crash of the whiskey decanter being smashed onto the grate.

The pair stared at the closed door and then to each other, biting their lips like naughty children caught tormenting the cat. They then convulsed into silent giggles. Holding hands, they dashed upstairs before their laughter was heard.

***

The snow did not retreat for over two weeks, the first layer lay soft and pristine like diamond dust, before freezing to a solid blanket of frozen sleet. Trips to and from the Hall were burdensome and only made upon necessity. For some, the growing tension within the expansive walls of the home was compounded by this sense of imprisonment.

Lord Charles felt cornered by Anne's revelation. His period of well-being and optimism now truncated, negated and twisted inside out. He paced his study now, chewing his nails with mixed feelings of frustration, constraint and reluctant compliance to the will of his coercive daughter.

He had offered various alternate options and suggestions that would serve to rid themselves of the Hall and secure a temporary solution for the young couple, and their collective impending dilemma. None of which were received with any degree of satisfaction by Anne. David usually remained silent, but loyal to all of her desires.

The ignominy of the extra-marital conception did not particularly rankle Lord Charles, he was always independent of thought and far removed from the backwards and often cruel convictions on the predominantly catholic island. Shame did not enter the argument, particularly as Anne was in a committed relationship to a upstanding and devoted young gentleman.

No, it was the timing, and the delay to his plans that the pregnancy incurred that was his primary cause for concern. In the end though, Charles yielded to his daughters unwavering request to protract the sale or transfer of the estate from beneath their feet until the child was born and given some time to gain strength.

Since his reluctant concession, Charles began spending most of his time in his study, updating his affairs in his journals and drafting letters to his family and solicitors. Mr Delaney also found himself replenishing his Lord's whiskey supply, and emptying the ashtray in his office with far more regularity.

Treasa had not returned to her duties, reports of her shredded nerves and night terrors quickly filtered back to the house. Michael's frozen corpse, less than half a mile from the gardens, had still to be found. Mr Delaney and Missus Meades ably picked up the slack around the house, though now a dark wariness clung to them, like soot to the hearth.

Anne and David were quite happy to self cater most of the time, David proving himself to be quite gifted around the hob. Anne appeared oblivious to the hollow void that now filled the candlelit halls, the captivity enforced on them by the weather giving her ample opportunity to torment her murderous stepmother. Although Jane was seen less and less frequently outside of her bedroom, opting to have her meals brought to her room by Missus Meades or Charles. Her reclusive and agitated situation further adding to the Lord's aggravated state.

Anne took more to wearing her mother's old clothes, most of which fit her quite adequately now. She also wore her hair up in the fashion her mother favoured, and with some deft nuances to her make-up application the mirror could not fail to perceive her as her mother's visage when she walked before it. And neither could Jane.

From time to time, Jane would of course need to leave her quarters. In anticipation of this Anne began to loiter about, waiting to hear her footsteps or her door handle. Then, when Jane was far enough from her room not to retreat, Anne would appear, as might the ghostly wraith of Jane's poisoned victim, and glide towards her, silently with an unerring wide eyed smile. Jane would shriek, or freeze and cling to the wall, or crumble to the ground grovelling as Anne passed her by. While passing, Anne simply behaved oblivious to her simpering presence.

By mid January the thaw had reduced the snow blanket to a scattered white archipelago over the narrow flat landscape. As soon as the driveway was clear Detective Tynan arrived to interview the family about Michael's last movements. Once statements were taken, a search of the grounds was coordinated, David and Mr Delaney assisted while Lord Charles remained inside, brooding with his bottle.

It wasn't long before one of the constables was heard sounding his whistle.

Wexford agricultural land is pocked with deep ponds called marl-pools. These artificial trenches were dug by farmers in the thick claggy soil to access lime and serve as watering holes for cattle. It was out of the top of one of these ponds, just off of Loftus land that the remains of the gardener's son was discovered, the thinning ice still holding his bloated face above the surface, just high enough to allow the crows to perch on his head and pluck away his nutritious eyeballs.

The path Michael took home could be accessed a little quicker if the marl-pool didn't interfere with the route. It was assumed that in his haste to hurry home on Christmas Eve he chanced to cross the frozen surface which succumbed to his weight. The sequence of sad events appeared straightforward enough, however, upon inspection of the dredged body there was a couple of unpleasant findings.

Detective Tynan sat down with Lord Charles and Anne in a private chamber. He explained the matter how he perceived it had occurred. Anne buried her head into Charles' chest to weep while her shocked father comforted her. Tynan then broached the awkward matter of the items retrieved from Michael's remains. He unfolded a damp paper envelope containing two items, one, a sodden pair of ladies undergarments, and the other a pendant, specifically a rabbit's foot necklace.

'I'm very sorry to present these to you at the difficult time, Lord knows I don't wish to sully the name of Casey's son at this awful time, but I need to know if you recognise either of these items,' said the sombre faced detective.

Charles withdrew with an awkward grunt. Anne, fully recovered from her cry leaned forward, eyes wide and horrified. 'They are mine Detective, both of them, the pendant was a curiosity from childhood, I kept it hidden in a drawer containing my delicates. Do you mean to tell me he...' Anne cut herself off and covered her outraged expression behind her gloved hands.

'What is the meaning of this,' barked Charles. 'Do you mean to tell me that Michael had some, what, some depraved obsession with Anne?'

'Well, it would appear so, I'm very sorry to say. It seems he may have been in such a hurry to get home to...examine...his stolen items that he ran across thin ice and drowned.' Tynan suggested remorsefully.

Detective Tynan, at lengths to spare the Casey families shame, urged Lord Charles to keep the sordid details of the death under wraps for now, using the leverage that the less attention drawn to Loftus Hall on the untimely death, the better it would be for all concerned. No doubt, over time, the truth would leak out, it always did.

The official cause of death was announced to the Caseys as drowning by misadventure.

***

A small fire burned ineffectively in the freezing subterranean vaults where Father Broaders was concluding his studies. His few humble belongings packed neatly in a light case awaiting his departure, his pilgrim scrip however was heavily laden, crammed with notes and drawings, copied from the abbey's archives.

He recalled the letter he scribed to Lord Charles many weeks ago. The invite to return to Loftus Hall had never arrived and he had heard of no incident, fell or otherwise, reported from the estate over the Christmas. He decided this was a good thing, and despite his assertions, maybe Dr. Blake's visit to the Hall was without lasting consequence.

Wrapped and ready for his return voyage home to England he began extinguishing the many molten candles on their waxy roots, the sour aroma emitted from their dousing filed the stale air and blended with the musty atmosphere of ancient papyrus. Broaders stood in the solitary smoky beam of light from the door window, and regarded his dark underground study, curiously he would miss this dungeon, his mine full of intellectual treasures.

A sharp rapping shook him from his reverie. In the sunlit window an instantly recognisable shadow waited, the wiry wisps of white hair blowing in the wind. Broaders opened the door wide and welcomed again his comrade, Father O'Dowd. Without a word, O'Dowd's frown and sincere eyes told Broaders there had been a development at Loftus Hall, and a grim one at that.

The candles were relit and the two hurriedly conferred in the cold cellar. Their collusion was a brief one, bereft of small talk or comforting refreshments. When the two had concluded their meeting O'Dowd set off hurriedly on his hike home, his breath trailing like a steam engine behind him in the winter air. Broaders bade him farewell and retreated back down the three steps to where his belongings, were patiently waiting to leave.

But Broaders had already reconsidered. He would stay a while longer. His instinct told him he would be needed, and called upon soon, he would wait. Besides there was still far more undiscovered nutrition for his ravenous mind stored in this well preserved pantry of parchments. Snapping a candle from its waxy seat he got a flame started in the hearth again, then he took the light to inspect the spines of the tomes in the deeper recesses of the vault. He fingered the dusty covers until he reached the one he sought, *De Obsessis A Spiritibvs Daemo*. Roughly translated – Driving out the Demon Spirit.

***

David and Anne's relationship continued to thrive in the diminishing mansion on the wuthering peninsula. It was of little regard to them that their fellow dwellers chose to exile themselves to their rooms. Life was just beginning for the fervent young couple. They had decided, against their father's wishes, to postpone the wedding until after the child was born. They asserted that they could arrange the event properly, when they settle again in England, rather than a hurried celebration within Loftus's cold and unwelcoming walls. The proposition she dangled before her Daddy worked. His only goal now, to be ever rid of his foreboding fortress, each day he spent there, he felt peeled another layer from his sanity.

Anne sat upright in the library, absently rubbing her slight tummy as she leafed through books concerning native flora and fauna, and some recipe books too. Although Missus Meades was commended for her efforts in Treasa's absence, the meals had become bland and mainstay. Anne decided she would like to arrange a feast after the gloomy January, if the crocus and snowdrops were making an effort to cheer things up, than so shall she.

Lord Charles was due to take a business trip to Gorey where he would convene with the Chamber of Commerce on matters of great importance. He yearned for time away from the coffin-stale atmosphere and had arranged to meet with his old solicitor friend Diarmuid Devereux to discuss how to expedite the sale of the house. Councillor Devereux was also an enthusiastic ale and rye imbiber, and just the sort of jolly company the Lord needed at present. With a night of good cheer in mind, he would protract his stay and secure a bed in the Loch Garman Arms Hotel for a couple of nights.

Anne approached her father who was scrawling intensely in his study. 'I'm sorry to disturb you Father. I know you are busy making arrangements for your visit to Gorey.'

'What is it dear?' he replied tersely without looking up.

'Well, I know things have been fraught of late, and David and I shoulder the blame for much of this. We would like to prepare a special send off meal before you leave. It may even coax Jane from her bed for a pleasant evening with kin. To this end, we would like Mr Delaney to take us to Kilmore Quay to get some fresh produce.'

'And you wish me to arrange a coach for you?'

'Yes Father, that would be wonderful,'

'Very well dear, is that all?'

'Yes Father, unless you would like me to pour you a drink?' she suggested.

'Thank you dear, I can quite manage myself. Please close the door properly when you leave, this damned place is like a tomb,' he grunted. When she had turned to leave he glanced up at her, her resemblance to his dead wife made his heart swell and ache, after she had secured the door tight tears fell from his eyes. He poured himself a whiskey.

***

Kilmore Quay is as quaint an Irish village as you may find. Its narrow winding roads lined with idyllic cottages, all decorated with their own unique thatched roofs. This cosy nook by the sea was also a thriving fishing harbour and a gastronomic hub for choice local produce, fresh fish and epicurean meats.

Mr Delaney arrived around noon with his well groomed cargo in tow. As Anne and David stepped gracefully from the coach their cheeks met with the whisper of spring warmth which teased the frigid gusts stealing in from the turbulent sea.

Traders would remember Lady Anne Loftus, who was frequently seen perusing the wares in the markets with her two daughters, the graceful one and the sprightly one. These same traders and shopkeepers, many years older now, stood gawking, unsure if their eyes betrayed them, as the very apparition of the long deceased Lady graced their stalls. Anne, was that raggedy little scamp no more. With her cocoon shed and her alluring wings unfurled, fluttered nonchalantly past her onlookers. Anne the radiant, yet chilling reincarnation of her mother greeted their stunned expressions with self-assured poise and purpose.

'Miss Anne?' Mrs Bolger the butcher's homely wife greeted her timidly, 'Begging your pardon Ma'am, I was given to not trusting my own eyes for a moment Ma'am. I'd have not recognised you from the playful girl I remember such is the beautiful young lady you have become.' David hovered close by, lazily enjoying eavesdropping while perusing her selection of game meats. Anne noticed Mrs Bolger sucking her fat, chapped lip as her eyes drifted wantonly over David's fetching features.

'You are too kind Mrs Bolger. My dear mother always hailed your counter as the most enticing in Wexford. I am very pleased to see you still trading such exotic meats. Tell me, I am looking to have a special meal prepared, one particular to our family, Do you supply wild boar?' Anne smiled pleasantly.

'You happen to be in luck Ma'am, it's not native I'm sure you'll know, the boar has gone the way of the snake on our fair island. But it's cured and salted, and just off the boat from Wales. You'll not taste finer ma'am.' Mrs Bolger fussed as she pulled a drop-cloth off the smoked pig and slapped its hide with her thick red fingers, 'I was just about to carve him up, what can I get you? Loin? Rump? Belly?'

'Why not the lot Mrs Bolger, hooves and all, I wish it to be quite the centrepiece.' Anne enthused and motioned for Mr Delaney to take the swine away. 'David, would you be a dear and give Mr Delaney a hand loading this,' she added kissing his cheek, his ego swelling at the public display of affection. Again, Anne caught the burly butcheress scanning David with a fanciful eye as she sharpened her cleaver. 'Eyes on your own meat Mrs Bolger, I would hate any distractions to cause you to lose a hand. Goodness knows Mr Bolger has few enough of your assets to depend upon for his relief.' Amused by her brazenness, David swivelled to guard his guilty grin.

'Why I never...' the aggrieved biddy began, but Anne cut her off matter-of-factly.

'Please Mr Delaney, pay this handsome woman quickly for her kindness, the odour of rotten old flesh over here is beginning to nauseate me.' Anne fixed the meat handler with burning stare, the effect of which muting any rebukes, Mrs Bolger snapped shut her heavy gawp. When the Loftus party had moved on, the trembling Mrs Bolger clung to the crucifix around her neck and mumbled an Our Father.

Arm in arm, the pair waltzed languidly around the stalls and shops, sourcing vegetables, berries and herbs, before stopping in a cosy tea-house for some warming refreshments. All whom they encountered offered them smiles and courtesy, none could refuse the capture of their youthful magnificence and enigmatic splendour.

However, there were those, safely out of earshot of the couple, who had heard tell of the dying man in the big house. Gossip of he ghostly castaway brought back from the dead by the devil. Whispers of the icy haze that clings to the grounds on that fell estate. Further tales of the hardship, suffering and death that tormented the few that still dwelt within.

The pair, though aware of the admiring, the envious and the malicious stares, remained indifferent to them all. It was in one another's eyes they spent most of their time captivated. Anne reset her china cup on her saucer, 'This has been a wonderful day, darling, so nice to breath new air and see new faces, regardless of how ugly they are.'

'Anne Loftus-Tottenham! You truly are a wicked woman,' David laughed, 'How glad I am of it. I fear I would seize and topple over with boredom where you in anyway less.'

'It takes a rogue to spot a rogue darling,' she winked. 'Now I wish to stop off on the way home to gather some wild shrubbery to compliment my wild boar dining table display. Will my wild man be kind enough to snip me a few lashes? Holly, Ivy, Yew, plenty of berries, festive, that sort of thing.'

'Of course my lady, your wish is my command. And I suppose I should get used to demanding cries,' he said nodding to her barely visible bump. 'How is our cosy little monster today?'

'He's positively giddy today, must be all this sea air. He's been performing acrobatics since the meat counter, I think he's hungry, I'm sure he's dying to get a taste of this pig.'

***

From the side of her bed Jane watched Charles prepare some overnight essentials for his short escape to Gorey. Her eyes followed his movements frantically as she ground her nails with her neglected teeth. Charles had noticed she was paying little attention to her appearance lately, so as well as becoming mentally unhinged she was also beginning to appear wasted and bedraggled. Over the past few weeks he attempted to broach the cause of her fall into melancholy and sloth, however Jane always deflected or digressed from the topic, or blamed her disorder on the long bleak winter. He had encouraged her to spend some money, to buy new clothes or try a new hairstyle, but she batted away all his suggestions with disinterest.

He could feel her twitchy eyes tracing his steps, she asked him again, 'Please Charles, let me accompany you, you'll not even know I'm present, I'll busy myself shopping, I'll buy that gown you suggested. Please, Charles, I'll fall asunder if I've to stay in this mausoleum alone,' she begged.

'You know I'd love to have you along darling,' Charles lied. 'This is not an occasion for wives, the A.G.M. is being held in the Market House. Chamber members only. Matters of great commercial import need my steadfast attention. Besides, it will be tremendously dull, and you won't be alone here, Anne and David are having a feast prepared to lift our spirits before I leave.'

Jane shivered at that prospect and fought down her rising hysteria. She began her protestations again but Charles hushed her quiet and urged her to make an effort with her appearance for dinner, citing, 'Dear sweet Anne is going to great effort for us, we must show our appreciation and arrive to the dining table looking our best.'

When Charles had bent to tie his shoe Jane imagined *Dear sweet Anne* and clawed her bony hands in a mime of strangulation. She had not eaten a proper meal since Christmas Eve, even the thoughts of a plate of stacked food made her stomach wretch and head dizzy. *Anne – her bane, the sorceress and witch, the source of her endless well of misery.* For a month now she believed that for her own sake and sanity, the only return path to happiness lay in destroying Anne and her bastard child. She fantasised scenarios involving her impaling, drowning or falling from the balustrade. But she could not overcome her fear of the dauntless, indomitable and omniscient young vixen.

Defeated by herself, she threw back on the soft bed whimpering. Charles watched her with little pity, imagining instead a foamy head of ale in the carefree company of his witty old friend.

Eventually Jane did make an effort of sorts to prepare for dinner. She donned an evening gown and tied her strawberry blonde locks up in a dainty fashion. Her powder and rouge helped to mask her deteriorating complexion, but her light blue eyes belied her fragile state, darting from this to that, like an irate bird desperate to escape her cage.

It was an early dinner, to leave Charles with good time for his long trek to Gorey. Charles and Jane followed the sweet gamy aroma down to the dining room. The dining table was immaculately placed, the silverware catching glints from the candles, the place-mats and coasters complimenting the wild garlands that Anne had prepared as a centrepiece. It looked like the celebratory Christmas dinner that never happened, and certainly the visual and olfactory sensation served to lift the mood of the small dinner ensemble.

Anne, as was now the norm, looked darkly enchanting, and as much like her mother as she could possibly be. She welcomed them all to be seated. Chill fingers already began scaling Jane's spine just being in Anne's presence.

Missus Meades served, the meal began with whole fried spatchcock rabbit for all, served with mushrooms and chives. The golden crisp, flattened conies were greeted with *ahhs* of delight and devoured with gusto, by all but Jane of course. She toyed with the spreadeagled lepus, its crusty legs twitching as though alive. From the tiny morsel she sampled she spat out gristle and a tiny bone.

Mr Delaney next wheeled the heavy main course from the kitchen under a giant silver cloche, the smells of garlic, onion and rosemary quickly in pursuit. He gestured towards Anne for permission to unveil the dish. She smiled and nodded, Mr Delaney lifted the lid to reveal the suckling boar. Presented in bizarre fashion, its roasted head was bent upright, its elongated canines, like horns, wrapped around its charred upper lips. It was a tableau to the Loftus family crest. The head and eye sockets had been hollowed out, and within it was placed a candle, affecting the glow of a jack-o-lantern, its demonic eyes staring forth at its rapt audience. Its trotters too, were positioned unusually. The hocks had been cleaved from their knee joints and placed radially beneath the upturned head, creating a macabre floral effect and showcasing the cloven feet. If Treasa prepared this we may have assumed it as an abstract tribute to the last sighting of Baggy.

Anne, pleased with her design, stood to address her dinner guests, her almond eyes smiling as she leisurely moved from person to person, 'Thank you all for indulging my culinary ambitions on this fine afternoon. I know that I have presented you with unforeseen challenges lately. This meal is both mine and David's gesture of our endless appreciation for your kindness, your compassion, your understanding and your unwavering patience with us. I thought I would pay tribute to the great Loftus name and the heavy mantle my Father has carried with such dignity...' she glanced quickly to Jane, '...since the death of his precious wife and my beloved mother.' At this point Anne rose a glass to summon a toast to the dead.

Jane's eyes dropped and fixed on her fidgeting fingers.

'To Anne,' Charles and David said solemnly, while Jane, her bowels now writhing with anxiety, mumbled some response then fumbled with her glass and clumsily spilled her wine, dying her place setting blood red.

Charles, on his third glass of wine, set her a scornful look.

'Not to worry,' Anne continued unfazed. 'Accidents will happen Jane. Missus Meades will see to that. Now before we carve up this delicious beast. Let me tell you a little about the boar. The Greeks favoured her as a symbol of motherhood, a vigilant and fierce defender of her brood. But the Erymanthian Boar was not only a savage maternal symbol, it was also a creature of wrathful revenge, the goddess Hera summoning the vengeful beast to lay waste those who may seek to usurp her.' Anne paused to observe her attentive audience.

Jane, aghast and verging on insanity, could not take her eyes off of the grotesque roast.

'I for one, as an expectant mother, feel heartened to have such a powerful symbol as our family totem, and looking at the small, but beloved remaining members of the Loftus family, I feel honoured to be soon adding my own new branch to our distinguished family tree.'

Anne's words encouraged and buoyed her fatigued father, who rose to his feet to offer her a rousing cheers, 'Here here Anne. Here here. We have been glum of heart and down of mouth for long enough now, let this fine feast dispel the icy grip of this desolate winter. Here's to Spring! To the Boar! To Anne, and to my wonderful grandchild to come!'

Anne smiled demurely. 'Thank you Father. Now, if you please, I've excused Mr Delaney while we dine, would you care to carve the beast?' she asked motioning to the sharp silverware.

Lord Charles paused, 'Darling, I'd love to, but as I will be absent this evening I am going to relinquish, temporarily, I'd like to stress, my status as man of the house to this fine upstanding young gentleman,' placing a hand on David's shoulder. 'And his first official duty will be to slice up this delicious, if somewhat gothically gilded delicacy, before it's as cold as the third floor guest rooms.'

David, stood up and received the knife and prongs with his chest full of pride. In his thoughts he harked back to the last time he gutted a pig, that one named Roberts, and pondered the ironic twist in faith that led him to this victorious moment. He felt a magnificent swell of triumph over his adversities and adversaries. Taking the honing rod he began sharpening the blade with expertise, drawing impressed looks from the diners, then, holding up the shimmering steel he asked, 'OK then, anyone for a nice piece of crispy jowl?'

Jane watched in horror, feeling like a paralysed fly, caught in the black web of a nightmare. As the blade sliced through the pigs cheek, the crusty rind fell to reveal two gnashing rows of the beasts rear teeth.

Once again, she passed out.

***

Mr Delaney carried Lord Charles' valise to the coach and waited patiently by the horses, their breath puffed small clouds into the chill air. The loyal valet rubbed his cold hands together vigorously. If the families hijinks were troubling Mr Delaney he did not show it, today it was just the sharp easterly that appeared to ruffle his feathers.

Lord Charles did not allow Jane's capitulation at the dining table to adjourn his daughter's arrangements. Missus Meades was summoned to fetch the smelling salts and Jane revived almost immediately, but appeared less certain of her circumstances and even less fit to further her presence at the banquet table. She began mumbling nonsensically, Charles muttered excuses for her then had her escorted back to her room.

The remaining three dined heartily, Charles quaffed back another three glasses of wine to wash down his second helping of loin, David attempted a third portion of crackling but found himself happily defeated by the bountiful boar. Charles rambled on, jocular at first, then wearily he regaled to them his joys and woes, the amused young couple tolerating his tales, pleased to see the lift in the masters mood.

After several attempts to remind him of his appointment, his tardiness, and his frozen butler waiting in the courtyard, Charles eventually rose unsteadily from his seat at the head of the table and readied himself to leave. It took another fifteen minutes before David and Missus Meades got to wave him his safe farewells as his carriage trotted hurriedly towards the gates in the fading light.

Finally alone, Anne encouraged David to have another celebratory drink. Happy to oblige, she had Missus Meades wheel in the drinks trolley then suggested she dismiss herself for an early evening, congratulating her on her successful undertakings in the kitchen. Anne sat David in the plush chesterfield sofa by the fire and poured him a large single malt. 'A chesterfield for a Chesterfield, Master.' She chirped.

David purred contently, 'The temporary Lord of the Manor feels like the cat that's got the cream, and way too many helpings of it. I hate to admit it, but your banquet has me fit to burst, and fit for bed.'

'I'm not at all surprised darling, I never imagined such a slight young fellow to possess such a rapacious appetite. You had better not bloat and become also, like our fat, cloven hoofed swine after we're wed,' she prodded. 'Very well, get you to bed and beneath your blankets, I wish to linger a while here and cluck dreamily over my adorable little bump. I think I'll dig out my needles and begin a few tiny hats, the nesting instinct awakens when the sun has set.'

They kissed and parted, David retiring with another nightcap, destined to sleep like a bear.

***

Anne sat for a while, cupping her belly, delighting in her circumstances. The glowing fire projected her shadow into a dance on the ceiling, a fitting representation of her ebullient spirit.

It was time for tea at last and she would not drink alone tonight. Anne stole light-footed to her room and changed her ensemble and tip-toed away again. David snored in a meat induced oblivion, unaware of her visit.

Jane was awoken from her fitful sleep by soft fingers, gently rubbing her cheeks.

'Mummy? Mummy please wake up.' A small voice whispered.

The voice was childlike and pleasant, Jane opened her sleepy eyes and turned to see a familiar girl sitting beside her on the bed. It was Annie. Unnerved, Jane retreated from her placid smile in fear and confusion.

Petting a small furry toy, Annie sat innocently in her crumpled old mud-stained pinafores. She was without make up, save for a couple of freckles she had dotted onto her cheeks. Her hair hung loose and unkempt beneath a floppy cloth sun-hat she created when she was twelve.

'Hello Mummy, I have missed you so. But I am everso pleased to see you return, I think you have a lot of making up to do with me.' She pouted playfully. 'Let's start with a tea-party shall we?'

Jane's mouth quivered silently in shock, eventually words came out, 'Annie? Annie dear, I'm not Mummy, you seem to be confused...'

'Nonsense Mummy, you just look a little fatigued is all. See here, we just need to revitalise your spirit with an invigorating cuppa. I have readied your favourite gown and shoes, you slip into them and then I'll get to work on your face with your powders and paint, you look a hundred years old.' Annie smiled wide eyed and quite insistent that Jane play along. 'You want to make it up to me don't you Mummy? You are sorry for the wretched things you have done, aren't you Mummy? It's time to make amends Mummy.'

Jane felt sure she was caught up in an insane dream, or maybe she had finally snapped after weeks of mental turmoil. She was held in a hypnotic trance by the coaxing waif. Jane obeyed through fear and the child's twisted persuasiveness and did as Annie commanded.

After dressing in Lady Anne's lavish brocaded silver threaded dress, Annie skipped behind her and regarded her in the mirror, 'wonderful Mummy, now lets get you made up for the Royal Ball shall we? The Queen has finally arrived.''

Annie sat Jane down in front of the vanity desk and from the drawers pulled forth every cosmetic product they stored. Annie opened them all and began applying them to Jane's twitching cheeks in an exuberant and slapdash manner, as a young child might apply to herself without her parent's permission.

Jane began to cry as she endured the torture, witnessing herself become painted as a circus freak or some squalid whore from the docks. All done, Annie squeezed cheeks with her and shared her view in the mirror, 'Oh Mummy, you do look beautiful again, I've already forgotten who that idle sow in the bed was. Now put on your hat and take me to the tapestry room for playtime.'

Annie handed Jane a black wide brimmed bonnet, with a lace veil, a funeral hat. It was the one Jane had worn to Lady Anne's funeral, she preferred it then as it helped to disguise her indifferent feelings towards Lady Anne's death. Now, with her spirit truly broken and enslaved to Annie's mania, she donned it again without protest. Annie pinned back the brim and lace cowl so Jane was not afforded the luxury of her absurd face being hidden today.

All set, Annie clapped excitedly. She then took Jane's feeble hand and led her downstairs like a blind old dog to the candlelit tapestry room. A small gathering awaited them by the fireside to begin the parlour games. The party consisted of her favourite old dolls, cuddly toys and stuffed animal figures. They were arranged in a semi circle around two steaming pots, some neatly arranged cups and saucers, and a large bowl full of berries. Annie gestured to Jane to take her seat.

'These,' Annie held up two dolls, 'these are the King and Queen of Elizaland. They've come at last to visit us and all the woodland creatures. Isn't this such an honour Mummy?'

Jane grimaced with an attempted smile.

Annie held up the one eyed doll she called Button and mimicked a squeaky voice for her, 'Oh Annie look, it's your Mummy. Mummy is back at last to play with us. She must be parching, lets all take tea. Hooray!'

She held up another doll she called Henry, a plump sailor-boy, with a toy crown placed on his china head. Mimicking an authoritative voice she commanded, 'for crimes against the Loftus family – OFF with her head!'

Replying to herself Anne said. 'Steady on 'enry, your highness. Even Jesus was granted his Last Supper.'

Jane began to blubber again as her reality melted away, she twisted her fingers in knots, they popped a little as her knuckles cracked. Chewing the inside of her lips and lowering her head she then burst into heaving sobs. 'I'm so sorry Annie. I'm sorry. I'm sorry. I'm sorry.' she blurted as tears streamed down her farcical face.

Annie then held up a different toy, a knotted, knitted, three legged bunny with a stitched over mouth, again Annie mimed, 'Gmmph Gmm Mmmph?' Then she continued in her own voice, this is Mr Mumbles, and he's a mute, and despite his lovely longs ears he's also deaf. I think he wishes you to write a note so he can understand you.' Annie slid Jane some paper and crayons. 'Come on, write neatly please. What are you sorry for?'

Trying to comprehend the latest insane request she wiped her tears, then she began scrawling. All done she returned the note in red crayon. I'M SO SORRY I KILLED HER.

'There, there Mummy. You dry those silly tears. You can make it up to Mr, Mumbles, and me, and Button, and all the thirsty toys waiting for their tea, by playing with us. I promise that if you are a good Mummy and drink up all your tea, then all your sins will be forgiven. What say you Mummy? Aye?' Annie pipped happily.

Jane just snuffled through her snots and tears, swallowing wads of phlegm gathering in the back of her throat, thoroughly undone by the hideous charade.

Louder this time, shocking Jane alert again, 'WHAT SAY YOU MUMMY?'

Jane whimpered a meek, obedient *Aye*.

Annie, resumed her calm and poured from the pots, 'Good Mummy, good. Now, let me pour the tea, while you chat to Button. I've made special toy tea for their delicate tummies and yummy berry tea for you. Say thank you Annie.'

'Thank You Annie.' Jane repeated as she took the cup of steaming infusion from her.

Button spoke up again, 'Mmm, your tea smells yummy Mummy. Ha Ha. Yummy Mummy. Drink up before it gets cold you old pig.'

Annie snapped at Button, 'Now that's just plain rude Button. I'll have to punish you for that.'

Button squeaked, 'No Annie, please, I'm sorry. I'll be a good dolly.'

But it was too late for Button's apology and Annie cast her into the fire, her blond curls first to singe and flame and then stink out the room. 'Naughty Button,' Annie pouted, then righted her floppy hat.

Jane watched Button's face melt, and shook hopelessly.

'Well, Button did have a point Mummy, your tea will get cold, and it is a special brew that will help with those nasty shakes you have. Sip up now quickly.' Annie tipped the cup towards her lips and Jane obediently drank up. 'We spent ages crushing and mashing up the berries and steeping them before boiling them up for you. Or should I say Yew. Yew for you Mummy! Here eat some too.' Annie fingered a handful from the bowl through Jane's thin lips. 'Good girl. Crunch them up and swallow them all now.'

Jane in the deepest pit of despair continued to sup and chew the mildly sweet berries, if she attempted to spit out the seeds Annie would get cross with her. After all, that's the poisonous part.

The mad hatter's tea party continued for a short while longer, until Jane began experiencing cramps in her tummy. Within very little time, the pain became unbearable and she was convulsing on the floor clenching her gut in agony. 'Oh God, Oh God help me Annie, please.' she cried.

'Oh that is a nasty pain Mummy, lets get you some fresh air before you pass out on us completely.'

Annie took Jane's hand firmly and dragged her to her feet. Jane remained crippled with the pain and Annie had to support her to assist to the door to the rear of the house. Still in character Annie chirped, 'Nearly there Mummy.' Jane collapsed to the floor, delirious from the pain. 'Oh dear, it looks like we'll have to do this the hard way Mummy.'

Annie threw away her hat and grabbed her semi-concious stepmother by her ankles. Annie found her surprisingly light after her months fasting, and it made her pleasantly easy to drag out into the garden. Once outside the fresh night air pepped Annie up even more and she began to warble a ballad about a raggle-taggle gypsy.

Across the wet lawn and over the cracked pavement slabs Annie dragged Jane until they reached Lady Anne's plot in the family cemetery. She then propped Jane directly over her mother's grave, fixing her black hat and resting her lolling head against her headstone. 'There Mummy, comfy?'

Barely lucid, Jane strained to reply, 'Help me Annie, please. Please help your Mummy.' These may have been her last words, it was hard to tell, so faint was her voice, her circulatory system was misfiring, sending her into convulsions.

Annie's countenance transformed under the pale moonlight, leaving Anne towering over her broken and deranged stepmother. Rubbing the rabbit's foot between her graceful fingers she responded to her limp victim, 'Help me? Help me, you say. Did you for once consider helping my Mother as she lay dying for weeks in her bed? Of course you didn't, after all it was you who put her there' Anne stated plainly, 'I'd like to help you *Jane,* I'd like to. But you are already beyond saving, and added to this Jane…YOU'RE NOT MY FUCKING MOTHER.'

Jane grumbled her last desperate plea, raising her hand a couple of inches off of the cold earth. Anne smiled at her politely and placed the note she had written to Mr Mumbles into her hand. At her leisure, she then returned to the warmth of the house. She enjoyed watching her moonlit shadow accompany her as she went. By the time she reached the hearth to warm her hands, Jane was already dead.

***

By a smouldering turf fire in the lobby of the Loch Garman Arms Hotel Lord Charles and his salacious solicitor friend supped down their ale with merry gusto. Their collars and their tongues loosened as they boisterously bevvied into the night. When Mr Devereux upped to empty his bladder, and refill their tankards, Lord Charles reflected on how good it felt to be far from the constraints and burdens of his chilly home and his withering, withdrawn wife. His jolly comrade returned, spilling ale just as two fetching ladies graced through the lobby. The two gormless drunkards did their best to feign sober smiles and nods in their direction. The well dressed ladies courteously returned their smiles and hurriedly continued towards the reception desk, giggling as they strode closely together. The boys guffawed and clapped their shoulders, believing the ladies bashful reaction was a measure of their unfaltering masculine prowess.

How Charles wished he could follow them to their room. He longed to feel the warmth of a big hearted, comely woman in his bed. An eager maiden, full of figure and full of life. To feel passion and vigour pump hot in his veins again and to never have to breathe a word of his misadventure to Jane for the rest of his life.

Little did he know, he would never have to.

The Grieving Lord

In St. Ibar's cemetery in Foulksmills, daffodils and apple blossoms were in abundance by the time Jane's remains were ready to be interred.

After her subsequent discovery by Missus Meades, there followed an extensive inquest, post mortem and autopsy. Arrangements had to be made to source a burial plot far from the family home after conclusions were decided on the cause of her death. The official cause - suicide by cardiac arrest induced by ingestion of excess neurotoxins.

The reason for her disturbing death seemed to explain itself by the bizarre theatre involved prior to Jane's demise. Overwhelming guilt and regret, mimicry and self-defacement, and an unyielding desire to trade places with the woman she poisoned a decade ago. What triggered the sudden flaring of her guilty conscience remained guesswork, not that Lord Charles could care less anymore. Jane murdered his first true love and wife, her corpse could not rot quick enough for him.

No member of the Loftus family attended her burial, her brother, Thomas Cliffe amongst the meagre showing of her relatives. Some looky-loos turned up from nearby parishes to poke their snouts into the murky trough, scavenging and spreading the gothic gossip as they went. Within minutes of the priest closing his bible the cemetery was vacant, leaving only the cawing ravens on her headstone to mourn Jane's death.

As one holy book shut, another one, far less holy, opened. Lord Charles, from the old family library sourced a small pile of ancient books which referred to the Dark Arts, Mysticism, the Occult and Necromancy. It wasn't until he leafed through *The Book of Abramelin* that he found a match for the illustration, now only ash, that Broaders had posted to him. Baal – First and Principal King of Hell. Lord Charles compared the accompanying text with the words on the letter Broaders had sent, now retrieved from the bin and uncrumpled again.

The menacing image immediately set the besieged Lord further on edge. He had not met the dread Doctor Blake, but he imagined Baal's fiery countenance carved onto the shadowy fiend who stormed into his home six months ago.

Paranoia had began to seep into the edges of Lord Charles' thoughts since Jane's death. The initial high he felt at Anne's maturing and pairing with David had since been eroded by the series of deteriorating events. Baggy mutilated, Michael drowned, Jane's suicide. *Was HE behind it all?* Broaders' warning whispered to him in the night and by day he scrutinised the pair with increasing suspicion.

Anne and David continued their lives, unfettered by the losses and revelations. Anne's belly grew large and David's devotion grew in size with it. They remained in blissful oblivion to the dreary Hall and the prospects of leaving it to start anew. Lord Charles felt, that regardless of the discovery that Jane most likely murdered her mother, the pairs behaviour was anomalous and very strange considering the bleak circumstances.

David's presence had corrupted and poisoned his little Annie's mind, Lord Charles concluded. *Had he always been corrupt or had the grim visitor infected him with darkness that stormy night? Was he even the Squire Chesterfield he proclaimed to be?* He had made inquiries to his son William in Wales, instructing him to probe into David's assumed identity, but to no avail as yet. *Was he a charlatan, or was he a manifestation of the King of Hell?* The question itself felt foolish to the level headed Lord. In certainty he had no answers, but he knew, that before his daughter had encountered her new lover, Anne was an innocent. An exasperating and precocious pixie, but still an innocent. The cold, and self-assured madam she became manifested itself directly upon his arrival and influence.

After digesting the grim details and the significance of the Demon Baal, Lord Charles slammed shut the offending book, clasping Broaders' letter between the leaves like a bookmark.

He slid open his drawer and took his pen and paper to daft the necessary correspondence, ignoring the lure of a whiskey bottle also in his drawer. He needed to maintain his focus, and if contacting the Catholic priest was the path to ridding his home and his daughter of the accursed spell that dwelt within them, then this is the path he would take.

He rang the bell to summon Mr Delaney to his office.

'Mr Delaney, I entrust you with a private errand. Please take this to Tintern Abbey for the immediate attention of Father Broaders. Within our very own walls there are matters that need attending by persons more qualified than you or I, or detective

Tynan for that matter. I know I can continue to count on you for your discretion.' Lord Charles said sincerely.

Mr Delaney placed the note safely away and reassured his master of his trust and confidence. Turning then he left the gloomy office and prepared the horses.

Lord Charles surveyed Baal's malicious mouth again, leering from the pages of the old tome. He deliberated the urgency of the matter further and a surge of fear gripped his heart. He shot from his seat, leaving his desk askew, as he raced after Mr Delaney.

By now Mr Delaney had bridled and saddled up. He was trotting halfway down the drive when he heard his name being called. Over his shoulder he found Lord Charles dashing after him. He halted the carriage.

'I think it may be better if I accompany you. I have wasted enough time. I believe it'd be best if we could drag the priest here this very day.' Charles panted then boarded his coach, 'Onward my good man, make haste.'

***

Around the dining table Anne and David gathered. Anne was feasting again. Her appetite was avaricious now. She had just devoured bread and corned beef and was now biting into her second boiled egg, she had been craving eggs since she woke. David marvelled at her intake, he felt pride and joy watching her grow in health and abundance. They continually doted on her rounding belly, each eager to experience the next kick or wriggle beneath the swollen dome.

Anne knew it to be boy. She knew the day he would appear. She knew a lot more than she pretended. Her sense of knowing had been growing for a long time. She knew of David's devotion, she sensed her father's suspicion and artifice. She sensed the hunger of the child within her, it burned not just with a hunger for food, but for life, for sensations, for tactile and rapacious experiences. And a lust. It burned with a dark-red lust to pervade good people, to ravage the world and then set it on fire.

David spoke in good humour. 'If you continue feeding like this I think we'll have to drag timid little Treasa back into the kitchen, Missus Meades can scarcely keep up.' Anne smiled and picked up an apple, 'As for our darling child, at this rate of consumption, I fear he may grow too large to squeeze out.'

Anne slapped David's shoulder, 'Cheeky boy. Are you alluding to gluttony? How dare you prod your darling fiancée.' she laughed, 'Anyway, I'll let you in on a little secret, our little bread-loaf is almost fully baked. He shall be out far sooner than the midwife predicted.'

'What?' How do you know? He? Have you unholy magical insights?' David blurted happily.

'A woman just knows these things my darling. So be sure all is ready in the nursery. Fatherhood looms. Are you ready to become an honest and responsible family man?' Anne teased.

'Oh darling, I have thought of nothing but.' He held her hand and gazed at her sincerely. 'Let me tell you this my love. Since I met you, since you took my hand on my deathbed, since I purged my sins unto your trust, I have only ever endeavoured to become a person that I never dared to believe I could be. Confessing to you, all that I have done, my wickedness and deceit, I found myself liberated like never before, as though you had baptised me. I dream of fulfilling a lifetime of dedication to you and to our baby. I dream of becoming the type of father for my child that I would have wanted when I was a but a babe. Devout, attentive and pure. That vile boy *Dafydd* drowned last year. What washed up on the shore was akin to Moses in the reeds, and you are the Pharaoh's daughter that found me, you are my salvation.'

Anne withdrew from his hand and regarded him with a trace of disgust. He had never before witnessed from her anything but looks of adoration and love. His stomach immediately twisted and panicked. 'My darling, whatever have I said to distress you? Know that I am devoted to you, and wish only to secure your faith in me for evermore.'

Anne regained her pleasant countenance. 'Of course darling, forgive me, I am unaccustomed to such proclamations. I think the thoughts of being someone's saviour overwhelms me.' She took his hand again, 'David my dear, I am ever grateful you entrusted your secrets in me. But I wish you to know I did not find Dafydd abhorrent. On the contrary, had you been a church going dullard I think you would not have magnetised me to you so. I assumed that all this time you were playing the role of a puritan, as have I. Tell me dear, what do you truly believe happened to Jane?'

David confessed that he believed the theory that the police derived at. He admitted that he never held any particular fondness for her and as the truth about her came forth he was pleased that some sort of justice was served by her death. Anne laughed at his innocence, a condescending guffaw that left him cold. She then proudly proceeded to enlighten him about her teddy-bears picnic and Jane's final resting place.

'I found your tales from sea quite inspirational David. I had first considered using the sash window as a makeshift guillotine to lop Lady Jane's head off. But it was far more convenient for us all not to introduce any suspicion of foul play.'

A familiar horror overcame David, he thought of Roberts' rancid breath and his own indifference towards running him through. It was a world David wished he had left behind, a world he believed he had traded for true love and a family, a world that had now mutated and manifest itself behind the bewitching beauty of the woman he loved.

'Anne?' he whispered trying to discern where this revelation left their relationship, she appeared to be drawn towards the darkness that he had let sink deep into the sea, 'Anne, sweetheart, I have committed wretched acts out of necessity and desperation and at times for sheer malicious delight, but with each sin I further damned my soul. I have known little true peace until I came to rest in your arms. I truly understand your lust for vengeance on your mother's murderer, truly I do. But the deed is done now, let the rage settle within you now, do not allow it to fester and grow. You know my secrets, now I know yours. We can entrust in one another, and move forward into our new life free of further atrocity,' he said ruefully.

Again, Anne's mouth stretched to a display of disdain upon hearing his feeble plea, 'David, I find this watery whining very displeasing. Where is the pirate rogue I love, the slayer of tyrants, the destructor of lives. Tell me, you believe this act upon Jane to be my only crime since we met? Do you? I've been having lots of fun while no one was watching. Shall I tell you what became of Michael?'

David's eyes widened while his throat constricted, 'He didn't plunge beneath the ice by accident?'

'No, no, silly. It's far more juicy than that,' she chirped. 'After your little male bonding excursion on Christmas eve, I hurried after him. I didn't at all like the way he was casting his disapproving, sneaky glances at you, at us. The impertinence of that cheeky, cock-eyed garden-hand. He had forgotten all sense of place. Well, I caught up with him as he walked home and we talked. Of course he was very happy to see me, the poor simpleton did dote on me so. I brought up, in a friendly fashion, the issue of his mistrust in you and, just as you had regaled to me, he also confirmed that you spent a fine afternoon together and he subsequently felt that he had misjudged you. I then suggested we take the short-cut via the frozen marl-pool.' enjoying her recollection, she paused. 'Shall I go on dear, you're looking pale?'

David *was* looking pale, and had slunk from her into the corner of his chair, 'please do my love, there is so much more to you than I ever imagined.'

Anne thrilled. 'Oh, there truly is David. Now where was I? Oh yes. So, off down the narrow path under the hoary trees we meandered. I decided to have a little fun with the foolish oaf before bidding him a final farewell. We reached the edge of the frozen pond and I pointed out the short-cut to his house, but he was wary to cross the ice, on account of its thin crust. With that, I showed him this.' Anne flipped the rabbit's foot from between her swelling breasts. 'Ample room for hiding things down there these days,' she giggled, then continued. 'I said to him this, "When David first arrived to us after his miraculous sea adventure, he was wearing this." Michael was struck mute as I handed it to him, I knew that he had recognised it at once, but he couldn't comprehend how it could have returned. "It's magic Michael. We made it so. David would have drowned without it. It permits you to walk on water Michael." I handed him it to him. He regarded it with his simple awe.'

"Lucy-fur" he recalled, mesmerised by the preserved appendage

"Yes Michael, Lucy-fur. You remember." As he stood gawping I changed tact. Firstly I praised his heroism for looking out for me, for wanting to protect me and other gratitudes a distressed damsels might proffer. He was puffed up now, so I said, "In truth Michael, I have duelled with myself over who would better suit me. David, or you." Well, the lad was stupefied, nearly tripping over his step. "Do you know why I chose David, Michael?"

"I suppose because he's smart and proper, m'lady."

"Not that. Forgive my candour Michael, but it boiled down to his eyes. He has beautiful eyes, haven't you noticed? And well, I'm afraid yours just frustrate me. Please forgive me Michael. I just feel I need to be very honest with you."

'The poor sod was close to tears, so I continued in a kind and hopeful voice. "Michael, you know I know magic, don't you? I crafted that magical charm, and lured David to our shore, and I know other spells...I know of a way to un-cock your eyes. Then if it works, maybe *we* could be together." Well, he gave me such a goggley look of hope I nearly laughed, but I remained stoic and caring. "Michael, have you ever seen a woman before? I mean, really seen a woman, without her clothes? Don't be shy. You haven't, have you? You're a virgin aren't you Michael?"

"Uh, uh, um, yes m'lady. No m'lady. The girls don't really take to me on account of my eyes. Can you really fix me? Can you?" he trembled.

"I can. Here is what you must do. The legend goes, that a virgins crossed eyes will straighten immediately at the sight of his true loves naked body. Do you believe me? Am I your true love?" I said, placing the rabbit's foot around his neck. He nodded like a dog waiting to be thrown a stick. "Well then you must trust me, the foot is magic, I want you to walk across the ice, then I'll show you. And so you know you can trust me, I want you to hold these." At this point I shuffled out of my knickers and handed them to him. Well, if you saw his look as he clenched my warm linens, I thought he'd shot his bolt right there.'

David felt queasy and struggled to refrain from showing it.

"Now, off you go, you can do anything now, you can walk on water now. Go now and I'll show you the rest" He obeyed and turned diligently, as though locked in a spell, the thick ice at the edge did well to support him, but as he ventured towards the centre I could hear faint cracking. When he reached the centre I told him to turn around. "Now Michael, lets straighten those silly eyes of yours." He stood transfixed on me as I hoisted my petticoats in the freezing air. I must say David, for a moment I thought the sight of my quim was actually going do the bloody job, his eyes nearly popped out of his head. He barely even noticed the ice giving way beneath him. Well, I'd say the frigid water then put a quick halt to any developments in his trouser department.' Anne giggled as she recalled.

'He came up and down a few times hollering. But I'd swear each time he rose he seemed to be more interested in copping another eyeful of my bush rather than screaming for help. Eventually he stopped bobbing up and I covered up again. Let me tell you, it was nippy down there. But it was hilarious David. Though I can see that you're not amused now. I'm sorry I displayed myself to another. But I couldn't bare that little upstart giving you mean looks. Besides my little trick served its purpose, didn't it?'

David sat dumbstruck, his world in disarray after the whirlwind announcements, his core beliefs regarding the nature of his bride-to-be, strewn in tatters amidst the devastation. He felt less alert, less reactive, less capable of formulating a counter response than Dafydd the artful dodger once was. Bangor, Tenby, The Rapscallion, he was wily at every turn. Now he lilted, canon-fire had tore open a hole in his hull and yet again, he felt he was sinking.

'Oh, yes, and the dreadful old dog too, I got so fed up with him snarling at me that I twisted his scrawny neck and flung him down that icy chute. I know, I'm a right rotter. I realise now, that this must all be quite a shock for you, you seem not to be the man you once were. I think for now you need to go and consider the man, the father, and the husband you wish to be for me,' Anne smirked as she gestured for him to leave. She picked up another apple and set her teeth in deep, the juice draining down her angular chin, 'Go! It seems you have even more to digest than me,' she cackled. 'And don't go running to Daddy, *Squire Chesterfield*, don't forget - we all have our secrets.'

***

Anne peered out of the third floor window, the same window where she once eagerly awaited the arrival of her mystery pirate guest. Her melancholy fiancé was slumped on the bench, staring into nothing. She pondered her Moses in the basket. Anne knew David could not revert to his villain heart. She could relate to this quite easily, the door between her and Annie had been sealed off too and there would be no return for her. Her whimpers from behind the great seal growing fainter every day.

Although Anne wasn't really Anne either. There were many metamorphoses the night Doctor Blake arrived, and brave Annie did not escape his attentions unscathed. It is true that Annie spared Dafydd an unholy transfusion when she pierced the demon with the puny knitting needle. However, the interruption only served to deviate from Baal's original intentions unto him, and change them, into an altogether more cunning, elaborate and potentially enduring strategy.

The naive female unconscious at his feet was ripe for corruption. The dying male with the nefarious heart would serve to fertilise her. The spirit of Baal would gestate within. The debauched parents would nourish, protect and serve the child, and the will of Baal, until adulthood. His reign would be long, magnificent and calamitous.

With Annie faint on the floor, Baal used his black power to burn the fever and infections from Dafydd, ensuring his return to full health. He then clasped his wicked claw around Annie, and as her brothers pounded on the door to enter the stifling room, he transferred his wretched, carnal spirit into her, sending Annie retreating to the sanctuary of her inner world and allowing the alter-ego of Anne to dominate.

And so now, as she watched her lover bury his head in his hands, on the bench they so often shared on the lawn, she realised that he could no longer serve purpose. No righteous man, father or otherwise, could bear the burden of the abomination she would soon bring unto the world. She gently petted her bloated tummy, feeling the knuckley squirm of hard bones twist within her. David had done his bit she thought, time to move on.

***

The postman, over the past few months, had become very fearful about making his deliveries to Loftus Hall and was happy to see the pleasant young man that he'd come to recognise walking along the driveway. He nervously handed the days mail to David and hastily sped back towards the rusting gates.

David's mind was elsewhere, its cogs ensnared in the mire yet again. Memories of fleeing Bangor and Charlotte haunted him. His dreams of a rosy future with a wife and child in shambles. He was bereft of energy and will. The murderous witch behind the beautiful veil he could no longer love, her father had turned cold on him, and even if he had the strength and desire to run, there was nowhere left to go.

He thumbed idly through the manilla envelopes. A beige letter with an English stamp caught his eye, he recognised the postmark from Anglesey stamped across it. He flipped it over out of curiosity, it was addressed to Lord Charles, with the word URGENT underlined twice.

***

The mild spring evening was drawing in and birds took to roost in branches far from the Halls darkening walls. Mr Delaney and his master had still not returned from their quest to the Abbey. Missus Meades clattered about the kitchen preparing a joyless supper. The two remaining servant's loyalty was a tribute to their devotion to their employer and desperation for a weekly wage.

Missus Meades delivered a bowl of stew to David in the dining room and informed him that Anne will not be joining him to dine this evening, adding that she had requested his company in the tapestry room when he has finished eating. He thanked her, finished the note he was writing and tucked into his fatty broth.

Eventually he made his way to his fearsome fiancée, a hollow terror rising within him, he swallowed it down. The tapestry room was eerily chill and Anne was sat comfortably in a beautiful red gown by the fire, she regarded him pitifully as he entered as you might a cripple or orphaned child. 'Sit with me David. Say hello to your child. He will be with us very soon,' she purred.

'Thank you darling, let me sit facing you so I can behold your radiance,' he answered as he took a seat in the chair beside her knitting utensils.

'Of course you may my dear. Soak it up by all means, you may not get to enjoy it for very much longer,' she smiled coyly. 'I'm afraid your change of heart has put me in quite a quandary darling. You see, I need a strong man to protect me and guide our baby. A resolute man, a man not given to charity or clemency. A driven man who will not allow anything, or anyone to impede his, or his family's destiny. You were once this man, now I just see a shell, an obedient lapdog, given to kindness, leniency and notions of guilt. I see no way in which you can serve me, nor our child now.' Her tone cold, her confidence and malice abundant.

'And what of our love my dear, what has become of that. Do you no longer care for me?' he whispered.

'Hah,' she sniggered. 'Well, I suppose there was that. I was prone to these feelings at first. Enjoyable as they were, but they are of no further use to me. Caring for you is no longer my business, nor is love my currency in this pathetic human realm. I now have but one duty. To raise this child, to serve him and see his ascent into glory.'

David's fear twisted into something else, a dread realisation that any semblance of the Anne he knew and loved had entirely dissipated. Sat glaring at him now was something else, something not even human. An uninvited power, a hideous corruption of the soul, staring out from behind her fierce eyes was a fiery beast, a savage succubus, bent on carnage and ruin.

'You see me now don't you David? I am of the fire and the fire is of me.' She stood up, her copious crimson dress gathered in crumpled trails by the grate. Her belly on full display between the wide reveal in the seam, the pregnancy had completed its cycle in a matter of hours. David stood now in astonished marvel at her straining skin, the contours of the foetus twisting violently against its fleshy cage, readying itself to burst free at any moment. The appalling sight sent David into deja-vu, Charlotte on the hill, her dragon dress billowing amongst the clouds, *what comes next*…he tried to remember.

'It is almost time David. Do you care to witness your son's arrival unto this world. It is a moment of great celebration. It is your honour to witness his almighty coming, as a volcano erupts or lightning strikes the earth, you are privy to behold an event of such obscene magnitude.' She opened her arms wide to welcome David in an embrace, her long sleeve swinging into the fire and catching flames. Her dress started to burn.

David watched in bewilderment as the flames lapped up her arm. 'Do not anguish my love, I am of fire, our child is of fire, and shall be born into flame. Come to us. Come from the cold and join us in the flames.' She sighed seductively as she pulled open the full front of her smouldering dress, exposing herself fully.

Entranced by the flame and enslaved by her feral beauty he approached the unbearable heat, her arms widened to welcome him into her burning embrace.

Just before she ensnared him, David drew upon his last sliver of sanity and brandished a long knitting needle high above her breast, as he drove it down towards her heart, she snatched hold of his wrist with ease. Her fiery grip sizzling his flesh.

'Foolish boy! The girl tried this puny implement on me already. Even if I allowed you pierce me, I would endure its feeble sting.' Pure evil poured from her grin, 'You are truly an unworthy sire to this child of Satan. We will engulf your insipid soul in fire and the newborns first feast will be on his father's charred flesh. Know before you die that the only seed you've sown on this earth will wreak havoc and chaos to all it touches.'

Anne pulled him in tight as they drowned in flame, she laughed at his screams.

As David's skin blistered and bubbled in her clasp of fire, he fought the pain, just as he had done so on the doomed Rapscallion and summoned from his gut the strength to utter his last words to her. 'I did not confess to you *everything*, Witch. Your filthy womb was not the only one I fertilised. You can read minds can't you, Demon Whore? Search mine, search mine and call me a liar.'

Anne's inflamed features turned to disgust, her wicked beauty at last warped into an image of grotesque abhorrence. As David burned away in her arms she pulled the last thoughts from his waning mind and she saw...*across the sea, guarded by a beautiful crimson dragon, lay a child, a creature of goodness, cradled in love.*

David could no longer smile, as his face had been scorched clean from his skull, but the last image Anne saw, before his soul evaporated from him, was a fanciful image he had once conjured as he hiked his way across Snowdonia. It was of he and Charlotte, dressed in their finest clothes, off to have a picnic on a lush pasture with their happy little boy skipping along beside them. The three waltzed around their picnic blanket smiling. Dafydd's beautiful face, filled with sheer contentment, turned to wink cheekily at his dreams intruder just before she snuffed out his light.

The Exorcism

Mr Delaney whipped the reins to speed the horses homeward with his pious passenger in tow. Father Broaders and Lord Charles bounced in the carriage, apprehension creased across Charles face, focus drawn onto the priests. They sped through the gates and galloped up the long muddy driveway, as the intrepid trio neared the bleak façade, the sound of a crash drew their attention to the third story windows, a furious scream or a roar, it was hard to tell if the loud, raging yell was even male or female.

The horse came skidding to a halt in the courtyard and the passengers spilled out, their necks craning towards the line of top windows just in time to see the centre pane explode and a fireball spat forth from the smashed frame. It flew from the building into the dusky sky, trailing sparks and flames in its wake before crunching to land in the arboretum.

Lord Charles involuntarily grabbed hold of Broaders' arm in fright as they gawped at the crumpled pyre amongst the thorny vines. Mr Delaney was first to react, leaping from his box seat towards the fire, carrying with him a luggage pike that he kept snagged onto the coach roof.

The Lord and the priest caught up behind as Mr Delaney poked carefully through the fallen flames. The fire appeared to consist of long cloth, possibly the heavy red curtains that draped that upstairs room. The brave butler continued to poke through the material to unearth the ballast that was wrapped within.

Catching the edge of the drapes with his pike he flapped them away to reveal the heavy, charred contents.

It was difficult to identify the blackened coagulation in the fading light, but the trio's instinct, along with the beefy stench of cauterised skin told them it was human remains, the skin still sizzling and spitting in the intense heat. Charles clasped a hand over his open mouth, grief-stricken by the knowledge that this could well be his beautiful daughter. Broaders crossed himself and muttered some prayer, or curse, in Latin.

Under the circumstances, Mr Delaney remained very even-headed and went to comfort his master. 'Sir,' he said, as he laid his hand on Charles' shoulder, 'This may not be Anne, it is impossible to recognise. Let us get quickly inside. She may yet need our help.' He then ushered Charles inside.

Before Broaders followed he sniffed the foul smoke rising from the scorched flower beds. His nose flared as he sifted a familiar scent from the bouquet of burning cotton, hair and human flesh - sulphur.

***

Lord Charles' anguish was quickly dispelled, he and Mr Delaney had just began mounting the staircase when Anne rounded on them, tears streaming down her tormented face. On the landing she threw herself into her father's arms. 'Daddy, Oh Daddy,' she cried.

'Anne, Oh thank heavens you're alright,' Lord Charles held her in a tight embrace. Reassured that his beloved little girl was not simmering outside in the rose garden, Charles squared with her, 'My darling, what on earth has happened? The fire? The window? There's a body, there's…someone, in flames in our garden. Has Doctor Blake returned darling? Is it…Is it David?' He gently searched her eyes.

Anne broke from his gaze and sobbed again. Eventually she blubbed, 'Father, I had no idea he was capable of such things. David lied to us all. He's a conman, a thief, and…and a murderer. He confessed to me everything. He was deranged. Oh Father, he was going to kill me and my baby.'

Lord Charles' eyes hardened, he scorned himself for leaving her alone with the Machiavellian brute, he chastised his judgement for ever welcoming the charlatan into his home. He and Mr Delaney escorted Anne into the tapestry room and Charles continued to comfort her while she relayed her version of events. She was now dressed in a copious cream linen gown with long sleeves, it served well to hide her now greatly distended belly. Mr Delaney stoked the fire and lit candles.

According to Anne, David had grown impatient waiting for Lord Charles to find him gainful work. He was accustomed to having money, and craved having it at his disposal again. He believed her father had no intention of financing their future and that they should run away like he had done before. She then told Charles that he had fled from Wales and assumed the identity of a friend he had murdered. She went on to say that he admitted killing Michael and Jane, and that he would murder her too unless she left with him now.

Charles' eyes enraged, he wanted to go out now and smash in David's still burning skull with his boot. He fought to restrain himself from thrashing the ornate furnishings in the room. 'Mr Delaney, fetch Brandys,' he ordered tersely, he wished to toast the death of the miserable, cremated cretin on his lawn.

Mr Delaney strode off. By now Missus Meades was alerted to the calamity and joined Father Broaders waiting in the hallway. Mr Delaney appeared then and fixed them a stern, *don't even ask*, glance.

Back in the tapestry room Anne, still whimpering and snuffling against her loving father's lapels, finished her tale. After she refused to elope with him, David flew into further fury. Like a madman, he swore to cut his baby out of her and toss it into the fire. He then dragged her towards the flame as if to prove that he would. She was so close that her dress caught fire and, in her panic to wrest herself from him, she somehow became entangled around him and his clothes too caught light. In a flash he was a screaming ball of fire, and in his disorientated desperation to flee the flames he bound through the window.

The drinks were wheeled in and not before time, Charles, forgetting his manners, necked a full glass before offering his forlorn daughter a nerve soothing beverage. He then called all to gather and ensured all present were offered a glass. In his vast and rapidly dwindling household, companionship was a comfort Lord Charles yearned for at this moment.

Anne sipped her spirit, maintaining her *distressed damsel* demeanour until she caught sight of Father Broaders. He noticed the faintest flash of venom in her glance before she re-assumed her doe eyed display. 'Oh, Father Broaders, I didn't think we'd see you again. What a dreadful day for you to return,' she sniffled.

'Yes my child. Please, if there is anything at all I can do,' he said kindly.

Lord Charles spoke, 'Father, I am sorry to drag you out here on this fools errand. It seems it's not the clergy we need, it's the constabulary. We need to get in touch with the police at once. Mr Delaney, I'm sorry but you'll need to turn the horses back around directly after they're watered, you can take Father Broaders. My apologies again Father for dragging you into this carnage.'

'Don't apologise Lord Charles, said Broaders. 'Your instincts were correct to be wary of the boy. I'm only sorry we didn't arrive sooner. Please, if it's fine by his Lordship I would like to stay on a while, I might like to give a statement to the police when they arrive, and maybe I can be of some comfort or assistance in the meantime.'

'Indeed Father, very good of you, of course you're welcome to remain here,' said Charles.

Anne smiled weakly, 'Thank you Father.'

'Missus Meades, can you stay with Anne for a moment, I wish to write a note for Detective Tynan to send with Mr

Delaney,' said Charles. Missus Meades nodded, finished her drink, and took her turn consoling the behaving bereaved young woman in the rapidly warming room.

The men exited the stuffy atmosphere, Mr Delaney to tend the horses, and Charles to his study. Broaders itched to ask Lord Charles' permission to examine the room from where the body was hurled, he was sure it was the same room he had already investigated with Father O'Dowd, but knew it would be an unwelcome request at this point. So he said, 'Lord Charles, It may be prudent to make sure the fire is safeguarded on the third floor, may I dash up to ensure that all embers have been doused?'

Charles agreed absently and made for his study.

***

Such was the chaos of Lord Charles' thoughts he could hardly remember what it was he came into his study to do. He immediately noticed something irregular about his bureau. His Jameson bottle, normally discreetly confined to his middle drawer was placed on top of some letters, beside it sat an empty glass.

Sitting down to examine the staged items, he found a letter addressed to him resting beneath the bottle. It had been opened. The hand writing was familiar and the return address on the envelope belonged to his son William who lived in North Wales. The word URGENT was underlined twice.

It read.

William Henry Loftus   23 March, 1884

Dear Father,

I write to you on the matter of great concern and urgency with information pertaining to the letter you wrote me last month.

You asked me to inquire about the man claiming the name of David Chesterfield, now residing in our family home and engaged to my beloved sister Anne.

I have contacted the Chesterfield Mining Company in Hirwaun, with a view to meeting the heir to the mine, a Mr Herbert Palthrow. When eventually I received a reply, it appeared that, broadly speaking, the characteristics of our Mr Chesterfield very much matches the identity of the tearaway character of Mr Palthrow's long lost cousin. However, I was invited in his letter to join Mr Palthrow for luncheon to discuss the matter in greater detail.

I have just left the office of Mr Palthrow and I am presently writing this letter from a teashop in Hirwaun. After our discussion, Mr Palthrow believes, though the details you have been told about Mr Chesterfield are accurate, the physical resemblance is very far from that which Mr Palthrow recalls, it is our deduction, and we are in complete accord on the matter that you have in the midst of your home ~ an imposter.

Mr Chesterfield was last reported seen at a sports engagement in Glyn Garth and there he was spotted with a young man very much matching your guests description. It is now feared that he may have murdered the real David Chesterfield, stolen his money, and his identity.

Father, do not reveal the contents of this letter to him, or to Anne until the police have arrested him and have him locked far from your home. He may be very dangerous and liable to strike out if put into a corner. I am making arrangements to visit at my next opportunity. I pray this letter is received safely, in good time and before more tragedy befalls our noble family.

May God be with you.

Your Loving Son

George.

Tuppence tardy and thruppence shy, thought Charles when he was finished reading. Still, at least the vicious snake was now roasted alive and died screaming, and beyond committing any more harm on his family from his death pyre amongst the roses.

As he cobbled together David's devious manoeuvres in his mind he scolded himself for having not spotted the serpent to whom he gave sanctuary.

But the question then returned to his head, *who opened the letter? who was at his whiskey?*

Charles flipped the note over. To his surprise there was a further correspondence on the back of Georges' letter. A different hand, but the ink Charles thought he recognised as that from his own well.

This note said.

My Dear Lord Charles.

I am exposed. By now you will have read that I am not who I have claimed to be since you took me into your home and nursed me back to life.

Today I had a choice, to run or to confess. I think I had decided to confess prior to opening your son's letter. Forgive the intrusion. But I suppose this is the least of the matters I should be asking your forgiveness for. You have shown me a kindness that, in my short life, I have rarely known. For a while you became as close to a Father to me as I've ever felt. It was, my sincerest wish to live happily ever after in the bosom of your kind family, and to model myself on the kindness and grace that I have witnessed from you this great estate.

My name is Dafydd Alwyn Jones. I have committed an uncountable number of crimes, I am a fugitive and a fraud. Up until I arrived in Ireland I did whatever I had to do stay alive. Today I asked myself could I become that person again. In truth I cannot.

Other than my false identity, I have perpetrated no crime nor act I am not proud of whilst under your roof. Being with Anne made me better, made me want to be an honest person. I have been living a dream for the past six months. The manor, my beautiful fiancé, my baby arriving, but I was a fool to believe we could sustain this.

I noticed your letter from Father Broaders slid between the pages of the book on demonology on your desk. Now, having read it and the pages it bookmarked I now suspect I know where you have hurried off to with Mr Delaney and what you hope to achieve upon returning with Broaders...ridding me of my demon spirit via the exorcism ceremony.

It is a worrying truth that my arm bears the mark of Baal's grip. But it is faint, he did not complete the possession he had intended with me. He was diverted by your daughter. It was Anne, or Annie, who thwarted his goal, and he made her suffer for it.

Anne, is not who you think she is, she is not who I thought she was. She is a slave to Baal's will, or she is *He* incarnate, I am as new to this chicanery as you are, but I assure you, their is a terrible evil at the helm of all her actions.

She has confessed to me the slaying of Michael and her stepmother Jane. If I am still alive by the time you read this, please do not waste Broaders time on me, I have never felt as pure of spirit in my entire life. Look to your daughter Charles, she still bears unhealed burns on her arm, and I have seen the hellish fire burn from behind her eyes.

Though I proclaim my innocence, no one deserves a death sentence more than I. This wickedness has followed my every step for many years, I brought it to your doorstep and it poisoned your family on my account. I am sorry beyond words and beyond your forgiveness. Today, I believe, I will join all whom I have wronged ~ in Hell

Truly,

Dafydd Jones.

PS, I did not kill David Chesterfield. He was very drunk and slipped into the tide without any assistance from me.

PPS, I truly loved Anne.

The double-sided letter sent Lord Charles into a tailspin. It was like flipping a coin, only both sides were minted tails and presented solely a lose/lose situation. Only now he faced the even greater loss of his daughter's immortal soul. He swigged directly from the bottle, the days of etiquette had long expired.

***

Even at a cursory inspection Broaders' keen eye detected inconsistencies within the accursed room. Making a mental note he quickly turned to return downstairs. He had decided not to broach his suspicions with the traumatised Lord until after the police had arrived. He reckoned there had been ample upheaval and disaster for one day.

David is still smouldering on the outside lawn for Christ's sake.

As he hurried down the oak staircase he encountered Lord Charles in his ascent of the stairs. Broaders started, 'Ahh your Lordship, all is fine upstairs. Has Mr Delaney gone to fetch the police yet?'

'Nevermind that now, I've told him to hold off. I need to talk to you.' Broaders detected that any relief the Lord had felt earlier had flown, and was replaced with a new graveness, 'Read this,' Lord Charles reluctantly passed the letter to the priest.

When finished reading the missive, Broaders raised his eyes to meet Charles. For a moment there was silence as they both digested the ramifications of the note. Charles spoke first, 'If this is true, which it may not be, it may very well be the last testament of a madman, but IF there is any truth to this, then I may yet need your expertise before this awful night is done.'

'We must determine if she bears the mark of Baal on her arm your Lordship. If she has been infected, as the letter suggests, she will have foresight - an unnatural knowing. She will anticipate our intentions.'

'So what do you suggest man? We can't afford to dilly-dally on the matter,' he spat, beginning to tear at his seams, the unfathomable stress straining his nerves to their limits.

Broaders placed a calm hand on his arm attempting to compose the untethered Lord. 'I know we can't, nor shall we. Call Mr Delaney, I have an idea.'

***

Missus Meades, more than just Anne's maid since her infancy, spoke gently to her, soothing words to salve the broken hearted maiden's despair. Anne's rapid breath and spilling tears quelled and subsided, She sipped from her brandy glass and thanked Missus Meades for her attention and kindness.

Mr Delaney entered the tapestry room with a tray and placed it on the side table, on it sat various ointments and balms. 'Before I leave for town ma'am, your father asked me to administer you with some medicines to help calm your nerves. You are very likely to be suffering from shock''

Anne detected no perfidy from the mild mannered manservant, and after a feeble protest, declaring herself just fine, she agreed to take the sedative tonic. After she took two spoonfuls he returned the medicine to its tray, then he proceeded to hand Missus Meades a small vase containing a cooling aloe salve. 'Please Missus Meades, if you'd be so kind, could you massage this into Miss Loftus hands and arms, she may very well have suffered superficial burns during the incident.

'Of course Mr Delaney, the poor thing needs all the attention we can afford her.'

The sedative, combined with the brandy had already relaxed Anne and now she was enjoying the fuss been made over her. Missus Meades began to massage the salve along Anne's forearms, she closed her eyes and savoured the pleasant cooling effect on her skin. When Missus Meades raised the long loose sleeve on her right arm Anne flinched as she remembered the distinct scars that she had kept hidden for so long.

'Oh Miss, that looks nasty, you were seared after all, we'll have to get the doctor to tend to that.'

Anne flared and snatched her sleeve back down, 'Thank You Missus Meades, really, I'm quite fine. Please leave me now, I very much need to rest,' she snapped.

If she was shocked at all, Missus Meades did well to conceal it. 'Very good ma'am, you just call us if you need us at all.

The servants retreated with the treatments, leaving Anne to seethe alone by the fireside.

Once the doors to the tapestry room were securely closed the pair were accosted by Lord Charles and Broaders. Without trying to appear alarmed Lord Charles quizzed them about the administration of the medicines. When the news of the scarring on her arms was revealed Lord Charles felt his strength drain from him and he collapsed against the thick wooden newel.

Mr Delaney, as alert as ever rushed to support him, 'Sir, I've got you, Miss Anne is resilient, she appears fine, I'm sure the scarring is just superficial, her nerves are shred, she needs rest and our support is all.'

Broaders spoke up, solemn and authoritatively, 'I'm afraid she needs more than that.'

***

Anne glared into the fire, fuming at herself for her lapse. She finished off her brandy then smashed the glass into the flames and began pacing the stifling room frantically while rubbing her enormous tummy. She delayed her labour earlier that evening but felt now that she could not postpone the advent of her spawning for much longer.

I can feel you twist in me my love, I can feel your growth has peaked, and your desire to burst forth this nigh. I can feel you strain against the frail fleshy restraint of my womb, you would tear and slash and rip me asunder to free yourself and begin your reign. I pray you be patient. Let me deliver you, let me nourish, guard and guide you through your infancy. You may discard of me on maturity, but let me usher you to that zenith.

You have waited a hundred years to take human tenure, wait a moment longer my Lord.

She calmed herself. Her instinct was to find a dark and isolated nook, as would an animal, to discharge her young. She would give birth on the third floor in the dreadful room where she was first turned, where Annie was dispelled, and the bloody virago was borne by her Master. She would do it alone, she would do it now, before the police arrived. Soon, she would be mother, the mother to evil incarnate.

Wishing to avoid detection, Anne slipped stealthily up the back staircases, her gown billowing wide, exposing her ripe nakedness on the stairs. The effort of her ascent inducing the first powerful contractions of her abominable labour. She doubled over with the pain from its seizing grip. She strained not to cry or scream. *This must be done silently.*

Reaching the dark, acrid stinking quarters once more, she turned quickly inside and secured the door shut. Once inside, she spun around to prepare herself on the bed, only to find all four of the houses occupants gathered ominously in the breezy room. She feigned a yelp of innocent surprise, and covered herself up modestly, making sure to catch the holymans eyes as she tucked away her engorged breasts. Presenting herself as the coy and traumatised waif, she gasped at her steadfast onlookers, she feared this ruse would not hold for long.

'Father, what on earth are you all doing mustered in this awful place? You've frightened the life from me.'

The audience remained stoic and unconvinced by her performance. Mr Delaney edged nearer to the door.

'Where are you sneaking to *butler*?' her breathy tone levelling out.

'Sleuthing for clues again are we Father Broaders. Has anything caught your eye yet?' she suggested as she glanced down towards her swollen bosom, the trace of acid in her voice enough to finally engage her rapt inquisitors.

'Anne my love, you've had a tremendously stressful evening, we're gathered here to help you through this ghastly time in your life. Please, sit on the bed and take some more tonic,' offered Charles nervously.

Anne detected the deceit, detected the ulterior goal. detected Mr Delaney behind her, preventing her leave. She felt more like a wild beast ensnared by predators than a lady shielded by her allies. She focused on the priest. 'Is this little party your idea then, Priest? Convinced these good folk that I'm troubled, amoral, corrupt, have you? Convinced them that I should be tied to a bed and bathed in prayers have you? I'm sure you'd love to see me tied to the bedposts wouldn't you Father?'

'My Child, I am here by request of your Father. These people love you and wish to see you well. Please sit, take some tonic, ease your mind and let us help you,' Broaders said calmly, offering her the small glass of dark emollient.

'Of course Father, I'm sorry for my behaviour, please forgive me.' She took the glass from his outstretched hand smiling. She then brought it to her nose and winced, then flung it to the wall. 'Poison!' she hissed. 'You would anaesthetise me and tear the child from my womb and cast it out the same window from which his pathetic father dived, screaming in agony. Fuck you Priest. Fuck you all.' She snarled savagely. This exertion induced another fierce stomach cramp and she creased to the floor.

The aghast onlookers took this opportunity to seize her and carry her to the bed. Despite her agony she managed to kick and buck with formidable strength. Eventually Mr Delaney and Broaders managed to restrain her on the bed. She writhed against the tethers the men had used to tie to her limbs and then to the bedposts. Her gown opened again, exposing to her father the perverse acceleration of her pregnancy. He watched in horror as the small, bony knots protruded aggressively against her stretched abdomen.

'Daddy, Daddy, don't let them do this to me, please Daddy,' she pleaded. Charles' heart was ready to rupture, seeing his darling daughter, now heavily pregnant, thrust up like a pig on a spit. He wailed at Broaders, 'No! This is madness. There must be another way. This is my little girl. This will kill her. Untie her. For God's sake, you must end this lunacy,' he bawled.

'Lord Charles, we must act now to try and save her. Look at her, see her scars. You know in your heart the words in David's letter to be true. Look into her eyes and tell me if you can see any trace of the girl you remember. Tell me truly if you believe that this is wholly your daughter.' Broaders commanded.

Lord Charles looked deep into into her eyes. Yes they were the same captivating crystalline wells, brimming now as they pleaded for pity, for mercy. But he could not fully convince himself that her harrowing tears were not entirely farce. He searched deeper, searching for Annie. 'Annie.' He cried, 'Are you still in there. Daddy is here precious. Come, come and talk to me, I miss my little ragdoll, please, talk to Daddy.'

Anne could not maintain her pitiful performance in the face of Lord Charles' pathetic attempts to commune with the lost little girl. Contempt lifted the sham cowl she wore, changing her grieving grimace to reveal a widening, baleful sneer.

Lord Charles started and retreated from her lewd mocking smile, 'Daddy Daddy,' she squeaked in a fake falsetto, 'Save me, Daddy, save me. The big bad wolf has swallowed me hole and I'm all alone. Come on Daddy, rescue me. Rescue me like a heroic prince. Save me, save me like you saved Mummy, and Elizabeth, and Jane.' She cackled then her voice deepened to a rumble, 'What say you me hearty? Say Aye. Say Aye Daddy!'

The Lord reeled back at the cruelty of her words. 'Pay no heed, your Lordship, that is not your girl that vents this vitriol, it is the demon that his taken her, your daughter may lie within, lost, as the demon mocks. But I must begin the ritual now, as his grip on her soul is almost complete.'

'Very Well, Priest, you have my permission, do what you must to bring forth my little girl from within this beast.' Lord Charles gasped when he finally gathered himself.

Anne at this moment seized into another torturous spasm, her limbs straining against the tight restraints, her whole body flushing redder as she bellowed unnaturally in labour pain. She pulled up and apart her knees as much as the ties would allow, flooding the filthy sheets with embryonic fluid.

The child was coming.

***

The motley assembly were scarce prepared or equipped to assist in Broaders' archaic ritual, let alone the premature delivery of her baby. Nonetheless, it was coming, the contractions were actually visible through the taut skin of her clenching stomach.

Mr Delaney mustered some control and leadership over the dire calamity. He ordered Missus Meades to act as midwife and Broaders to begin his ritual, while he and Lord Charles would try to hold her flailing body. Missus Meades, known for her resolve and fortitude, found herself struggling to fathom and function during the incomprehensible nightmare. Switching to auto pilot she obeyed the butlers command and took her station between Anne's writhing legs, the heat from her widening groin was like a stove.

Father Broaders was experiencing his first wobble now, his posturing of authority and surety being truly tested by the wild, wailing woman. For years he had read the case studies and visited the sites of just such occurrences, but, to have all of his senses exposed to, and tested by, her vile corruption was a world away from the scripts and stories he had for so long studied. The rising sulphuric odour, the gaining heat, Anne's bloated body buckling, the sweat pooling on her reddening skin, the intensifying howls - how could he perform amid this clamour.

'Broaders,' Mr Delaney yelled, 'What ever you came here to do, do it now for Christ's sake.'

The command jolted the priest back to his senses. He prepared to begin the exorcism. Conducting such an act without express permission from the Vatican could result in his excommunication from the church. But this matter was beyond consideration for the young priest now.

Retrieving his effects from his leather case he produced the rosary, a vial of holy water, a bible and the exorcism scriptures. He draped his purple stole around his neck. Firstly, before he may read the rites, he must provoke the demon to name itself. He brandished the crucifix before Anne's face and commanded, 'What call you Demon. Expose yourself before Christ. What vile serpent slithers within this child, this child of the one and the only divine God of man? Speak Demon. Lest you fear the might of the risen Lord.'

Anne laughed hysterically at the small wooden cross. 'Oh my dear little cleric, I am but an innocent, what harm do you intend me with this tiny artefact? Will it burn me upon touch?' she raised her head, then protruding her long pink tongue she licked the contours of the cross. 'Mmm, I bet your God enjoyed that. Would you like me to lick you next, priest?' she laughed.

Broaders was struck by her resistance to the rosary, he momentarily questioned his faith, his will, his ability to complete the exorcism. Anne sensed it and seized on it. 'See Holyman! Even YOU doubt your feeble God, you doubt your own urges, you doubt your strength,' she mocked, her voice an impossible tenor now, 'My God lets me wield power, satiate my urges, my God sustains me in my hour of need.'

'Beast,' Broaders countered, 'You are a coward. You hide your wretchedness behind the veil of the innocent and the weak. You have no place upon Gods holy kingdom, I will draw you from under your rock, and cast you back into your filthy pit. Name yourself, Demon of Phoenicia.'

'Soooo, you know me already? Filth! Sodomite! You are a clever boy.' She toned down and hissed at him.

Boosted by this change in temperament, Broaders wet his thumb from his vial and daubed the sign of the cross across her bare chest, 'NAME THYSELF DEMON.'

The skin beneath the holy water seared and steamed, Anne screamed and spat at the priest, the pain causing yet another excruciating contraction. 'Fuck your mother Priest. Fuck your God. I will tear off your head and spew lava into your soul. You pathetic paedophile. I saw how you looked at me. Virgin. Do you want to feel me? Taste my sweat Father Broaders. Please Thomas, I want you in my mouth Thomas.' She leered viciously, showing him her open mouth, lapping her tongue lewdly.

Lord Charles and Mr Delaney were frozen by her guttural virulence. Disbelief awash on their drained faces, any roosting beliefs that this was their sweet Annie beserking on the bed had now finally flown.

Broaders continued with more confidence, he was close. 'You will free this woman beast, I will draw you from her like venom and spit you back into damnation. You will know no domicile nor quarter here on God's green land. Your powers count for nothing beyond your sunken ring of fire. You are but a rabid dog, a diseased rat, a powerless sprite upon Earth and Gods Holy Kingdom. Are you so low in Hell's pecking order you do not even warrant a name?'

Infuriated by the lowly clergyman's pious insubordination, Anne managed to tear one arm free of its restraint and immediately clawed it into Broaders' right eye, gouging deep and tearing the skin from cheek to neck. She then bellowed forth her authority, drowning out his bloody, agonised wailing. 'Dare you question my might, filth? I am the fire around which the universe spins, I am the black root of man's darkest desires, and the red fruit of his lust. I am the principal King of Hell, Duke of sixty six legions, I am older than time and my will shall be done on earth.

My name...is BAAL.'

***

Hiding in a hollow, under a blackened tree, deep in Elizaland, a frightened girl cowered. To there she had retreated, in the abandoned wasteland, for what seemed like an eternity. Around her were small piles of dark coloured hats, fashioned from rags and the remains of the creatures that once dwelt in this vivid kingdom. There was no longer colour beneath the swarming grey sky, never a scent bar the stale powdery cloy, never a noise, but the howl of the wind. Only silence filled the airless realm.

Until now.

Annie flinched when she heard the roar like distant thunder. A putrid burning smell followed in its wake. Did it come from the east, from the huge oaken door from which she fled so long ago? Her instincts told her to stay safe in her darkening world, down with the roots and her hats, far from the burning beast that prowls beyond the gate.

But, she found herself watching her hands, tentatively testing the earth, her fingers digging down and crawling through the charred soil of her own apocalypse. She found herself following them, hunched on her knees. She scrambled through the undergrowth towards the thunder and the distant portal.

***

Anne's wardens managed to secure her wild, flailing arm to the bedpost again, horrification etched across their trembling faces. Anne relaxed then, sighing with glee and accomplishment at the sight of the priest's torn and bloodied face. 'You won't be eyeing up the boys with that eye anymore, Father.' Anne cackled.

Broaders, now blind in one eye, had no time to lament his loss nor heed the pain of his burning injuries. With assistance from Mr Delaney he prepared a makeshift gauze and bandage using a handkerchief. He doused it with holy water, wrapped it around his head and carried on courageously. Despite his debilitating wound, Broaders felt encouraged by his progress in the ritual and returned to his texts, one good eye still intact.

Having divulged his identity to the exorcist, Broaders could begin the ritual in earnest. The process required the priest to command the demon, in Gods name, to expel itself from its host. He must recite the psalms and prayers, five thousand words from the Roman scriptures and deliver them with the conviction of Jesus Christ himself.

In essence, the exorcism is a battle of wills, a prolonged duel between mortality and immorality, a test of strength, faith and rectitude in the face of torment and unrelenting hostility. Baal had faced countless pious pretenders over the millennia, vanquishing many, falling to few. The priest was a novice and the demon smelt it.

The bout began, Broaders recited the verses while Baal hurled obscenities, from threats of unimaginable violence and abuse, to lurid suggestions of carnal decrepitude. With the increasing roars and cries Anne's face warped into impossible contortions, her eyes bulging from their sockets, her mouth gaping, her lips stretched agonisingly back, revealing her back teeth, her tongue tasting the air like a snake.

Broaders was tested and though a greenhorn, he had stomach and backbone and a will of iron. His faith in his Lord's word was undeniable and he continued to deliver the prayers with uninterrupted certainty. A holy clipper ship, slicing through a raging tide of abuse. Moses carving through the Red Sea.

The priest had another advantage, unprecedented in the history of exorcisms, the host was heavy with labour. The violent contractions tolled on Anne's strength, her vitriolic tirades staggered and halted by the painful seizures and the urge to dispel the infant.

Missus Meades, her thin grey curls stuck to her sweating brow, witnessed the head crowning. Where once she may have offered calming words of encouragement to the birthing woman, these was far from normal circumstances. All she could do was try to safely rescue the child from its insane mother while avoiding injury from her wild, bucking body. Mr Delaney came to her assistance and despite Anne's feral strength, he managed to harness her knees still, using two long lengths of curtain chord. The bed shifting beneath her. It was easier for him to wrestle in troublesome coach horses.

After almost an hour the battle of wills had taken a heavy toll on all. Broaders had aged ten years during the ordeal, flecks of grey now littered his thick dark hair. The servants, pooled in sweat from their efforts and the increasing heat, had exhausted themselves in the efforts to retrieve the child, its huge head still ripping Anne wider in its bid to free itself. And her father, the stoic and upright Lord, knew he was operating on his body's and his soul's reserves. He would give his all, purge his all, in this arcane quest to retrieve Annie, knowing that when done, success or no, he would be spent, void, and forever changed.

Anne too, was at last listing, the convulsions easing under the weight of Broaders' verbose chants, her foul profanities waning as she now mumbled and babbled in obscure Aramaic, foam draining from her loose lips onto the soaked bed.

The defiant priest drew upon his fading energy to deliver the final verse with commanding gusto.

'Humiliare sub potenti manu Dei contremisce et effuge, invocato a nobis sancto et terribili nomine Jesu, hunc quem inferi tremunt, huius nominis cui Virtutes, Potestates et Dominationes subjectæ caelo subjectæ sunt; quem Cherubim et Seraphim indefessis vocibus laudant, dicentes: Sanctus , sanctus, sanctus Dominus, Deus exercituum.'

It sent Anne into an epileptic fit. Quick, small jerks that shook her spasmodically, and reverberated through her squealing voice, the baritone fading to a sound more befitting a woman.

Annie, hearing the squeal from behind the great round door, with smoke streaming from its seams, ventured nearer. Daring to peer through its keyhole and through the ring of flame on the other side, she could see faces, familiar faces, strewn with fear, anguish, and compassion. The chanting man she did not know. But over his shoulder she recognised the other man, distraught, yet full of pity and love...Daddy.

He and the priest uttered the final words of the prayer and Annie pushed with all her might against the scalding portal.

From the snares of the devil,
-Deliver us, O Lord.
That Thy Church may serve Thee in peace and liberty:

-We beseech Thee to hear us.
That Thou may crush down all enemies of Thy Church:
-We beseech Thee to hear us.

Heat rose from Anne like steam from a doused fire, in the effort to expel the demon she erupted into one last booming, volcanic spasm, and fell still.

Annie stood in the doorway, the door destroyed, her kingdom in ruin, then walked through the ashen wasteland, a figure shrouded in smoke awaited her. The wind unfurled him from the dark fumes. Lord Charles stood before her, his arms open.

Annie opened her eyes, Baal was banished. Her father awaited. Her eyes now witnessed the truth of the world, she was back, free from her long, dark purgatory. Lord Charles rushed to take her frail body into his arms as her bonds were untied.

He wept.

They all wept.

There was but a fleeting moment to enjoy this pause in the chaos. Annie, finally drawn from her malevolent mire was granted no time to ascertain her bearings nor any context to comprehend her situation as she was quickly plunged into the pain of her final contractions.

Missus Meades at last could offer her those soothing words of comfort, 'Oh darling, you are so close. Breathe sweetheart, just breathe slowly now, and it'll all be over with one last push.'

Annie breathed, Annie closed her teary eyes, Annie took her father's hand and pushed. Annie gave birth to a baby boy.

***

Are you still with us? I know it has been gruelling, and you have done well to stomach the arduous journey thus far. I'd like to tell you that you are over the hump and we can now float gently down to a wildflower meadow or a lilly kissed lake, where Annie laughs with her father and her beautiful babe in arms, the traumas they have encountered now but a nightmarish memory to them both. I'd like to write THE END now and be done with the damned tale. You may even chose to close this book now with this relatively pleasant scenario screening in your minds eye.

But it is a falsehood.

The final chapters will leave you feeling none the richer for poor bedevilled Annie and her encumbered father. So, if you must know, and if you have the onions ~ then read on.

The Late Spring

Why Mr Delaney and Missus Meades remained within the bleak and misery soaked walls of Loftus Hall one can only surmise. Of course they had given twenty years of devout service to the Loftus family through the good and the grim, but considering their knowledge that the *Devil* had walked their very own halls and hid, disguised as an angel amongst them, wreaking havoc and tearing souls asunder, it would have seemed more likely they would have sought refuge far from the peninsula, joined a convent or monastery or become sectioned in some asylum.

Maybe this place became their asylum, to which they willingly committed themselves. For no one in the outside world would give merit to their tale. Their experience was their bond, one that they would take to their graves after seeing out their sentence in the vast empty mausoleum.

Father Broaders, who left The Hall scarred, depleted and withered by his unsanctioned ceremony, chose exile. His prematurely aged figure was last seen boarding a ferry to the continent. Though he had triumphed over evil, his spirit was broken and defeated. His will was tested, bent and mangled, and when he at last thought he had banished evil from under the roof of the stately home, he beheld the homunculus child and fled.

And so, it was the broken Lord Charles and his two servants that held ground in Loftus Asylum with their patient, a frightened, confused and deranged young mother. Annie had returned yes, but she was no longer the Annie they once knew. The ghost of Annie that returned to her mortal shell was the antithesis of the dynamo, the sprite, the pixie that had energised the dull corridors so long ago.

Annie, a frail, silent, and lobotomised version of her former self retained but one discernible human trait, her protective maternal instinct.

The child, when thrust upon the world, was not greeted nor welcomed in the customary manner with smiles, relief and wonder. Those who witnessed his expulsion from the womb drew back, hand to their faces, grimacing in loathsome horror at the aberrant child.

It was not that it was unlike the general resemblance of a greasy newborn babe. It was of the approximate size, the correct number limbs and appendages were present and untwisted. All other inconsistencies could have been forgiven if their sum didn't induce a feeling of lurching unease at the very sight of it. The child was abhorrent and wrong. If it were not for Annie, it would have been beaten and hurled from the window without hesitation, like a snapping shark from a trawler having been caught up in the herring net.

The features of the infant were thus, its skin, redder and more leather than the tactile softness of a newborn, as though it had calloused over from intense heat within the womb. It was stretched ill fittingly over its bulbous bones, and twisted into uncharacteristic creases around the joints, and over the face it seemed too tightly grafted causing its eyes to squint and pulling the lips into a hideous leer.

Behind the vile mouth it was born with the points of sharp black teeth already protruding, these proved useful immediately after birth, when blindly, the infant fed the umbilical tether into its own mouth and gnawed itself free.

Its nails were similar, small black and pointed and not soft, as Missus Meades found out when pulling him free. The accursed child clawed and raked at her arms as it savagely scrambled out, she could not bear the horror and dropped it onto the filthy sheets. Already it moved abnormally, attempting to crawl towards its mother's breasts.

As it lay silently on Annie's exhausted chest, chewing the umbilical like a dog slobbering over a gristled cartilage, she cradled it. Thick black hair matted its huge crown, beneath lay hidden a circle of small protrusions, knots on the skull. More evident, were the ones along its spine, a ridge of knuckley bumps that tested the elasticity of its venous skin.

Annie instinctively pulled some sheets over her abhorrent baby, shielding his irregularities from the aghast audience, though she could not disguise its putrid sulphuric smell. It did not at first cry nor suckle, silent save for the small slurping sounds of small teeth severing through offal.

***

The mansion now nestled in an almost permanent grey mist, was barely visible from the roadside. At night a dim solitary light faintly lit within its walls.

In house meetings, a state of emergency was declared and martial law descended on Loftus Hall. It was decided the gates to the Hall should be locked, no one would be permitted entry, a box to retrieve and collect post was mounted onto the padlocked entrance.

Groceries and essentials would be obtained via messages and lists. A brass bell was secured to the gate pillar to be used when the delivery boy had delivered his cargo.

Lord Charles corresponded via post to his sons, forestalling them from any plans to visit. He assured them that the matter with the imposter had been dealt with and he would resume full communications again when his many domestic matters had been resolved, assuring them all was well, and that he would leave Wexford, bound for England, soon.

Until they devised a decisive strategy to deal with the demon offspring, they would try their best to nurse Annie back to health and to sanity.

The remaining three had become more akin to orderlies, in attendance to the enormous asylum's only patients, Annie and her monster child. She did not communicate with her carers but could be heard muttering sweetly to her baby, she was at times heard whispering his name...Dafydd.

The two were inseparable. It fed voraciously from Annie, its pin like teeth gnawing painfully on her raw nipples, and when they bled it was content to drink the blood too.

Such was her protectiveness of her baby that she devolved into a feral-like creature, and would hiss and snarl upon the approach of her carers. They managed to lure her to a bedroom they had prepared for her on the ground floor in the tapestry room, there they could guard and tend to her needs with greater ease. The room was kept locked at all times.

A rudimentary toilet was placed in her quarters and rotated twice daily, all taking an even turn to maintain the miserable confine and its inhabitants. Annie maintained a sanitary condition for the child, but let herself go unwashed. Her nightshirts smudged and ragged, her hair grew matted and wild, her fingernails thick and encrusted with black grime.

As she scarcely moved, save for a slow rocking motion, bedsores began to welt and blister beneath her buttocks and eventually burst. Her left nipple, close to chewed off, had become infected, claw-marks flecked her chest from the child's ravenous efforts to suckle.

She would not permit assistance bathing, nor the touch of another person, she was liable to whip out an offensive arm or leg should anyone come too near to her and her beloved child. The room stank with heavy wet smells, rotten eggs, stale sweat and human waste.

Ensuring she took food and water was an essential errand for the carers while the infant drained her.

'I'm leaving porridge on your locker Annie, there's a jug of milk on the tray too,' her father spoke quietly in the dank, gloomy room. 'Would you like anything else dear?' he did not expect a reply, as she no longer communicated with others, she only doted in a lolling crouch over the rapidly developing child.

Annie did not look at him, her still figure a shadow in the dark. 'Eggs, Meat, Liver. Bring them to us.' It was the same everyday, occasionally she demanded fruit, but she always craved sulphur rich foods. Mr Delaney once found her crouched over the grate, licking and gnawing the coals, her face blackened from the slack.

At times she was heard crooning softly, lulling the rasping thing at her bosom to sleep.

-it was late that night when the Lord came in
  Enquiring for his lady-o
  And the servant girl she said to the Lord
  "She's away wi' the Raggle taggle Gypsy-o-

After some weeks it was clear Annie was wasting while the abomination thrived, the orderlies needed to reverse the situation, and reverse it fast.

The three sat in the study in casual attire, the dynamic was no longer master and servant, there was no pecking order. They were a family, brothers, sister, an aunt and uncles, united by a singular goal. All three had taken a silent pledge to do their damnedest to save Annie from her plight.

The mood was grim and sombre, the staple atmosphere in the lachrymose House.

'The time is at hand Charles, Annie will wither and fall unless we act,' Mr Delaney said.

'I agree,' said Missus Meades, 'The tyrant child swells, your daughter shrinks and sickens, we cannot summon the doctor nor the police. It rests upon us to set the matter right.'

Charles twisted his uncouth moustache upon his lips, 'don't you think I would stamp on the beast like a rat to see my darling Annie well,' he cried.

'We all would sir, we all love your little girl and as she is in a far worse state now, it is time to rid her of her burden,' said Mr Delaney.

'We have discussed the options before sir. To wrest the beast from her would prove too traumatic for her delicate state,' whispered Missus Meades, 'we must poison the child, let it die in her arms, let her grieve.'

'Then we must pray that Annie will wake from her stupor, to climb from her pit of despair and madness. And for God to forgive us,' said Charles gravely.

'The beast is ravenous sir. She can barely feed it such are the wounds to her breasts. The brute would feast on her flesh if it could. I am certain she could coax it to take solids. With your permission I'll prepare the pâté we discussed,' said Missus Meades.

Charles scrutinised his palm, the skin still scarred from the red hot door handle he grabbed so many months ago. 'Very well Missus Meades, let the poison be the cure.'

***

Missus Meades would have preferred if it were she who would deliver the poisoned chalice, sparing Lord Charles the grim charge. But as it was his turn to bring the meal they decided to keep their usual rota to avoid any hint of suspicion, although they were unsure if Annie even registered their coming and going most of the time.

Charles carried in the tray. Missus Meades and Mr Delaney waited outside the doorway, listening.

Mr Delaney, on one of his few excursions to town, procured a vial of arsenic from the same dispenser Jane had bought hers so many years ago. Missus Meades had mashed pigs livers and kidney into a thin paste before adding the poison, its garlicky aroma not at all awry in pâté dishes.

The dish was brought upon the tray alongside a pitcher of water. The contents clinked slightly, though resolute, Charles was nervous. His conscience protested against his intentions. Poisoning an infant was, in his life, not an act he had ever envisioned committing. 'Annie dear, it's Daddy, I was thinking your child is ready to take solids, and goodness knows you need the rest my love. You are drained and he'll find little sustenance from you now.'

Prior to the exorcism, Anne's uncanny astuteness would have sniffed out her father's ulterior intent with ease. But Annie, mumbling inanely to herself just rocked, bent over the sleeping child, then slowly turned her head towards her aged father without expression. Charles was almost in tears beholding her bedraggled features. 'I'll just leave it here my dear, Mr Delaney will be in next with supper.'

Anne's big eyes, caricatured larger by her dark, sleep deprived lids, moved slowly towards the meal, she surveyed it slowly and cocked her head a little. She turned back to Charles and made eye contact with him, her eyes holding the first sign of lucidity he'd witnessed since the birth. He froze.

Annie pulled back her lips and began a silent snarl, her teeth greying in her receding gums. She saw her father's fear, and though Annie's mind was a dark knotted web of torment and malady she somehow honed in on the pitiful look upon Charles' pensive face. Despite his deceit, she detected nothing in his heart but love for her. The fugue mist that long dulled her eyes seemed to dissipate and clear.

She spoke. 'Daddy?'

Tears flooded from Charles eyes, his lips trembling, his daughter at last recognising him. 'Yes Annie my love. It's me. It's your Daddy.' He held his distance, still fearful that he might spook her.

Annie looked again to the offal paste meal, its thick, fatty smell awakening the child, hungry again. It coughed a skin-crawling, retching plea when it was hungry, like a cat hacking up fur. It whined with avarice to be fed, the meaty scent sending it into a frenzy, clawing its huge hands along Annie's torn breasts. She winced, and rocked the mutant child to calm it.

'Come Daddy, come close to me. Come close to Dafydd.'

Charles stepped closer, entranced by her voice, absent from his life for so long. 'I'm here my darling,' he said calmly, ignoring the stench and the heartbreaking sight of his ripped up daughter.

'Hand me the dish Daddy, my little boy is hungry...so hungry.'

Charles swallowed hard and gave her the dish and spoon. He had not seen the creature this close since birth, though the sight still repulsed him, he hid his disdain.

It looked about eighteen months old, but its squinted eyes still looked blind. Its skin sat better on its skull now, although the head was even larger and more elongated. The true horror lay in its rows of dark teeth, now gnashing blindly towards the smell of the food, they were more fitting to some vile creature from the murky depths of the sea than any child on earth. Charles wondered how its mother could bear the heat emanating from its dragon-like mouth. He tried not to flinch for Annie's sake, he risked putting his arm around her thin shoulder, she did not flinch either.

Loading the spoon, Annie looked at her father with happy-sad eyes, and then to her son, Dafydd's son, whose father she loved intensely for the briefest moment, before she was corrupted by evil and before evil corrupted their son. She was seeing him for the first time as the spawn of the fire serpent, an abomination on earth and she was ready to end its unholy torment.

'Come now, Dafydd, Mummy has something yummy for you,' she cried.

The demon child opened its huge mouth as the smell from the spoon grew close to its flaring nostrils. Sensing no danger from the food, it swallowed greedily until the bowl was clean. Anne wept as it settled, its furnace stomach satisfied fully for the first time since birth.

'Sleep now Dafydd, Sleep, Mummy has you, Mummy loves you.' Annie gently cradled the creature's peaceful body as it slept, deeper and deeper, its breathing slowing, slowing until it could slow no more.

Annie kissed her dead baby's head and cried him a song.

I'd rather have a kiss from the yellow Gypsy's lips
I'm away wi' the Raggle taggle Gypsy-o!

Bala, Wales, April 1884

Across the Irish Sea, in the peaceful village of Bala, deep in the Welsh countryside, smoke rises from a quaint Tudor cottage. Inside a midwife stokes the fire and places over it a kettle to prepare tea. Resting by the glow is a pretty young woman, she is nursing her newborn son, who arrived into the world without fuss nor fury during the night. A perfect pink baby, hale and hearty, Madonna and Child. The quintessential picture of harmony and love. The mother cooed in wonder as her infant gently suckled.

She was considering two things. One, her disapproving, militant father and two, names for her infant. Her conclusion took but an instant. 'Oh, To hell with your stuffy old Grandfather,' smiled Charlotte as she kissed his sweet, downy crown, 'I'm naming you Dafydd.'

Annie Awakens

The golden morning sunbeams illuminated Loftus Hall and lifted the leaden fog like a veil from its grey façade. A pleasant solitary trill danced through the late spring air, a blackbird sang from the third floor sill. The scene almost befitting a bright new beginning, if it weren't for the crows scavenging on the few charred remains of Dafydd senior, splayed on the flower beds.

It was to be an errand filled day, Mr Delaney began by digging a deep hole far out back. The tarp he had used as a temporary cover over the roasted cadaver long since blown off. It was time to bury the scant blackened leftovers. The incredulous events had become matters far beyond the comprehension of the church, law and state. After filling the hole he returned inside.

Annie had stopped weeping several hours ago, but she would not relinquish the cold remains of her child to the small party that sat in her attendance.

She had not spoken, but welcomed comfort from her father, clasping his hand as he held her, remembering his familiar masculine cadence.

Mr Delaney and Missus Meades also at last received glances of recognition, dappled with kindness from her. Their strong Annie had survived the torment of two demons. Those who knew Dafydd better, may say three.

But she was not the same, how could she be.

When all had acclimatised themselves to the sea-change in atmosphere and became comfortable in Annie's company again, they began the menial tasks of airing the room, cleaning the grate, disposing of the soiled linens. All the while Annie remained still, like a tableau to Michealanglo's *La Pieta,* with an antichrist corpse-child in Jesus's stead.

When the day drew late Lord Charles ventured to talk to his daughter. His hope, to coax her to consider to allow himself and the others to take her burden from her, offering her rest, sustenance and comfort. Patiently and gently, he continued reassuring her of their support and unconditional love for her.

The sun had dimmed before she finally spoke, her cracked voice little more than a whisper. 'You may take him Father, do what you must with the remains, I am at peace.'

Charles gently held her sunken cheeks in his hands, staring deep into her lost eyes, willing his little girl to skip back from the deep dark woods, but he knew she would never skip again.

'I'm afraid you will have to pry him from my embrace, I fear I cannot move my arms.'

Charles looked at his girl, confused and troubled by her latest ailment. He attempted to move her emaciated arms, indeed they were quite locked. Her entire body shifted when he tried moving them. Despair raced to his face. Seeing Charles' distress, Mr Delaney came to assist him and between them they slowly and gently prised the foul infant from her frozen grip.

Mr Delaney and Missus Meades wrapped up the remains quickly out of sight of Annie and hurried it to a faraway corner of the house, somewhere it would never be found again.

When they returned they found Annie was still in situ from when they had left, Charles was doing his best to conceal his despair, stroking her lank hair, kissing her pale forehead. Annie had become almost completely petrified, like a clockwork doll after completing her wind-up dance. Whether through her trauma - an accursed side effect from Baal's tenure, or her sloth-like movements over the last few weeks, the cause remains far from certain.

There was still some looseness in her fingers and wrists, her feet and neck, but her back had become as rigid as a cane, her major joints fused, holding her paused in an eternal moment, an awkward crouching pose, seated upright, arms arching down, her head staring onto her empty lap as though a sudden gust had stolen her baby.

Thankfully, she could still verbalise, 'I appear to be frozen Daddy, I remember fire, now I am ice. Oh, what's to be done with the poor urchin Annie!'

Her father smiled sadly at her attempted levity. *Annie the kidder.*

'Would you be a dear Daddy and have my effects taken from my bedroom and to the room on the third floor. Make it pretty for me, take your time, then when it's ready maybe you could assist me up the stairs.'

'Of course my darling, whatever you need.' he replied breezily, his heart filled with lead.

'In the meantime, I am neither use nor ornament and it appears I badly need to bathe, maybe dear Missus Meades might prepare a bath. Who knows, I may at least become somewhat ornamental after a good scrub.'

***

Although loathe to enter the *demon room*, they did not protest nor delay in seeing to Annie's requests. Mr Delaney looked particularly uneasy with the proposition, and hoped the large hole he had just plastered over would dry in time to take paint. The able footman saw to the many repairs, then he covered over his recent plasterwork and the stained wall paper with leftover paints from the workshed. Annie's favourite tapestry, depicting a boar and dragon, was taken from downstairs to hang over the clean coat of pink paint.

Lord Charles hauled in her bed from her old room, the old one would soon become fuel for the fire. Missus Meades saw to freshly laundered bedding, floral in design, then replaced the smoky old curtain with light and brightly coloured drapes. A large plush rug was used to conceal the heavily tarnished floor.

When done, the room was as fresh and welcoming as it once may have looked when they expected the Queen to come a-knocking. Annie's dresser was bedecked with jewellery, brushes and cosmetics, her wardrobes were stocked with her clothes and hats. Her dolls and plush toys decorated her bed and armchairs.

Beside a table they had also placed a basket they prepared containing all of her knitting and millinery accoutrements, along with various materials and wools. Flowers, a hamper of fruit and a water decanter rested on her tabletop.

They asked her permission to light a fire, wary that the fourth element may trigger hellish recollections for her. 'Of course you may, can't you tell I'm frozen to the bone,' she joked.

Missus Meades discreetly tended to her ablutions and attentively nursed and salved her sores and cuts. After her mahogany hair was washed and brushed it regained much of its previous lustre, then Annie asked her doting carer to apply some blush and rouge to her wan and sunken cheeks.

Dressing her was somewhat challenging, with her limbs locked like that of a dead tree, but as Annie requested loose fitting bedclothes it made the effort a degree easier.

All done and Annie almost looked like Annie again.

When the gentlemen were permitted to see her, their hearts filled with a heavy happiness. Their encouraging smiles of pleasure at seeing her looking so well after her previous cadaverous appearance masked the grim weight they bore.

'You look beautiful Annie, it's so good to have you back.'

'Thank You Daddy,' her face angled away and down, but her eyes towards him, 'I don't plan chasing or bounding around the gardens today, I'd very much like to take tea in my splendid new room, if you please.'

Lord Charles and Mr Delaney had prepared a makeshift stretcher, and though Annie weighed very little, her rigid frame made transporting her an awkward task and a highly distressing experience. Nevertheless, they stifled their feelings and carried on as respectfully as possible.

When they finally placed Annie, in her mannequin-esque pose, onto her bed, they found her fixed neck brought her line of sight to the wall, so they lifted her and the entire bed around so she could face into her room and out the window.

'Open it please for a moment Daddy, you know how the fresh air invigorates me.'

Charles slid open the newly fitted sash and a cool gust ghosted in.

Annie, shored up by an arrangement of pillows, enjoyed the harmony of her new abode, surrounded by familiar furnishings and her favourite things. She longed for Baggy to jump up and lick her, and although she could not remember any details or specifics since the time she stabbed the dark stranger, she knew, or rather she felt, that many bad things had happened, and that she had somehow been involved in all of them. So about these matters she would not speak. Her minders, by some telepathic arrangement, also agreed not to exhume nor address the recent disconcertions, of which there were many.

It was not so much denial, as it was a beneficial burial of events for all. The occurrences were far too perplexing and acroamatic to ponder or rationalise, it felt far more therapeutic to return to menial tasks, uphold a couple of rooms in the house and tend to Annie as best they could.

Without doubt it was bizarre, behind the locked gates in the colossal Hall, a few ghostlike figures, remnants of its twisted past shuffle around. They dust and dine and cater for a petrified lady in pigtails. Just the latest in the mansions long list of atrocities, but what place could these good folk fill in the outside world now.

The calcification of Annie's joints meant she needed to be fed, maintained and cleaned by her attendants, and to them, it was not even a chore. But while her fingers could still clasp a little they would place familiar items in her hands for their tactile and reminiscent values.

Her soft toys, fabrics and wools, the clothes and crafts she fashioned, a hand mirror. Alas, it did not reflect the pretty young scamp she remembered. She beheld all her trinkets with great affection, but what she yearned to hold most was the pendant she found around Dafydd's neck. She would never mention this as it was one of the many items on the exclusion list of taboo subjects. Anyway, she could not even remember where she had it hidden.

And so their life in limbo continued for a time, no one came, no one left. The grocery bell would occasionally chime and the post collected. It was a remedial harmony, an interim respite for those who had looked for too long in to the abyss. Charles did not fool himself that this state of purgatory would be perpetual, nor even prolonged.

During this period Charles' forlorn musings wandered often into abstract and allegorical domains. He contemplated, amongst many bleak things, his daughter's plight and the rationale he had mused when Annie was just a sooty little tyke. He believed that had he applied enough pressure, his darling little pebble of coal could be squeezed until she became a shining crystal of pure, unadulterated carbon. He had since learned that the theory of deriving diamonds from coal to be, on the whole, bunkum. In truth, diamonds are formed deep within the earth's mantle, where magma and extreme forces condense carbon into its most pure form, and only a tiny fraction of these splintered stones are ever forced to the surface.

Fire, lava, and relentless force, deep beneath the earth. She had been to Hell and back. The pressure subjected on, and suffered by Annie was enough to transmogrify anyone. She had escaped to the surface and though not the same girl, she would always be her Daddy's purest and most precious thing.

Charles sat by Annie, now propped at her window. His eyes followed her locked gaze to the world outside. Looking out over his overgrown gardens he caught site of the delicate white bells of the *lily of the valley* squeezing through the dense wild foliage. He considered its sweet, innocent scent, and the brief pleasure the sight of its white, poisonous pitchers bring in Spring, knowing full well its fragile beauty would soon wither and diminish.

He could no longer despair at the prospect of its departure, for his heart was already too broken and beyond repair. His spirit was akin to scorched earth, where love, nor hate, nor hope cared to dwell anymore.

Now, such things were simply maintained and tended to, until their time too came to perish and fade. Then, as such things must, and as all things must, return to the ground.

Where maybe there, forgotten underfoot, their seed may oneday begin another life, in another time.

***

A few weeks later, toiling in the workshed, we find Mr Delaney and Charles, both having already worked up quite a sweat, and there was still the digging to be done. At least it was a pleasant day for outdoor work.

Lord Charles had never used a handsaw before, but with his sleeves rolled up he found that hacking through the timber was quite cathartic. When done, he held the carefully measured boards in place and allowed Mr Delaney to the hammer them together. Now, with a taste for manual labour Lord Charles insisted that he may also get some time sinking nails into wood.

Missus Meades, brought them a tray of refreshments, she glanced at their progress and quickly retreated before they could see her tears welling up.

They carefully followed the design for their irregularly angled box, and, once assembled they were pleased with their efforts with the large wooden casket. After sanding and varnishing they thought it quite suitable, no matter how macabre its function. They left the bulky, curiously shaped, coffin as they set off towards the family cemetery with their shovels.

The previous night, Annie's blithe spirit left her seized body. She endured with her endearing charm and waning health for almost a month. At this stage there is no need to go into her decline and eventual demise. But take heart and know she suffered no pain and that she died peacefully, with a smile on her face.

Her last request, before her jaw seized tight, was to have two items placed in her frozen embrace, dresses, one of her Mother's and one of Elizabeth's. These, she gazed happily at to the very end.

Her father, and devoted carers remained at her side until at last, her beautiful heart also became still, the last thing to freeze on her porcelain face was a tear, forced to the surface, like a perfect diamond.

There we will leave the distant past and the fallen House of Loftus. The devastation wreaked upon the remaining family began to yield from this point, the waves of their hardships becoming ripples, and eventually a calm settled on the surface.

Deep beneath the stillness lies the wreckage of sunken traumas, like the pulverised remains of the Rapscallion on its icy bed.

And always, slithering amongst the carnage, the opportunist beast lurks, waiting patiently to strike again.

The Blue Light Inn. September 1983

It is in the dark early hours in the Blue Light Inn on the Dublin foothills and the fire has dimmed. Rubin has finished retelling his portentous tale and his audience are still alive, though fretful and nauseas to their core.

Rubin was aware that Baal would not allow dawn to arrive without attempting entrance into the weakly barricaded bar. The ashen faced folk scrutinised the windows, the ceiling joists and the crack under the door with increasing unease and fear.

Having digested the eerie story, they realised that the demon wasn't laying in wait to seize his fiery hand on just any of them, it was the blow-in he sought to snare. Their self-preservation instinct had whispered to them to toss the welsh visitors out to the wolf, and though there eyes suggested as much, it remained an unspoken notion.

Sidney, weak and very weary, looked at the petrified faces, and then to his beautiful young wife, 'I should leave this place now my love. This demon, it's after me, my bloodline. It's clear he smells my ancestry, he wants vengeance for having been thwarted by my forefather. He wants to corrupt and destroy through me. I have brought danger to these innocent folk and to you my dear. If I wait, we may all burn alive, if I leave now, you will all be safe, or at least you'll have a chance.'

Nancy eyes fell away, distraught and contemplative, as always she fidgets with her necklace locket when under duress.

'No,' said Rubin, his thin, creviced face stern, 'That will not help us. He will attempt to see us all perish this night regardless of your actions. Then, what of you Sidney? You will be well again and carry within you his malicious will and you will become a force of unholy terror on the world. No. You must stay. We are stronger together, we must stare into the eye of his evil and stave it away.

The pressure within the room became erratic, the barometer strained, their inner ears began to squeeze and pop as though changing altitude, the demon was making his move.

Nancy turned to Sidney, conveying a dawning realisation through her doleful eyes, an urgency upon her, but she found she could not speak the words, her lips trembled and her tears welled. Sidney took her hand, he touched her cheek and implored. 'Hey now, this is not the end my love, we will survive this night, it is time for us to be strong, together, as Rubin says.'

'No, Sidney, my love, this…this is not your fault, the demon…it is not after you, it is not your soul he wants to ravage and possess…it's mine,' she wept.

Sidney frowned, mystified, 'Why on earth do you believe that my dear? You are an innocent, you are well, there is no reason at all for him to chose to pursue you.'

'There is!' She looked to Rubin, eyes drawn with fear. 'You told us how Anne flew into a fury with David, how she turned him to flame and flung him through the window when she found out he had fathered another child?'

'Well, yes, but there is much of the story that has been interpreted over the years, its accuracy is questionable in places...'

Nancy silenced him, and opened her locket. 'This heirloom was passed down through generations of my family, it was very precious to my grandfather, who was given it by his mother. We were never told the name of the boy in the photo, but I remember the name of my great grandmother, as I loved it so, and I dreamed I would oneday christen my first baby girl with that very name, Charlotte.'

Rubin and Sidney, peered at the antique silver oval, now split in two to reveal very old, sepia stressed photos. Though over one hundred years old the beauty of the pair was undeniable, the girl so fair and full of unadulterated joy, and he, high of cheekbone, with his raven locks and a mischievousness glint in his eyes. Dafydd.

The others in the room gathered round, all peering in wonder over the shoulders of the couple to witness the miraculous revelation.

'Well Holy fuck,' exclaimed Dennis, 'You're Dafydd's great, granddaughter!'

As they muddled round in wonder to glimpse the tangible link to Rubin's historic tale, and marvel at Nancy's genetic resemblance to the young man in the old photo, they did not notice, that behind them a stranger was now propped at the bar.

'Weren't you going to invite me to the party Nancy?' came the raspy growl from the heavily cloaked figure.

A collective gasp shot through the room as they all swivelled to behold the tall shadowy villain sneering smugly towards them. Rubin was cast back to his last memory of the Hellfire Club, and the raging host he saw turning to flame, Lord Blake.

'Good Evening Rubin, so nice to see you again, you left before I could thank you for burning my house to the ground. You must let me return your kindness.' he mocked, baring his long line of crocodile teeth.

'Blake! How did you penetrate our walls beast?' Rubin spat, 'I will torch you again demon and return you to hell for another fifty years.'

'Hah! Ol' Saint Nick is not the only one who can enter by chimney. And please. Call me BAAL.'

Baal's bellowing laughter shook the sweltering room. The punters crept under tables, cowered in corners and blessed themselves. Rubin stood defiant to his hideous blast. 'Fool of a Jew. Poor little orphaned kyke. I watched the slaughter of your parents during the pogroms in Kiev, I laughed as the gold was pulled from their dead mouths. They managed to slip you away before all the fun started. But you too will feel their agony this night.'

'Leave him be demon, your business is with me and you're the fool if you believe I will let you take my wife,' Sidney grabbed the small sacred blade from Nancy and raised it defiantly to the King of Hell.

'Look at you,' Baal laughed, 'An infected worm, weakened by one of the many diseases your God has inflicted on your frail, mortal existence. That pin you bear is no more a threat to me than the knitting needle your ancestor once poked me with.'

'But she defied you in the end, didn't she beast? She cast your wretchedness out of her. Murdered your wicked spawn and shoved him into a wall. We too, will defy you.'

Baal arose, his hoofed feet hitting the oak like mallets, his head almost to the ceiling, he shed a layer of clothing and the world grew hotter. 'Maggot! I wear seven layers, they keep the fires of Hell from turning you all to ash. Do you wish to witness my divinity naked? Your dear old aunt Annie, she saw me naked, she welcomed my embrace, and we had our fun together. It was I who discarded her. I have no interest in your bloodline, Sassanach. It is but spent. You are the last of your kin, and you will die the last. It is the seed of the Welshman I have come to claim. Nancy, my love, come, warm yourself.'

Rubin had began to chant in Hebrew, the incantation against the *Aynhoreh*, to dispel the evil eye. The faith in the Jew was strong, and within the scalding room began the rising of the maelstrom, around Rubin a small icy tempest whirled and met to counter with Baal's terrible heat. Within the inn the storm grew wild, lifting and thrashing stools, and sending the wall ornaments crashing.

Where the miniature weather fronts collided, electrical surges cracked and fired through the air, striking off the walls and the oak beams. Ambrose, quivering under a table dared to look up, only to be struck by a bolt in his eye, blinding it instantly. Marie tugged him back under the table and blanketed them both under their coats.

Seeing their comrade struck down, roused the military streak within the three brothers. Blood rushing to their heads, they nodded to each other, agreeing to carry out an unspoken order to advance on the enemy. Taking hold, of pokers and stool legs, the brave band of brothers charged over the top. Into the face of sheer terror they roared without fear. It was their finest hour ~ and also their last.

Their savage attempts to bludgeon and tear the brute apart were quite futile, their makeshift batons snapping like balsa wood, the poker that Jack used to pierce deeply into the mighty beasts neck as effective as it would have been poking the furnace of an almighty steam engine.

When Baal tired of there puny efforts he simply shed another layer of clothing and took them into his arms. They screamed in torture as his embrace engulfed them in flame. He dropped the three into a crumpled pyre on the floor and turned his attention to the bothersome Jew.

'The exorcists apprentice. He chose well, a cunning little runt you were. You have learned to wield prayer well, but you are old now, your candle has burned almost to its wick. And now it is time to snuff out your pitiful flame.' Baal reached towards Rubin, his hand like burning claw.

Rubin roared in Hebrew, '...*you have no permission to drink all the water, and you no longer have permission to harm him, nor his body, nor any one of his limbs...*' in doing so he produced a bottle, and doused the burning outstretched hand in Holy Water, and squirted the last drops towards its vile burning face.

On impact the flames hissed, steamed and quenched his fiery talons, and caused Baal to retreat in shock and pain. His hand and half his face were charred black and no longer alive with fire. *If only I'd had a bathful of the stuff*, thought Rubin.

Enraged by the impermanent Jew, Baal launched into a furious attack.

Dennis attempted to impede his path, but Baal just swatted him away, the blow propelled him crashing through a window pane, he hung on the smashed frame, half in half out, his severed body being held by splinters of frame and glass, as though on a fork, before his weight collapsed the window entirely. He slumped flat onto his beloved dahlias below, dying their yellow petals red.

Baal used the same charred hand to seize Rubin by his neck, the force of his grip garbling, then silencing the paladin's relentless chant. The storm subsided.

'Quiet now Jew, you've had your fun. You've told your story, and now it's time to end yours. Shall I just snap your bony neck?

Or just bite your shrivelled old face off?' Blake opened his huge mouth impossibly wide, revealing the long rows of sharp yellow teeth that led towards his volcanic throat.

Rubin looked into his fiery chasm, felt his searing breath and smelled the stench of brimstone. He had failed the pair, after fifty years, he had failed himself, too old, too weak. Blake's teeth were on his flesh when the demon suddenly recoiled back, this was no knitting needle, the spearhead, the holy Lance of Longinus, stung far more than Blake had reckoned.

Rubin was flung to the floor as the beast wailed in pain, Sidney had pierced his side deep, in the same approximate abdominal region where the Roman centurion had landed the spear in Christ almost two thousand years previously.

The tormented demon struck out at the enfeebled Welshman, smiting him to the flagstones and pinning him there with his monstrous hoof. '*Mochyn brwnt,*' Blake cursed him in his native tongue, but he had already been knocked unconscious by the terrific blow.

Blake continued to vent his vitriol while his blackened hand clumsily searched for the stinging spearhead buried in his injured flank, a molten ooze leaking from the tear. At last he gripped the knub of the blade and was about to tear it free when another javelin-like weapon shot into his heart.

Brave little Nancy held the long pike, a bona-fide artefact from the Irish rebellion that had adorned Dessie's wall for generations, until it was tossed to the ground by the chaos that night. Nancy Moss, stared the demon of sixty six legions square in the eye with defiance, contempt and spite. Something in her DNA triggered a sense of déjà vu, it was not the first time a member of her lineage impaled their persecutor.

Rubin, concussed and groggy, beheld the magnificent site, the towering Goliath about to be toppled by the diminutive heroine. Just before he passed out he believed he saw her halo, the last image he thought of before his head fell to the floor was that of Joan of Arc, expelling the British tyrants on her holy crusade.

It was a pleasant thought to send him into unconsciousness and he may have continued to believe in his dreams that this is how it ended. That the brave little Welsh woman, in the name of righting the wrongs of her forebears and in the name of innocence and righteousness laying to waste the mighty and merciless Baal, his burning spirit cast screaming back into the black endless abyss, and the champion, Dafyyd's successor, pike in hand, standing proud and victorious over the ashes of the marionette called Blake.

For when Rubin woke there were none remaining but he. Bruised, ribs cracked and skin bleeding, but still breathing, intact, alive. All around him had perished, Dennis had bled out on his flattened window box. The brothers three were but a dusty pile of ash and bones, Ambrose and Marie lay over one another and beneath a tabletop smashed to smithereens, their bodies like porcupines, perforated with a hundred splinters and wooden shards.

The concussed Jew, dried blood caking his wispy hair to his forehead, traced through the clutter for signs of the couple from Wales. Amongst the debris he found the Holy spearhead, the pike, and the necklace of skull-bone, but no other sign of either them. Were they amongst the smouldering ashes, were they obliterated by their infernal foe or did she vanquish her oppressor and flee? He stumbled to the door and eased it open, the morning sun making him squint.

He scanned the roadside, their mint green Capri had gone. This bode well, thought Rubin. They have fled, they united in battle, they combined forces to slay the dragon.

A fine Welsh story.

Rubin shielded his eyes against the golden morning light. He peered down the slope, to where the road wound down to the sea and the harbour, the ferry sounded off and began to trace a path of foam towards Wales. Rubin prayed they were on it, for Sid's safe return to health, and for a long and happy life with Nancy and God willing, a baby oneday.

***

Loftus Country House Hotel – Reprise

The gaudy green Capri sped down the mountain, Nancy was driving, ebullient and exhilarated after escaping the night of mayhem and murder. Lying across the back seat where she had dragged him was her Sidney, sleeping soundly beneath a blanket, his colour had returned and his coughing stilled.

She screeched to a halt at a signpost. Were she to go straight she would reach Dun Laoghaire harbour in 2 miles, were she to take the right and drive for 120 miles she would reach Wexford town, another hours drive from there would return them to the place they fled the previous morning, the Loftus Country House Hotel. Nancy smiled and bore right at breakneck speed.

She fiddled with the AM-FM stereo and the limited music stations it boasted. She tutted as she tuned in and out of tunes, The Pretenders, Planxty, The Waterboys. Eventually she found a track that suited her velocity, and very apt. to Sid and Nancy, the pirate radio station Big D were blasting the Sex Pistols, *Anarchy in the UK.*

'...I AM THE ANTICHRIST...' was one of the lines from the punk classic Nancy found herself belting out triumphantly. All the way south her singing and the music did not once disturb Sidney, although some of her erratic manoeuvres on the twisting roads nearly sent him toppling off the leather upholstery a few times.

It wasn't until she ground the sporty car to a stop in the gravelled carpark that he finally woke. Groggy and very much bewildered, but apart from a pain along his forearm, which he'd been sleeping on, he felt as good as new.

'Nancy?' he yawned, 'Why am I on the back seat? What time is it? Christ! What DAY is it? He looked around. 'Where are we?'

'Oh my, don't you have a head-full of question this morning. Just how much did you drink when I wasn't looking last night?' she chirped.

'Huh? Oh God dear, I don't remember a thing past checking in here yesterday.' Sidney rubbed his bleary eyes and cleared his dry throat, hacking the brown gunk out the car window.'

'Well that's just charming Sidney, this is a classy joint don't you know. And, Mr Amnesia, we checked in two days ago. Don't you remember? We checked out, but then we agreed that we'd stay another few nights?

Sidney scratched his thick tussled hair and shook his head, stumped.

'I'm never taking you to the pub again. C'mon lets get you into bed,' smiled Nancy.

'That's a good idea pet. We'll take a wholesome stroll around the 'ol family gardens later eh? I must say I'm feeling a lot better, apart from from this sting along my arm.' Sidney began to roll up his sleeve to investigate the irritation.

'Nevermind that now. C'mon, let's get you inside and I'll nurse you properly then, my brave little dragon.'

They hauled in their luggage, again. Michael Devereux was manning the reception desk, head down and scribbling. When he looked up to greet his guests his broad smile flipped to a look of rigid surprise.

'Good morning Michael,' Nancy pitched.

'Oh, em, yes, good morning, erm, welcome back Mrs Moss. So lovely to see you again.' The hotel manager lied, half expecting to see the police, or a team of beady eyed hotel inspectors swarm in behind the pair.

'We've decided to stay a while longer in your charming hotel, is our old room still available?'

The flummoxed manager had to shake himself to respond. 'Erm, yes, I believe so,' he ran his finger over the register, 'Yes. Yes, room 307, freshly turned down and awaiting guests. Are you sure you want...this particular room, we have many fine suites available on our second floor?'

'Quite sure, it has the most wonderful view of the horizon,'

Bemused and suspecting a ruse of some-sort Mr Devereux carried out her instructions, then handed her the key fob and wished them a pleasant stay.

The valet left them at their room and retreated. Sidney turned the key and in they went. 'I am embarrassed to admit that this is ringing no bells, we stayed here two nights ago?'

'Go and shower you numbskull, I'll be waiting for you under the covers…naked,' she winked. 'And brush your teeth, you smell like catfood.'

While Sidney washed, Nancy recalled the room, not as it was presented now, but how it looked one hundred years ago. She walked to the wall and removed the painting of Hook lighthouse, she slid her hand over the floral wallpaper. Her heightened tactile sense could feel the irregularities in the plasterwork, where Mr Delaney had hurriedly patched up the large hole.

Under her hand, behind the drywall, and wrapped in worn sacking, lay the skeletal remains of a child. Its skull abnormally large and spiked with a ring of small bumps. Where its metatarsals and phalanges should have been, lay coffin bones, more commonly known as *hooves*.

'I'm home son,' Nancy whispered to the wall, 'and I'm about to make you a brother.'

As Sidney dried off, he scrutinised his arm, the skin appeared pink and blistered and did not at all enjoy the hot water from the shower.

Nancy too bore the same markings, but they seemed less of a mystery to her. When he would ask what happened, she would claim their involvement in a very drunken game of *Indian Burns* in the pub the previous night.

As she undressed she cleared a few things away into an old vanity table, there was a familiarity to it, as though it was a restored piece of original furniture. She nosed through the drawers, and tapped her knuckles against the base of the middle drawer on the left, it sounded hollow. She slid the false bottom aside and inside lay a very old trinket. She smiled and removed her once beloved silver locket.

Sidney, dried off and entered the bedroom, wrapped only in his towel. Nancy was sprawled invitingly across the freshly made bed, naked, apart from an odd looking necklace.

Sidney smiled, already growing in enthusiasm to join his very desirable young wife. He slid down beside her, appreciating her soft willowy figure, he toyed curiously with the furry stump around her aquiline neck, 'What is such an ugly thing doing on such a creature so beautiful?'

'I found it in the drawer. Isn't it me lucky rabbit's foot, t'be sure,' Nancy chimed in her best Irish accent, 'It'll bring us the luck of the Irish when we're making our baby.'

'Well in that case me hearty, I want you to wear just that, and nothing else from now on.' Sidney took up her mimicry of the brogue, but all he could manage was a pirate snarl 'Now, have I permission to board your very fine ship Cap'n Nancy?'

Nancy threw her arms around him and kissed him playfully. 'Aye, Aye! All aboard, you raggle taggle gypsy.'

Acknowledgements

To my patient wife,

My dynamic son,

My loving/lovable family.

My thirteen year old computer.

Notes.

References inspired by and borrowed from Herman Melville, Bram Stoker, Lewis Carol, Emily Brontë, Chrissie Hynde and the Sex Pistols and all the other sub-conscious influences that I'm accidentally omitting.

Printed in Great Britain
by Amazon